TIME FRAME

Douglas E. Richards

Paragon Press

PART 1

"Does anybody really know what time it is?
Does anybody really care—about time?
If so, I can't imagine why
We've all got time enough to cry."

> —Chicago, *Does Anybody Really Know
> What Time It Is?*

"For those who think the world is obsessed with 'time,'
the Oxford dictionary added support to the theory
Thursday when they announced that the word *time* is
the most often used noun in the English language."

> —NBCNEWS.com (6/22/2016)—based on an analy-
> sis of almost three billion words culled from the
> Internet.

With respect to knowing what time it is, or caring, the currently
accepted worldwide definition of one second is: "The duration of
9,192,631,770 periods of the radiation corresponding to the transi-
tion between the two hyperfine levels of the ground state of the ce-
sium-133 atom." This is measured by atomic clocks that are accurate
to within one second over a period of fifteen billion years—roughly
the age of the universe.

1

The two naked women who were sprawled out at provocative angles on the huge bed were spectacular. Flawless. Both in their early twenties, with curves in all the right places, beautiful faces, and soft, silky hair. And the positions they assumed left nothing to the imagination.

The lone man who completed the threesome took them with a frenzied abandon, allowing himself to operate on lust and instinct alone. His passion was so fierce and unbridled, he was so consumed by pure, mindless animal need, that he was able to achieve his goal: temporarily forgetting he was a prisoner, condemned to death.

A prisoner whose sentence would be carried out with chilling efficiency in less than three weeks.

True, he was imprisoned in a veritable palace, a luxury resort that the richest men alive would envy, but knowing that his execution date was imminent, and set in stone, did tend to put a rain-cloud over the sunniest day.

But at least for now he would be fully occupied satisfying a primal need as old as time, responding to the softness of the women, their warmth, their writhing bodies, and their groaning and other squeals of ecstasy. Not to mention their exhortations for him to *take them*, along with explicit instructions for how they wanted him to accomplish this task.

He had become the star of his own porn movie, and he allowed himself to believe that their performances were real—not letting his intellect spoil the perfect fantasy.

Finally, unable to hold out any longer, he achieved the release his body so desperately demanded. He closed his eyes and tried to maintain a state of pure relaxation, basking in the recent memories of the fierce ecstasy he had experienced.

Even so, his rational mind couldn't help but return from its exile. He gazed at the women, who made no effort to cover up. They had done their job well, but *of course* it had all been an act. For twelve thousand dollars a day, one could get prostitutes who looked like centerfolds and who would pretend to be in lust with the man to whom they were assigned. And these pros had been worth every penny.

Death row inmates were traditionally given a last meal. His warden had given him a *month's* worth of last meals, with an expanded menu that included the hottest call girls in existence.

He dressed, told the two girls he'd be back in a few hours for another round, and made his way to the pool, just outside the luxurious main residence. He took a seat inside an egg-shaped wicker lounge chair, and stared off at the nearby Rocky Mountains, still capped with white despite the warmer weather at lower elevations. The late afternoon Wyoming sun glistened off the snow and hit the incoming storm clouds at various angles, creating a bruised purple mosaic in the sky.

It was magnificent.

But all he could think about was death.

The endless mansion, the size of a small hotel, faced the mountains that he loved while being stocked with everything else that he loved, not just the world's priciest and best call girls, but even his favorite mattress and pillows on the bed. The temperature and agitation level of the Jacuzzi's jets had been finely tuned to his preferred settings. Gourmet meals were brought in fresh by drone every day, each one a favorite. He had his own movie theater and the best automated massage chairs money could buy.

Everything precisely tailored to his tastes.

And why not? The callous bastard who had trapped him, who had written his death sentence, knew everything there was to know about him.

His executioner wanted him to be as happy and comfortable as possible for his last weeks among the living, not fully understanding how staring into the abyss, knowing Death was rapidly approaching, made every luxury a double-edged sword, reminding him of how great life truly was just before it was snatched away forever. No luxury could make him forget that eternal night was coming.

The man holding a knife at his neck had made attempts to soften the blow, but this didn't change the fact that his executioner was cold and pitiless, a man of blind ambition. A man certain he could utterly transform human civilization. A man who thrived on control, selfishly guarding his command and unwilling to share a single iota of his authority.

"God damn you, Edgar Knight!" the condemned man whispered to the mountains, but this was spoken more in resignation than in hatred. Hatred wouldn't help.

He could hate Edgar Knight all he wanted. But this didn't change the fact that he *was* Edgar Knight.

And that the decision to imprison him in this gilded cage, awaiting a swift and imminent execution, was one that he, himself, had made.

2

Edgar Knight shifted his gaze from the mountaintops and lowered his eyes to the sand-colored limestone tiles surrounding the pool. He remembered the thinking behind his death sentence, every step of the decision-making process, as if it had been his own.

Because it *had* been.

Although Knight had reached his fateful conclusion seven months earlier, it seemed like yesterday. It was simple, really. He was a great man, one who would be pivotal in determining the future course of humanity. In fact, the *most* pivotal to ever live. Which meant the most irreplaceable. If he was ever stricken down, the only man great enough to take his place was . . . himself.

So he had made plans to give himself repeated one-month death sentences. Death sentences that had now been carried out six times over six months. The version of Knight now recalling this reasoning had come into existence in this frame of time just over a week earlier, the seventh repetition of this exercise. Like the others, there would be no escape.

Almost three years earlier, Edgar Knight had discovered a way to tap into the mysterious dark energy that physicists had found made up more than half of all energy in the universe. Well hidden, but all-pervasive, it was a power source that existed even in the vacuum of space. As nearly infinite as a human mind could comprehend.

By finding a way to tap it, Knight had cemented his status as the most brilliant, intuitive experimental physicist and inventor to ever live. He knew it was considered bad form to think of oneself in these glowing terms, but he had to recognize reality, and no one familiar with his work would ever deny the truth of this assertion.

Knight was born to parents who reproduced like rabbits, the seventh child of ten, in a backwater town in the heart of Kentucky. He didn't believe in tales of gods impregnating women, either in Greek mythology or in the case of the Virgin Mary. But if someone *were* trying to prove this was possible, Edgar Knight would have been offered up as *exhibit A*. His parents and many siblings had the combined IQ of a lump of clay, and far less talent, while he had a genius for invention the likes of which the world had never seen.

By the time little Edgar was thirteen he had come up with inventions that had netted him millions, allowing him to buy a mansion for his family with a guesthouse all his own. He left as soon as the law would allow, emancipating himself from an environment that taught him nothing but to despise both overpopulation and ignorance, which was all his home life had to offer.

His high school was worthless, so he taught himself, absorbing the equivalent of a PhD level education in several scientific and technical disciplines. He was admitted to MIT, where he completed a degree in electrical engineering in two years despite attending classes only when this was mandatory.

His genius for invention became so obvious, so early, that he was snapped up by the head of Black Ops R&D just after graduation, who made him an offer he couldn't refuse. Year after year, Knight proved the wisdom of this choice, coming up with one breakthrough invention after another.

Then, four years earlier, he had joined up with a man named Lee Cargill, who had earned a sterling reputation for managing interdisciplinary teams in pursuit of impossible goals. Whatever the latest Moon-shot or Manhattan project, Cargill would be put in charge. This time he was tasked with finding a way to tap into *dark energy*, and Q5 Enterprises was born, a Black Ops initiative under cover of a tech company.

It was believed in the highest towers of academia that this enigmatic dark energy could never be tapped. Knight had been determined to prove this wrong. Just because you didn't know where or what a force was, didn't mean you couldn't find a way to use it. An electromagnet would still pick up a car, even if the magnet's maker knew nothing about magnetic fields and lines of force.

Using nothing but instinct, Knight had forged ahead, a blind man attempting to tap into an invisible energy source, which often seemed more mythical than real. And he had succeeded, although it had taken a while for him to realize that he had, and longer still to understand the nature of the effect—an effect that no one could have ever predicted.

Metaphorically, he had placed an energy collector in the center of an exploding nuclear bomb without managing to collect any energy. It was like standing on the surface of the sun and not even getting a *tan*.

Eventually he came to realize that the energy was doing work, just not on the *spatial* axis of space-time.

Instead, he was releasing mind-boggling amounts of energy, enough to meet the power requirements of the entire planet for *months*, but this energy was accomplishing one thing only: pushing matter within a contained space just over forty-five millionths of a second into the past.

Edgar Knight had done nothing less than invent a time machine, albeit one that could only send matter back precisely 45.15 microseconds.

Still, it was astonishing. Miraculous. And while its limitations meant there would be no trips to witness the birth of Jesus or to watch dinosaurs frolicking about, it was inarguably the most stunning, breathtaking discovery in all of history.

3

Knight continued to reflect on these vivid memories, which belonged as much to him as to the Edgar Knight who would survive him.

Lee Cargill, the head of Q5, had raced to understand the potential of this new capability, and had taken great pains to secure this earth-shattering secret. Only after Cargill had transformed his organization into the most isolated black program in the history of black programs did he turn his full attention to finding ways to exploit and advance Knight's discovery.

Knight had continued to perfect the technology, building it into the trailers of eighteen-wheelers to give the system mobility, and had immediately seen far beyond the obvious possibilities. He knew just how to use these newfound capabilities to utterly transform the world, lift the species to new heights.

But try as he might, he could not persuade Lee Cargill to subscribe to his views.

Cargill was pathetic, *worthless*. The man could not have been more short-sighted if he were blind, and his sense of caution bordered on paralysis. He was also bound by an antiquated sense of morality, not relevant in this day and age and given the possibilities that time travel created.

Knight, on the other hand, was supernaturally talented, daring, and visionary. It had driven him mad that Cargill had been too squeamish to make the best use of what he had created. Unwilling to push the technology to its limits, especially when it came to sending a human being back in time to create a universe with two copies of him or her.

The term *creative differences* didn't begin to cover it.

So Knight had taken his technology, and a number of members of Cargill's team, and had left. Not that this had been easy to do. When you're part of the most secretive project on Earth, housed within the blackest of Black Ops groups, and you've come up with a technology capable of altering the structure of the universe itself, the very *fabric* of reality, separating from the pack and freelancing isn't exactly an available option.

But Knight didn't let that deter him. After careful planning, and considerable bloodshed, he managed to extricate himself from the womb Cargill refused to leave, and eventually set up shop on an island in Lake Las Vegas, a man-made lake that was seventeen miles from the fabled Strip.

No one knew that he controlled this facility, and his headquarters couldn't have been more impregnable.

Even so, Knight was a cautious man. Human beings were frail, easily killed. He could fall and hit his head on the edge of a table, killing himself instantly. He could electrocute himself during an experiment, despite careful precautions.

So why not make a backup—just in case? Why not send himself back in time so there were now two of him?

Not that he would ever let a second Edgar Knight roam free to interfere with his efforts. He would not allow any meddling, even by a version of himself a fraction of a second younger. Two of him would lead to confusion. Who would be in charge?

The second him, the duplicate, wouldn't just share his DNA, but his bank accounts and legal rights, his every memory—his very *mind*. The duplicate would be him just as surely as *he* was, simply one frame—or forty-five millionths of a second—behind him in the film reel of his life.

There was no way he would ever consider sharing power, especially not with someone as brilliant, ambitious, and formidable as he was.

So he decided to make duplicates of himself and imprison them. Let each lead a life of luxury while trapped, one month at a time. At the end of each month, the current duplicate would be dispensed with and he would create another, who would be fully up to date on all of the thoughts and experiences he had had during the preceding month. A fresher backup, so to speak.

Once a month he had his helo pilot fly him from Nevada to his backup headquarters compound in Wyoming, chosen for its spectacular mountains and sparse population.

Once he arrived he would step into the back of a big-rig, which housed a time machine, and send himself back forty-five millionths of a second.

And the computer would dutifully carry out this order. Knight would be pinned on the spatial axis of space-time, but would slide a single frame backward on the time axis. He would remain on the spatial coordinates at which he had begun, but when he arrived in the near past the Earth would be in an entirely different location.

The Earth never stood still. In fact, it hurtled through space at far greater speeds than any human plane or rocket had ever achieved. It spun on its own axis and revolved around the sun, while the entire Solar System raced around the center of the Milky Way Galaxy at breakneck speed.

All in all, the Earth was traveling through the cosmos at two hundred forty-two miles per *second*. Even in forty-five microseconds the Earth traveled a distance of fifty-eight feet, meaning Knight would arrive in the past fifty-eight feet ahead of where he had begun. Gravity played a role that wasn't fully understood, such that objects sent into the past ended up fifty-eight feet away, but always landed on the ground rather than above it.

If fifty-eight feet would put an object inside a tree, matter's strong repulsive force would deflect the object a short distance away, so that it would end up *beside* the tree instead. If the destination was dense with matter, like the middle of a mountain, with no open space near enough for a slight deflection, time travel wouldn't work at all.

Remarkably, the directionality of the effect could be changed by adjusting the polarity of the time travel field. The jumps were always fifty-eight feet, the exact distance Knight's fledgling theory suggested would be the case based on the movement of the Earth over forty-five millionths of a second, but the direction of the jump could be dialed in as desired. This wasn't something either predicted or predictable, but an effect discovered by trial and error alone.

How this was possible was currently unknown, with the going theory being that time travel didn't cut across the space-time axis, per se, which would be through the four common dimensions, but rather through a fifth dimension. Movement through this dimension translated into unexpected and counterintuitive results, which none of their scientists could yet adequately explain.

Once Knight had landed in the past, there would be two of him. When he arrived, the very slightly younger version of himself would still be in the semi awaiting the computer command to send him back, which would commence in less than the blink of an eye.

But Knight's arrival in the past would instantly trigger the computer to abort, so his younger self would now never be sent back, ensuring that a third edition of Edgar Knight didn't come into existence. Instead, his younger self would be locked inside the trailer, soon to find himself a prisoner in a luxury resort.

Scientists, logicians, and science fiction writers had always believed that the universe had two primary choices when it came to dealing with time travel. It could branch out into two separate universes, beginning at the point in the past that had been changed due to time travel.

Or it could fight to stay self-consistent.

Neither had turned out to be correct. It turned out the universe found branching into multiple universes wasteful. And it didn't care a whit about paradoxes. When Knight's arrival in the past changed events, aborting his future time travel jump, he should have disappeared. After all, he had changed things so he was never sent back. So how could he still be there?

The universe used a different logic. It could not have cared less how the second Knight had come into existence. It just accepted his presence in the new reality, resetting time in its general vicinity and moving forward once again from there, as if there had always been two Knights—forging a brand-new future. If the computer had not aborted, when the universe moved forward forty-five microseconds it would send him back in time yet again, introducing a third copy into the past. And then a fourth. And then a fifth . . .

If future time travel was then aborted after the fifth, the five Knights would remain, and the universe would move forward on this basis.

If Marty McFly had changed past events so his parents had never married, so he had never been born, neither he nor his image in a photo would have vanished. The universe would have reset in the local vicinity of 1955 Hill Valley, where Marty had disturbed the timeline, and created a new future from there. It wouldn't care that Marty was an interloper from an erased future, and that his parents had never, and would never, give birth to him.

He was there, and that was good enough for the universe. It wasn't checking birth certificates.

Six times Knight had sent himself back into the past, each time imprisoning and eventually killing the version of himself that he joined there. Just over a week earlier, Knight had begun this exercise for the seventh time. And like the six versions before him, who had each lived their allotted month before being erased in favor of a fresher face, the seventh would soon die. An irrevocable death sentence, perhaps made even worse from the knowledge that he had bestowed it upon himself.

The idea of becoming a disposable backup was horrifying to Knight, but far easier to swallow in the abstract than when his head was locked inside a guillotine and the blade was inching its way toward him.

Star Trek had made it clear from select episodes (although this was never brought up directly) that Kirk and Spock died every time they used the transporter, with a new, identical version materializing in the new location, constructed from their *patterns*.

In principle, Knight's own situation wasn't that different from the use of such a transporter device. One version was killed to make way for another—identical—version.

But at least in the case of the *Star Trek* transporter, this was instantaneous, which was a lot less troubling. Vaporize the original man or woman on the *Enterprise's* transporter pad, copy him or her on the planet below, and no harm, no foul. When Kirk beamed down to a planet, he could convince himself that he hadn't really died, that he had just disappeared and reappeared.

But it was the cruelest of tortures to remain alive after such duplication, to know that death was imminent, and the exact time it would take place.

Knight wanted to scream at the top of his lungs. There was no way out. His death sentence was immutable, and the means for carrying it out unstoppable.

One of dozens of speakers hidden throughout the residence came to life. "Edgar Knight?" said the male voice of Lazlo, his personal digital assistant, so advanced it made earlier PDAs, like SIRI, seem like pull-string talking dolls.

Knight was instantly at attention. Lazlo was always there in the background, awaiting his instructions, but for his AI to initiate an interaction on its own—well, this was highly unusual.

"Yes," responded Knight, letting the AI know he was listening.

"Sensors show a recent cessation of all life signs coming from Edgar Knight One. Video footage streaming from his office, along with my personal observations, indicate that Knight One was killed in a massive explosion at the Lake Las Vegas compound. Just to be sure there is no mistake, this has been confirmed by seismic sensors and news reports. I would have informed you sooner, but I was housed primarily in a mainframe on this same site, which was also vaporized. It took me almost two minutes to fully reconstitute all of my functionality within the mainframe housed at the Wyoming site."

Knight's mouth dropped open. His namesake had been killed? How could this be?

It was a huge setback, at least when it came to achieving the goals that he shared with the version of himself forty-five microseconds older, whom he and Lazlo had dubbed *Knight One*. But he couldn't help but be elated. He was no longer expendable. Instead, as Knight One's only backup, *he* would now be running the show.

It was time for the understudy to take the stage, for the heir to ascend to the throne.

The king was dead.

Long live the king.

Knight blew out several deep breaths in relief, and if he had believed in God he would have been thanking this deity profusely.

"Full control of all operations has now been transferred to you," continued Lazlo, "and I will respond to your commands only. You also have sole access to all of the deceased Knight One's assets, financial and otherwise. I have sent a signal to the capsule in your skull, and it has been fully nullified. You are now free to leave the premises and operate at full autonomy."

A slow smile crept over Knight's face. "Tell the two girls on-site I won't be needing their services further and they're free to leave. Organize all information you have on what Knight One has been up to since leaving me here. Transfer it to the computer in the home theater."

Knight paused in thought. "Does the video taken before the explosion contain any clues as to how this happened? Who might have been responsible?"

"More than clues," replied Lazlo. "I am sure you will find it very illuminating."

"Good. Get rid of the girls and send the footage to the big screen in the theater. I'm going there now. Also, to save time, prepare an executive summary of all information you think will be relevant to my full understanding of the events culminating in Knight One's death?"

"Prepared and ready," said Lazlo immediately.

4

Knight's strategy for creating, and dispensing with, his understudies was ingenious, ruthless, and unstoppable, three adjectives that fit him well. He would begin the process by entering a trailer and setting the computer to send him back in time. As soon as he arrived a split second in the past, a signal would be sent aborting time travel for the version of him who was still in the trailer, on the verge of being sent back again. The signal would not only abort time travel, but cause the release of a knockout gas inside the compartment.

Once the Knight inside the trailer was out cold, the Knight who had landed fifty-eight feet away would use a robotic device to inject and implant a tiny titanium capsule into his skull. The capsule was divided into two equal compartments. One contained a toxin that, if released, would kill the younger Knight instantly. The other compartment held an agent that could be combined with the toxin in the first compartment to nullify its effect and render it harmless.

Knight called this his *table salt* strategy. Sodium by itself was deadly. So was chloride. But combine the two into *sodium chloride* and you ended up with a crystalline substance that was not only harmless, but delicious when sprinkled on french fries and pretzels.

Once the capsule was in place, the backup Knight would awaken in the main building of the Wyoming compound, where he would be forced to wait out his month. Lazlo was set up to monitor his every activity. If he made any attempt to leave the general vicinity of the mansion, the AI would immediately send a signal releasing the left compartment of the implant, killing him instantly. If he found a way to shield the capsule from Lazlo's signal, the same thing would happen automatically. If he stayed put, at the end of a month, the capsule would be triggered as well.

The only way out was for Knight One to die. If this happened, Lazlo would do as it had just done—open the partition between the two compartments and allow the neutralizing chemical to mix with the toxin, thereby defanging it.

The chemistry and mechanics of the system had been perfected by several members of a large group of geniuses Knight had dubbed his *Brain Trust*. These were acclaimed scientists he had sent back into the past without their knowledge, effectively making copies of them for his own use, while the originals went about their lives, none the wiser.

The duplicates—or, more accurately, the versions brought back from a split second in the future, often multiple copies of the same scientist—represented the greatest collection of human ability the world had ever seen. Knight provided them with unlimited funding, the ability to work with the best people in the world on the most challenging problems, and treated them like royalty—at least for the most part.

While they were technically prisoners, their only responsibility was to pursue their passions, and many wouldn't have left if they could have.

Knight made sure the two call girls had left the premises and took a seat in one of ten cushioned, reclining chairs in his private theater. "Lazlo, give me the executive summary you prepared," he ordered, feeling giddy from having just escaped death row.

"In short," began Lazlo, "Knight One's people managed to capture Aaron Blake and Jenna Morrison out from under Lee Cargill and bring them to Lake Las Vegas. Cargill and several other members of Q5 were killed in the process."

Knight's eyes widened. Outstanding. And completely unexpected.

Not long before the Knight in Wyoming had come into existence, Lee Cargill had intercepted an email message that indicated a leading physicist named Nathan Wexler had come up with the theoretical basis for time travel. The physicist's short email left no doubt that the work was groundbreaking. Monumental. Because Wexler had arrived at the period of 45.15 microseconds based on *theory alone*.

This was *extraordinary*.

Knight had stumbled across time travel and had discovered that the length of time traveled back was always of this duration. Always. But he knew this due to experimental measurement only. Neither he, nor anyone else, could ever figure out *why* this was the case.

Until now. The intercepted email indicated that Nathan Wexler's purely theoretical equations had pointed to this exact interval of time as being special. More importantly, his theory indicated that the reach of time travel could be *extended*. It should be possible to travel back in time, in forty-five microsecond intervals, to a maximum distance of almost *half a second*.

Half a second! This was more than ten thousand times farther back than Knight had achieved.

This was *huge*. Being able to effectively send a person or object fifty-eight feet away was one thing. But in a *half-second*, the Earth moved over *a hundred miles*, dramatically increasing the system's scope and versatility.

When Knight's moles within Q5 had alerted him of this development, the race to acquire the brilliant physicist was on. But as he and Cargill battled over the man, Wexler was killed, leaving his fiancée, Jenna Morrison, as their only hope. She possessed a flash drive that contained Wexler's work, but had hired a man named Aaron Blake to protect her, an ex-special forces operative turned private detective.

Even so, both Blake and Jenna had ended up in Cargill's hands, and Knight had been convinced Q5 would soon have Wexler's work as well, giving his former boss a tremendous advantage in their ongoing struggle.

But Knight One had apparently managed to wrestle Jenna and her hired protector from Cargill, after all, killing him in the process.

Everything appeared to have been going Knight One's way.

So how had he ended up dead?

"Rather than continue with an executive summary," said Lazlo, "I recommend that you watch the recording of Knight One's meeting with his two captives. I believe it will tell you what you need to know. It was streaming to the cloud right up until the instant of the explosion."

"Understood," said Knight. "Show it now," he ordered.

5

An ultra-high-definition image of the inside of Knight One's lavish penthouse residence in Lake Las Vegas appeared on the massive home-theater screen in perfect 3D. On the screen, Knight One's men strapped Jenna Morrison and Aaron Blake to two of four steel chairs at one edge of his office and left.

As Knight watched the footage, he was struck by just how unimposing Blake seemed to be. The man was just over five foot seven, and looked harmless, like a man who might get sand kicked on him at the beach. About as dangerous as a nursery-school teacher.

But Knight had learned the hard way that this impression couldn't be further from the truth. Aaron Blake was a highly decorated ex-Army Ranger, seventy-fifth regiment, who had served within various counter-terrorism groups in Yemen, Somalia, and Iraq before deciding to leave the military to become a private detective in LA.

He was smart, tough, and brave, and had bested some of Knight's most talented soldiers. His appearance couldn't have been more deceiving.

Knight took a moment to study Jenna Morrison's 3D image on the screen as well. This was the first he had ever seen of her, other than a few stills. She was almost as tall as her PI companion—which, at five foot five or so, wasn't saying all that much. Her brown hair was cut short, and while she wasn't classically pretty, she was still in her twenties, and there was something attractive about her. Perhaps it was her perfect complexion, or the easy intelligence reflected in her brown eyes.

"Where are the others we were with?" she was demanding as he watched.

"I'm afraid they're all dead," replied Knight One. *"Including my old friend Lee Cargill."*

"*All of them?*" said Jenna in horror. "*But why? They were helpless.*"

Helpless? thought the Knight watching in annoyance. Cargill may have been a lot of things, but he was hardly helpless. The man had been a sleeping lion, and Knight One had just applied the law of the jungle.

Just as these thoughts flashed through his mind, Knight One denied that Cargill had been helpless, right on cue. "*When you're being stalked by a lion,*" his predecessor was now saying, "*and you chance upon him sleeping, you kill him. The difference between me and Lee Cargill is that I'm willing to make tough choices, own up to tough realities.*"

Knight couldn't help but smile. Great minds thought alike. Especially when those minds were identical up until one week earlier, when their life experiences had begun to wildly diverge. Even so, he and the man on the screen would be expected to have virtually identical reactions to anything the prisoners might say.

With one caveat. The Knight in Wyoming knew something his predecessor had not known. He knew that Knight One only *thought* he was in full control of this situation.

"*Compassion is great,*" continued his predecessor. "*I'm all for it. But if we let it paralyze us from making rational, logical . . . necessary decisions, we deserve to go extinct as a species.*"

"*Just the opposite,*" said Jenna. "*Compassion will make sure we don't go extinct.*"

"*If everyone were compassionate,*" said Knight One, "*this would be true. But there are ruthless people in this world. People who relish the idea of Armageddon and are moments away from having the means to make this happen. Compassion in the face of that is suicidal, which is the exact path we're on.*"

"*I agree with you in many ways,*" said Blake. "*But the answer isn't setting one man up as absolute dictator.*"

"*Why not? Right now we have democracies in the world, but we also have any number of countries run by dictators and worse. Irrational, power-hungry people, with only their own interests at heart. At least with me running the show you'll have rational decisions.*"

"*Like sterilization of anyone below a certain intelligence level?*" said Jenna.

"*Yes. First you wipe the barbaric, destructive extremists from the planet. Simple decision. Kill them, or they'll kill you later. As for controlling the coming swarms of unintelligent, ignorant masses, our planet is a tiny lifeboat in a vast ocean universe. But our boat is getting overcrowded and taking on water. When the crew members who aren't capable of bailing any water reproduce ten times faster than those who can, it doesn't take a genius to see that the boat will eventually sink.*"

"Well said," whispered the Knight watching, fascinated by the restraint his predecessor had shown in referring to those he planned to weed out as *crew members unable to bail out water*, rather than calling them what they really were: ignorant, dim-witted slobs reproducing like cockroaches. He couldn't help but wonder how many kids his nine moronic siblings had produced. He hadn't checked in with any of them for over a decade, but even then they had collectively brought more than forty new mouths into the world. He wondered how much this number had grown in the time since.

Even though Knight didn't have any children, he had engaged in reproduction all the same. Only *he* had reproduced exact copies of himself, and copies of the best minds the planet had to offer, rather than swarms of high-school dropouts who were future reality-show stars.

"*So what do you want with us?*" asked Jenna on the screen, pulling Knight from his reverie.

"*You have a copy of Wexler's work in the cloud,*" replied Knight One. "*I want you to open it.*"

After an exchange in which Jenna Morrison made it clear she would never cooperate, Knight One had two additional prisoners brought into the room, both bound and gagged. One of the prisoners was Jenna Morrison from a different frame of her life. The other, a duplicate Nathan Wexler, another version of the fiancé she had seen die in her arms.

An interesting development, but not one that the Knight watching hadn't expected.

Knight One went on to explain how he had come to possess multiple copies of Nathan Wexler, each of whom he forced to try to recreate the breakthrough the deceased version had made. None had succeeded in finding the random insight that had led this other Wexler to his eureka moment.

"*I'm sure Cargill told you all about human duplication,*" Knight One was now saying on the screen. "*The difference is, Cargill is too weak to actually do it. Another idiot who blathers on about slippery slopes while our ship is hitting an iceberg. So what do you say, Jenna? I need that file. But I'm willing to make this easy on all of us. I'll offer you the deal of a lifetime. Get me that file, and I'll reunite you with the man you love.*"

"*This is all so . . . wrong,*" said Jenna.

Knight One turned toward the duplicate version of Jenna Morrison in the room, drew a gun, and shot her twice in the chest.

"*That's better,*" he said calmly.

On the screen, blood erupted from one version of Jenna while the other filled the room with a horrified shriek.

"*No one wants to share their man, after all,*" continued Knight calmly when Jenna's scream subsided. "*Even if the person they're sharing with is themselves. So now that he's all yours, Jenna, how about it?*"

"*You're the sickest bastard who ever lived!*" she screamed.

"*I'm just a man willing to do what's necessary to save the species.*"

Exactly right, thought Knight as he watched.

On the screen, Jenna's face was taking on a new resolve, and she proceeded to offer Knight One a deal of her own. She would willingly provide the passwords he so desperately wanted if he would let Aaron Blake and Nathan Wexler go, giving them a head start before alerting his security they were loose. She would make this deal, she told him, because she was confident that his entire security apparatus wouldn't be able to stop an unarmed Aaron Blake and an egghead physicist from escaping.

Knight One had agreed, of course. The idea that these men could really escape—head start or no head start—was *ludicrous*. The Knight watching couldn't fault his predecessor for taking this bargain, even though it was now clear he should have refused.

Somehow, this decision had marked the beginning of the end for his predecessor.

Yet as he watched, Knight still couldn't imagine how Aaron Blake could have possibly prevailed.

6

"I advise advancing the footage by twenty-six minutes," said Lazlo, interrupting the video.

"What would I be missing if you did?" asked Knight.

"After Knight One had Blake and Wexler deposited outside of the high-rise and cut loose from their bonds, Jenna Morrison directed him to where her fiancé's work was stored in the cloud, and gave him the appropriate passwords. While this was happening, Blake and Wexler reentered the building, blinded video monitors, and proved more elusive to Knight One's security than he had anticipated."

"Why am I not surprised?" mumbled Knight. "So what's happening at the twenty-six-minute mark?"

"Knight One has downloaded Wexler's file and is about to review it."

Knight considered. Surely, based on what had happened, this file couldn't have been the genuine article. But either way, Lazlo was correct in assuming this was footage he didn't want to miss.

"Okay," said Knight. "Skip ahead."

There was static on the screen for just an instant, and then the scene in Knight's Lake Las Vegas penthouse continued to unfold, twenty-six minutes later. On the screen, his predecessor was studying a tablet computer in silence, his head looming over it as he held it at chest height, inadvertently blocking out the various cameras taking the footage that the Knight in Wyoming was now watching.

As hard as it was for Knight to believe his predecessor was really viewing Wexler's work, Knight One's body language left no doubt. His eyes were large and his growing excitement clear. He was more than excited. He was amazed. *Euphoric.*

Knight continued to study his predecessor on the screen with great interest.

A violent earthquake shook the home theater, accompanied by a deafening explosion. Knight nearly dived to the theater floor in a reflexive act of self-preservation.

A moment later he realized that the theater wasn't under attack, after all. The shaking and exploding had all happened at the Lake Las Vegas high-rise. The 3D scene had shaken on the screen, not the screen itself.

The footage continued, showing a stunned Knight One, still alive, shouting for Lazlo to tell him what was going on. But Jenna Morrison answered, instead. "*What's going on is that Cargill just played you for a chump,*" she said triumphantly. "*He orchestrated all of this. We wanted to be captured.*"

"*Why?*" responded Knight One. "*How has this helped you?*"

Remarkably, the Knight watching *still* found this to be a valid question. He knew a train wreck was coming, yet he still couldn't see the train.

On the screen, his alter ego continued. "*If Cargill was the puppet master here,*" he said, "*he didn't do a very good job of it. Because I know for certain he's dead, along with a number of his key people.*"

"*Come on, Edgar,*" said Jenna in disdain. "*You're so much smarter than that.*"

"*Are you suggesting Cargill was a duplicate?*" said Knight One incredulously. "*He would never allow it.*"

"*To stop you he would,*" snapped Jenna. "*He'd still never allow two copies of the same person to coexist. But he knew you'd kill everyone but me and Aaron.*"

"*Okay,*" said Knight One slowly, considering her words. "*I believe you. But I still don't see his end game,*" he admitted.

"*Aaron and I knew we would never be safe as long as you were alive. More importantly, the world would never be safe. So I agreed to be the bait. To sacrifice myself to get to you. Aaron volunteered as well. All I asked was that before we completed the mission, we be allowed to do everything humanly possible to try to save Nathan.*"

"*Blake may be good, but he's not that good.*"

Jenna smiled. "*Isn't he? That explosion means he did it. It means that Nathan is safe.*"

"Pause the footage!" the Knight watching in Wyoming command-ed. "I need to think."

The pieces were finally falling into place. The only way Wexler could be safe is if Blake had fought his way to the time machine on the first floor and had altered it, making use of Wexler's discovery to teleport many miles away. Knight now knew precisely what the rest of the footage would reveal. Still, he needed to watch it unfold.

"Resume," he barked to his PDA.

On the screen, at least part of the truth was now dawning on Knight One. "*Cargill found a way to extend time travel beyond forty-five microseconds,*" he said. "*Didn't he?*"

"*That's right,*" said Jenna. "*The explosion was Blake's signal. It could only be triggered if the teleportation was a success. He used a little explosive that you actually brought to our attention: octa-nitro-cubane. Ring a bell? The most explosive non-nuclear substance known to science, but impossible to make without a time machine.*"

Knight One glared at Jenna in contempt, still having no idea what was coming. "*Cargill's plan may have been flawless,*" he said, "*and it will set me back, but he still can't win.*"

"*You still don't get it, do you?*" said Jenna scathingly. "*You poor psychopathic asshole.*" She shook her head. "*Here's the thing, genius, Aaron and I are duplicates also. The goal was to get Nathan out, if possible, and destroy you. We signed on for a one-way mission. Aaron sent Nathan to safety and stayed behind, knowing he would die in the explosion.*"

Knight One's eyes widened in horror, and the Knight watching these events unfold knew that he finally—finally—understood. But too late.

"*It's finally dawning on you, isn't it?*" said Jenna. "*You think the explosion Aaron triggered was epic? Well, I'm carrying a hundred times as much explosive.*"

She glanced down at a diamond ring on her finger, one she had been fiddling with throughout. "*I push down hard on this diamond and enough octa-nitro-cubane is triggered to flatten this building and at least the three key buildings around it.*"

"*But you'll die also,*" said Knight One. "*Horribly. Your body torn to shreds. Are you really prepared for that? Another Jenna may get to live, but it's you who takes the full brunt of the explosion. You who gets vaporized. It won't hurt any less because there's another of you inside Cheyenne Mountain.*"

Tears began streaming down Jenna's face. "*I know,*" she said. "*And I am terrified. I don't want to die.*"

"*So don't do it,*" pleaded Knight One. "*The world is a fucked up place. The inmates have taken over the asylum. You know it's true. I'm the only person who can save humanity from itself.*"

"*You might be right,*" whispered Jenna, now sobbing. "*But let's hope like hell you aren't.*"

And with that she pushed down hard on her diamond, and the footage abruptly ended, leaving a backup Edgar Knight with his fists clenched, staring at a blank screen.

7

"Lazlo," said Knight, blowing out a long breath, "how long has it been since this explosion?"

"Exactly fifty-seven minutes, fifteen seconds," the PDA replied.

"Did any structure at headquarters, or any people, survive?"

"Yes," replied Lazlo. "But only buildings and people on the periphery. Your central high-rise and the three buildings surrounding it were obliterated, with no possibility of survivors. Some of the outlying structures survived, along with the members of your group housed there."

Knight scowled. The central high-rise and three buildings that had ringed it were the nerve center of his operation, and while many of the people in these buildings were relatively unimportant workers, all of the key members of his organization were housed there, also, including every last member of his vaunted Brain Trust.

Most of his team had never been duplicated and were now gone forever. One copy of each famous scientist from his Brain Trust still lived, going about their normal lives throughout the world, but this setback was absolutely devastating. Duplicating these scientists one at a time without their knowledge had been a daunting task, impossible to repeat until he could rebuild his strength and his organization.

"Swarms of helicopters are descending on the island now," continued Lazlo. "They aren't painted black, but their serial numbers and registry are untraceable, indicating a high likelihood of being part of a Black Operations group."

No shit, thought Knight miserably. It had to be Cargill. He knew in advance what was likely to happen and had a team waiting to go in and mop up the moment it had.

Knight struggled to remain calm. He closed his eyes in supplication. "Please tell me that we still have the copy of Nathan Wexler's work my predecessor was reading," he said, his voice taking on a pleading quality.

"I'm sorry, Edgar, but it was destroyed in the blast. And the former Knight One hadn't yet saved it to the cloud."

Knight grimaced as though he had been stabbed in the neck. "Why can't you retrieve it from the cloud the way he did? Don't you still have footage of the instructions and passwords Jenna Morrison provided?"

"I already tried that, and failed. I knew this would be of vital interest to you. Cargill's team must have rigged the site to delete the file the moment it was downloaded. I've analyzed all footage taken while the former Knight One was reading the file on his computer, to see if I could recover some of the content from glimpses of it on his tablet. This was also unsuccessful."

Knight issued several sharp curses that echoed around the spacious home theater.

The loss of real estate and associates hurt, but nothing like the loss of this data.

Knight forced himself to calm down. He needed to look at the big picture, keep things in perspective. In his struggle with Cargill, he was now playing from behind.

But so what? An hour ago he was nothing but an expendable backup, facing certain death in three weeks' time. Compared to that, his current situation was a blessing. Getting out from behind the eight ball and finding a way to get his mission back on track wouldn't be easy, but it was certainly achievable.

This had been a blow to him, his organization, and his goals. He had lost hundreds of millions in real estate on Lake Las Vegas, his entire Brain Trust, and countless soldiers in his growing army.

But the Wyoming backup headquarters complex could be upgraded to serve his needs. He may have been confined to the main residence, but there were additional buildings and warehouses on-site. Now that he could reach these other structures without triggering his own death, he had access to working time machines and a storehouse of advanced technology created by members of his Brain Trust. He may have lost *them*, but he hadn't lost the astonishing advances they had made in almost every field.

And while he had lost most of his lieutenants and mercenary soldiers, a handful of these were on assignment away from Lake Las Vegas. These men knew all about time travel, supported his goals, and could be pressed into service once again.

With respect to the hundreds of millions of dollars the loss of his primary headquarters had cost him, this didn't matter in the least. He had billions more. It was easy to make money when you could, literally, *make* money.

Rebuilding human resources was the more difficult challenge, but in time he could recover the ground he had lost. Even so, he felt a rage within unlike any he had ever experienced. Cargill, Blake, and Morrison had outsmarted him. Had played him for a fool.

Well, had played Knight One for a fool. But this was a distinction without a difference. He would have fallen into their trap just as surely as his predecessor had. Even knowing the end result and watching it all unfold, he still hadn't been able to figure it out in time.

Allowing himself to be deceived by the likes of Cargill stung like nothing ever had, like a splinter buried deep within his eyeball. It was a monumental blow to his pride. It was *intolerable*.

Cargill was a buffoon. The thought of being outplayed by this man was *galling*.

But not *entirely* outplayed, Knight reminded himself. After all, here he was, still standing.

And as savvy as Cargill was, there was no way he'd suspect another version of Knight was still alive. He'd have a blind spot about this, believing he knew Knight well enough to know he would never allow a double of himself to run around.

Which was true. Knight hadn't allowed it. But Cargill would never guess that his rival had the intestinal fortitude to create, imprison, and kill a series of backups.

Even so, Cargill was a cautious bastard. So Knight would have to tread carefully. It was critical that the head of Q5 not get even a hint that he was still alive. Ideally until the prick was drowning in his own blood. But, at minimum, until Knight regained full strength and the noose had already tightened irreversibly around Cargill's neck.

Knight was confident he could still take Cargill down. In fact, he was the only person who could. Only he had intimate knowledge of Q5, as well as access to working time machines and Brain Trust technology.

So he would stay in full stealth mode. Regroup. Rebuild his strength and bide his time.

But even as these thoughts came to him, the seed of a plan began to form in his mind. With any luck, perhaps he could get his revenge and also destroy Cargill and Q5 faster than he had first thought. And most importantly, finally get his hands on Nathan Wexler's work.

Cargill hadn't won yet. He may have won this round, but there were more rounds to come.

Lee Cargill, Jenna Morrison, and Aaron Blake had managed to deliver a devastating blow.

But now it was his turn.

PART 2

"I don't know what weapons will be used to fight World War III. But World War IV will be fought with sticks and stones."

—Albert Einstein

8

Lee Cargill sat in his office inside Q5's temporary headquarters, deep in the bowels of Cheyenne Mountain, arguably the most famous underground facility in the world, although the word under*ground* didn't quite do it justice. Under-mountain might do. Or better yet, within-mountain, as it had been carved out under a ceiling of granite almost a half-mile thick, with an extensive array of three-story buildings constructed on a system of giant springs, protection against earthquakes and pesky nuclear attacks.

Q5 currently shared the surprisingly extensive space inside the impregnable Colorado Springs facility with a number of other Black Ops groups, although the organization had been allotted one entire wing out of four. Cargill worked out of a space that was more war room than office, with state-of-the art communications. His temporary office was surprisingly large, but its ceiling, while smoothed, had been left natural and uneven—not that he needed such an unsubtle reminder of the millions of tons of rock above his head.

Cargill rubbed a fifty-two-year-old hand through a still-thick head of salt-and-pepper hair and inhaled sharply. His anxiety was causing him to hold his breath for extended periods without his conscious knowledge, gasping in air only when his body's involuntary demand for oxygen became too great for his troubled subconscious to ignore. And then his breath would become stuck in his throat once again—sleep apnea without the sleep.

He didn't read much fiction, but even so, he had read the overused expression, *waiting with bated breath,* many times before. Was this what he was now doing? Or was this phrase meant to describe something else?

He closed his eyes, glad he had chosen to wait this out alone. Joe Allen, his second-in-command, was tied into his ear with a comm, but he didn't want Allen to see his tension, his uncertainty. Didn't want to discuss the tough questions with him.

He had just received a call from Nathan Wexler, at least one version of the man, who had teleported blindly, as planned, and found himself somewhere in the Mojave Desert, a location so barren it could well have been on another planet. As it turned out, it was just sixty-nine miles from the Las Vegas Strip. Since the plan had been for Blake to send the physicist just over a quarter second into the past, which would land him sixty-two miles away from the time machine, it was possible that Knight's command center was very close to this dense population center.

Of all the locations Cargill had expected for Knight's headquarters, Las Vegas wasn't it. Given that Knight's ego was the size of Texas, Cargill had half expected him to build a secret lair within a volcano, taking a page from *The Incredibles* or a James Bond movie.

On the other hand, Cargill should have known better. These bases had been constructed by the villains of these movies, after all, and Knight had fooled himself into thinking he was the *hero* of this drama. That his ruthless behavior wasn't that of a psychopath, but simply the behavior of a pragmatist striving to save the world from itself.

Holing up in Las Vegas, hiding in plain sight under the most blinding concentration of neon lights in North America, would be just like the man. Assuming Jenna and Blake had been taken to his headquarters, which was not a sure thing. Nothing was a sure thing.

Cargill's plan was bold, with a significant chance that it would end in disaster. They were attempting to bring Knight down by first giving him exactly what he wanted, what he needed, to destroy Q5 for good. If he figured it out in time, they would have delivered Jenna Morrison to him on a silver platter, and more importantly, Nathan Wexler's work.

For the plan to succeed, everything would have to go perfectly right. So far, it seemed that this was the case. Cargill had been confident Knight would let Blake go and give him a head start in exchange for access to Wexler's work, something he had already gone to herculean efforts to get.

In this quest, at least, Cargill couldn't blame him. Knight had spent so many hours struggling to understand the time travel he had tapped into, it was a wonder his brain hadn't burst into flame. Getting a chance to peek at the answer key was understandably irresistible. Like another, legendary, bite of knowledge that had been offered up in the Garden of Eden, Cargill was counting on *his* apple to lead to a downfall similar to the one a serpent had brought about.

And it seemed to be working better than Cargill had any right to hope. Because even assuming Knight would give Blake a head start, and assuming a duplicate Nathan Wexler had been negotiated into the mix, the odds against the private eye making his way through the phalanx of guards and security that Knight was certain to have, and managing to beam Wexler to safety, seemed astronomical.

Blake must be even better than Cargill had thought. He doubted the term *miracle worker* was much of an exaggeration.

Cargill had just finished a brief call with an ecstatic Jenna Morrison. He had given her the news that her fiancé was alive and they were even now racing to Wexler's GPS coordinates to retrieve him, scrambling a helo from nearby Nellis Air Force Base to pick him up.

While Cargill's identity and the nature of his work were kept in the shadows, he possessed command codes that could get US military bases around the country, and their commanders, to jump to carry out his every order. The commander would know better than to ask any questions about how the man he was retrieving had ended up in the center of a desert without any means of transportation, and why Nellis had been assigned to act as his personal chauffeur.

But just because this part of the operation had gone much better than expected didn't mean they were out of the woods. Knight could have knocked Jenna unconscious so she couldn't activate the explosive. Or perhaps he wasn't inside the blast range.

Regardless, what was now eating away at Cargill's stomach like so much battery acid was that everything might go *right*. If Jenna truly was in a dense population center in Las Vegas, this would be his worst nightmare.

Cargill had been *certain* Knight's base would be secluded. When Jenna and Blake had initially balked at his plan, he had assured them that this would be the case. The dose of octa-nitro-cubane explosive he had embedded in Jenna's ring was enough to vaporize a broad circle of real estate around her, the expected size of Knight's headquarters.

Even if Knight's base was secluded, there were sure to be scores of innocents surrounding him who would lose their lives if the plan succeeded. But at least in this case, most of the casualties would be people who had sided with a man determined to thin the human herd, kill every member of Q5, and ultimately ride roughshod over all of humanity.

But what if Knight had taken Jenna to a penthouse suite on the Strip? If she didn't realize where she was, and activated the ring, she could wipe out tens of thousands of innocent tourists, causing a blind panic around the world as a veritable crater appeared in the middle of one of the most iconic locations in the US.

Cargill shuddered.

Had he become as big a monster as the man they were trying to stop?

Bigger?

It was he who had pushed Jenna and Blake into accepting this degree of overkill—just to be *sure* that Knight was within the blast radius.

But Cargill had to admit to himself that this wasn't all of it. He also knew that a larger blast zone would have a greater chance of eliminating the scientists Knight was thought to have duplicated, as well, getting rid of a problem Cargill wasn't equipped to handle.

If these scientists lived, Cargill would be forced into making impossible choices. Imprison them, as Knight was doing, or go public with time travel. There was no third option.

Five identical copies of Elon Musk, with his exact memories up until recently, would be impossible to explain away. All of these Elon Musks would believe, rightly, that they were the father of Musk's children, the owner of his assets, the rightful resident of his home.

And this would repeat itself for hundreds, or even thousands, of famous scientists. It would be mayhem. Anarchy. Insanity.

And when time travel was revealed, as it would have to be to explain how so many duplicates of so many geniuses had sprung up like copies of newspapers rolling out of a printing press, it would throw the world into a panicked frenzy. This would be a shock to civilization, to the status quo, that would be too sudden, too profound to readily absorb.

By advocating for the use of so much explosive, if the plan did work, Cargill hoped to eliminate a problem he couldn't imagine being able to adequately solve.

But knowing that one copy of these scientists would all still live, knowing that the duplicates had no right in any sane universe to exist in the first place, and knowing that his actions had prevented a disclosure that would tear the world apart, didn't make him any less a monster. These scientists were innocents, prisoners, and he had put a plan into place knowing it could result in their deaths—worse, *hoping* that it would.

And now it might end much worse than he had thought. If Jenna was in a population center, there could be no good outcomes. If she realized where she was and never pushed down on her ring, Knight would survive, and they would have handed him a potent tool. And if she didn't realize where she was, Knight would die, but at the cost of many thousands of additional innocents.

Cargill tried to tell himself that if this were to happen, it would still be for the greater good, would still prevent far more loss of life later on, but the constriction of his throat, his inability to breathe correctly, suggested his subconscious would never be fully satisfied with this rationale. Because this is exactly how Edgar Knight justified his heinous actions. In Knight's mind, the world was headed for almost complete self-destruction. If Knight truly believed he had to eliminate twenty percent of the population to save the other eighty, was he any worse than Cargill?

Shakespeare had written, *Heavy is the head that wears the crown,* and Cargill never imagined he'd learn just how true this was. He didn't wear a crown, but he led a group that controlled time travel, and had virtually unchecked authority, making him the most power-ful man on Earth.

Assuming, of course, that Knight was taken down in the next few minutes.

If not, Edgar Knight would hold this title instead, and Cargill's days would be numbered.

Cargill gritted his teeth as he noticed the time ticking away on a digital clock in the corner of a large monitor on his wall. Almost five minutes had elapsed since Wexler had teleported into the desert. If Jenna did intend to trigger the explosive, she had already delayed it much longer than he would have expected. Did this mean the mission had failed?

This question was answered an instant later as Joe Allen's trium-phant voice materialized in his ear. "She did it, Lee!" said Allen excit-edly. "I have reports of a massive explosion in a region called Lake Las Vegas. Incredible!"

"Lake Las Vegas?" repeated Cargill uncertainly. "What the hell is *that*? Please tell me it isn't near any population centers."

"It's not. It's sixteen miles from the Strip. Knight's headquarters was on a man-made island in the center of a man-made lake."

"A man-made lake in the Mojave Desert? That's ridiculous."

"I agree," said Allen. "But also true. It was part of a massive con-struction project, decades ago, that not many people know about. The site of a multi-billion dollar resort that went bust. The island lat-er became home to a number of commercial buildings, most of them abandoned. Until recently. Nine months ago the island and every-thing on it was purchased by an anonymous entity for private use."

Cargill blew out a breath he felt he had been holding for centuries. This anonymous entity had to be Knight. So his base had been rela-tively secluded, after all. Thank *God*.

Cargill had still punched his ticket into the bowels of hell, had still joined the ranks of history's greatest mass murderers, but it could have been so much worse.

"Well done, Jenna," he whispered, trying to focus on the positive. What they had accomplished was nothing short of a minor miracle. They had brought down a man, and protected a secret, that could well have had a devastating impact on far more than just a tiny man-made island.

Cargill just hoped that if there was a God, He didn't judge that this had come at too great a cost.

9

Cargill closed his eyes and allowed himself to feel at least some relief at the successful conclusion of such a bold and risky Op, but only for a few seconds. There was much still to be done. "Send in our team to mop up as soon as they arrive on-site," he instructed Joe Allen. "You know the drill."

He had scrambled a team to head to the general vicinity of Las Vegas the moment they had pegged Wexler's GPS coordinates five minutes earlier, and they were already in the air. "Just make sure they land on the outskirts of the blast," he added. "By the time they get there, the periphery should have cooled enough for them to be safe. But make sure."

"Roger that," said Allen.

"Inform Aaron and Jenna that their duplicates succeeded. That Knight is no longer a threat. And tell Aaron that I'm pretty sure he's superhuman. Also, find out when Nathan Wexler is due to arrive on the runway, and make sure Aaron and Jenna are with us to greet him."

"Will do. Did you decide to give President Janney a heads-up on this Op?"

Cargill frowned. He had made it a policy to tell the president as little as possible about Q5 and his activities, not being shy about withholding key information, including their recent ability to travel almost a full half-second back in time. The president had known about the battle to acquire Nathan Wexler, but Cargill had told him only that he had discovered a theory that could help them develop the technology, without telling him the specifics of how.

"I decided against it," he said. "The odds of success were too low. Why risk upsetting the apple cart for nothing?"

"Sure," said Allen, who knew him only too well. "But mostly you didn't tell him because it's better to ask forgiveness than to ask permission."

"There was that too," he admitted.

Normally, this exchange would have brought a wide grin to Cargill's face, but he was torn in too many directions to find it amusing. At the moment, he felt more like vomiting than celebrating.

"Wait five minutes to be sure news of Lake Las Vegas has reached President Janney," continued Cargill, "and then organize a call between the two of us as soon as you can. Tell him it's urgent I speak with him about the explosion."

Cargill was left alone with his thoughts as his second-in-command began to carry out his orders. Seven minutes later, Allen informed him that the president was ready for his call. The moment Janney's computer-generated holographic image appeared, made to look as though the man himself was seated across the table from Cargill, the president began, wasting no time on greetings or pleasantries. "Jesus Christ, Lee! What the hell happened in Nevada?"

Cargill frowned deeply. "You're acting like *I* had something to do with this, Mr. President," he said, as though deeply offended at the mere implication.

One of the critical elements of lying effectively was to fool even yourself that you were telling the truth, thereby reacting to others the same way you would if your story *were* true, with the same indignation, surprise, concern, or outrage. The lies and misinformation he had already fed Janney about Q5's activities would get him fired, or worse, but the ones he was about to tell now would get him tossed in jail and the key thrown away. Or perhaps get him executed. He could make arguments as to why he thought his actions were valid, but even he appreciated that these arguments might not win the day.

"Just because I contacted you to discuss this tragedy," continued Cargill, "doesn't mean that I caused it."

Janney's pissed-off expression didn't change in the slightest. "But you know who did, right?"

Cargill nodded reluctantly. "Yes. I do know. Edgar Knight. He stole some advances we were working on to make the duplication process more effective." Even though the process involved traveling back in time, the words *time travel* were rarely spoken. "We happened to have some dark energy detectors in and around Vegas," he continued, another lie, "and the signature of the explosion reeks of it. We think Knight was probably headquartered at the epicenter of the explosion, and tried to modify one of his time travel devices using the data he stole from Q5. But the parameters weren't fully perfected. We're all but certain that it blew up in his face."

"*Are you kidding me?*" shouted Janney from his holographic perch in front of Cargill's desk. "This is almost worse news than if you *had* been responsible."

Cargill blinked rapidly in dismay. "I have trouble understanding how you could possibly say that, Mr. President. I know there was considerable loss of life," he added hastily. "I'm not trying to sugarcoat that. It's absolutely horrible. But if there is a silver lining, it's that we're nearly certain that most of those who were killed were affiliated with Knight. Not to mention Knight himself. We've been working night and day to find and eliminate him. We never could have guessed that he'd do it for us. Regardless, the biggest threat to the US and the world is now gone."

"Is it?" said the president in disgust. "Why isn't time travel *itself* the biggest threat? Jesus, Lee, did you hear what you just said? You think Knight didn't use the right settings and it created an explosion so devastating it could have been caused by a small nuke. I'm not enough of a scientist to understand everything you and Knight presented to me about the process after its discovery. But I *am* sure about this: you *swore* to me that the immense energies you were tapping into could only be used to push objects back through time. You guaranteed that they could never be released explosively."

Shit! thought Cargill. He had been sloppy. He had underestimated the president and made up a cover story that opened a huge can of worms. He would have to backpedal in a hurry.

"You're right, of course," he said. "And I fully intend to give you all the reassurance you need that this can never happen again."

"Like you did the *first* time?" said Janney dubiously.

Cargill winced. He had made an idiotic choice of a lie, and he had his work cut out to recover from it. "I deserve that," he said. "But our best people are sure they have a handle on what happened. This was a freak anomaly that might never be repeated, even if someone were *trying* to repeat it."

He sighed. "And I promise you, we're done tinkering. If this doesn't scare us straight, nothing will. We've sent matter into the past millions of times now without even the hint of an energy discharge. If it isn't broken, don't fix it. From now on, we'll be sticking with what we have."

Janney's glare didn't subside, but Cargill could tell his response had reduced the president's anxiety.

"Make damn sure you do," said the president. "You've made it clear that you're dealing with energies that could destroy the planet, maybe the solar system. And yet you're playing around with it like a five-year-old with a flamethrower."

"Apologies, Mr. President. You're absolutely right. Given the stakes, I was far too careless. But you can believe that I've learned my lesson. With Knight out of the picture, Q5 will spend all of its time using the current capability—which we know to be absolutely safe—to achieve our strategic goals."

"I'm well aware of how much good this technology can do. That's the only reason I'm not pulling the plug this instant. But see to it that you don't make another misstep, no matter how small."

"Understood, Mr. President," said Cargill. Then, after a brief delay, he added, "Before you go, I recommend that you ask your communications director to send the press my way. I'll use the alias Shawn Goodwin, and I can give you a phone number they can use to reach me. I'll go on record as an anonymous top-secret source within the government. I'll say it was a civilian scientific experiment gone awry, and assure the press that the odds of another inventor repeating this mishap are one in a million. I'll assure them it wasn't terrorism and that there is no radiation or other harmful fallout."

"And when you're asked the nature of this scientific experiment and how this could have happened?"

"I'll make it clear that we don't intend to make this public. If we reveal details, others might try to repeat it—on purpose."

"In that case, everyone around the world will immediately assume we're lying about it being civilian, and that it was a secret weapons site."

Cargill nodded. "Let them. We'll deny it, but it might give America's enemies something to think about."

The president considered. "Okay," he said finally, looking as miserable as Cargill had ever seen him. "You can take point initially, but I'll pick a few others I'll want you to work with to spin this, so you can pass the baton very quickly."

"Understood, Mr. President," said Cargill, relieved that his meeting with Janney had come to an end. "I know how bad this is," he added. "But rest assured, with Knight out of the picture, there will be nothing but smooth sailing from here on out."

10

The Lake Las Vegas explosion continued to be the biggest news story around the world, and would be for days and months to come, garnering wall-to-wall coverage on the networks, cable channels, and social media—but the spinning of the tragedy was now out of Cargill's hands.

Since so little real information was coming out of the government, speculation and conspiracy theories abounded. Many of these theories were preposterously farfetched. On the other hand, given the truth—that a duplicate of Jenna Morrison from another frame of time had triggered the explosion to kill the inventor of time travel, who wanted to use it to rule the world—no conspiracy theory could possibly go far *enough*.

As much as Cargill wanted to regroup and begin to move Q5 forward, he gave Nathan Wexler a full day and night to roam around the inside of the mountain, meet various members of the team, get reacquainted with his fiancée, and discuss and absorb the history and potential of Q5.

The second morning after Wexler's arrival, Cargill had a lengthy conversation with the unparalleled physicist and Jenna Morrison. Wexler agreed to join Q5's efforts, but only after making it clear how troubled he was by the loss of life that had taken place. He also acknowledged that they were in a brave new world, one presenting challenges that no ethicist or philosopher had ever dreamed of. He was well aware that the decisions they had been forced to make were treacherously difficult, and that the ones going forward wouldn't be much easier—which was why he wanted a seat at the table to be sure that this capability was used in the best way possible to benefit humanity.

With this new addition to the ranks of the senior management team, Q5 officially completed the most comprehensive management change in its history, even including the aftermath of the bloody civil war that Knight's violent secession had brought about.

The ranks of true senior management had dwindled down to three: Lee Cargill, his second-in-command, Joe Allen, and Daniel Tini, who was the most accomplished of the physicists on staff and had been serving as the head of the science and technology teams after Knight had left.

Cargill did have an Inner Circle of six members who were also in the know, all ex-commandos in charge of security and other clandestine operations. This number had recently been significantly larger, but, tragically, many of these men had been lost during the recent tug-of-war to acquire Nathan Wexler and his breakthrough.

But if only senior management were considered, the team had more than doubled in one fell swoop. Along with Jenna and her brilliant fiancé, Aaron Blake had been added as Cargill's number three, in charge of the Inner Circle soldiers and all non-scientific aspects of the team. Finally, Dan Walsh would also be joining, becoming the number three scientist on the team as soon as UCLA's semester ended and he joined them for good.

Despite Tini's demotion to the number two scientist, he had wholeheartedly supported adding Nathan Wexler and putting him in charge. Tini didn't believe for a moment he should remain the lead when a once-in-a-generation superstar was available.

Greg Soyer, a master computer hacker, was about to be married and had elected not to join the senior management team, but would act as a consultant to Q5 as needed.

A few hours after Wexler had agreed to come on board, Cargill held the first meeting of the new senior management team in a large conference room within the mountain, and welcomed the newcomers.

"I called this get-together," said Cargill after preliminaries had been dispensed with, "because we have much to discuss. We've just seen a number of dramatic developments."

He paused. "One," he continued, ticking each point off with one of his fingers, "we now have the capability to extend time travel almost a half-second into the past, thanks to Nathan's groundbreaking advances. This theoretical framework also opens up a few other intriguing possibilities that we'll get to in a moment.

"Two, Edgar Knight is out of the picture, so we'll be able to carry out our agenda in peace. The threat he posed is hard to overstate. He was wealthy, resourceful, and ruthless, and we suffered devastating losses during our recent war with him."

"I can attest to his ruthlessness," said Wexler. He went on to describe the horror he had witnessed inside Knight's penthouse, when Knight had shot one version of Jenna Morrison in cold blood, before the other version of her had worked a deal that had ultimately saved his life.

"Knight spoke of culling the human species like it was no more troubling than trimming an unruly hedge," continued Wexler. "If we hadn't stopped him, he would have wiped Q5 out without a second thought. And I was part of his Brain Trust, so I know just how remarkable some of the advances he was working on truly were. He would have been unstoppable."

"I have no doubt," said Cargill.

Wexler nodded at the head of Q5. "Sorry for interrupting your flow," he said sheepishly. "I believe you were about to list point three," he added with a smile, gesturing to Cargill's hand, which still had two fingers extended.

Cargill returned the smile. "I guess you really are good at math," he said in amusement. He held out his hand and made a show of adding a third extended finger to the collection. "And three," he continued, "after our Palomar headquarters was compromised, we've taken up residence here, but this is only temporary. We need to begin construction of a new headquarters tailored to our special needs. One that will have the right labs, facilities, and security we need to advance our agenda."

"We'll be looking for considerable input from everyone in this group," said Allen, "so we get the details right."

"With this said," continued Cargill, "let me move into the meat of the meeting. Our capabilities have changed dramatically. Our team has changed dramatically. I feel that we're at a crossroads, but also lost in the wilderness. Aaron pointed out when we first met that there is no real oversight of Q5. As the head of this group, this means no oversight of me—my power, my decisions. We all know what history teaches about the perils of a person or group having as much power as we do. Especially when this power comes with an almost complete lack of accountability."

Cargill sighed. "So Aaron was right to be concerned. I'm concerned also. At the time he brought this up, I offered Jenna a key role if she would join our efforts. She's had extensive graduate level training in molecular biology. And while this science isn't part of what we do here, she's shown herself to be brilliant and well trained in the rigors of analysis and critical thinking. So I asked her to make what is likely the most significant contribution of all: to study the ethics of our situation, and find ways to keep me honest."

Jenna shook her head and lowered her eyes in shame.

Cargill pretended not to notice. "So as a first order of business today, I'd like to ask Jenna to begin playing this role, in consultation with the members of this team and anyone else who might prove useful. I'd like her to begin putting together a moral and ethical framework to govern our actions."

Jenna shrank back and shook her head once again. "How can you possibly think I'm still fit for this job?" she said, looking like she might vomit. "After what I agreed to do to take out Knight? After the innocent lives my duplicate destroyed on Lake Las Vegas? If this doesn't show how wrong I am for this role, nothing will."

"Lake Las Vegas only goes to show just how badly we need an ethical framework," said Cargill.

"We may need it," said Jenna, "but asking me to take the lead now is like putting Jesse James in charge of railroad security."

"Who then?" said Cargill. "We're all tainted by this. And we're all struggling with it. I know you and Nathan have discussed it at length. I've discussed it with Aaron as well. You're still more worthy than any of us," he continued, and then with a wry smile added, "not that this is such a high bar to clear. But we all have other assigned tasks that are critical, and we aren't about to read in a trained ethicist to the most secret program in the country. So who better than you? Who better than someone who was forced to make this kind of impossible ethical decision? Someone with some amends to make?"

"We need to get this right," said Jenna morosely. "Daniel and Nathan are the best choices. Both brilliant, both analytical, and neither of them have innocent blood on their hands."

"As I said, we need them elsewhere," replied Cargill. "But even if we didn't, Jenna, I've studied your past more than I care to admit. Your character. Everything I've seen so far, along with my instincts, tell me you're perfect for this role. I know you fell from grace—or more accurately, I shoved you from grace—but that doesn't change the fact that your actions were necessary and heroic."

"I *thought* I was being heroic," she said. "But now all I can think about are the innocents who died."

"You were one of them," Cargill reminded her. "Willing to sacrifice your own life to take down a monster. And this is a natural reaction. In the heat of battle people do things that seem barbaric to them in cold after thought. This is happening to all of us. When we made this decision, the stakes were off-the-charts high. Knight was a threat, not only to all of our lives, but a real threat to the entire planet. It's natural for us to sober up afterwards and second-guess this decision. It's easy to be outraged by cannibalism while pondering the concept from your sofa. A lot harder when you've survived a crash landing and your choice is cannibalism or starving to death."

"Is this a rationale you've used to forgive yourself?" asked Jenna.

"No," said Cargill, shaking his head vigorously. "Because I *haven't*. I never will. None of us will. Which at least tells us we aren't totally lost causes."

Blake sighed. "I have to agree with Lee," he said reluctantly. "I've thought a lot about all the innocents that were killed at Lake Las Vegas, as we all have. But Lee is right, context is critical. Second-guessing a brutal decision after the fact is common. Harry Truman ordered two atomic bombs dropped on Japan, which ended World War II. These bombs led to the deaths of over two hundred thousand Japanese, including scores of women and children. So was Truman a monster?"

He didn't wait for a response. "Of course he was," he continued, answering his own question. "But should he have done it? This isn't as clear. The preponderance of the evidence suggests that by putting an immediate end to the war, this act saved many more lives than it cost. Estimates made before this decision was reached varied. But if the bomb had not been used, some at the time believed the additional losses on the American side would have been as high as a million."

"Based on what?" asked Tini, not challenging this assertion but expressing genuine curiosity.

"Prior to having the atomic bomb as an option," replied Blake, "America had planned two D-Day-style land invasions of Japan, and was determined to carry them out. The casualties on both sides would have been enormous, as they had been on D-Day. Japanese forces would have amassed at the point of these landings, turning them into bloodbaths. Not to mention that a Japanese Field Marshall had let it be known he would execute all one hundred thousand American prisoners of war if Japan was on the verge of losing."

Blake paused. "Nowadays, it's easy to second-guess this decision, easy to suggest the number of lives saved on the American side were overblown. Or even if they weren't, this still didn't justify such a horrific attack on women and children. But furthering Lee's point, it's easy in a time of relative peace, sitting on a comfortable couch, to do this second-guessing. But if you had lived during that time, when the threat was real, you'd have a different appreciation of why the decision was made."

"You mean beyond just the saving of American lives?" said Nathan Wexler.

"Exactly," said Blake. "Because the Americans didn't just estimate their own casualties if the atomic bombs were left unused. They estimated Japanese casualties, as well. These came in even higher than on the American side. If true, this would mean that the net loss of life on both sides would be far less if the bombs *were* used than if they weren't.

"Again," continued Blake, "it's critical to remember the context. Japan was using Kamikaze fighters, something the Americans had never run into before. Warriors willing to commit suicide to kill the enemy. Today, with our long experience with Jihadism, we've become accustomed to this reality. But back then it had the Allies rattled. The fear was that this mindset would cause Japan to fight to the death, to the bitter end and beyond. It didn't help that Prime Minister Tojo had issued an emergency declaration calling for millions of kamikazes and suggested that the entire Japanese population should be prepared to die."

Jenna listened in horrified fascination. "Why have I never heard about any of this context?" she asked. "I've always been ashamed of this episode in our history."

"History is barely taught in schools anymore," said Blake. "I only studied this episode because I'm in the military, where the history of war is an important topic."

"But even knowing the full history," said Cargill, "we *should* be ashamed. All of humanity should be ashamed of what the species was forced to become. But that's also the point. Sometimes there are no good decisions, only impossible ones. Which doesn't—necessarily— make those forced to make these decisions evil."

Jenna considered for several long seconds and then turned to Blake. "What do *you* think about the bombing of Japan? Do you think it was justified?"

He paused in thought. "Everything considered," he replied finally, "yes. Truman and the Allies warned the Japanese leaders they planned to use the bomb and gave them plenty of chance to surrender. They issued something called the Potsdam Declaration, which outlined surrender terms that were quite reasonable given the circumstances. I believe that using these bombs might well have been the best call for *both* sides. There is a writing that has become famous, made by an aging Japanese professor who was recalling the war. He said at the time of the bombings, he and multitudes of other Japanese civilians were starving to death. Literally. His weight was down to less than ninety pounds. The Japanese were starving their own people to fund the war effort, much like North Korea is doing today. He claims that, ironically, the atomic bomb saved him and millions of other Japanese lives. He said he couldn't have survived another month. That if the

Japanese military had its way they would have fought until every last person in Japan was dead."

"Which is exactly what the Americans feared," noted Jenna.

Blake nodded. "And there were many in Japan after the war who shared the professor's view. But even this doesn't help put the decision into proper context. I could go on for hours, because there were numerous other factors. WWII was bloody hell on earth. The Japanese had killed thousands at Pearl Harbor, stabbing America in the back at the same time they were engaged in diplomatic negotiations with the State Department. By the time the bomb had been developed, the war had gone on for six years, and hundreds of thousands of Americans had been killed. During this time, the Nazis and Japanese never hesitated to bomb cities filled with civilians. The Nazis rained rockets down on England for years, killing tens of thousands. We think of Japan today as a friendly, democratic, peace-loving country. But at the time, its rulers weren't so . . . civilized. Japanese soldiers committed any number of atrocities, including mass killings and rapes of helpless civilians in China, which I'll leave to you to look up if you want, but which would sicken you to your very core."

Blake paused to let this sink in. "All of this was against the backdrop of the Nazis gassing millions of innocent Jews to death. It was the ugliest stretch of years in human history—and Truman had the chance to end it once and for all."

He shook his head. "So again, did he make the right call? It's impossible to know for sure. There are any number of people today who think this was a clear war crime. And it probably was. But it was also likely to have been the right call, the *unavoidable* call."

11

As Blake finished his analysis of the first and only use of an atomic bomb in anger, the room became absolutely silent. Everyone was both spellbound and horrified to be reminded of the extended carnage and barbarism that had taken place during humanity's last world war, something certain elements of the species always seemed hungry to repeat.

The ex-soldier, ex-private eye had certainly given everyone much to ponder, and Cargill left the group alone with their thoughts for almost a full minute. "Thanks, Aaron," he said finally. "This helps put things in perspective. I hadn't considered this era, but it does give one food for thought."

He turned to Jenna. "So back to our own actions. I believe we made the best decision we could at the time. The most moral. We didn't make this choice because we get off on killing. We made it *despite* how much it sickens us."

Jenna nodded woodenly.

"I pushed you and Aaron into it," continued Cargill. "Not that this absolves you, but it puts this into further perspective. The bottom line, Jenna, is that I need you. *We* need you. So maybe let's shift the focus of your job. Instead of focusing solely on ethics, maybe focus instead on the broad goals Q5 should be pursuing going forward. With the ethics of these goals being a key component of the analysis."

"You're really willing to delegate something as important as our future goals?" said Jenna.

"My plate is full," said Cargill. "I have to focus on the specs for the new headquarters. I have to pull strings and create cover stories so you and the other new members of our team can seamlessly leave your old lives and join us without causing any eyebrows to shoot up. Aaron has agreed to let me erase any evidence that he even exists. I could go on and on. But even if I had the time, I'm not the right person. I've been at this too long. I need a new set of eyes. A different perspective."

"So you'll just agree to adopt whatever goals I come up with?" said Jenna.

"Absolutely not," said Cargill with a wry smile. "You'll get to set the tone. To lead the conversation regarding where we go from here. But I expect that you'll consult liberally with all of us as you perform your analysis. And I expect the goals to change and evolve as we all give our input. I want your ideas, your framework, as soon as you feel like you've completed a solid first-pass analysis. Folding in ethical considerations as needed along the way."

He paused. "But this isn't a democracy. So I'll have final say as to our direction. Even so, I could well agree to follow your exact prescription. At minimum, it will serve as a good starting point."

"What do the rest of you think?" said Jenna, her head swiveling to take a survey of the meeting participants. "Are you comfortable with me doing what Lee has asked?"

The response around the table was immediate and unanimous. All wholeheartedly supported her playing this role.

Jenna sighed. "Okay," she said to Cargill. "I guess I'm in. I'll try to deliver something as soon as I can."

"Thank you," said Cargill. "And remember this is supposed to be a work in progress, so don't wait until you think it's perfect."

"Understood," said Jenna.

"Before we adjourn," said Cargill, "I do have one other topic I'd like to address. I mentioned that Nathan's discovery opens up other possibilities. The obvious is going back in time a full half-second, which functionally allows us to project matter a greater distance. Another possibility that isn't as obvious is using the fifth dimensional connection we believe we are creating to develop faster-than-light travel, which Daniel and Nathan are evaluating now."

"Sure," said Blake, rolling his eyes. "Because everyone knows the fifth dimension is a magical place. Whatever that is."

Wexler laughed. "Sorry, Aaron. I know it sounds like total bullshit," he said, surprising all but Jenna with his down-to-earth phrasing. Only she knew that the most brilliant man in the room would never put on intellectual airs.

"The term, fifth dimension, sounds like new age hooey to most people," continued Wexler. "But it isn't. It's a very real concept, with very real mathematical implications. Now isn't the time, but I'll prepare a quick presentation for everyone on what this means. It will help you understand what might be going on. The mathematical framework is intensely complex, but I can provide a conceptual framework. Enough to help you understand why bizarre things can happen in higher dimensions, and why it even makes sense—sort of."

"If you can get a dumb grunt like me to understand any of it," said Blake, feigning humility, "then you're an impressive teacher."

Wexler shook his head. "You forget that your double helped me escape from Lake Las Vegas, Aaron. He was about as far from a *dumb grunt* as it's possible to get."

"Well, he was forty-five millionths of a second more experienced than me," said Blake with a grin.

"Just to finish my point," said Cargill before this side discussion could continue, "there's another new possibility that's come up. One Daniel realized had come out of Nathan's work."

"It's no longer just a possibility," corrected Tini.

"Right," said Cargill. "It became a reality just hours ago, when Daniel finished testing some recent modifications."

"What possibility are we talking about?" asked Wexler.

"Daniel used your theories to solve what we call the *nesting problem*," replied Cargill. "One that you and the other newcomers to the team didn't even know existed."

"Here's the problem in a nutshell," said Tini. "We can use a kettle to send an object back in time," he said, using *kettle* as a convenient shorthand for *time machine*, one that had begun to catch on within the group. Q5's time travel devices didn't resemble kettles in the slightest, but the term had been chosen to pay homage to a very old time travel novel that was a favorite of several scientists on the team. "As you know," he continued, "when we send something back, we end up with two copies. But there is one object we were never able to send back." He paused for effect. "A time machine itself."

Wexler nodded in sudden understanding. "Ah, I see how this would be useful. This would allow you to use a time machine to duplicate an unlimited number of slightly smaller time machines, basically at no cost."

"Except this turned out to be against the rules," said Tini. "Like using one of your three wishes to ask the genie for more wishes."

"Which we all know is the ultimate, unbreakable genie rule," agreed Blake with a grin.

"The devices can only operate if they have a continuous connection to dark energy," continued Tini. "If they've opened a tiny hole into the fifth dimension, so to speak. We couldn't send back a kettle within a kettle because the dark energy connection of the inner kettle always interfered with the outer one, and disrupted the process. We couldn't figure out a way around it."

"So we had to construct each device from scratch," said Allen.

"But you're saying that my theory allows you to circumvent this supposed rule," said Wexler.

"Exactly," said a beaming Tini. "As Lee mentioned, I just finished testing it before I got here today, and it works like a charm. Time machines for everyone," he finished with a smile.

"Not as exciting as the possibility of faster-than-light travel," said Joe Allen, "but a huge development."

Cargill frowned. "But one that also makes future security more difficult," he said. "We guarded against infiltration by Knight or his men by ringing our facility with dark energy sensors. Far enough away that we'd have plenty of warning if a kettle was being maneuvered to within fifty-eight feet of us to attempt to teleport in. Even inside a fast-moving truck."

"But now you have to deal with over a hundred-mile range," said Blake.

"That's right," said Allen. "The good news is that we've continued to improve upon the original dark matter sensors that Knight invented. They're now so cheap and sensitive we can deploy enough of them to make it feasible to detect dark energy in a three-hundred-mile radius around us."

"But nesting still leaves us vulnerable," said Wexler, catching on with his customary speed, "even with a three-hundred-mile sensor perimeter. Without nesting, any enemy time travel device—um . . . any *kettle*," he amended, like the rest of the newcomers still becoming used to this odd stand-in, "crossing the perimeter would trigger our alarms. Since the enemy would still have to travel almost two hundred miles to be close enough to use their device to breach, we'd have plenty of time to stop them. But when an enemy can nest kettles like so many Russian dolls, they can get within range in less than a minute, taking multiple hundred-mile jumps."

"Meaning we'd be totally exposed," said Blake.

"Not just us," said Cargill. "Everyone in the world."

"That sounds even *less* good," said Blake.

Cargill actually shrugged. "Don't worry about it too much. I just pointed it out as an academic exercise. With Knight out of the picture this isn't an urgent problem. For this to come into play, someone from Q5 would have to go rogue. Even if this happened, only the people in this room know how to program the devices for longer than forty-five millionths of a second. And at the moment, only Daniel knows how to get nesting to work. Even if a rogue learned how, I'm the only one with the codes necessary to work the devices. So it's not something we need to panic about at the moment."

"That would be a nice change of pace," said Jenna wryly.

"Even better," added Cargill, "I think we might ultimately be able to protect ourselves, even from this."

"Hard to imagine how," said Blake.

"Q5 began life under the auspices of Colonel Hank Vargas," explained Cargill. "He's in charge of all black secret weapons programs in the country. After Q5 became . . . independent . . . Vargas and I both built Chinese walls around our organizations. But when I was part of this larger group, I was aware of a team making great progress upping the power, speed, and precision of lasers. I'm pretty sure they've perfected a laser system fast enough to stop a series of nested kettles from getting close enough to reach us."

"The reason we have any chance," said Tini, "is that once a nested kettle is sent back through time, there's a little over a six-second delay before it can repeat this with another nested kettle inside of *it*."

"Why is that?" asked Jenna.

"I'm not sure," replied Tini. "I suspect Nathan will be able to figure that out."

Blake eyed the head of Q5 skeptically. "So what are you saying, Lee? That Vargas's lasers can kill these devices in less than six seconds?"

"Again, I'm not fully up to speed on recent advances," replied Cargill, "but I'm pretty sure they can. The laser's computer should be able to receive a signal from a dark energy detector and pinpoint the kettle's location in under a second. The laser system itself is designed to be powerful enough to reach down from low Earth orbit. If we mount it on a tower centered near headquarters, it should have more than enough stopping power to kill the kettle in two or three seconds."

Blake nodded appreciatively. "Impressive," he said. "I heard rumors about this Colonel Vargas in my past life," he added. "Supposed to be a real hard-ass."

Cargill smiled. "I didn't interact with him all that much, especially considering I reported to him for a time. Hard-ass for sure, but also hard to read. I *can* tell you that he had a reputation for killing weapons programs. Not because they were *too* terrible to use, but because they weren't terrible *enough*."

"Sounds like the kind of warmonger who makes Edgar Knight look like he's Amish," said Jenna.

Cargill laughed. "Unfortunately, this is true. But if his laser program ends up helping us stay secure, then he'll have done a good deed." He paused. "But, again, a problem for another time."

The meeting continued for almost thirty minutes. When it ended, Cargill thanked everyone for their time, making sure to catch Blake before he filed out behind the rest of the team. "Aaron, could you hang back for a while," he said quietly. "I'd like to speak with you privately for a few minutes."

Blake frowned. "Why do I have the feeling that I'm not going to like what you have to say?"

Cargill forced a tired smile. "I'm pretty sure you're going to *hate* it," he replied. "But I'm glad to see your intuition is as good as ever."

12

Blake waited for the last few team members to exit and close the conference room door behind them before turning to Cargill, who was gesturing for him to take a seat once again.

"To what do I owe this honor?" said Blake as he sat.

He had been impressed with the first formal meeting of the new senior management team. Cargill had known they were all second-guessing themselves regarding the loss of life at Lake Las Vegas and had made it a point to address this head-on, in the context of asking Jenna to be a planner/watchdog. In a sense it had been group therapy, and more effective than most, especially for Jenna Morrison.

Wexler and Tini each had a clear conscience, since they weren't involved. He, Cargill, and Allen had all made life-and-death calculations before, so could handle things better. Not necessarily well, but better than a lifelong civilian.

Blake had killed many times, and had made peace with the necessity, as long as he deemed he was killing the right people, for the right reasons. He had given up war—or at least had *tried* to—because he found that battling fellow humans, especially gifted warriors, was the ultimate challenge, and had become so stimulating that everything else seemed boring by comparison.

Except for time travel. That had yet to become mundane.

Blake was grateful to Cargill for pulling Jenna back from the emotional brink. In the short time he and Jenna had worked together, he had come to develop quite an affection for her.

His friend, Greg Soyer, had surrendered to the fairer sex and would be tying the knot relatively soon. He was worried about Blake's lack of dating, which Blake had excused by saying he was putting all of his energy into getting his nascent Private Investigator practice to be taken seriously. The cases he had been forced to take while building his practice could sour *anyone* on the idea of a relationship.

Before Jenna had come along, he might as well have been a porn photographer he had taken so many videos of cheating spouses— soon to be divorced spouses—screwing other people. Not exactly an endorsement of relationships, nor of the PI business. He could never have guessed when Jenna Morrison had walked into his apartment office, looking like a battered wife, how profoundly she would change his life.

"Aaron," began his new boss, "you know I meant what I said to Jenna. I want her to help guide us. I want to get back on track helping the world rather than killing people. I want out of the monster business."

"But?" said Blake warily.

"But . . . I want to act the assassin one last time before I hang up my spurs."

"I take it you mean you want *me* to act the assassin one last time before you hang up your spurs."

Cargill displayed a reluctant smile. "Okay, that is a more accurate description, I'm afraid. Before we get ourselves out of the muck, the least we can do is take out the two most dangerous men on Earth. We've taken out the *most* dangerous—Edgar Knight. And I take full responsibility for not doing more to limit the collateral damage. But we now have the means to take out the *second* most dangerous. This time with far less breaking of glass. We have the chance to make partial amends for any stains we have on our souls. To potentially save millions of lives, in addition to the millions we've already saved by ending Knight."

"You mean in addition to those you *believe* we saved?"

Cargill shook his head emphatically. "No. In addition to those I'm *certain* we did," he insisted.

Blake stared into Cargill's eyes for several long seconds, and was happy to see that the man's conviction on this point was unwavering. "What do you have in mind?" he asked.

"You mean *who* do I have in mind. Given he's now the single most dangerous man alive, it should be obvious."

Blake paused to consider, but only for a few brief seconds. If he had been asked to name the second most dangerous man left after Knight, this would have been tricky. But the *most* dangerous was head and shoulders above the rest: Kim Jong-un.

This tyrant, considered evil even by those who abhorred the use of this label, wielded considerable power and was thought by many to be insane, an unholy combination. But there was an even more chilling possibility—that the dictator was, in fact, quite sane, and also extraordinarily cunning. That the persona of this chubby, grinning dictator with the stilted walk and ridiculous haircut was one that he had purposely cultivated.

There were credible sources who claimed that the once-trim Kim Jong-un had purposely packed on pounds to match the weight of his grandfather, the first North Korean monarch to come to power after Russia liberated the country from Japanese rule in 1945. After gaining weight and adjusting his hair and mannerisms, Kim's resemblance to his grandfather was *uncanny*. Since this first monarch had been considered semi-divine, and this divinity was passed on through the bloodline, many were convinced that Kim's striking resemblance to his grandfather was the single biggest factor in cementing his ascendancy over his two older brothers.

Scarily sane or utterly mad, either way he was erratic, unaccountable, and utterly unpredictable, seemingly willing to burn down the world if it achieved an objective. The dense population of the metropolitan area of Seoul, South Korea, only a stone's throw away, gave him the equivalent of twenty-five million hostages to kill if anyone tried to use military force to rein him in or remove him from power.

And few doubted that he would destroy Seoul without hesitation, at minimum, before turning his sights on America and other targets. He was known to have conducted purges in his government, to have ordered hundreds of brutal executions, including orchestrating the deaths of his uncle and half brother, all in an effort to settle scores or consolidate his power. He was relentless in his saber-rattling and his pursuit of nuclear weapons, ignoring those in his country who were literally starving to death as the fruits of the economy were spent on weaponry and lavish palaces.

"So you want to target North Korea's Supreme Leader," said Blake. It wasn't a question.

Cargill nodded grimly. "Can you think of anything else we could possibly do that would better relieve global tensions? Let's get rid of this maniac once and for all."

13

Blake and Cargill, alone in the abandoned conference room, stared deeply into each other's eyes, studying each other's resolve and body language.

When Blake didn't speak for several seconds, Cargill pressed on. "No one is more of a powder keg than Kim Jong-un," he said. "We all know it. Ruthless, demented, and totally arbitrary."

"And sitting on a growing number of nuclear weapons," added Blake, "and the intercontinental ballistic missiles to deliver them."

Cargill's lip curled up in disgust. "I have a dossier for you to read. However ruthless and brutal you *think* Kim is, the unreported intel we have on him shows that this is just the tip of the iceberg. It's a miracle he hasn't nuked millions of people yet, just for grins." He shook his head. "It really is time for him to go. In fact, it's now almost a decade overdue."

"Isn't this something that Knight recommended?" said Blake. "Something you rejected? When we first met," he continued, "you said that using teleportation to kill someone like Kim was an example of a slippery slope you didn't want to step onto."

"Yeah, well, that slippery slope wasn't *teleportation*. It was human duplication. If teleportation could have been achieved without duplication, I'd have no problem with it. And as you know, I've now broken my own rule against duplication. I've taken such a giant step onto that slope that I've slid straight down to the cesspool at its bottom. I *will* climb back up again. But before I do, we need to take advantage of a golden opportunity to rid the world of this asshole. And things have changed since I ruled out this kind of operation. *Beyond* the fact that I've already duplicated humans when I swore I never would."

"What kind of things?" said Blake.

"It hardly seems possible," replied Cargill, "but we both know that Kim is getting even more unstable lately. Perhaps *bold* is the better word for those who believe him to be fully sane. We've been running out of time for a long while, but it's hard not to think we've reached the two-minute warning. Besides, Knight's plan for taking him out wouldn't have worked. It was too risky, requiring someone to get within fifty-eight feet of him with a kettle. Next to impossible. His protection detail makes the US Secret Service look like one elderly man with a walker."

Cargill shook his head and continued. "And even if such an assassination attempt did succeed, killing Kim isn't enough. Not when we don't know how to disarm his country. Where all of his nukes are hidden. Or who might fill the vacuum left when he's gone. We don't know if the dictator who replaces him would feel the need to retaliate to cement his hold on power. The eventual repercussions of an assassination could be even worse than what we're dealing with now."

"So your quarrel with Knight wasn't that he wanted to use this tech to take out a dangerous tyrant," said Blake. "It was just that you didn't find his plan an effective one."

"No. Again, I was pure as a virgin and wanted a total ban on human duplication, then and forevermore. And even though I broke my own rule, I still want the same thing. But before I put this genie back in the bottle, we have an unprecedented opportunity to end a North Korean nightmare decades in the making. Because we now have a range of over a hundred miles, and the ability to nest kettles. So we should be able to assassinate one version of Kim and kidnap and keep another."

"You're certainly ambitious," said Blake. "I'll give you that."

"If we're behind an assassination," said Cargill, "it's a clear act of war. Pyongyang might retaliate, perhaps striking at Seoul, or at us directly."

"But if a bomb blows up in Kim Jong-un's bedchambers," said Blake, "it's hard to blame the US. Unless someone can explain how we did it. Which no one would be able to do."

"That's one possibility," said Cargill. "If we went with that, North Korea and the world would assume that those around Kim finally got tired of serving a madman. In the days and weeks it will take Pyongyang to sort it all out, fill the power void he leaves behind, we could be milking this sick bastard for intelligence. We could make multiple duplicates of him so we can see what drugs or torture or inducements work the best. We could get all the intel we need to make sure we disarm the North Korean powder keg he left behind."

"Maybe," said Blake. "But what if you find that squeezing the right intel from this maniac is more difficult than you anticipated?"

"Then we'll just have to try harder," said Cargill simply. "We'll get it, and quickly, one way or another. Of that I have no doubt. We can make five copies of him and use cross interrogation. Glean one nugget from one of them and use it with another to show we know a lot more than he thinks—really get inside this tyrant's head. Plus, I'm still in touch with a number of scientists within black weapons groups. Scientists who used to work for me."

"And they'll still talk to you?" said Blake with mock incredulity.

Cargill laughed. "Working for me was a little less challenging for them than it has been for you, I have to admit. But yes, I'm still close to many of them. The point is, there's a new experimental truth serum I've become aware of. It's called T-4. Supercomputer simulations that take into account everything we know about the brain, and neuronal mapping, suggested it would be absolutely effective. The perfect truth agent. So it was moved into limited human testing."

"How limited?"

"Very. Because the simulations also indicated that it would kill roughly half of those who got it within a minute of administration. An unfortunate little side effect," added Cargill sarcastically.

"If it kills half the people," said Blake, "it's a poor interrogation drug. A dead subject is *really* good at keeping secrets."

"Which is why it's still being perfected."

"Given it's as lethal as it is, how was it tested?"

"Six times only. It was used twice in terror situations where this was the only choice. And four times on inmates about to be executed, who agreed to be guinea pigs in exchange for a commutation of their death sentences."

"Assuming they survived T-4," noted Blake dryly.

"Right. Anyway, these six, while a small number, give its developers confidence the simulations are correct. Half died, and the other half spilled their guts. All the information provided by the half who survived checked out as one hundred percent accurate. There is no doubt that if a subject survives the first five minutes, T-4 works like a charm."

"So you plan to check in with your scientist friend," said Blake. "See if he's made any progress on improving the drug."

"Correct."

"You said that blowing Kim up was one possibility. You have another?"

"Yes. One that I think will buy us more time—and create tremendous discord in North Korea. What if we jumped in and hit him with a slow poison after we knocked him out? There's a new one I know of. Inject him, and he'll feel just fine for three or four days. But he won't be. At some point on the third or fourth day, he'll drop dead abruptly from a massive heart-attack."

"How does a drug like that work?" asked Blake.

"I have no idea. All I know is that it does. So we could teleport one copy of the unconscious Kim a hundred yards away from the palace, one that we've poisoned. And we could teleport another copy of Kim out to be interrogated. Then we could blow the kettle, taking the palace with it."

Blake nodded thoughtfully. "Remind me not to play chess with you," he said, a mixture of admiration and horror in his tone. "Wow," he added as he continued working out the implications. "So Kim wakes up, alive, having no idea how he ended up outside the palace, but thinking someone tried to take him out. Convinced he was the target of an attempted coup."

"Think about how pissed off *that* will make him," said Cargill with a smile. "He won't be looking at us, he'll be looking within. Not knowing who to trust. Interrogating his most trusted lieutenants. Purging his own government."

Blake nodded. It was brilliant. The word *diabolical* came to mind. Much more paralyzing and destabilizing than even an outright assassination would be.

"Meanwhile," continued Cargill, "we'll have a copy of Kim to play with. And we'll have bought ourselves three extra days to get intel. When Kim dies from a heart attack, the country will be even more disoriented. Then we can strike at his nukes and missiles. Whatever it takes to defang North Korea. Bombing runs. Special forces boots on the ground. He'll show us where all of North Korea's family jewels are kept, and we can crush them in one fell swoop. Kill the chicken while its head's cut off."

Blake stared at him, deep in thought, but didn't respond.

Cargill inhaled deeply. "But let me get back to your comment about Knight," he said. "Don't forget that my refusal to use time travel as an assassination tool was the least of the points of contention between us. He also wanted to form a world government with himself at the helm. Or behind the scenes pulling the strings. He wanted to duplicate whoever he pleased without their knowledge and against their will. He wanted to institute a widespread eugenics program. And so on. So when the North Korean threat is neutralized, we'll have eliminated the two biggest threats to civilization this century. *You'll* have eliminated them."

"Is that an appeal to my ego?" asked Blake.

"No. Just a statement of fact."

"How far along is your planning for this Op?"

"It's nearly complete," said Cargill. "I started before we took out Knight. The key to moving forward was Daniel's confirmation that nesting is now possible. Not that we'd want to nest more than a single kettle. Making a series of jumps makes cleaning up after ourselves that much more difficult."

"Why would we even need a series of jumps?" said Blake. "Having a teleportation range of one hundred twenty miles turns this Op from impossible to relatively straightforward. Isn't Seoul within this distance of Pyongyang?"

"Just barely, but yes. Unfortunately, it won't be that easy."

"Why not?" said Blake. "Just to be clear, exploring this idea further doesn't mean I've agreed to the mission. But just for the sake of argument, I could land with two nested kettles in Seoul. I wouldn't even have to leave the runway. I could teleport into Kim's bedroom inside the inner kettle, while he's sleeping—say at three or four in the morning—drug him, shove him into the kettle, and send his chubby ass back out to my plane in Seoul."

Cargill frowned. "It *would* be this simple, except for one wrinkle. It's not common knowledge," he said, "but Kim doesn't sleep inside the palace at Pyongyang anymore. Hasn't for almost a year. He's more paranoid than ever."

Blake raised his eyebrows. "It isn't paranoia if there really are people who want you dead. In his case, it would be hard to find people who *don't* want him dead." He paused. "So where *does* he sleep nowadays?"

"At another of his palaces, northeast of Hyangsan, which itself is northeast of Pyongyang. Built at the foot of a mountain."

"How far away from Pyongyang?"

"Just under a hundred miles. Hyangsan is almost the exact geographical center of the country. I don't blame Kim for sleeping there. It probably is the safest region in North Korea. And it's only a thirty-minute helo ride to the capital, so still fairly convenient."

"But it puts him out of teleportation range of any border," said Blake.

"I'm afraid so. You didn't want this to be too easy, did you?"

"So what did you have in mind if I were to agree?" asked Blake.

"I'd want you to cross into North Korea from China. China is Kim's benefactor, and its border with North Korea is more porous than the border between the two Koreas. Not to mention that the two Koreas have a demilitarized buffer zone between them."

"And you have all the logistics buttoned up?"

"Nearly," said Cargill. "Just a few finishing touches. But once you're across the border, you could carry out the exact plan we just discussed. Get within range, teleport into his palace in Hyangsan, and teleport him back out."

"To where?"

"Still working out the details, but probably either the Swedish or UK embassies in Pyongyang. America doesn't have an embassy in North Korea, of course, but we can get operatives inside the embassies of our good friends. We could have you teleport Kim into an empty room and have our guys smuggle him to South Korea and on to America."

"By our guys, I assume you mean members of our Inner Circle."

"Yes. Specifically, Eric Beal and Chris Entwistle. They both have extensive interrogation experience."

Blake nodded slowly. "You do seem to have this all worked out."

"I've tried," replied Cargill.

"Give me some time to think," said Blake, before lowering his eyes to do just this.

Cargill waited patiently as his colleague mulled this over.

"If what you've outlined was all there was to it," said Blake finally, "it'd be an easy decision. But we have to vaporize the Kim that will remain in the bedroom after the two copies have been teleported out. We'd want to blow up the kettle left in the palace as part of the clean-up regimen in any case."

He frowned deeply. "Which also means vaporizing the Aaron Blake left behind. The *two* Aaron Blakes left behind, since I'm sure you'll want to also blow the kettle I use to jump inside the palace in the first place."

Cargill winced. "I know what I'm asking, Aaron. You've already made the ultimate sacrifice. Asking you to go on another suicide mission is the last thing I want to do. But you've proven just how good you really are. We need someone with your remarkable abilities. There can't be any mistakes. You know the old saying, 'if you're going to shoot at the king, you better make damn sure you don't miss.'"

"I'm not sure I'm as good as you think," said Blake. "And there's always a risk of failure. So what happens if we put a time machine into the hands of North Korea? Talk about blowing up in our faces."

"That wouldn't be . . . ideal," said Cargill. "But it wouldn't be catastrophic. They would have no idea what it was. Especially since the kettle I plan to use for this mission has been disguised to look like a large refrigerator. One without any inside shelves, of course."

"What's the matter," said Blake with a grin, "you couldn't fit it inside a DeLorean?"

Cargill smiled back. "I'm having a few more of these refrigerator kettles made for our possible use in the States. Along with some other configurations for emergencies."

"Emergencies?" said Blake.

"Look, I'm getting off topic. The point is, while I don't want a kettle to get into North Korean hands, it wouldn't be the end of the world. We booby trap all kettles, anyway, so that reverse engineering isn't possible. And they'd never be able to use it without the proper passwords. But you'd be under no such restrictions," he hastened to add. "In case you had to improvise, I'd give you total control of the kettles, first the outer and then the inner. They'd be linked to your vital signs and programmed to respond to your voice commands like a favorite PDA."

Blake nodded grimly. "You pamper me way too much," he deadpanned.

"I know how much of a sacrifice this is, Aaron," said Cargill softly, lowering his eyes. "And I'm truly sorry to even have to ask. But you're not just my first choice, you're my *only* choice. The only operative I'm confident will not fail, no matter what the circumstances."

Blake frowned. The man didn't exactly have a limitless group of soldiers to choose from. Given that only a handful of people knew about Q5 and time travel, *of course* Blake was his top choice.

"You should know, Aaron," said Cargill, as though reading Blake's mind, "that if I could choose any commando in the world, I'd still pick you. You're remarkably resourceful. You can make lightning-fast decisions under fire. And you always seem to find a way to win. This puts you in your own class of formidable."

"So all I have to do is agree to condemn other versions of me to death," said Blake. "I just have to send a duplicate or two off to get blown up for me, like I did before, while I sit here drinking umbrella cocktails. What could be easier?"

"Just about anything," said Cargill. "I'm well aware. You weren't the only one who allowed a duplicate to be knowingly killed on this last Op. So did I. Remember, one of me was shot in the head. I know how hard it was to allow this to happen. Because while I wasn't the one shot, I committed my double to being a human sacrifice. We both know the copy of you sent on this mission will remember this discussion, know that you—he—agreed to saddle himself with a suicide mission. And his love of life will be just as strong as your own."

Blake scowled for several long seconds, but this was suddenly replaced by a look of amusement. "Remember that guy in the Revolutionary War?" he began. "The one who said that his only regret was that he had but one life to give for his country?"

"Yeah, Nathan Hale," said Cargill. "What about him?"

Blake grinned. "Well, he's really beginning to piss me off. Because *my* only regret is that I seem to have an *infinite* number of lives to give for my country."

"It does suck to be yous," said Cargill, also breaking into a grin. "Sorry. Couldn't resist. Gallows time travel humor."

"Hilarious," said Blake dryly. This was followed by a long silence. "So if I did agree to this mission," he said finally, "when would I start?"

"You'd leave in two or three days," replied Cargill. He shrugged. "No time to waste."

"A quick operational question," said Blake. "Won't Kim have security cameras in his bedroom that will pick up my arrival? Sensors that his security team will be monitoring?"

"The kettle will have the ability to disrupt cameras, but based on our intel, this won't be necessary. He has multiple women in his bedroom—frequently—engaging in acts of debauchery that make Sodom and Gomorrah look like Disneyland. He's a man of large . . . appetites. He likes his privacy. So no cameras and no sensors. He locks his room at night more securely than a vault. And he is secure. From anyone but us. Because outside of his room, and throughout the palace, he has explosive sensors, poison gas sensors, and guards who are well paid and loyal."

Cargill paused to see if Blake had more questions. When he saw that none remained, he went in for the close. "So what do you say?" he asked. "Are you in? I promise this will be the last mission of this kind. You'll have removed two of the biggest threats the world has ever seen. After that, the world is on its own. We go back to helping little old ladies cross the street."

There was a long silence. "*Okay,*" said Blake finally. "I'm in." He rolled his eyes. "*Of course* I'm in. You had me at Kim Jong-un."

Cargill grinned. "I can't thank you enough, Aaron."

Blake pursed his lips in thought. "You made it a point to meet with me in private," he noted. "Even Joe Allen isn't here. Is it your intention to keep this Op just between the two of us?"

"Yes. Why not err on the safe side? If no one else knows, no chance of a leak."

"And President Janney?"

Cargill shook his head. "Not so much," he replied. "I'm not exactly on his good side at the moment. I need to tread carefully. To be honest, I'm not sure I'd involve him anyway. The less he knows the better."

"If I succeed, you'll have to tell him," said Blake. "He'll need to direct forces to act on the intelligence we get from Kim."

Cargill sighed. "I'm well aware. That day will not be pretty for me, I can tell you that."

"No, I'd imagine not," said Blake, unable to keep himself from taking satisfaction in the thought that Cargill would suffer also, even if it was the tiniest fraction of what he would be forced to endure. "I guess we all have our crosses to bear," he added with the hint of a smile.

PART 3

"To everything there is a season,
and a time to every purpose under heaven:
A time to be born, and a time to die;
A time to kill, and a time to heal."

> —Partial excerpts from Ecclesiastes 3:1-8, King
> James Bible

"Time flies like an arrow . . . but fruit flies like a banana."

> —Unknown (often attributed to Groucho Marx)

14

Aaron Blake was strapped into a jump seat within the nearly empty hold of a small cargo plane, on approach to Beijing Capital International Airport. "We'll be landing in ten minutes, sir," said the pilot, his voice coming through the tiny comm embedded in Blake's ear.

"Acknowledged," he replied to the head of a military piloting duo. He had never met either pilot, and neither had been told anything about him other than he was a VIP—whom they assumed was also military.

He suspected they were eager to drop off their unknown passenger, with his unknown cargo, and get their asses out of Chinese airspace as quickly as possible. Active military pilots flying with false uniforms—those of the cargo company they were pretending to work for—weren't treated particularly well if discovered on foreign soil, especially if the owners of this soil tended to be rivals of America on the world stage.

After Blake had agreed to the Op, Cargill had wasted no time whisking him back a split second, creating two Aaron Blakes an instant earlier, and prepping one of these Blakes for a one-way assassination/kidnapping mission. Despite his preparation, Blake spent the first six hours of the flight continuing to study up on the mission, the six hours after that making sure he slept, and the final two hours playing through various ways the mission might go wrong, and planning out the best way to react if this did happen. Since it was a rare mission that went precisely by the numbers, this exercise had saved his life a number of times.

He was wearing a gray jumpsuit with the logo *International Freight Services* stenciled on the pocket in bright yellow, and was carrying a relatively small leather bag. He felt naked going on an

Op without body armor and without weapons of any kind, but this was par for the course for a spy mission behind enemy lines, and he would acquire these other items soon.

Blake pulled a small plastic well from his right pocket, opened it, and considered the contact lens inside, floating in an unknown fluid. He fished out the small lens, carefully set it on the tip of his index finger, concave side up, and touched it gently to his cornea, where it remained.

The tiny device was insanely impressive. He had practiced with it during the early stages of the flight and had quickly become adept at controlling its functions with simple voluntary blinks, which sensors inside could easily differentiate from the *involuntary* variety.

Numerous companies were working on smart contact lenses that would do Google glasses one better—Google, Sony, Samsung, and a host of others. One version of such a lens had even been put on the market fairly recently, in 2023, but this one only had a rudimentary functionality. Not that it wasn't a miracle of technology, but it was primitive next to the smart lens Blake was now wearing.

Cargill had told him he had gotten his hands on this tech under the table, without going through proper channels and without going through his old boss, Hank Vargas, although he didn't specify how he had managed this sleight of hand. Blake was beginning to appreciate the varied skills Cargill brought to the table more and more as time went on.

The lens contained a nearly microscopic onboard computer and an invisible antenna, allowing it to connect to a peripheral device like a phone. In this case, since the kettles Blake was bringing with him in the cargo hold possessed supercomputer level processors, both his phone and contact lens connected to the outer kettle of the nested pair, which he had named K-1. Once the inner kettle—K-2—was sent back in time, his lens and phone would connect to this one, unless he specified otherwise.

Along with an in-eye display and access to computer programs carried on the kettle's supercomputer that were extraordinarily advanced, the lens could send pulses, invisible to the human eye, that would prevent video cameras from recording a clean shot of Blake's face, and also allow him to see in the dark, using thermal imaging. Both capabilities were truly extraordinary.

"Where have you been all of my life?" said Blake affectionately to the lens, blinking in such a way as to temporarily deactivate it until they were on the ground.

He didn't have to wait long. Only seconds later he felt a momentary jar as the wheels touched down, followed by a rapid deceleration.

"We've landed on runway six of Beijing Cargo Transportation Station, sir," said the pilot, unnecessarily. "We'll be coming to a stop shortly."

"Thank you," said Blake.

He looked up the station on his phone. "Beijing's Cargo Transportation Station," he read, "undertakes warehousing, loading, delivery, transit, and land transportation for international and domestic air cargo. In addition to other types of cargo, the Station is capable of handling super-big and super-heavy loads, freezing, refrigeration, hazardous materials, live animals, valuables, and air mail."

Blake noted in amusement that time travel machines were absent from this list.

Not anymore, he thought, as his smile vanished and he braced himself for the true beginning of his mission.

15

As planned, Blake was greeted by a man named Zhang Ping on the runway before moving on, alone, to a nearby inspection station. The inspection and approval of Blake's passport and false papers went smoothly, as expected. Zhang had assured Cargill before the mission had begun that the inspector had been bought and paid for, threatened and rewarded both, and would rubber-stamp Blake's arrival and onward trip even if he were Attila the Hun.

Even so, he was relieved when he was finally waved on.

Blake forced an appearance of relaxation as he supervised the transfer of his time travel devices to Zhang's plane. Both nested kettles had shells of stainless steel. The inner kettle was identical to the outer, just a fraction smaller. Both contained two doors that opened in the middle, and both had been engraved with the words, *Sub-Zero Commercial Refrigeration, Final Prototype*.

The Final Prototype part had been a nice touch on Cargill's part. Had Blake flown all the way from America with what appeared to be a single commercial refrigerator in his cargo hold, and nothing else, this may have raised some eyebrows. But if this refrigeration unit was marked as an advanced prototype, such special treatment would be expected.

The kettles had been designed to look just like actual Sub-Zero restaurant units, with the exception that refrigeration motors and coolant systems housed in a closed-off section on top had been replaced with whatever technology allowed for time travel, and an electric power system replaced by a connection to a power source the Sun would envy.

The inside of the second kettle, the inner layer of the time travel onion, was large enough to fit four men inside, or, more importantly, one glorious North Korean leader sprawled out unconscious, even if said leader were to double in size.

Both kettles also included a tiny, stainless steel video camera and mic, centered above the doors, blended to look like they were part of a design flourish. These would provide Blake a much-needed window on the outside world, especially important when he arrived at the palace inside K-2, since he would be deaf and blind otherwise.

During the cargo transfer, Blake appeared as carefree as a tourist at the beach, but inwardly he was at full attention, prepared to issue a one-word code that his phone would transmit to detonate the kettles, which had been rigged with octa-nitro-cubane.

This explosive was impossible to synthesize in the quantity needed. Q5 could only acquire enough for their needs by putting an infinitesimally small amount of it in a kettle and running it through billions of duplication cycles. This resulted in pushing back a local eddy of the universe forty-five millionths of a second, not once but *billions* of times. Even so, since the local reality reset each time, from the perspective of the universe and all observers this extensive duplication occurred without any time passing at all.

The kettles contained less than a gram of octa-nitro-cubane, but this was enough to create an explosion that would obliterate them and take out a significant portion of the surrounding area. Importantly, this would also disrupt the kettles' connections to the dark energy field, leaving no evidence that they had been anything but a Sub-Zero prototype—albeit one that would no longer be moving toward the market.

Blake wasn't an expert, but he had to believe that an appliance that could spontaneously explode and take out half a city block would not be highly valued by refrigerator connoisseurs.

While Blake waited for his cargo to finish its short journey to Zhang's plane, he passed the time testing out the advanced capabilities of his smart contact lens and phone. He blinked three times in succession to activate the lens's translation feature, designed to allow him to read Chinese with flawless efficiency, and couldn't help but grin as his eyes sought out Chinese signage at the airport. The system worked like a dream.

The lens was now in constant communication with K-1, the outer kettle's supercomputer, which converted any Chinese characters Blake spied into English with breathtaking speed. The lens then displayed the translated words in perfect clarity just beyond his retina.

His phone could perform the same task with spoken words. When activated by a single touch, it would open a two-way connection to the kettle supercomputer, which would listen for the Chinese language, once again converting anything it heard into English and transmitting this to the comm in Blake's ear.

After twenty minutes of testing both systems, he marveled at the speed and precision of this technology. The translations, at least from Chinese to English, were nearly flawless, and the military translation software far surpassed any civilian efforts Blake was aware of. He knew enough about the severe challenges inherent in this type of flawless translation to be more impressed than most would have been.

The hardware was one thing, but perfecting a program that could accurately translate complex ideas from one language to another, idiom included, was astonishingly difficult. Languages were hard. Even without idioms and adages, words had multiple meanings, and only an intimate knowledge of a culture and word-context, learned since birth, would allow full comprehension.

One example of why perfect translation was so difficult was the phrase, *time flies like an arrow . . . but fruit flies like a banana*, which demonstrated just how many wildly different meanings a simple sentence might convey.

What would a non-native speaker of English make of the five-word phrase, *Time flies like an arrow*? Did this mean that time moved quickly, like an arrow? Or was this advice to use a stopwatch to *time* flies, just like one would *time* an Olympic sprinter, or an arrow?

Or was a "time fly" just another fly species, like the housefly? If so, did these *time flies* happen to harbor affection for arrows for some reason? And just how much *did* time flies like an arrow?

What about *fruit flies like a banana*? Did this mean that all fruit, when thrown, flew through the air as a banana would? Or did members of the fruit fly species just happen to have an affection for the yellow fruit? Or did fruit flies like bananas only in the sense of wanting them on their personal dinner menus?

Putting the two phrases together would probably melt the most accomplished translation computer ever created.

Although of questionable veracity, additional urban legends of translation follies had become widespread, suggesting that using a computer to translate English phrases into other languages and then back again could yield ridiculous results. *Out of sight, out of mind*, could come back simply as *blind idiot*. Or maybe *invisible insanity*.

The spirit is willing, but the flesh is weak might come back as *the alcohol is good, but the meat is rotten*.

Blake continued to experiment with his new toys until the nested kettles had been transferred to Zhang Ping's jet, secured, and he was ready to board. The entire process, from landing to being ready to take off again, had taken just under an hour.

16

Junior Technician Yang Tan jumped as if he had been stung by a hornet. He shook his head to be sure he wasn't dreaming and checked his monitor once again.

Sure enough, the upper left corner of the screen was still flashing red and beeping noisily. He had just returned from lunch, but the monitor indicated this had been going on now for almost an hour. His initial shock subsided as he realized that this must be a glitch. The next test wasn't scheduled for three more hours, so the odds of this being a real signal were probably one in a trillion—and that was on the conservative side. A SETI researcher would have been less shocked to receive a message from deep space saying, "We're aliens from Tau Ceti and we'd like to pop over for a visit."

Yang checked the settings once again, and when these checked out he rebooted his computer. Yet the flashing and beeping remained.

Yang was just an ant in an enormous colony, a sprawling campus at which China was trying to out-DARPA America, invest in breakthrough technologies of all kind, even those believed by most scientists to be decades away or so outlandish as to not be taken seriously. DARPA's mission statement was "to make pivotal investments in breakthrough technologies for national security," and China had plagiarized this statement almost word for word.

China's Advanced Science and Technology Institute had been hastily constructed in 2021, twenty-five miles from Beijing's city center, and only five miles away from Beijing Capital Airport. This airport proximity facilitated the rapid comings and goings of important members of the Chinese military, as well as Chinese scientific consultants working at labs throughout the country and around the world, and even the occasional Politburo member, underscoring the facility's importance to the future of China.

But of all the wild science and technology projects being pursued here, Yang was a tiny cog in the most speculative wheel of all: one whose goal was to tap into dark energy.

As expected, after two years of employing China's best minds, the Institute's Dark Energy Initiative, or DEI, had gotten exactly nowhere. Not a millimeter of progress had been made, and most scientists thought the project made less sense than one devoted to surpassing the speed of light. How could they tap into something they couldn't measure and didn't understand?

The only breakthrough had come in the development of a sensor array, the size of a small home satellite dish, which the groups' scientists believed would detect dark energy, confirming their success if they *did* somehow manage this impossible feat. *Maybe*. Again, not knowing precisely what they were dealing with, the array operated on theory and educated guesswork alone. They would never know for sure if it worked until they managed to tap into a local dark energy field, and if it *didn't* work they would never know it.

Still, it was the only tool they had. So they forged ahead and deluded themselves that the sensor array really would magically indicate if they had achieved their impossible goal. They tried one pie-in-the-sky experiment after another, sometimes several in a single day, each a wild-assed attempt to tap into the field, taking a page from Edison, who tried over a thousand filaments for a light bulb before finding one that worked.

Perspiration over inspiration. And if there was one thing China could do well, it was perspiration. It was throwing ridiculous amounts of manpower at a problem for as long as it took to solve it.

They tried using lasers in combination with magnetic fields, controlled explosions within chambers cooled to near absolute zero, exotic electromagnetic pulses, and endless other blind attempts to achieve their goal, each ending in failure. It was worse than shooting in the dark. They were blind men trying to locate a single off-color piece of hay in a haystack the size of Jupiter.

So far, as expected, the sensors had yet to detect the slightest hint of a signal, although, for all DEI scientists knew, they had managed to connect with the field and had never known it, because the sensor array was nothing but a joke.

But this joke had just come up with a new punchline.

Because, at long last, the sensors had apparently detected a signal—*but at a time when the Institute wasn't even running an experiment.* Good trick.

Junior Technician Yang forced himself to remain calm and think logically. "Computer, identify the precise location of the signal," he commanded, doubting this would help. He knew it wasn't coming from any experimental chamber within the institute, and the sensor array was thought to have a fairly limited range, seven to fifteen kilometers at best.

"Working," replied the computer, and then only a few seconds later added, "The signal is concentrated within the Cargo Transportation Station of Beijing Capital International Airport."

Yang bolted upright. The signal was coming from the airport? This possibility had never even crossed his mind, despite the airport's proximity. And it wasn't just coming from the airport, but from the cargo section.

Surely there must be some combination of factors that could account for this, that could provide a mundane explanation, but for the life of him Yang couldn't find it.

"The signal is now moving," reported the computer in a calm, soothing voice, unaware of what a bombshell announcement this truly was. "It is traveling southeast at a speed of twenty kilometers per hour—and accelerating." Pause. "Forty-five kilometers per hour." Pause. "Eighty kilometers per hour." Pause. "One hundred ninety kilometers per hour."

Less than a minute later, after several additional updates, the computer added, "The signal can no longer be detected."

Junior Technician Yang's eyes widened and electricity coursed through his body. Given that the signal was detected on a runway, it didn't take much imagination to figure out what had happened. The source of the signal had accelerated rapidly until it was out of range of the sensor. The conclusion was inescapable: the object in question must be on a plane, now flying away from Beijing.

Yang stared at a monitor that no longer indicated anything unusual, but which had just shaken him to his core.

So what should he do now? If he brought this to the immediate attention of the higher-ups, he would do so at great risk to himself. If Yang had overlooked something obvious, some way that made it clear this was a false signal, he would surely lose face, and probably his job. The Chinese government didn't tolerate mistakes or incompetence, especially among those who had been given the honor of working for one of the Institute's forty-eight different science and technology projects.

Yang would rather kick a dragon in the teeth than interrupt a superior with a false alarm.

On the other hand, if he failed to report this signal promptly, and it turned out to be as important as he feared, it would go even worse for him. Besides, the strange behavior of the signal indicated the dark energy connection was taking place within a cargo jet, moving as the jet moved. If there really was an object that could fit within a cargo hold capable of opening a hole in the fabric of space-time, assuming the sensor really could detect the proper signature, they needed to know about it.

Junior Technician Yang Tan swallowed hard and rushed out of the lab, moving toward the office of the head of the entire project, Director Chang Yin, bypassing the usual channels in an effort to save time.

Yang hoped that going directly to Director Chang with this information would be lauded as a bold move, saving precious minutes that could prove decisive as the DEI sought to understand what they were dealing with.

But he was well aware that he might be doing nothing more than racing toward the maw of a wood chipper, bringing about career suicide with all possible haste.

17

Blake's face was glued to a window as the jet climbed into the sky. Within seconds the seemingly ever-present layer of smog that plagued Beijing and its vicinity blocked out the ground, and he turned to face his fellow passenger.

Zhang's plane was a unique hybrid, half luxury passenger jet and half cargo aircraft. Its tail opened like a crocodile mouth at the back for ease of loading and unloading, and it had a transparent hull between passengers and cargo, perfect for VIPs with precious cargo they wanted to keep an eye on at all times. Blake refused to even ponder what kind of dark, illicit goods may have also taken a ride in this hold over the years.

Blake was seated in an impressive leather chair across from Zhang in the luxurious passenger compartment. Although the compartment seated twenty in spacious comfort, he and Zhang were its sole inhabitants, and a large prototype refrigerator its sole cargo. A refrigerator that couldn't even keep an icicle cold, but which did have a few tricks up its sleeve.

Zhang eyed the unit with great interest, but knew enough not to ask its importance.

"Now it is safe to talk, Mr. Blake," said Zhang in perfect English, dispelling any notion Blake might have had that the man was partially mute. He hadn't exactly been chatty over the previous hour. "It's unlikely anyone was listening in down below, but I'm *certain* they aren't now. I am honored to share Sun Yee On's plane with you."

"Not at all," replied Blake, schooled in both the importance of praising guests and the deep humility expected in the Chinese culture. "The honor is all mine, Enforcer Zhang," he added, also aware of the Chinese penchant for using honorifics followed by last names—which were given first—the opposite of the Western system.

When the jet leveled out, Zhang removed a green nylon duffel bag, almost five feet in length, from the overhead compartment and handed it to Blake. "This contains the weapons and other gear that you requested. I encourage you to inspect it, and hope that you will find it worthy."

Blake smiled, not even glancing at the heavy bag, stuffed to the gills. "No need, Enforcer Zhang. I'm sure everything is there, and is more than satisfactory."

Zhang was tall and muscular, with fine black hair and other features that were unmistakably Chinese. He appeared calm, self-confident, and moved with an athletic grace. Despite the studied passivity of his face, there was an aura of menace about him.

Zhang's lack of expression was also not unexpected. The Chinese people had long been stereotyped as inscrutable, not entirely without reason. Many Chinese did try to appear emotionless whenever possible, wearing neutral, unreadable expressions that would make the best poker players jealous. This showed that they were taking their guest seriously, exuding harmony, and adhering to the Confucian dictate of balance in all things.

"I was instructed not to take a direct route to our destination," said Zhang. "I don't expect any trouble, or that anyone will try to follow us, but I believe this to be a wise precaution."

"What *is* our route?" asked Blake.

"We are heading southeast toward Shanghai. This is the flight plan that was filed with authorities. But when we are halfway there, we will circle back and head northeast to our final destination, a private airfield on the outskirts of Shenyang. A *very* private airfield. One that is four hundred of your miles closer to the North Korean border than Beijing. Our transponder has been modified so we will appear to be continuing on to Shanghai, as planned."

"How close is Shenyang to the border?" asked Blake.

"About two hundred kilometers," Zhang replied, momentarily forgetting to do the conversion for his American guest. "A hundred twenty miles," he amended. "But we won't be pursuing a direct route. The truck you requested will be awaiting us on the runway. We will cross using a tunnel under a remote part of the border, two hundred twenty miles from our landing. I will then drive you to a secluded area within a hundred miles of Hyangsan, as agreed, and leave you there."

Zhang paused. "Can I assume you have a phone, and that it is untraceable?" he asked.

"Yes. It mimics the latest Apple model, but it has a number of enhancements and safeguards. No tracking, no hacking," added Blake with a smile.

Zhang's face remained impassive. "Good. Give me its number and I'll send the precise route I plan to take to get you where you want to be. We should also link our phones so we can communicate, if necessary, while I'm driving the semi and you're in the back. The *trailer* as you call it."

Blake was impressed. He knew Zhang would be competent and experienced, but the man was also more careful and meticulous than he had expected. Zhang sent the route he planned to use to Blake's phone, and they set up communications so their voices would come through the comms each wore in their ear if this proved necessary.

"You mentioned we'd be using a tunnel," said Blake when this process was complete. He looked uneasy at the prospect. "Can you elaborate?"

"Please do not be concerned, Mr. Blake. The tunnel is well concealed and drivable. Even with a truck the size that we will be using."

"Are there no runways closer to the border-crossing than Shenyang?" asked Blake.

"There are many," replied Zhang. "But the private airfield we will use is guarded and controlled by our people. Unfortunately, this marks the easternmost edge of our . . . influence. It is a territory we have only recently begun to expand into. The airfield was completed only a few months ago. We have a policy of steady expansion. Only by continuing to grow, continuing to gain strength, can we ensure our long-term prosperity and survival."

"This is a wise strategy," said Blake, not sure what else to say about this. He detested everything Zhang and his group stood for, but in this case, clandestine operations made for strange bedfellows.

During his brief mission prep, Cargill had explained that American Black Ops had long had a relationship with Sun Yee On, one of the most powerful of the numerous Chinese Triads. This had come as a shock to Blake, but he realized that it shouldn't have. Collaborations between the US government and the American-based Mafia were known to have occurred in the past, so forging an unholy alliance with Chinese organized crime wasn't breaking any new ground.

And it made strategic and tactical sense. Spies could be recruited in China, but could they be fully trusted? For the most important Ops, could America really be sure the agents they *thought* they had turned weren't really double agents? Agents waiting for the highest-stakes missions to reveal themselves?

A Triad, on the other hand, would be expected to have far less loyalty to the homeland, and far clearer motivations. Sun Yee On, formally and euphemistically known as the *New Righteousness and Peace Commercial and Industrial Guild,* had arisen in Hong Kong, as had many of the most powerful Triad groups, and had quickly spread. The organization now boasted over seventy thousand members in China and around the world, where it was involved in counterfeiting, gambling, narcotics, human trafficking, prostitution, smuggling, and extortion.

So the head of Black Ops had opportunistically forged an alliance with this group to get intel on China, and in-country contacts for US operatives with missions on the ground there. The US government could offer Sun Yee On much more than just money in exchange for its services. America could provide the Triad with intelligence on activities outside of China that only the world's predominant super-power could obtain, and technology that could enhance the group's capabilities. In the US, it could influence prosecution of members of the American branch of Sun Yee On, which was growing quite nicely, offering several get-out-of-jail-free cards each year to high-ranking America-based chieftains.

No one on the US side was thrilled with this arrangement, but Cargill had indicated they were willing to hold their noses and live with it. The alliance had proven invaluable over and over to

US intelligence efforts within China, and worth ten times what it cost, financially and ethically.

This wasn't to say that the Triad didn't have *some* loyalty to its homeland. The group reserved the right to refuse to help US efforts if they thought such help would cripple China, but for the most part they believed that spy-vs-spy operations, a never-ending jockeying for position among superpowers, did nothing to truly hurt their country or affect the balance of power, and so were more than happy to assist—given the right inducements.

Blake stared at Zhang and wondered how any of this could possibly have become reality. Hadn't it only been last month that he was a PI in Los Angeles? Now, fast-forward just a brief period of time, and he was in China working side by side with Sun Yee On's top enforcer, a man who ranked only two levels down the organizational chart from the mob's Dragon Head, its CEO equivalent.

And this was one of the *least* surreal things that had happened to him during this time.

As much as Blake hated to admit it, the mob enforcer did exude an air of competence. And the American did feel secure from a double-cross. This would not have been the case had Blake been working here with a Chinese intelligence operative the US had turned.

Blake decided that this would be the rare mission that went off without a single hitch.

He sighed. When mission success meant returning home to hearty congratulations and well-earned R&R, nothing ever went smoothly.

But in this case, when his only reward for successful completion of the mission was *death*, when his most sacred duty was making sure the kettles and excess copies of Aaron Blake were eliminated, *of course* the mission would run like a Swiss watch.

The universe was nothing if not ironic, Blake decided.

18

Colonel Li Ming stared at the three-dimensional image of Director Chang Yin, the head of the Advanced Science and Technology Institute's Dark Energy Initiative, who was unable to hide his urgency and excitement. The colonel couldn't even venture the first guess as to what the call might be about.

Li headed military operations for the Institute, which included attempting to hack the computers of top tech companies and top scientists around the world, and buying, stealing, or otherwise acquiring critical technologies. In short, anything directors at the Institute needed to advance their goals that required muscle, or force, rather than strictly brainpower, was in the colonel's purview, and he wasn't shy about deploying soldiers or spies to fulfill his duties.

The Institute hosted forty-eight different programs, a number that was rapidly climbing, which tended to keep Li Ming and his handpicked team fully occupied, although Chang had yet to require his services. Not surprising since the director of DEI led a program that was so outrageous it wasn't clear what technologies not already in hand might help his team achieve success.

The colonel was bald and in his late forties, and had earned a reputation as a no-nonsense performer who got the job done no matter what it took. A man who wore his fierce loyalty to China on his sleeve, and one who was expected to continue to rapidly climb the ranks in the years ahead. The importance of his current assignment was underscored by the manpower and resources he was able to access to accomplish any goal.

"What can I do for you, honored Director?" said Li.

"Colonel Li, something very . . . unusual may have come up," said Chang immediately, forgoing the usual self-effacing back and forth. He explained how DEI had invented what they were confident was a dark energy detector, but had so far failed in their attempts to open a pathway to this mysterious field. He went on to explain how he had been notified that a signal had been recently detected, quite unexpectedly. Given that someone had succeeded in tapping the dark energy field where the DEI's efforts had failed, this was a development that was as troubling as it was earth-shattering.

"Forgive my ignorance, Director Chang, but I believe you just told me you could not be sure your sensor device even works. Isn't it more likely this is an error?"

"A wise question, Colonel, and one I had my team expend considerable effort to explore. We've analyzed the almost sixty minutes of data stored in our computer. We first picked up the signal about eleven kilometers out, which is consistent with our estimates of the detector's probable range. It was moving, but rapidly decelerating, with the exact deceleration profile expected of a plane on approach to landing. Given that less than a minute after the signal appeared it slowed to a stop in the middle of the cargo section of Beijing Airport, this assessment seems . . . likely."

The colonel's expression changed very little, but the newfound intensity in his eyes showed that this last had gotten his full attention.

"Thirty-four minutes later the signal began moving again," continued Chang, "but only a short distance, and at a snail's pace, before becoming stationary once more. This is consistent with cargo being transported to another plane. This was followed not much later by a rapid acceleration, exactly matching the acceleration profile of a plane taking off. We lost the signal when it traveled more than eleven kilometers from the detector, as would be expected."

Colonel Li pondered this information for several seconds. "Go on," he said finally.

"We ran multiple computer system diagnostics and visually inspected the sensor array. Everything checked out. Before and after these anomalous readings the detector was silent, as it has been since the system was first deployed. Because the signal was dead center within the cargo area of an airport, and because the deceleration and acceleration profiles so perfectly match a plane, we deem the chances that this was nothing but a detector malfunction to be *extremely* low."

"Is it possible the detector is mistaking a more standard signal emanating from a jet or from cargo as a dark energy signature?"

"Yes," replied Chang. "This is trillions of times more likely than that the detector really did identify a genuine connection to the dark energy field, one arising from out of nowhere. But the array has been in use for more than three months, during which time countless planes, filled with an endless variety of cargo, have landed and taken off from the airport. And yet never before, and not since, has the detector stirred from its slumber. For all of these reasons, I tend to take these readings seriously. If this detection is accurate, I don't need to tell you just how monumental this would be."

Li pursed his lips in thought. "Thank you for bringing this to my attention, Director Chang," he said. "There is no question this is worth investigating with a high degree of urgency. Even if it does turn out to be a false alarm. Send me the exact moment the plane landed, and when it took off again, and I will look into this. I will do whatever it takes to locate this plane and whatever cargo it may be carrying."

"Thank you, Colonel Li," said Chang, relief in his tone. "If you locate the plane while it's in the air, let it land, and capture it on the ground—using extreme caution. Whatever you do, do not shoot it down. Dark energy is a force of nearly unlimited power, and if something within this plane *has* tapped into it, a violent disruption of this tap might be very . . . dangerous."

"How dangerous, Director Chang?"

"Possibly dangerous enough to make the aftermath of a worldwide nuclear war seem pleasant."

The colonel swallowed hard. "Understood," he said. "I'll check in with you as soon as I learn anything more."

* * *

"Have you found it?" said Chang the moment Colonel Li had established a video connection between them once again, less than an hour after the first had ended.

"Not yet," said Li grimly. "We identified the plane that landed and the plane the cargo was transferred to. What I find astonishing is that the registrations of both planes are false, leading nowhere. I've done considerable digging, and I wouldn't have believed a plane could exist that Chinese intelligence couldn't trace back to its owner. Until now." He paused. "And the news gets worse."

"How so?" said Chang worriedly.

"The plane that took off from the airport, the one carrying the signal away from Beijing, filed a flight plan indicating Shanghai was its destination. It was scheduled to have landed there forty minutes ago. Yet it never did. Even so, the plane's transponder indicates the plane landed in Shanghai, on schedule."

"Does this mean it changed course?" said Chang. "And found a way to hide this fact?"

The colonel nodded. "Yes. Unless someone was actively looking for it, no one would have been aware of this deception."

"What does that mean?" said Chang in alarm. "That this plane could be anywhere? That there is no way to track it?"

"That is basically correct," admitted Li. "But there is a bright side to this. The level of skill, of sophistication, exhibited by the people behind this cargo is extremely high."

"Forgive my ignorance, Colonel Li, but why is this a good thing?"

"Because the odds of this being a real signal have gone up considerably. If whatever you've identified can truly tap the dark energy field, on purpose, one would expect those responsible to have a very high level of stealth and sophistication."

"I was already convinced it was real," said Chang.

"Good. Now I am, too."

"Do you have any leads at all, Colonel Li?"

"Yes. The only cargo transferred between the two planes was listed as a prototype commercial refrigeration unit. Sub-Zero brand. Two meters wide and two and a half meters tall. Stainless steel. Not packed in any kind of crate." He paused. "Would I be correct in saying that one doesn't need dark energy to keep one's vegetable crisper at the right temperature?"

Chang smiled grimly. "Unless the temperature you want to achieve is a million degrees Celsius, no. A temperature I wouldn't recommended for keeping vegetables crisp."

Li also smiled, but only for a moment. "The man who accompanied this . . . refrigerator, had technology that blinded cameras at the inspection station when they looked at his face. His passport listed him as John Smith, the most popular name in America."

"Is he American?"

"He had an American passport, but we can't be sure. People with this level of sophistication could easily be using false papers. The inspector checks through hundreds of people of all nationalities, and can't recall this exact one. I don't blame him. That's why we have video cameras."

"Anything more?" asked Chang.

Li shook his head. "That's the extent of it."

"Can you locate this plane, Colonel Li? This cargo?"

Li's jaw tightened in determination. "I *will* locate it," he said emphatically. "I assure you. If I have to turn over every blade of grass in China." He paused. "But I will need a dark energy detector that can be made portable. One that can fit inside a plane or helicopter."

"I will see to it that you have one as fast as is humanly possible," replied Chang.

19

When the Sun Yee On jet was minutes away from landing on the outskirts of Shenyang, Blake changed into casual clothing and discarded the gray *International Freight Services* jumpsuit he had been wearing. He removed a Sig Sauer nine-millimeter handgun from the green duffel bag Zhang had provided and shoved it into his waistband in the small of his back.

"Feel better now?" said Zhang with a smile.

Blake nodded. "Much," he replied, zipping the massive bag back up, for the moment ignoring the rest of the gear inside.

He studied the airport as the ground approached. The sky was darkening but was crystal clear, a nice change from the smog layer that had hovered above Beijing. Blake guessed night would fall in less than an hour.

The airport was even more secluded than he had expected, as though it had been carved out of the center of a dense forest. Toward the south side of the facility four runways crisscrossed in pairs like a giant hashtag. To the north of this concrete hashtag was a wall of buildings, including a traffic control tower, several gleaming new warehouses, administrative offices, and any number of hangars.

Scores of planes and helicopters, along with a wide variety of ground vehicles—some to gas planes up, some to transport passenger baggage, and some to load and unload various types of cargo in various weight classes—were parked on concrete slabs either on, or very near, portions of the runways, leaving less room for pilot error but enhancing the efficiency of the operation.

The facility was unmistakably new, even from a distance. Zhang's Triad had only just begun to expand into the Shenyang area, but Sun Yee On thought big, and the airport was like the paws of a newborn

Great Dane, much too big for the puppy's current needs, but just the right size for the fully mature version soon to come.

"Your people control the entire airport?" said Blake as the plane continued its descent toward the runway, guided by two Sun Yee On pilots.

"Yes. Every security station, checkpoint, and inspection station is manned by loyal members of Sun Yee On."

"Impressive," said Blake. "But how can you be sure your government's police or military will leave you alone?"

"We can't be," said Zhang. "Not entirely. Chinese authorities can do as they please. But they haven't bothered us yet, and we don't believe they will. We have an . . . understanding. We aren't officially sanctioned, but they look the other way."

"I have to admit that this surprises me," said Blake.

"This is a special case," said Zhang. "We're doing the government a favor here. North Korea is a client state of China, as you know. But China has agreed to severely restrict trade across the border to comply with growing pressure to abide by international sanctions."

"I see," said Blake. "So your government pretends to comply, but ignores any black market trade that a Triad like yours may want to pursue."

"Yes. Such trade is good for the Chinese economy. And this way our leaders can prop up the Kim regime, increasing their influence and using the dictator as a wildcard on the world stage. Not that even China has full control of him."

"So your Shenyang operation is strictly about trade with North Korea? Food and clothing and the like? What in other times would be considered legal?"

An amused twinkle showed in Zhang's eyes. "Not entirely. Twenty percent of what comes through here is illicit. Even so, as long as we keep crime and violence in the area to a minimum, the local authorities have been instructed to leave us alone. We help ensure this remains the case using generous bribes." He paused. "Along with . . . *unpleasant* . . . punishments to those who cross us."

Blake ignored this last. "Just how good *is* your security?" he asked.

"We have over a dozen trained soldiers on-site who are very well armed, Mr. Blake," said Zhang as the plane hit the runway and began grinding to a halt. "There is nothing to worry about. You and your cargo couldn't be any safer."

The eighteen-wheeler Blake had requested, which was painted with green and white swirls, began moving toward the plane even before it came to a full stop. These colors, and this pattern, would signal to those in the know in North Korea that the truck was transporting black market rice to an underfed population. Or at least it was *supposed* to be.

Blake and his enforcer companion exited the plane and walked a short distance to the truck to oversee the loading of Blake's cargo, which would be affixed to the back wall of the trailer, the portion nearest the cab. A powerful dual sport motorcycle, built for both highway and off-road driving, was already strapped to a side wall, along with a helmet. Zhang would use this bike to re-cross the border back into China after he deposited Blake and the truck in North Korea.

Given Sun Yee On's black market activities, the North Koreans weren't likely to give him any trouble, even if he announced himself, but why take any chances?

A small truck worked its way toward the jet to refuel it. The pilots made no move to leave the cockpit, clearly intending to launch the plane back into the air as soon as possible.

Two large men boarded the cargo compartment of Zhang's jet and muscled the large stainless steel appliance onto a forklift truck. Both were visibly armed.

Blake smiled. Sun Yee On airlines did seem to value their security. Like a mafia-controlled dock, all those at the airport were armed to the teeth, but at least the mafia made *some* effort at concealment.

The two cargo handlers exited Zhang's plane, rolled up the large door at the back of the green and white eighteen-wheeler, and affixed a long steel ramp to the trailer. One of the men slowly drove the forklift with its precious stainless steel cargo up the ramp and deep inside the open compartment. Once the cargo was deposited and the forklift truck driven back out of the trailer, both men began strapping the Sub-Zeros into place with practiced efficiency.

Zhang encouraged Blake to inspect their work before they left, and informed him that he had arranged to air-condition the trailer so Blake could ride in comfort to his North Korean destination. "Nothing but the best for our American friends," said Zhang wryly.

Blake chuckled as he stared at the time machines that would finally erase Kim Jong-un and his cruel regime from the world stage.

A thick red spray suddenly burst onto the surface of the kettle Blake was facing, instantly turning a large swath of the stainless steel a vibrant shade of scarlet, like a bag of bank money after an exploding dye-pack had been triggered.

Only the red spray wasn't dye. It was blood and brain matter erupting from the heads of the two men in the truck, both dead before they hit the floor.

A maelstrom of sound pounded at Blake's eardrums at the same instant: explosions, pistol fire, machine gun fire, so much of it, coming from so many directions, the most chaotic war zones in Iraq seemed tranquil by comparison.

He and Zhang both dived behind the semi at the same time, putting the steel behemoth between them and the incoming gunfire.

The attackers had struck in several locations at once, a multi-pronged assault coordinated down to the second. A hundred fifty yards away, to the north, machine guns and explosions raged on, echoing through the line of buildings there. Zhang's vaunted, heavily-armed associates were putting up a spirited fight, but they had been blindsided and were outmanned and outgunned.

To the south a number of men were pouring from the tree line, moving toward the green and white eighteen-wheeler, taking cover behind various vehicles parked near the runway. They continued to work their way forward with caution, laying down a dense line of fire as they did so.

The poor bastard about to refuel Zhang's plane was caught in no man's land and took so many bullets he was practically vaporized.

Shit! thought Blake, annoyed that he had left the duffel bag Zhang had prepared for him next to the plane. He had let the confident assurances of his Chinese host, and the Sig Sauer in his waistband, lull him into a false sense of security. An inexcusable mistake.

Zhang returned fire. Inside the plane, one of the pilots took a messy bullet through his jugular, killing him instantly, while the other, severely wounded, managed to crawl from the cockpit to temporary safety.

Blake moved from the front edge of the trailer, where Zhang remained, to its back edge fifty feet away, but didn't yet return fire. Firepower alone wouldn't get him out of this. He only wished he knew what might. Sometimes even the most talented, creative soldiers could be left without any options, overwhelmed by superior numbers.

He manipulated his phone to activate his comm link with Zhang, the only way he could now communicate with the man. Even if they were side by side screaming as loudly as they could, their words couldn't penetrate the deafening shield of noise surrounding them.

"Zhang, who's behind this?" said Blake rapidly. "I don't see military or police uniforms."

"Don't know," grunted Sun Yee On's top enforcer as he continued to return fire, trying to keep the wave of death at bay, but only delaying the inevitable. "But very sophisticated. Cell coverage beyond the airport has been blocked."

The second pilot managed to tumble down the stairs that still extended from the door of the aircraft to the runway and crawl to cover behind the truck on Zhang's end. The pilot braced himself against the green and white vehicle, adding a handprint of blood, and began to return fire. Blake was astonished the man was still alive, but he was losing blood in a hurry and wouldn't be for long, no matter what else happened.

The bursts of machine gun fire and explosions ended abruptly to the north, suggesting to Blake that Sun Yee On forces had finally succumbed and the battle for the main terminal buildings was over.

This suspicion was confirmed seconds later.

"We have taken over this airport," boomed a voice coming from a hidden loudspeaker system, amplified enough to be heard over gunfire that had suddenly diminished. Blake's phone translated these words into English almost as quickly as they were spoken. "I hereby claim it in the name of Shui Fong."

Blake noted that the group of men who had been steadily getting closer—now down to six after Zhang had managed to kill two who had temporarily left their cover—were no longer firing, explaining the welcome reduction in the noise level. The man on the loudspeaker, no doubt the head of this assault, had surely been responsible. Zhang and the pilot followed suit, quieting their weapons and honoring this temporary ceasefire.

"To all survivors on the runways," blared the speaker, and for the first time, Blake took a panoramic look at his surroundings and noted that three other pockets of men were still alive on other runways, taking cover behind planes or equipment, and engaged in firefights of their own. "If you surrender now, you will not be killed, and we will not ask you to betray Sun Yee On. It is true that we *will* leave you with several broken bones, but you will be left alive, to send a message to your dragon head. A message that we will not tolerate this expansion into our territory. I know you have struck a deal with a faction of the Politburo. But Shui Fong has offered a much better deal to prevent your encroachment. We have been given permission to . . . *explain* to you that your services here are no longer needed."

Blake had never heard the words, *Shui Fong*, before, but any idiot could figure out from the context that this was a rival Triad. A very pissed off rival Triad. The one danger even Blake hadn't considered. Apparently the Politburo could be fickle, and didn't mind allowing survival of the fittest to determine who controlled black market trade into North Korea.

"You have three minutes to disarm," continued the amplified voice, "and come out in the open with your hands extended over your heads. Those who do not comply in this time will not be given a second chance."

With that, the loudspeaker abruptly fell silent.

"We need to surrender, Enforcer Zhang," said the American into the man's comm.

"Never!" spat Zhang. "Our dragon head would kill us himself for showing this kind of cowardice. And rightly so."

"My mission is of vital importance," said Blake. "If I'm killed, your US allies will be furious. Would your dragon head wish you to jeopardize his alliance with us?"

"Some missions fail," said Zhang simply. "Your people will know we did our best. The alliance will remain."

Without another word the Sun Yee On enforcer began firing once again, and the pilot, still hanging on by a thread, followed suit. Having caught the attackers somewhat by surprise, and not having to avoid an incoming wall of fire, Zhang demonstrated extraordinary accuracy, picking off two more of the remaining six.

Still, the four attackers who remained were well covered behind a cargo truck, and could wait for the arrival of large numbers of reinforcements from the north. The situation was still hopeless, and Zhang's left leg, pierced by return fire, was now drenched in blood.

It was getting darker by the minute. Given the night-vision setting on Blake's contact lens, this could play into his favor. Unfortunately, nightfall was still twenty minutes or more away, and he doubted he could hold on for nearly this long.

It was time to act. Now or never.

"Zhang, you know your pilot has only a few minutes to live, right?" said Blake.

"What's your point?" came the curt reply.

"Follow my lead," said Blake as he moved quietly toward the enforcer's position, deciding his only hope was to use deception, to count on being underestimated. "When I shoot at you, pretend to die. Then lie low and wait for an opportunity."

"I don't do theater," said Zhang bluntly.

"Well I do!" spat Blake. "And it's our only chance. I can turn the tables. Trust me."

"Even if you do, their forces in the terminal will cut us down before we get to the woods."

"One miracle at a time," said Blake as he made his way toward Zhang and the pilot. "Play dead when I shoot at you," he insisted, coming up behind the pilot who was now slumped against the truck, no longer even going through the motions of returning fire.

Not waiting for agreement, Blake shoved the pilot roughly past Zhang and into view of the four remaining assailants, shooting the pilot in the head the moment he became visible. Blake was sickened by having to execute a helpless man from behind, but it was an ugly necessity, and he had only hastened the man's death by a matter of minutes.

Before the dead pilot even hit the runway, Blake changed his aim and fired at Zhang, who played his role to perfection, after all, falling forward into a trailing pool of the pilot's blood, a third of his body visible to the enemy. He twitched twice and then remained perfectly still.

For someone who didn't do theater, Zhang could have won a Tony Award.

Blake walked slowly out from behind the truck, visibly shaking, both of his hands raised above his head, including the one still holding the Sig Sauer.

He dropped the gun as though he didn't realize it was still in his hand, as though it were a repulsive cockroach that both disgusted and terrified him. "I surrender," he said in English, hoping that one among the group could translate for the others, not that his raised hands and panicked expression needed much in the way of translation. "Don't shoot."

20

Blake sighed. This wasn't the first time he had been forced to play a panicked civilian to try to stay alive, and he was getting more than sick of it.

"Please!" he pleaded when there was no response to his declaration of surrender, making a face as though he were on the verge of bursting into tears. "I shot their last two soldiers for you," he added, gesturing with his head toward the fallen pilot and Zhang, who was still playing possum.

If the pilot's exploding head hadn't sold this ruse, nothing would. After seeing Blake shoot one man from behind at point-blank range, the Shui Fong attackers would have little reason to believe he hadn't done the same with the second.

"*Please*," said Blake again, his voice thin and whiny, "I'm trying to *help*."

He stumbled forward toward the four assailants, aware that he was now at their mercy and bracing himself for the end. But instead of filling him with holes, all four stepped out from behind their cover, guns extended toward him, and rapidly closed the distance between them.

"Frisk him!" ordered the tallest of the four in Chinese, which Blake's phone dutifully translated and sent to the comm in his ear.

Two of the men frisked him roughly, finding nothing but his phone, which they left in his possession, thinking it harmless. And why not? They had ringed the airport with cell signal disruptors, after all, ensuring no outbound calls could be made.

For the first time since the battle had begun, Blake was glad he hadn't removed more items from the green duffel bag. If one wanted to play the freaked-out helpless civilian, the reluctant killer who had only succeeded by sneaking up behind his victims and shooting them at can't-miss range, it wasn't ideal to be armed to the teeth.

After rapid cross talk in Chinese, the tall leader identified the shortest of the group as the best English speaker among them, and turned him into his spokesman. Blake concentrated on not reacting to anything they said to each other, not wanting them to know he could understand.

"Find out if he's an American," ordered the leader.

"Are you American?" asked the designated translator in English.

Blake nodded, trying to force himself to tear up, which he wasn't quite able to manage. Instead, he quivered his chin, something he had seen television and movie actors do before sobbing. "Don't *hurt* me," he pleaded. "I can help you. I know details of Sun Yee On's inner workings. Now that you've started a war with them, you *need* me. I can be a huge asset."

"*Impossible!*" said the group's leader in Chinese. "How would an American know the first thing about Sun Yee On's activities in China?"

"He could not, Enforcer Liang," said the short translator. "But one has to wonder how he got these men to trust him enough that he could sneak up behind them."

"Ask him!" demanded the leader, apparently named Liang. "Find out why he's here."

"What are you doing here?" demanded the shorter man in English.

"The Sun Yee On Triad is a growing menace inside America," replied Blake. "The US has pretended to partner with them to get intel in China. But it's a trick. We're really piecing together an elaborate map of the organization. To give to Chinese authorities."

"For what purpose?"

"So they can destroy this Triad in China. Once they kill the tree *here*, at its roots, we can chop off the branches in America and they'll never grow back."

When all attention was focused on the interpreter, who was relaying the gist of this response to his associates, Blake risked communication with Zhang. "When I fall to my knees," he whispered rapidly in English, "fire."

He waited for any sign the four men had noticed this whisper, and found none.

Now it was all up to Zhang. He just prayed Sun Yee On's top enforcer was as good as he thought.

Blake's luck was holding—so far. The men he was facing should never have accepted this situation at face value. They should have planted a bullet in each fallen adversary's head for good measure. Blake had been on too many battlefields, too many counterterrorism Ops, to ever make this mistake. You only had to be surprised *once* by someone rising from the dead to attack before you made *certain* those you hadn't personally killed were truly deceased.

The translator finished relaying Blake's words, and after a brief discussion among the four men, the short Chinese spokesman eyed Blake in disdain. "You can't really expect us to believe you're an operative," he spat. "I mean, *look* at you," he added, "your display of fear is a disgrace."

"I *am* an operative," insisted Blake, careful to still seem terrified. "Why else would I be here? I'm a logistics expert. I'm pretending to work with Sun Yee On, but I'm really planting bugs in their facilities. They would smell a soldier. But not someone like me."

After Blake's answer was translated into Chinese, Liang grew visibly angry, moved forward, and shoved the barrel of his gun against Blake's elbow. He turned to the man doing the translations. "Tell this coward I don't trust a word he says!" he shouted. "That if he doesn't tell me the truth, he'll never bend his arm again. Tell him!"

The short interpreter did as instructed.

"*Please*," blubbered Blake. "I *am* telling you the truth. Please don't hurt me," he pleaded.

Blake braced himself and then fell to his knees in supplication, as though begging for his life, delivering the promised signal to his enforcer ally.

Without hesitation, Zhang snatched up a gun and fired from his position on the ground, taking out two of the four men before they even knew he was alive.

Blake, ready for this opening, burst upright from his knees and used a martial arts move to twist the gun from Liang's outstretched hand with a speed and purpose that was truly extraordinary. The instant he controlled the gun he whipped it toward Liang's last remaining associate, a seamless continuation of his initial move made with the fluidity of a dancer. The man was swinging his gun around to shoot Blake, but the American beat him to the punch, planting two rounds in his head just as he was about to pull the trigger.

Blake dropped to the ground even as he was squeezing off the second shot, instinctively aware that Zhang would be ready to take his own shot. Sure enough, the moment Blake wasn't in the line of fire, Zhang put one round through Liang's neck and one through his head, and the man slammed into the concrete runway like a felled tree.

Blake rushed to Zhang's position and took a quick survey of his surroundings. Sure enough, Liang had been the last of the Shui Fong soldiers. At least for the moment.

Blake reached down and took Zhang's hand, helping to pull him up from the puddle of blood. The enforcer's left leg was still adding to the total.

"Let's go," said Blake when Zhang was on his feet, favoring his right leg, as expected. "Help me disconnect the ramp," he added, gesturing to the back of the semi. "Then you can drive us out of here."

They quickly managed to dislocate the heavy ramp and drop it to the concrete runway. The instant this was complete, Zhang moved toward the cab as quickly as he could in his hobbled condition.

Blake was preparing to enter the trailer and roll down the door when another barrage of gunfire pounded against his eardrums, coming from the vicinity of the terminal buildings to the north. About twelve Shui Fong soldiers, who had no doubt seen Blake and Zhang turn the tables on their associates from afar, were moving toward them, laying down another dense curtain of fire.

They were still too distant to achieve any level of accuracy, but several stray bullets found Zhang as he was climbing into the cab, and he fell back down onto the runway, dead. Blake took a bullet to his left arm as he was entering the trailer, but it only grazed him and wouldn't cause more than a minor nuisance.

Blake ignored the corpses of the two workmen who had installed the fake Sub-Zero inside the truck, and the slick red lake their pooled blood had created, and quickly took stock of his situation. If he now tried to reach the cab he would be cut to ribbons. The woods were far enough away that attempting a mad dash to the tree line would be equally suicidal. He would be out in the open for too long, and there was too much firepower concentrated against him. Even if he somehow made it, the forest extended for more than ten miles, and he'd be hunted like a dog until Shui Fong finally managed to kill him.

He only had one option left, one that he hadn't been able to use on Liang and his men because they had been too close to his own position. But the men coming for him now were not too close. At least not yet.

"K-1," he yelled hastily, "confirm that you're receiving this."

"Confirmed," said the outer kettle supercomputer into Blake's ear, responding to the name he had given it.

"Commence time travel on my order," he said.

He risked peeking his head around the edge of the open trailer to make a quick estimate of the mob's position and closing speed in the dimming light. He guessed the throng of men, still firing, still slowly closing in, were a healthy percentage of a football field away, maybe eighty yards—a good two hundred forty feet. Good. Far enough away that he and the truck might both survive if he acted quickly.

"Prepare to send K-2 one hundred thirty-five microseconds into the past," continued Blake. "Set the polarity so that it lands due north of your current position. If, however, after I've given you the command to proceed, you detect another dark energy signature in the vicinity, you are to abort time travel immediately."

Blake was so well versed in the strange vagaries of time travel he didn't even need to pause to check the logic. The outer kettle would send the inner kettle three increments of forty-five microseconds into the past. Because the inner kettle, K-2, would come from the future, from a position the Earth had moved to, it would land one hundred seventy-four feet away. When it arrived in the past, however, one version of the inner kettle would still be inside the semi, an instant away from traveling in time.

But when K-1 detected the presence of the kettle to the north, arriving from the future, it would follow Blake's order and now abort, never sending the inner kettle back in the first place. Despite this, the local universe would reset—accepting the existence of the new kettle in its midst from a frame in the future without any fuss.

"Understood and acknowledged," said the computer.

"Good," said Blake. "Once you've detected another dark energy signature and have aborted time travel, prepare to detonate the kettle responsible for this other signature, which will be approximately one hundred seventy-four feet away. Detonate it exactly five seconds after you hear me say the word, *mark*."

After just the briefest of pauses, during which the computer reconfigured the outer kettle's settings, it responded. "Understood and ready," it said.

"Commence time travel," said Blake, peeking around the edge of the open trailer. Seemingly before he had even finished speaking, the K-2 kettle materialized in the midst of the oncoming horde. Blake had witnessed this kind of magic before, but it never failed to amaze.

Far too fast for human comprehension, K-1 detected this new kettle the instant it arrived and aborted further time travel with thirty-nine millionths of a second to spare.

The oncoming Shui Fong soldiers stopped in their tracks as the large stainless steel refrigerator appeared out of nowhere within their ranks. Many had their mouths hanging open, and all of them were too stunned by this impossible event to continue firing.

Blake guessed that not even Confucius could hide his shock after seeing a large appliance teleport into his midst.

The men were stunned now, but would snap out of it and continue laying down a curtain of fire any second. Blake jumped to the runway and began sprinting away from the horde, taking advantage of this momentary respite, well aware that a bullet could tear through him without warning.

After allowing himself to work up a head of steam for three seconds, he decided he couldn't risk waiting any longer. "Mark!" he shouted as he continued running, a word his phone relayed to K-1.

He began a mental countdown from five seconds. Four. Three. Two. One.

A massive explosion rocked the airport and shook the runway like an earthquake, the shockwave slamming into Blake like a giant's fist, launching him off his feet and knocking him nearly unconscious.

Blake came to moments later, his head and ears ringing, and struggled to gather his senses. He wanted nothing more than to lie still on the runway, moaning and licking the numerous cuts and bruises he had acquired since the attack had begun.

Had it really been only fourteen minutes ago?

Despite wanting desperately to rest, he conjured up his full resolve and forced himself to stand, fending off wave after wave of dizziness.

Blake turned and grimly surveyed the destruction he had wrought, once again sickened by its necessity. His timing had been excellent. The men coming for him had all been wiped out, and while the semi had been nearer the blast than he had been, it seemed to have weathered the storm.

Even so, it was thoroughly pockmarked by bullets, creating such a dense pattern it almost seemed as if these dents and holes had been imprinted there on purpose. Miraculously, only three of its tires were blown, turning the vehicle into a fifteen-wheeler. Given that its cargo hold was nearly empty, despite being built to carry up to forty tons, Blake guessed that it was still drivable, even on this lessor number of tires.

He retrieved the green duffel bag Zhang had prepared for him and then scrambled back to the truck, not waiting around to learn if Shui Fong had more men beyond the blast zone. He took Zhang's phone from his dead body so it couldn't yield clues that would help Shui Fong find him. He then dragged the two corpses inside the trailer to its edge and pushed them unceremoniously onto the runway, before rolling down the trailer door and making his way to the cab. His ears were still ringing and he was still suffering through periodic bouts of dizziness.

Thankfully, nightfall was finally arriving. He needed to get as far away from here as he could, and traveling through the night, under cover of darkness, was his only hope of not being stopped. If driving a truck that had been through a war—and *looked* it—wasn't bad enough, any inspection would reveal many quarts of blood inside the trailer.

Blake let out a sigh of relief as the truck started up and he was able to get it moving. He accelerated as quickly as he could across the runway to the airport's main access road, swerving as he did so, possibly because he was still as addled as a drunk, or possibly due to the loss of tires.

Once he hit the speed he wanted and was no longer accelerating, he managed to wrestle the truck to a draw and keep it on the straight and narrow—more or less.

He made it to the road without incident. After the dramatic display of destructive power on the runway, he didn't expect to be followed too closely, if at all. At least not by any members of Shui Fong still at the airport.

Blake let out a string of curses he had been holding back. Arriving in Shenyang just in time for a Triad war was the epitome of bad luck. Yet he had somehow managed to do what he always did—find a way to prevail.

Not that this was the end of it. It was only the beginning. This was shaping up to be the ultimate test of his skill.

Blake shook his head in disgust. He had tempted fate by anticipating that the mission would be one of his smoothest ever.

He was beginning to think that this optimistic assessment might have been a bit premature.

21

Colonel Li Ming bolted awake as his ringing phone finally registered in his consciousness. He accepted the call, audio only, keeping the lights off in his bedroom.

"What's going on, Major?" he said to his second-in-command, Long He, in the darkness, knowing that none of his underlings would be bold enough to call at this hour without very good reason.

"Sorry to wake you, sir," said Long, "but we've found the plane you've been after."

The colonel still hadn't shaken off the last vestiges of sleep, but this statement blasted him fully awake. "Has it been secured?" he asked immediately.

"Yes, but it was empty. No refrigeration unit. In fact, no cargo of any kind."

Li considered. "Where is it? And how did you find it?"

"It's on a private airport just outside of Shenyang that we are now certain belongs to the Sun Yee On Triad. Apparently, Shui Fong didn't appreciate this encroachment into their territory and waged war for the facility. It was a bloodbath almost beyond description. I've sent photos to your phone."

Li scrolled through the images carefully, barely able to believe what he was seeing. Dead bodies were strewn about everywhere, and a massive explosion had obliterated trucks, planes, and equipment within a thirty-meter radius of its center. Men had doubtlessly been killed in the explosion, also, but the number was impossible to gauge, as they had basically been turned into paste.

"Quite a scorched earth campaign," he noted, almost in awe.

"The airport is private and secluded," continued Major Long. "Because of this, local authorities didn't learn of this battle until two hours after it was over. When they did, they traced the ownership of all planes that had just landed, in the hope of better understanding what they were dealing with."

"I see," said Li. "When they weren't able to trace the registry of one of the planes, you put two and two together and explored this further."

"Precisely, Colonel Li. I was able to confirm that the mystery plane in Shenyang was, indeed, the same plane that took off from Beijing. The one you are after."

"Excellent work, Major," he said.

"Thank you, Colonel Li, but this was due to luck more than anything. Had this Triad war not broken out, we may not have found this plane for weeks, if at all."

"Luck favors the prepared mind, Major Long," said Li, quoting Louis Pasteur.

"I've benefited from your example, sir."

"You flatter me," said Li, one of several nearly automatic responses to praise. "How long has it been since this plane landed in Shenyang?"

"I believe just under four hours. Which means the cargo could be anywhere by now. It could have been transferred to yet another plane, which left before the conflict began."

"How is it that you don't know this for sure?" asked Li.

"I tried to pull satellite footage of the airport during the time of the attack," replied Long. "But there is none available. Apparently this area was ordered not to be surveilled by certain unnamed authorities. My sense is that an order such as this must have originated from within the Politburo."

Li considered this in silence, wondering what to make of it. "Do you have men guarding the plane?" he asked.

"Yes, Colonel Li. No one will come near it."

"Good. Wake DEI Director Chang. Have him and anyone he selects flown to Shenyang to inspect it. Also, for the moment, assume the cargo we're looking for is still on the ground. I want a swarm of men watching the roads, looking for a vehicle capable of transporting a two meter by two-and-a-half meter stainless steel box."

"Understood."

"Set up roadblocks at every major and minor artery within two hundred kilometers of Shenyang," continued Li. "I want every vehicle examined by at least two soldiers before they're waved through. Any vehicle in the size range we're after, or with a Caucasian inside, needs to be pulled out of line for special attention."

Li's calm tone suddenly disappeared. "I want this man contained!" he demanded. "And I want these roadblocks established five minutes ago!"

"Sealing up an area this large will require enormous manpower, Colonel Li."

"I'm aware. I'm also aware that a very sophisticated group has smuggled something into China that we believe can tap into the dark energy field. Director Chang believes that such a connection might be used to unleash explosive energies that would put nuclear weapons to shame. And we have no idea who is responsible, what they're doing here, and what they intend."

Long let out a small gasp as the true gravity of the situation hit home. "I'm sorry, sir. I didn't know. I will set speed records getting these roadblocks in place."

"I know you will, Major Long."

"How much time until Director Chang can supply a dark energy detector for us to use?"

"Several days to get the first one, I'm afraid," said Li unhappily. "After that, additional ones will come faster, but not much. They are delicate and labor intensive, and only a few DEI scientists have the required expertise to put them together. So they can't be mass-produced. At least not yet."

"Understood," said Long. "I'm signing off now. There are a number of fast-response military units I need to awaken."

22

Aaron Blake was exhausted. Cut, bruised, nearly concussed, and mentally depleted.

Driving a hobbled semi that wasn't fully balanced didn't help, requiring unrelenting focus on his part to keep it on a straight path over narrow roads, cutting through nearly absolute darkness.

Zhang's route to the tunnel under the Chinese-North Korean border had been mostly over highways, a sensible path if Zhang had been driving and the truck had been undamaged.

Blake didn't have this luxury.

A smattering of other motorists, other trucks, would be using the highways, even during the wee hours of the morning. And highways were more brightly lit than smaller arteries would be. Blake needed to minimize the chances that his Caucasian face and battle-scarred truck could be seen. Even if this wasn't a consideration, highways were still out, as he didn't want to risk pushing his wounded vehicle to anywhere near highway speeds.

So Blake had instructed K-1 to tap into the Chinese Internet, whose content, while heavily censored, did contain programs that provided accurate driving directions, and plot out a course that would take him to the tunnel he needed over backroads, as lightly traveled and off the beaten path as possible. Roads that even in America would be poorly lit, but which, in China, were as dark as the inside of a cave and perfect for his needs.

Like most eighteen-wheelers, the green and white truck had small running lights, often called *marker* or *clearance* lights, that illuminated the trailer, delineating the rig's dimensions for other motorists to see as a safety precaution. Blake pulled off the road soon after he was away from the airport and destroyed any of these lights that hadn't already been shot out during the battle. Now, only the headlights of the truck were visible, and the damaged body of the semi disappeared into blackness. After four hours of driving he had seen only a handful of other vehicles, and he was confident that he hadn't aroused suspicion.

"K-1," he said to the kettle supercomputer, "estimate when I will reach the tunnel using my average speed over the past four hours. Question: will I make it there before sunrise?"

"Negative," came the reply in his ear. "Based on your expected time of arrival, and known time of sunrise, you won't reach it until one hour twenty-seven minutes after."

Blake nodded. He had expected as much. "Can you access the Chinese equivalent of Google Earth?"

"Yes. Although there are a number of areas that are not accessible due to the presence of military installations or censorship for unknown reasons."

"Understood. I've gone past and through many miles of woods. Is our route going forward equally wooded?"

There was the briefest of pauses. "Even more so," said K-1.

"Excellent. I'm looking for a place to hide out during daylight hours. The ideal location would be as follows: Isolated. Tens of miles from the nearest residence or other sign of civilization. An area that is minimally traveled, if at all. Better if it is roughly on our route, but if I have to go an hour or two out of my way, I'm willing. Ideally, I'd like to enter a woods on a gravel or wood-chip road—the kind that is almost never used. The idea is to be able to reach a more secluded area of a woods than a paved road could manage. Are you with me so far?"

"I believe so, yes," replied the AI.

"I want to leave such an unpaved road at some point and proceed into the woods. The ideal location would be where trees are fairly sparse, but get denser as I go. I want to be able to pick my way through the tress for at least twenty yards without having to bulldoze any over. After this, if I have to knock down some small trees to get to where I can't be seen from any road, I'm willing. Understood?"

"Understood," said K-1. "But even if you don't leave a trail of broken trees, you will leave tire tracks."

"Thanks," said Blake. "I'm well aware."

Tire tracks emanating from an unpaved road that might not get used more than twice a year, anyway, was a risk he would have to take, and one he would minimize by covering the tracks with leaves, pinecones, loose branches, and other foliage. This would normally be a daunting task, but he could make unlimited copies of these materials to ensure a supply adequate to the task.

But as he thought about tire tracks he realized he had missed an important point. It had been dry in this part of China for at least several days and the ground was hard, but if this changed the truck might never make it back out of the woods. "K-1, access the local weather forecast. What are the chances of rain tomorrow?"

"Zero percent," replied K-1. "This is true for the next six days. On the seventh day, there is a forty percent chance of showers."

"Outstanding!"

"Is that everything?" asked the supercomputer. "Or do you have additional parameters for me to consider?"

"That's all," said Blake. "Proceed now. Give me the five possibilities you believe come closest to matching my specifications."

"Working," said K-1, and Blake was not surprised that it didn't spit out an answer immediately. This was a daunting assignment, even for a supercomputer. K-1 would need to access road maps, the Chinese version of Google Earth, and numerous other sources of information, including patterns of traffic and human populations, and then pore over untold numbers of trees seen in satellite footage to find groupings in the proper location, and the proper spacing. It would have to analyze an enormous number of moving windows of one square mile blocks of area he would encounter along his route to the border tunnel, with only a few locations in this vast expanse of woods that might even come close to meeting his needs.

Still, only seconds later the computer had finished, and described the five best possibilities it had found. Blake had it walk through each, getting an understanding of distances to pockets of civilization, type of unpaved road, and frequency of traffic—along with what data K-1 had used to determine the same. He then had it send satellite imagery to his contact lens, showing the off-road path Blake would need to take in each case.

One of the locations was head and shoulders above the rest, a little more than an hour drive away. Perfect. Better than he had any right to hope for.

A few seconds later, K-1 had routed him to this new destination, and he was on his way, confident that he could hole up there for many days with only minimal risk of being discovered.

He was almost to his destination when he found himself on an access road that ran parallel to a major highway, about thirty yards to his east. "K-1, how long does this road parallel the highway?" he asked.

"Fourteen miles."

"I asked you to take me over backroads," he said. "Out of sight of any highway."

"You did. But you did say *whenever possible.* This road is not illuminated, and you are still far enough away that only your headlights can be clearly seen. I'm aware you prefer to stay much farther from highways, but in this case this is the only option. Unavoidable if you want to get to the destination you have chosen."

Blake sighed. He was still uncomfortable, but he didn't have a choice. After only a few minutes he settled back into the partial stupor he had been in much of the time, fighting exhaustion to stay awake and alert, and largely failing.

After driving for almost eight miles, he spotted a group of men and vehicles parked at an on-ramp on the opposite side of the highway, tiny in the distance. Adrenaline surged through his body, jolting him fully awake.

Was this a roadblock? It was too distant to tell for sure, but based on the dose of adrenaline now in his veins, his subconscious had already concluded that it was.

He pulled to the side of the road and brought a pair of high-powered digital binoculars to his eyes, which he had retrieved from the green duffel bag Zhang had provided. The binoculars were capable of automatically switching to night vision when the surrounding light became too faint. "Shit!" he said aloud as four men, each holding assault rifles, swam into focus, along with a concrete barrier.

Each was in uniform. Chinese military. It just kept getting better.

There was always the chance that this roadblock was due to a local issue and had nothing to do with him. But as he continued on his journey and passed two more roadblocks, exactly the same as the first, including the four armed men on patrol, it became clear that something big was going on.

Blake couldn't imagine how this could possibly be about him.

But he also couldn't imagine how it could possibly *not* be.

Fortunately, he was about to turn onto another road, much more secluded, which, twenty minutes later, would end within a wilderness populated only by animals. His daytime hideout.

He would need to perform reconnaissance and stay put until the coast was clear. But that shouldn't be an issue. He had planned to wait out the next day, anyway, and by tomorrow night, he felt sure the roadblocks would be gone.

Once he finally settled into his selected hiding spot, spent a few hours literally covering his tracks, and had gotten some sleep, he would phone Lee Cargill and report.

Cargill, and the Aaron Blake still at Cheyenne Mountain, were the only two people in the world who were aware of where he was, his mission, or even his existence. Not even Joe Allen or Jenna Morrison had any idea.

While there was nothing Cargill could do to help him now—not in the heart of China—the man needed to be kept apprised of his progress. Or the lack thereof.

Still, even though Blake would need to delay the mission by at least twenty-four hours, and there were some hurdles yet to clear, he was confident he would ultimately succeed.

He didn't care what it took. He wasn't about to blow this opportunity to rid the world of its greatest threat.

Cargill believed that Blake was the most resourceful operative he could possibly send on this mission. It was time for Blake to demonstrate that Cargill's faith in him had not been misplaced.

PART 4

"The first Matrix was designed to be a perfect human world where none suffered. Where everyone would be happy. It was a disaster."

—Agent Smith, *The Matrix*

23

Jenna Morrison walked into the conference room ten minutes before her first, "future of Q5" meeting was to take place, well pleased with the amount of progress she had made in just the handful of days since she had been given this assignment.

She had never worked harder, and that included when she was gearing up for a tough final, or even preparing for an oral exam in graduate school given by a professor with a reputation for being a human meat grinder. When she wasn't making love to Nathan, she was discussing physics with him and with Daniel Tini—discussing *possibilities*. She was reading about science, its history and the leading edge of where science and tech were headed, and also about ethics and human behavior.

Despite the mountains of research she had done, the nonstop thinking, the grueling hours she had been putting in, she had never been happier. When she busted her brain preparing for an exam, she was rewarded by the satisfaction of gaining new and fascinating knowledge, by the joy of discovery, and by the feeling of achievement when she aced a test or set a curve.

But any rewards she received from these academic activities paled in comparison to those she would earn for her efforts now. Her hard work and creativity in this case could dramatically change the world, the very course of human civilization. The stakes were so high that no effort on her part could possibly be too great.

Nathan felt the same way as he studied his own work, pondering its mind-blowing implications and applications, worked himself to blissful exhaustion. This mutual mental fatigue made for epic sex, which she and Nathan decided was the result of their conscious minds being so tired they fled into the background, along with even the tiniest of mental hang-ups about the primitive nature of the act, allowing it to unfold on an entirely unselfconscious animal plane. This was a reward that neither had expected.

This also served to help them fall fully back in love, as much as they had ever been. Helped them to recover from the effects of their separation and the traumatic experiences they had each undergone. They had been living together and engaged for some time before Q5 happened, but had now decided to take their formal wedding vows in two months' time.

Even so, Jenna found that she had developed an attraction to Aaron Blake as well, which, while small, was also persistent and annoying. She thought the world of Blake, but she wasn't in love with him by any means. It was more akin to being drawn to a dangerous, charismatic movie star. Nothing she couldn't handle, and nothing that would interfere with her love of Nathan Wexler.

Still, she found herself fascinated by this pull, and tried to self-diagnose the reason for it. She decided it had nothing to do with Blake's looks, although his looks were fine. It was that he was the ultimate bad boy. Badass was more like it.

Confident, competent, and self-assured. Decisive and deadly. She had seen him in action, and his boldness, his speed of decision-making under pressure, was breathtaking. He was a man she would feel safe with, even if they were unarmed and surrounded by three bigger men with guns, confident that he would manage to win the day.

She had always thought the idea that women were attracted to bad boys was a myth, despite certain experimental evidence that this was the case and theoretical arguments from her own field of genetics. It wasn't that the arguments and evidence were entirely without merit, it was just that she had never experienced this herself, and even found the idea insulting, so she naturally sided with the data and logic cited by those who were against this interpretation.

Jenna Morrison had always been attracted to *nice* guys, not men who lived dangerously and who could be overly aggressive. And *especially* not men like Blake, who were capable of slitting throats without a second thought.

But maybe she wasn't as immune as she had imagined. Blake had violent tendencies, but he was also sweet, and charming, and loyal, and brave. Perhaps she just hadn't met the *right* bad boy.

Given her graduate level education in genetics, she was well versed in sociobiology and evolutionary psychology. These fields espoused the idea that much of human behavior, social interaction, could be seen through the lens of evolution and evolutionary imperatives, like sex and survival.

One such theory to come out of these fields was often called, *sperm is cheap*. This theory was relatively simple, but also offensive to some. There were those who vigorously challenged the theory's conclusions, bringing counterarguments and data to support their positions. In the days in which any discussion of the sexes, scientific or otherwise, was fraught with peril and controversy, it took a certain amount of bravery, even among scientists, to engage in such a debate.

Scientists who did subscribe to this theory argued that reproduction was the cornerstone of evolution and species survival. Early humans who managed to pass on their genes won, and those who failed to do so lost. And genes influenced behavior. It was obvious that if you had a gene that caused you to be repulsed by the idea of sex, this gene would not get passed on to future generations. Those who had genes that caused them to become addicted to sex, on the other hand, would be very likely to pass these genes on.

This was just one of many behaviors that could help determine reproductive success. And the optimal strategies that might evolve to maximize this success could vary widely between males and females, resulting in antlers on elk and plumage on peacocks. Not that human males and females would be consciously aware of these strategies, which had been masterminded by genes and evolution without their knowledge or consent, and hardwired into their DNA.

A man could theoretically impregnate a different woman every day. Could father hundreds of offspring during his lifetime. Given this, proponents of the *sperm is cheap* theory argued that it was no surprise that males had an instinct to mount anything that moved. The genes of men who managed to sleep with hundreds of women over their lifetimes were more likely to be passed on than those of men who were exceedingly selective, and only slept with one. They argued that the reason a man could be sexually aroused by a slight breeze was that this hair-trigger horniness helped ensure he would mate with a greater number of women. If some of these women were relatively poor specimens, with less-than-robust genes, lessening the fitness of his children in these cases, so be it. It was a numbers game. Some of those he slept with *would* have good genes. Sperm cost so little to produce, why not spread it far and wide?

Women, on the other hand, had limited opportunities to reproduce, and each act of reproduction came at a very high cost. While a man could zip up his pants and walk away, the same was not true for a woman. Once pregnant, a woman had to put up with morning sickness, provide energy to a growing life within her, spend nine months carrying this life—increasing her physical vulnerability to environmental dangers—and risk death during childbirth. Afterward, a woman required extra calories to produce milk to feed her offspring, at least for many thousands of years before the advent of baby formula.

Given the high cost of reproduction for a woman, and the limited number of offspring that were possible for her, proponents of this theory argued that it was in a woman's genetic best interest to be more selective than a man. To choose mates with good genes, improving the chances that her offspring would survive. And to choose a man who was strong, aggressive, and self-assured. A man who could fend off the cannibal tribe over the hill while she was giving birth, and therefore helpless. Someone who could wrestle a bear to the ground, and then bring home bear steaks to help nourish her and the baby.

These differing optimal strategies created quite an interesting behavioral interplay between the sexes, one that was born out anthropologically. Genetic studies had found that about eighty percent of women throughout history had managed to reproduce, while only about forty percent of men had.

This finding was stunning at first, but made sense once human societies were examined through the lens of history. Kings, nobility, and sheikhs all had harems, hoarding numerous women all for themselves. Historically, a powerful man might father scores of children.

A peasant, on the other hand, might be shut out entirely.

Which could also explain why men were more aggressive and risk-seeking than women, on average. How did a man get to be a king? By taking risks. Winning wars. Embarking on dangerous journeys to explore and conquer new lands.

Passive men, nice guys, never earned enough resources and power, never showed a great enough ability to protect and sustain a woman through childbirth and beyond, to compete against those who did. Harsh, yes, but in earlier ages, life was short and often brutal, and competition for women could be one-sided when even the ability to *bathe* with regularity could be resource-dependent.

Women who were genetically attracted to powerful men, men capable of feeding and protecting them and their offspring, had greater success passing on their genes than those attracted to nice guys, who in more primitive, barbaric times, often *did* finish last.

It was good to be king.

At the genetic level, proponents of this controversial theory argued, a woman would be drawn to a well-heeled badass who cared enough about her to stick around.

At the genetic level, a man would be drawn to a woman he thought would be sexually faithful. When choosing to settle down with a mate, the theory argued, a man placed a high value on sexual fidelity because there were no paternity tests in nature. When a woman gave birth, she knew she was the mother. But a man . . . well, he never really knew for sure.

If a woman had been unfaithful and was carrying another man's baby, the fooled father would spend valuable resources raising a set of genes that were unrelated to his own. Evolution would thus reward a man who favored a chaste woman as a permanent mate, lessening the chances he would make this mistake.

Jenna had long been a critic of theories such as these. Even if certain elements had once been true, the days of harems were over. Nice guys really could come out on top, and often did. Brains and talents beyond just physical strength and ruthlessness could lead men to power and success.

Men like Nathan Wexler.

Jenna had always believed that ancient genetic instincts that may once have existed had not made their way into the modern world. But she was beginning to wonder if somewhere deep within her genes this barbaric instinct may have survived, after all.

She adored Aaron as a friend, and nothing more. But she couldn't deny that she found his competence as a warrior strangely attractive. Not that this was nearly strong enough to counteract her intellect, or the love she felt for the most brilliant man she had ever met.

Jenna grinned broadly as a new thought crossed her mind. Perhaps she could ask Aaron to teach Nathan some special-forces moves. Turn Nathan into a bit of a badass himself.

Now *that* would be having her cake and eating it too.

24

The Q5 management team filed into the conference room, one by one, and soon it was filled with the same members who had met before. Jenna thanked everyone for coming, said a few words of introduction, including her intention to keep the proceedings loose and informal, and then launched right in. She hadn't shared where she had ended up with anyone in the group, not even Nathan, because she wanted everyone to be on equal footing, to react organically to what she was proposing.

"I'd like to proceed by beginning with my conclusions," she announced. "Then I'll work my way backwards from there. Jump in at any time, of course."

Her fellow meeting participants looked intrigued, as she had hoped. Not every presentation led with its conclusions.

"In my view," she continued, "the most important two areas on which to focus our efforts are fairly unambiguous. First, I believe our highest priority *has* to be modifying the time travel technology to create an interstellar drive. Without a doubt. As you know, Nathan's work shows that faster-than-light travel is a possibility. As Daniel and Nathan would say, we might be able to use the immense energy we tap into to push us along the spatial axis of space-time, rather than the temporal axis. Time travel is great, but it hurts the head, and it messes with the universe more than anyone should be entirely comfortable with."

"Amen to that," mumbled Blake.

Jenna smiled. "In further conversations with Nathan and Daniel, I'm told that if they can solve this problem, we not only get interstellar travel, unlocking the cosmos, but actual teleportation as well. Think about it!" she added excitedly. "True teleportation! Yes, we can already manage it, but not without creating two of a kind. Which makes it useless. Teleport ten times a day, and in a year there are *thousands* of you running around." Her smile broadened. "Which does tend to make one's home a little crowded."

"Unless you adopt Knight's solution," said Cargill in disgust, "and incinerate the copy left in the kettle right after the jump."

Wexler tilted his head thoughtfully. This was the first he had heard of this idea. "As horrible as that sounds," he said slowly, "the idea isn't entirely unprecedented."

"Let me guess," said Joe Allen, "you're a big *Star Trek* fan?"

"Of course," replied Wexler, pretending to look confused. "Who isn't?" He arched an eyebrow. "So you've obviously already thought of the transporter machine."

"*We* didn't," said Cargill. "But Edgar Knight was a *Star Trek* fan, too. He said that if you incinerated the copy quickly and completely enough, you would basically replicate what happens when a character from *Star Trek* beams down to a planet."

"Exactly," said Wexler. "Two copies are produced. One of these is destroyed, and one ends up in a new location. But this all happens in a single instant. So the person being teleported is unaware of the actual mechanics of it."

"I'll let you be in charge of the marketing campaign," said Blake. "I can see the slogan now," he added with a wry grin. "Come for the teleportation. Stay for the fun of being melted down to your constituent atoms."

Wexler laughed. "I'm not saying we should do it," he said. "I'm just raising it as a point of interest."

"The important point," said Jenna, "is that none of that matters if we can use this tech to move through space *without* moving through time. No duplicates. No incineration. And we get interstellar travel, as well. The possibilities are too incredible for words. Mankind could spread our seed, venture into the galaxy. Turn *Star Trek* and *Star Wars* into reality."

"Q5 is already doing that," said Wexler. "Who says the dark energy field *isn't* the force from *Star Wars*? It's a mysterious force that pervades the universe, right? And we've found a way to tap it. So we and Luke Skywalker have something in common. The force is with us all."

There were loud groans around the table.

"*What?*" said Wexler innocently. Then, attempting a truly horrible Yoda impersonation, he added, "Get too carried away with this analogy, did I?"

"Just promise me that you won't create any lightsabers," said Blake in amusement.

"Why not?" said the physicist.

"Not very practical," replied Blake. "Miss your opponent and slice through a steal support beam like it was butter. The only thing *less* practical is that white body armor, which does absolutely nothing to protect its wearer."

Jenna gestured to both men and shook her head. "Are you two done now?" she said in mock exasperation.

Both men nodded, pretending to look chastised.

"To continue," she said pointedly as a smile flickered over her face, "within a thousand years mankind could number in the trillions. More. I guess I should have looked up what comes after trillion."

"Quadrillion," said Tini helpfully.

"I thought that was a made-up word," said Jenna wryly. "Good to know. The point is simple—we could take out the ultimate insurance policy against species extinction. I can't even imagine that our group wouldn't want to adopt this as our primary goal, hands down. For once, this would be an advance with unlimited upside, and no downside."

"Well, maybe one," said Wexler timidly after a few seconds passed, as though he really didn't want to bring it up and ruin Jenna's moment, but couldn't help himself. "There's always the chance that by venturing out into the cosmos we'll end up poking the bear. That one or more alien species out there, far more advanced than we are, will object to the possibility of trillions of humans traipsing around the universe, creating havoc as only humans can."

After pausing to let this register, he added, "I have to admit this is extremely unlikely. The universe seems to me to have plenty of room for all. And you'd think an advanced species would be welcoming. But it's impossible to say for sure."

"Okay," said Jenna. "A possibility I hadn't really considered. But assuming there aren't aliens out there who want to keep us in our cages, can we all agree that developing true teleportation, and a true interstellar drive, is our most important goal?"

As she expected, this statement quickly received unanimous support.

"Good," said Jenna. "So let me move on to what I view as our second most important priority. We need to find a way to suppress the time travel effect. I recommend that any resources not tied up on the interstellar drive initiative should be devoted to this."

"Why?" said Cargill. "Now that Knight's gone, we're the only ones with this capability."

Jenna nodded grimly. "For now. But do you honestly believe this will always be the case?"

Cargill remained silent for a few seconds and then sighed. "No," he replied miserably. "You're right. It will get into the public sphere at some point."

"Just for the sake of argument," said Blake, "what if we decided that the danger of this tech was too great, and chose to disband Q5 and bury it, destroying the kettle-building instruction manual along the way? Then there'd be no chance of a leak."

Nathan Wexler shook his head. "There's no shoving this back into the bottle," he said. "If Nature allows it, some other scientist will eventually discover it."

"That is my conclusion, also," said Jenna. "And the next scientist who discovers it might shout if from the rooftops. Or maybe turn into another Edgar Knight. Or worse."

"I have to hand it to him," said Cargill. "Knight did us a service by acting as a cautionary tale. Our memory of him ensures we stay properly paranoid."

"Which is why developing a suppressor field is so vital," said Jenna.

"Is something like that even theoretically possible?" asked Joe Allen.

"Yes," said Wexler almost immediately. "There are already cir-cumstances we know of in which time travel is prevented. One, send-ing back a kettle within a kettle couldn't be done until Daniel's recent workaround. Two, if an object would otherwise end up in the past within a block of granite, the process is . . . blocked." He paused. "*Blocked*, get it?"

There were blank stares all around.

"You know, you're *blocked* from ending up in a *block* of granite. Blocked?"

"Yeah, we all got it," said Blake, rolling his eyes. "We're just glad you didn't choose to be a stand-up comedian."

"Are you kidding?" said Wexler. "That joke *killed* in Vegas."

This finally did elicit genuine laughter all around.

Allen waited for the laughter to end. "I get what you're implying," he said to the physicist, "but just because nature can block this effect doesn't necessarily mean *we* can."

"But it does show it's theoretically possible," replied Wexler, "and it does give us hope. Actually, I have an idea of how to approach the problem already, making use of our ability to penetrate the fifth dimension. Gravity plays a role in time travel, as we know, which is why objects don't materialize in midair or underground. And gravity is conjectured by many to be a fifth-dimensional phenomenon. This has never been proven. But maybe this is our chance to change that."

"Just how many Nobel prizes do you need?" said Tini wryly.

Wexler smiled. "It's tough to get even one when you have to keep your discoveries secret from the Nobel Prize Committee."

"This is true, also," said Tini.

"There's nothing that says I have to understand this," said Blake, "even at a big-picture level. But I'd like to. Any way to dumb this down so I can get a sense how you might use the fifth dimension to block time travel?"

"I don't want to steal Jenna's thunder right now," said Wexler. "But I assure you, Aaron, I'll put that fifth dimension lecture I prom-ised on the schedule at some point during the next day or two."

Blake nodded his thanks.

"To continue," said Jenna, "let's imagine we never perfect a suppressor field, and the tech gets out. Either because of a leak or a discovery by someone else. Would this necessarily be a bad thing?"

"We've analyzed the wonders and dangers of time travel before," said Allen. "In many ways it would be great. But in many others it would be *exceedingly* bad."

"Just for the sake of this discussion," said Jenna, "I'd like to imagine a world with unlimited time travel. I'd like to look at the situation holistically." She paused. "By using bigger kettles to repeatedly send slightly smaller ones back through time, every man, woman, and child could have their own. Talk about your handy appliances. Anyone could copy anything. Diamonds, gold . . . food and water." She arched an eyebrow. "Hunger, thirst, poverty—these would all go extinct."

"And energy would become unlimited," said Tini. "We can't tap the dark energy field directly, but each person could use it to copy millions of charged batteries. And there are more sophisticated strategies for using time travel as an energy source, which I won't get into."

"If billions of people are resetting the universe forty-five millionths to a half-second back," said Allen, "wouldn't this eventually stall it out? Or keep it yo-yoing back and forth within a half-second interval forever?"

"Actually, no," said Wexler. "As you know, we think time travel only resets what is locally affected. If I copy a piece of string a million times, the rest of the universe isn't affected and rolls on its merry way as before. Only a very small chunk of the universe near me would notice that a million pieces of string had suddenly materialized. And I wouldn't even be aware that my local universe had been delayed, because it would reset at the earlier time period. When it resumed, I would never know that it had gone forward, and then backed up, even once, let alone a million times."

"If the rest of the universe isn't reset," said Blake, "wouldn't that result in time moving at different rates, depending on how close you are to the point of time travel?"

"This is true," replied Wexler. "But Nature doesn't see this as anything new. Einstein showed that time is running at different rates already, all over the place, depending on how fast you're going and depending on gravity. Time on top of a mountain runs faster than time at sea level, because the gravitational field is slightly less on the mountain. We now have clocks sophisticated enough to confirm this."

"Thanks," said Blake. "This is helpful. I'm sure we all have additional questions, but we should let Jenna continue," he added, gesturing to the woman in question.

Jenna nodded. "So to sum up," she said, "if we were to spread this tech widely, everyone would get unlimited food, energy, and wealth. No one would ever need to work again."

"Doesn't sound terrible so far," said Allen.

"If time travel were widespread," said Cargill, "there are people who would also advocate for making multiple copies of the greatest minds of our generation. Despite the legal and ethical issues."

"People like Edgar Knight?" said Jenna in disgust.

"You'd be surprised," said Cargill. "This wouldn't just find support among ethically challenged megalomaniacs. In my view, many ordinary, reasonable people would support it too. On paper, it would be very compelling."

"You're probably right," said Jenna. "Which just adds to the complexity of a world with time travel in it."

She paused for a few seconds to see if anyone else would jump in. When no one did, she continued. "Just to be complete," she said, "I'd like to quickly revisit the con side of the ledger, which we've discussed multiple times. Uranium could be copied. Weapons. Poison. Each person could make thousands of copies of themselves. Armies could be teleported inside buildings, behind enemy lines. The technology would bring total chaos."

"That sums it up pretty well," said Cargill. "Can I assume you've come up with additions to this list?"

"You know me too well, Lee," said Jenna with a twinkle in her eye. "One other side effect would be that wealth would lose all meaning. If everyone can make mountains of flawless diamonds, they become the *opposite* of rare. They lose all value. This applies broadly. In an economy of unlimited wealth, money means nothing."

"Getting used to this new world would require an adjustment," said Allen, "but we'd manage."

"I think Jenna is making a broader point," said Blake. "If every comfort is taken care of, what would be the incentive to advance any further? What would motivate people? Jenna mentioned that no one would ever need to work again, and Joe said that this didn't sound so terrible. But I disagree, and I think Jenna does too. It could be a devastating blow to the species. There are some who think we handle *hell* better than we handle *paradise*."

"You read my mind," said Jenna. "I based my concerns on my recent study of human happiness and human behavior. But go ahead, Aaron. I think you have an instinctive grasp of this."

"In my view," said Blake, "it's very simple. Unending leisure isn't all it's cracked up to be. It would drive me mad very quickly. And while it would take a lot longer for most people to grow bored and listless and unhappy, it would eventually happen to everyone. We're wired to get the most satisfaction from striving toward goals, from overcoming challenges. True, I'm an extreme case. I tend to get bored unless my life is on the line, which is something I'm fighting to change. But humanity isn't built for perfection. Our psyches aren't ready for everything to be handed to us."

"That about sums up what I was planning to say," said Jenna. "Until recently, I always thought that bringing about heaven on earth would be a *good* thing. Utopia. The goal of humanity throughout the ages. But it's possible unlimited wealth and leisure might not be utopia, after all. Might even be a bad thing."

Lee Cargill glanced down at his phone and grimaced. "Can we pause for just a moment?" he asked.

"Sure," said Jenna.

"Is this an emergency?" he said in low tones as he answered. After pausing to listen to a reply he added, "Okay to get back to you in just a few minutes?" When he ended the call a moment later, the answer he had received from the caller became obvious.

"Sorry," said the head of Q5, waving a hand at Jenna. "Please continue."

"As we've agreed," said Jenna, "time travel technology *will* get out there. Sooner or later. Look at the nuclear bomb. At the time it was developed, it was a greater destructive force than anyone had ever even conceived of. In the beginning, the US was the only country with the bomb, and did its best to keep it that way."

She shook her head. "But we all know how *that* turned out. Yet the world has survived, at least until now. So I say we have to assume our pet technology will get out there soon, and rush to find a way to survive the, um . . . fallout. More than survive. Benefit from its widespread use."

"Which is where your time travel suppressor comes in," said Cargill.

"That's right," replied Jenna.

"But if everyone on Earth has his or her own kettle," said Allen, "you can't possibly suppress them all."

Jenna Morrison raised her eyebrows. "Why not?" she said. "Put the suppressors on thousands of small satellites. Ring the entire globe. Produce one, and then make as many duplicates as you need. Many decades ago we found a way to connect every home in America to telephone and power lines. If we could accomplish that way back then, we can surely accomplish this now."

"You'd really want to turn the entire Earth into a time travel dead-zone?" said Blake.

"Not necessarily," said Jenna. "Let's get the suppressor fields up and running. Then we can decide how to play our hand. Perhaps you set aside a central location in each major city around the world where time travel is allowed. One small enough that authorities can maintain absolute control of it, ensuring the technology is only used for the common good. Authorized uses only, like duplicating food, creating unlimited energy, and so on."

"And countries like Iran?" said Cargill. "It's true that most of their territory would still be a time travel dead-zone, so at least they wouldn't be able to teleport arms or armies beyond their borders. But countries like this would be sure to use the process for ill."

"I agree," said Jenna. "Maybe you'd have a world body that would deny time travel zones to countries with massive human rights violations. Those wishing to destroy their neighbors, or those supporting terrorism."

"Even in approved countries," said Blake, "how could you ensure that the oversight of the time travel permissible zones was adequate?"

"I don't know," said Jenna. "Any group of people can be corrupted. So do we let AIs play a role in monitoring? Which begs other questions and concerns. Who would program the AI? Or should we put these responsibilities in the hands of those among us who are known to be compassionate, who have demonstrated a long history of charity and non-violence? Or do we have the time travel sites of each country managed by panels drawn from ten or twenty other countries?"

"Interesting ideas," allowed Cargill.

"Or maybe terrible ones," said Jenna. "I don't know. I don't have all the answers. I don't have *any* of the answers. I just believe we should build a suppressor field so we at least have the luxury of asking the questions. If this group agrees to devote itself to coming up with suppressor technology, second only to interstellar travel and true teleportation, I'll devote myself to finding answers. I can study the issues we've just discussed, with the expectation of leading many more meetings like this one to debate ideas as we move forward."

"And if you were able to lead us to a solution that we think is workable," said Cargill, "what then? Would you advise that we don't wait for a leak? That we just announce this to the world ourselves, along with our plan to ensure its safe use?"

"Yes," replied Jenna. "At that point, why not? The potential for good, the potential to change the world forever, would outweigh the potential for disaster."

Cargill nodded and then put on a thoughtful expression for several long seconds. "Does everyone agree with the initial priorities Jenna has laid out?" he asked the group.

"Absolutely," said Blake without hesitation, and the rest of the group chimed in with their wholehearted support as well.

"Very, very impressive, Jenna," said Cargill. "Well done. I thought you'd be the right woman for the job, but I had no idea *how* right. While I was thinking small, you were thinking big. I was expecting you to make recommendations for how best to keep this secret. Instead, you were thinking of how best to *reveal* it. I was thinking about how best to use this to do small things, like funneling money to anti-terror groups and duplicating large quantities of impossible-to-manufacture pharmaceuticals. You were thinking about how best to utterly transform human civilization."

The head of Q5 shook his head. "And you made your case so well that your conclusions seem ridiculously obvious in retrospect. It's hard to imagine now that I didn't see this instantly. Only I didn't. Not before you pulled up the curtain."

"Thanks," said Jenna, almost sheepishly, surprised and delighted by this reaction. "But setting out goals is the easy part. Now it's up to people like Nathan and Daniel to actually achieve them."

"True," said Blake. "But even the best marksman can't hit the target unless he knows what he's supposed to be shooting at."

"Spoken like a true warrior," said Jenna in amusement.

25

After the meeting concluded, Cargill asked Aaron Blake to hang back with him once again.

"That was your . . . *counterpart* who called during the meeting," he explained when they were alone in the room. "My phone pinpointed the call as having come from inside China. I only put it off because I knew the meeting was nearly over and I wanted you involved."

Blake checked the time on his phone and frowned. "Shouldn't he be in North Korea by now?"

Cargill nodded grimly. "Let's find out what's going on," he said, and then asked his phone to establish an audio-only connection.

Blake had studiously avoided his doppelganger while he was still within the confines of Cheyenne Mountain, and Cargill had made certain that no one else on the team would run into him either. Blake had no interest in seeing himself as others saw him, and he would only feel guilty that this man was being sent on a kamikaze mission while Blake stayed back, despite there being nothing to differentiate the two except for a split-second difference in their ages.

But given the operation had evidently hit a snag, Cargill was right to have him be part of the conversation, despite his wish to avoid talking to himself. Three heads were better than one, even if two of the three heads were identical.

The Blake in China answered the call, but only on the fifth ring, and his tone made it clear they had awakened him from a sound sleep.

"Sorry to wake you," said Cargill after a quick greeting, and after explaining that Blake was in the room with him. "But you did just call me a few minutes ago."

"I'm more exhausted than I thought," came the reply, and the Blake in Cheyenne Mountain grimaced. In his own head, his voice sounded much deeper. Like Idris Elba or James Earl Jones. But the voice coming from his double sounded nothing like these men. "The mission has encountered a few . . . hiccups."

"I gathered," said Cargill. "You sound like shit, Aaron," he added bluntly.

"I look and feel like shit, too," replied Blake. "Don't be too jealous, Aaron," he added wryly to his double inside Cheyenne Mountain. "The need for my death at the end of this Op puts a damper on things, but it's proving to be a real challenge. Plenty of excitement already. And there you are stuck behind a desk, probably bored out of your mind."

Blake smiled. It wasn't a joke. The truth was that he *would* have been jealous if not for the mission's finality. "Lee manages to keep things interesting enough around here that my envy of you doesn't get too out of control," he replied with a smile. "So what's going on?"

Blake told them. About the Triad war at the airport, how he had driven away—as far as he knew, the sole survivor—and how he had come to be in a truck in the woods, babysitting a refrigerator and waiting for roadblocks to be withdrawn to proceed. Roadblocks clearly established by the Chinese military.

"Impressive moves," said Blake when he had finished, and Cargill nodded his agreement.

"Not really," replied Blake. "Nothing any other Aaron Blake couldn't have managed."

The Blake in Cheyenne Mountain smiled broadly. His double may have been weary, but he still retained his sense of humor.

"I'll do what I can to explore the situation from here," said Cargill. "If we get intel on what's going on, I'll let you know. But I don't expect much. There was no way the difficulty at the airport could have been anticipated. But I can't believe it had anything to do with your mission. If it did, they would have focused their forces mostly on you, rather than spreading them out. And their goal would have been to capture you rather than kill you."

"Agreed," said the Blake in China. "But a rival triad isn't the problem anymore. It's the Chinese military. By now they've discovered the plane I was on when I arrived in Shenyang. They've learned that

I boarded it in Beijing. They've learned that the plane that brought me to China is untraceable. Not to mention that I'm most likely an American."

"No doubt you've piqued their curiosity," said Cargill. "But it's hard to believe they're going to *this* much trouble to find you. Especially since they have no idea what they're after, or how important you really are. And they have no idea what your refrigerator can do."

"My thoughts exactly," said Blake. "Which is why I expect this fishing expedition to end soon. I'm sure they'll dismantle their roadblocks by tomorrow night."

"Do you still believe you can carry out the mission?" asked Cargill.

"No question about it. Surviving the airport attack was the dicey part. Anyone could handle things from here. Even if they weren't Aaron Blake."

"Hard to imagine," said Aaron Blake.

The Blake in China chuckled, but even this sounded dead tired. "Once I'm off this call," he said, "I'll get some quality sleep. Enough so that I'll be fully rejuvenated. Then I'll do some recon. I've got a bike with me, as you know."

"How will you avoid your devastatingly handsome Caucasian face being seen while you're on the motorcycle?" asked Blake.

"When I planned out this mission," replied his double, "I wargamed out the possibility I'd need to use the bike, unlikely as I thought it was. I had Zhang prepare a duffel bag to my specs. I'll be wearing a helmet and goggles. I shouldn't stand out as a Caucasian."

"And what if the roadblocks remain up tomorrow night?" asked Cargill.

"Then I'll continue to wait them out. If they're still up for a *third* night, it'll be hard not to believe they know more about my cargo than they should. But this is a bridge I don't expect to have to cross."

"You really think you could keep a semi hidden for that long?" said Cargill dubiously.

"Yes. Maybe indefinitely. As I said, K-1 helped me find the perfect hiding place. And I've got all I need to live. A bottle of water, a piece of beef jerky, and a roll of toilet paper. With my trusty time machine, I can make enough copies of these items to supply an army."

"And what army wouldn't be excited about living on nothing but beef jerky and toilet paper?" said Cargill in amusement.

The Blake in China managed a weary chuckle yet again. "The Sub-Zero is truly a gift that keeps on giving."

"Enjoy your jerky, Aaron," said Cargill. "I'll leave you to get some sleep. But before I sign off," he added, "I want to commend you. Given what happened, I can't imagine anyone else making it as far as you have, as *well* as you have. Truly outstanding. Godspeed from here on out, my friend."

"Yes," seconded the Blake at his side. "Good luck."

"Luck?" said Blake to his alter ego. "You of all people know that when you're an Aaron Blake, you don't need luck."

"Very true," said Blake. "You're as wise as you are talented."

Cargill rolled his eyes. "Really?" he said in mock exasperation. "You guys are enjoying this way too much."

26

A holographic image of Major Long He appeared in Colonel Li's office.

"Did you find him?" snapped Li curtly in lieu of a greeting.

"No sign as of yet," replied Long. "Almost two thousand men have been activated. They're manning roadblocks and watching airports, train stations, and waterways. If he's within our perimeter, we *will* find him."

Li couldn't hide his anxiety. Every minute that went by increased the area they needed to cover exponentially. "Has Director Chang finished his inspection of the plane?"

"He and his team went through every millimeter. They are satisfied that it is just a plane. They are now certain that the cargo was responsible for the dark energy signature they detected."

"I assume you've gathered all cell phones and electronics from the airport?"

Long nodded. "All of them that weren't incinerated in the explosion. We haven't looked at every file on every device, but our initial analysis suggests these won't be helpful in identifying our mystery Caucasian."

"Send every last file to my computer here," ordered Li. "And keep pressing. I'm counting on you to net this prize."

"I won't let you down, Colonel Li."

27

Colonel Henry "Hank" Vargas sat in a relatively cramped office in CIA's Langley headquarters and studied the man who had just entered and was now seated across from him. To all appearances, Vargas appeared to be a mid-level CIA employee, even though he didn't work for the Agency and arguably wielded more power than its director.

No one who ever visited this office would possibly guess that Vargas headed up all black site secret weapons programs in America, and that's just how he liked it. He had numerous other offices at black sites across the country, but Virginia was where he made his home, and this was his primary office.

Vargas had served in the army in numerous capacities over the years, working his way through the ranks with startling speed. And why not? He was bright, shrewd, and brave, with extensive combat experience as an elite commando, an instinct for being in the right place at the right time, and an aptitude for politics.

It also helped that he looked the part. Handsome and serious, with dark, brooding features and a stern expression that seemed to be forever plastered on his face, suggesting he would never be frivolous with the grave responsibility his nation had given him. His hairline was receding, and the hair that did remain, once black as a crow, was showing hints of gray throughout, which he immediately dyed to its original color.

In other positions a bit of gray might be an advantage, a proxy for experience and wisdom, but not in his line of work. Leading-edge secret weapons programs were science and tech heavy, and a comprehensive knowledge of the state of technology was critical in his job. These days, nothing said *out of touch* like advancing age. He was in his early forties—plenty young in his mind—but in the era in which the public had far more confidence in a fourteen-year-old to solve a tech problem than they did in a sixty-year-old multinational CEO, gray was out.

Matt Mueller, on the other hand—the man who had just entered the colonel's office and taken a seat—was in his late twenties. Confident and energetic. But at this moment, also noticeably intimidated. This was only his second face-to-face audience with Vargas, and the colonel's perpetual scowl didn't make any visitor feel comfortable, let alone a young up-and-comer.

"Thank you for seeing me in person, sir," offered Mueller after Vargas made no move to shake his hand.

"I didn't do it for you," said Vargas bluntly. "I did it for me. I saw video of the results of the tests you did yesterday. So I wanted to see the man responsible for wasting four billion dollars of the taxpayers' money."

Mueller stared at the colonel in confusion, studying the older man for any indication he was joking. But the fierce glare that remained on Vargas's face made it clear that he was not.

"Are you sure you saw the same tests I did?" asked Muller in disbelief. "We aren't where we want to be, true, but this is an incredible start."

"Four *billion* dollars," continued Vargas as though Mueller hadn't spoken. "Down the drain. The government throws around the B word so much that four billion doesn't sound like all that much, does it? Sounds like a much bigger amount when you say four thousand *million* dollars."

The colonel shook his head in disgust. "So, instead of funding your program, we could have given four thousand people a million dollars each. Or we could have given *four million people* a thousand dollars each. That's about sixty football stadiums filled with people, each getting an extra grand."

"The orbital laser system performed *brilliantly*," protested Mueller, his professional pride overcoming any feelings of intimidation he was experiencing. "We weren't even sure it would work at all, and it surpassed our every expectation."

Just the day before the first prototype of the orbital laser system had been flown into space in the cargo hold of a private rocket.

"Performed brilliantly?" repeated Vargas skeptically. "Define *brilliantly.*"

"You saw for yourself. First, allow me to remind you that the satellite is compact enough that we'll be able to build and launch enough of these to reach every square inch on Earth. The laser reached all ten targets we aimed for, six on land and four at sea, including one the size of a baseball. The beam was extraordinarily accurate, held its cohesion all the way to the ground, and was able to burn through a quarter inch of steel in *twelve seconds*. Hell, we could use it to kill a fly that landed on your picnic table."

"Not if the fly felt a little toasty in the first fraction of a second and flew off," said Vargas in disdain. "Because the system is shit when it comes to moving targets, right? Can't shoot down a missile, or even a plane, can it?"

Matt Mueller's eyes were now burning even hotter than his laser. "You already knew that going in!" he barked. "No, we can't maintain an unwavering lock on a single point on a fast-moving target. Not for long enough. At least not yet. But we *can* kill a man who's in motion. Even one who's running."

"Taking how long? Twelve seconds?"

"Less. Probably five or six."

"And would a bystander see the beam?"

"Unlikely, but maybe."

"And can you spread the beam to take out larger targets?" pressed Vargas in obvious contempt. "Buildings? Terrorist training camps? Cities?"

"We already have weapons that can do that," protested Mueller. "I know you included in the program specs that the system should be able to take out buildings and other massive targets, but you've acknowledged these are stretch goals. *Extreme* stretch goals. What we've done is a remarkable first step. A total triumph. Think about what this system will be able to do. Our orbital cameras can already read the label on the underwear of every human being on the planet. Now we can pick off anyone we choose from space with absolute precision. Like the fist of God, striking from above. In what universe is this not a brilliant success?"

"In *this* one," snapped Vargas without hesitation. "Because if we use this system as a personalized assassination device, we can't hide the fact that we've weaponized space, that we have a ring of lasers pointed down at every living person. You can only drill so many holes through the tops of the heads of enemies of the state before intelligence agencies around the world figure out what's going on. Our potential targets already know how to avoid being seen by our satellites, so they don't get a drone strike up their ass, but they'll be even more careful. And you can bet the major powers will spend their every last dime—or whatever the hell currency they use—putting up orbital laser systems even more powerful than our own.

"It's not worth triggering this kind of worldwide panic," continued Vargas, shaking his head. "Not worth triggering this kind of arms escalation among major powers, just so we can deploy a half-measure like this. Or more accurately, a *tenth* of a measure. And that's being generous."

"So you're saying you'd only consider using this system once it's able to meet *all* of the mission goals you set up initially?"

"*Very good*," said Vargas, his tone scathingly condescending. "Glad I was able to make this simple enough for even *you* to be able to understand."

Mueller ignored the insult. "I thought you knew that many of these goals were all but impossible," he said. "Something to strive for, like a three-minute mile. But unrealistic. We've just shown that we can power a laser from low Earth orbit all the way down through mile after mile of ever-thickening atmosphere. With enough energy to kill! This is one of the greatest breakthroughs in history! Surely you can appreciate that. To use the system to take out an entire building, let alone a city, you'd have to widen the beam a hundred- or a thousand-fold. You'd be looking at many orders of magnitude higher energy requirements. Even at the rate technology is improving, it could take decades to get there—if ever. I know your ultimate goal, but you never told us that you consider all intermediary steps to be worthless. You have to walk before you can run. This system is performing beyond our wildest dreams!"

"Are you done?" said the colonel icily.

Mueller was still seething and looked like he wanted to rant for another ten minutes, but visibly stopped himself. "Yes," he spat. "I'm done."

"Good. Because I've made my decision. I want you to use the thrusters on your prototype satellite to push it into deep space, headed for the Sun. And I won't authorize the testing of another one until it's able to take down the fucking Kremlin. Do you understand?"

Based on Mueller's expression a visitor might have thought that the colonel had stabbed his first-born child—which wasn't far from the truth. Several long seconds passed before Mueller's rage had subsided enough to allow him to speak. "I urge you to reconsider, Colonel," he said, biting off each word. "Think it through. The current capability is far more valuable than you realize. And its deployment will lead to steady, incremental improvements, making it more and more valuable as time goes on."

"I agree it has a limited utility," allowed Vargas. "But not nearly enough to risk showing our hand." He shrugged. "And since you think what I really want it to do isn't possible, I'm going to kill the program entirely. Effective immediately."

Mueller looked ill. "But you knew what this test was designed to show," he whispered. "Why even test it if you knew this was your position?"

"Sorry to interrupt, Colonel Vargas," said the feminine voice of Marga, his digital assistant. "But you have an incoming call on your private line, audio only. You asked me to alert you whenever you received such a call."

Vargas nodded, not needing to be reminded of his standing orders. "Tell whoever it is that I'll be with them in a moment."

He turned to Mueller. "To answer your question," he said, "my thoughts weren't fully crystallized until I saw the system in action. That's when I realized just how relatively useless it is, even when it was successful. This test drove home how far it has to go before it can become the game changer I wanted."

The colonel gestured toward the door, indicating it was time for Mueller to leave. "Not many people have access to my private line, so I need to take this. Get this program shut down immediately. And I'll expect you to come up with a proposal for an entirely new project by this time next month. Am I clear?"

"You're making a mistake, sir," said Matt Mueller bitterly.

"Until you're promoted to my position," barked Vargas, "it's my mistake to make. So either do what I say, or look for another job. Just don't expect it to be in the tech sector, for the government or otherwise. By the time I finished blackballing you, you'd be lucky to get a job as a bag boy in a grocery store. Have I made myself clear?"

Mueller was so enraged he didn't even trust himself to speak. He managed to nod before giving the colonel one last look of thrilling hatred on his way out.

"Thanks for stopping by," said Vargas smugly. He waited until the door to his office closed, and then turned to take his call.

28

"Hank Vargas," said the colonel into the receiver of an untraceable phone he pulled from his desk. Marga had been programmed to stop listening in once he answered. Not only would his intelligent digital assistant not monitor the conversation, it would make sure that it was routed through an enhanced encryption system so no one else could either.

"Hello, Colonel. It's been a long time."

Vargas recognized the voice immediately and almost dropped the phone. "*Edgar Knight?*" he whispered in disbelief.

"I'm honored that you remember me."

"*Impossible!*" insisted Vargas. "You can't be Knight."

The colonel hadn't spoken to the man in years, and unless Knight had discovered how to communicate from beyond the grave, Vargas wasn't speaking to him now.

Knight had worked in the colonel's orbit on a number of occasions over more than a decade as both men were rising through the ranks. Knight was a brilliant experimental physicist and inventor, maybe the best ever, even if he did have an annoying habit of saying so himself. The last time their paths had crossed, Knight was working with Lee Cargill at Q5, an initiative that had originally been under Vargas's auspices. During its first year, the colonel had met with Cargill and his star inventor a number of times.

Then, inexplicably, the group was pulled away from him with little explanation, other than some hand waving that the attempt to exploit the mysterious force known as dark energy should technically have never fit under his purview in the first place, as it was never solely a weapons program.

He learned later through back channels that Cargill had been given a civilian rank and authority equivalent to Vargas's own, even though Vargas was responsible for all black site weapons programs and Cargill was only running one.

Not only was Q5 taken from him, but he was no longer authorized to know anything about the group's activities. Given the wide range of secret information he was given access to without hesitation, this was truly extraordinary. Every attempt he had made to investigate further had led nowhere. His boss, Kate Johnson, the Secretary of Defense, told him that the order to change the status of Q5 had come from President Janney himself. She insisted that she had nothing to do with it, and that Janney hadn't felt the need to explain his rationale when she had questioned him about it.

And that was that. Until now.

"You say I can't be Knight?" the voice on the line repeated in amusement. "Why is that, Colonel? What have you heard?"

"You know damn well what I've heard. That you died in a freak accident about nine or ten months ago, along with several other members of Q5."

Knight laughed. "You know better than anyone that you can't trust everything you hear. I'm afraid this was fake news, Colonel. A fairy-tale to cover up what really happened. Only Cargill and the president know the truth. And me, of course."

"So what *is* the truth?"

"Turns out I wasn't killed last year, after all. Go figure. It's a long story, but I'll be happy to share it with you. Here's the thing, Colonel. I've always liked you."

Knight paused. "Okay, maybe that's going a bit too far. But I *have* always respected you. I've seen your potential. You don't put up with bullshit. You're bright for a military grunt, and more visionary than most people I've known. You think big. I need that. So maybe it's time I tell you what's really going on with Q5. Why the rumors of my death have been so exaggerated. And, oh yeah . . . the real reason a man-made island near the Las Vegas Strip turned into a fireball last week. Interested?

Vargas's eyes widened. "You could say that," he replied evenly, making sure not to sound overeager. "Go ahead," he added, his tone so casual it almost sounded bored. "I'm all ears."

Knight laughed once again. "Over the phone, Colonel? Really? I'm afraid we'll have to do this in person. There's an abandoned warehouse at the corner of Mercer and Twain. Meet me in the lot behind the warehouse at eight tomorrow morning."

"I can be there in thirty minutes," offered Vargas.

"No, no. I just arrived in town after a long drive from Wyoming. Tomorrow will work just fine."

"You drove all the way from Wyoming?" said the colonel. "Suddenly afraid of flying?

"Driving was a necessary evil."

"What is it, about a thirty-hour trip?"

"Twenty-five, but who's counting? But don't worry, Colonel. I had a colleague of mine drive through the night while I relaxed in relative comfort. I'll explain everything when we meet. If you tell anyone about this call, I'll know it, and you won't learn a thing. By now, you have to be dying of curiosity, so don't blow this. And there's a huge opportunity for you here, as well, in addition to just satisfying your curiosity."

"Who am I going to tell?" said Vargas innocently. "I'll see you tomorrow morning."

29

Vargas found sleep to be elusive and welcomed the dawn of morning. He took a bracing cold shower to get his blood flowing and contemplated the meeting he would soon have with the ghost of Edgar Knight.

Cargill's project had gone as dark as a black hole, almost literally. Information could enter Q5, but none ever exited, not since the moment Vargas had been relieved of command. The secrecy Cargill had managed to keep was truly unprecedented, even for a black project. Vargas hadn't even heard a rumor about what might be going on there, not a single conspiracy theory among the ranks.

The group had been exploring a mysterious force that pervaded all of space. There were several theories out there as to the nature of this force, but they could all be summed up succinctly by the physics and cosmology community: we have no idea.

Vargas could only assume that Q5 had found a way to exploit this force, but if this had led to a new explosive or other type of advanced weapon, why had the group been pulled out from under him?

Knight had been right. Vargas was dying to know what this was all about.

He just had to be sure that the *dying* part of this idiom didn't become a reality.

Because there were few men he trusted less than Edgar Knight, and this was saying something. Vargas had always had a good radar for megalomaniacs—not just egotistical narcissists, which Knight obviously was, but true megalomaniacs. Knight was all of this, and more. He might have been able to keep his true nature hidden from almost everyone, but Vargas had seen through him very quickly.

What worried Vargas the most was that in the history of megalomaniacs, few were as formidable as Knight. The man was single-minded, ambitious, and flat-out brilliant. Maybe their interests were aligned, as Knight thought. But maybe not. Either way, the man was less trustworthy than a politician.

Someone had gone to a lot of trouble to convince the Black Ops community that Knight was dead, to disavow his existence at the highest levels. There must have been a reason for this. It stank to high heaven.

Perhaps Knight had become wildly unstable. So dangerous his existence needed to be expunged. Since he hadn't bothered to set the record straight, it was also likely he had gone rogue.

Vargas would be a fool not to prepare as though he were walking into a trap—or onto a landmine. And he was anything but a fool. He had been a special forces operative for too long, with too much combat experience, not to prepare for the worst now.

He put on a pair of tan cargo pants, civilian garb, but custom designed with several well-concealed pockets in addition to the many that were so prominently displayed, and began to arm himself. He first loaded up with weapons in all of the obvious places. After this was completed, he hid two small guns in two hidden pockets, and two combat knives, one sheathed in an ankle holster and one taped to his back.

The colonel looked into the mirror, satisfied, but knew he wasn't done yet. He fully expected Knight to confiscate his first, obvious layer of weaponry. He wouldn't even be surprised if the inventor went the extra mile to find and remove his more hidden layer.

Which is why he planned to add a third layer, one that wouldn't look like weaponry at all.

What was the point of being in charge of all black site weapons programs if you couldn't use a prototype now and then?

He hoped Knight's call was on the level. That all he planned to do was share information with Vargas and offer him a golden opportunity.

But if this *wasn't* the case, Hank Vargas would be ready.

30

Vargas planted himself on a grassy hillside and surveyed the specified meeting location, a hundred yards away, through high-powered binoculars. The abandoned warehouse itself was relatively small and windowless, and the parking lot behind it in disrepair.

There was no one in sight, and no vehicles. Heavy padlocks were still holding rusting doors closed, reducing the likelihood that Knight was inside.

He continued to recon the warehouse and its surroundings until it was time to move. As expected, when he arrived and parked at the designated spot, Knight was nowhere to be found, but this changed within minutes as an eighteen-wheeler soon joined him behind the warehouse, with the Amazon logo and orange swoosh on the side. If one wanted to choose a vehicle that would blend in, choosing one that mimicked what was quickly becoming one of the most often seen delivery trucks in the United States wasn't a bad choice. Unless this was an actual Amazon delivery truck that Knight had stolen, which was also a possibility.

But why a tractor-trailer? A sports car was much more Knight's style.

The man seated next to the driver in the cab's passenger compartment jumped out before the truck even stopped and pointed an automatic rifle at Vargas's gut. "Hands up, Colonel!" he said.

Vargas sighed and did as requested, while the driver stopped the truck and quickly joined them. Vargas's gaze shifted between them. Identical twins. What were they doing working with Knight? Shouldn't they be filming a chewing gum commercial somewhere?

The driver looked him up and down carefully. Vargas was wearing nothing but tennis shoes, cargo pants, and a black T-shirt. His dyed black hair was covered by a cap that was essentially a larger, military version of a baseball hat, decorated with a mottled, brown-and-tan desert camouflage pattern.

The driver began to frisk him while his partner continued to hold him at gunpoint.

"What's all this about?" demanded Vargas, pretending such treatment was unexpected. "I was told this would be a meeting among friends."

The twin holding the weapon laughed. "Really, Colonel? Then why did you come armed for bear?"

Vargas shrugged. "I have dangerous friends," he said evenly.

The man continued frisking him with admirable thoroughness, removing the obvious layer of weapons and eventually finding and removing the second layer as well, including the knife taped to his back.

When he finished, his twin rapped on the trailer door, which opened seconds later to reveal Edgar Knight in the flesh. It was unmistakably him. Vargas still hadn't been entirely convinced.

Until now.

Knight gestured Vargas inside. The colonel climbed up to join him, while the gun-toting twin followed suit, continuing to train his gun on Vargas when they were both inside the trailer compartment.

The driver waited until he was sure that Vargas was in his twin's sights and then retook his position behind the wheel.

"Thanks for coming, Colonel," said Knight inside the trailer, making no move to shake hands. "Happy to see me?"

"I only wish I knew," replied Vargas.

Knight laughed. "Never fear. You will soon enough. And you'll be glad you came."

Knight closed the door and the truck began to move. Vargas glanced around the surprisingly well-lit compartment, about fifty feet in length. The last ten feet, closest to the cab, held a transparent box made of what looked like Plexiglas, just six inches smaller in every dimension than the space within the trailer it occupied, clearly tailor-made to fit there.

The rest of the compartment could only be described as a traveling bedroom, with a beige area rug, a bed, a dresser, and a small table with a large computer monitor and keyboard attached firmly to its surface. Knight had said on the phone that a colleague had driven him from Wyoming while he relaxed in relative comfort, and now Vargas knew what he had meant.

After taking in his surroundings, Vargas turned back toward his enigmatic host. "Come on, Edgar," he said, gesturing toward the twin and the gun in his hand. "Is this really the kind of first impression you want to make? I'm unarmed. You've seen to that. So why don't you have Bozo the Henchman here lower his weapon."

"I'm afraid I can't do that," said Knight pleasantly. He nodded at the twin. "His name is Jack Rourk, by the way. He's a very skilled ex-soldier. But you're even more skilled, Colonel. Left alone in this trailer, I have no doubt you could overpower me. I plan to tell you everything I know. Willingly. After all, I plan to convince you to join me. But who knows, you might decide that gaining the upper hand is worth the trouble of having to drag it out of me by force. I can't let that happen."

He paused. "Besides, what kind of first impression does it make when someone has a fucking knife taped to their back?"

Vargas ignored this last point. He gestured to their surroundings. "You do know they make RVs, right?"

Knight smiled. "Thanks for the tip."

"Where are we going?" said Vargas.

"To someplace more . . . private. A farm that I purchased nearby, just for this occasion." He gestured toward the colonel's camo hat and smiled. "I guess you were expecting a desert."

"How far is this farm?"

"It's in Maryland," replied Knight. "About two hours away. But we'll make good use of this time. I can tell you about Lee Cargill. What's really been going on within Q5. And what really happened at Lake Las Vegas. You'll think I'm making it all up, at least at first. But trust me, you'll come around. Rest assured that when we arrive at our destination, I've planned a little demonstration. One guaranteed to turn you into a believer."

31

"I have to give you credit," said Vargas after Knight had spoken for just over an hour on the reality and intricacies of time travel, fielding dozens of Vargas's questions along the way. "If this is a twisted fantasy of yours, you've been able to present it well. Self-consistent logic and well-thought-out answers."

"It's twisted, all right, but it isn't a fantasy. You'll learn that soon enough."

The colonel nodded. He understood the duplication effect of time travel. Who didn't? Anyone who had seen even one time travel movie had come across a character who encountered an earlier version of themselves. But he still wasn't crystal clear on the rest. "Help me understand this translocation aspect a little better," he said.

"Perhaps I've been too technical," said Knight. "I forget how strange this is to the uninitiated. To make this as simple as possible, think of the Earth as a cruise ship, and space as an ocean. Imagine you're on this cruise ship, which is always moving. You begin at Island A and sail to Island B. A trip that takes exactly one day. When you arrive at Island B, you jump back in time exactly one day." He paused. "The thing is, time travel doesn't change *where* you are. It only changes *when* you are."

Knight waited for this to sink in. "So after you send yourself back," he continued, "*where* are you?"

"You're still on Island B," said Vargas immediately.

"Exactly. But where is the other version of you that you've joined in the past? Where was he a day earlier? Still on Island A, right? About to begin the journey you just took."

Vargas frowned. "Yeah, it's obvious now. I'm not sure how I missed it."

"You aren't the first," said Knight.

"If I'm understanding your other rules, if I send a quarter back in time your forty-five millionths of a second, I get two of them. But then the universe starts up again and sends the quarter back a second time. Then it does this again. Over and over. Forever. How is it that I don't end up with an infinite number of quarters?"

"I explained why an object can't end up in solid matter. Existing matter repels incoming matter from the future. But it can only deflect it so far. If you try to beam into a thick block of matter with no open space nearby, time travel is disrupted, aborted. This is basically what happens with your quarter. Each time you send it back it ends up in the same location. For the first ten or twenty thousand trips, its brethren already deposited in the past deflect it a slight distance away, adding to the bounty. But, eventually, you create a big enough pile of quarters that the incoming one can't be deflected far enough, and the process is halted."

Knight paused. "This is a situation I call runaway time travel. In practice, I rarely let this happen."

"How do you prevent it?"

"The time machine can detect an additional copy of an object when it arrives fifty-eight feet or so away. I can program it to abort the instant a second copy is detected. Or a third. Or whatever number I choose."

"But you only have forty-five millionths of a second to abort once your machine detects the proper number of copies."

"Plenty of time for a computer."

Vargas paused in thought. "You said Q5 can beam things a hundred twenty miles," he said.

"That's right."

"And they can still detect copies that far away and abort before a second firing?"

"Easily," said Knight. "Because, in this case, they have almost an entire half-second. I haven't done it in practice, because I'm currently limited to forty-five microseconds. But I developed sophisticated electronic signaling devices when I was with Q5. Imagine a tiny chip with an adhesive backing. One that can broadcast its presence at the same speed as your cell phone. Since your friend's voice can travel thousands of miles during a call without a noticeable delay, imagine how quickly a signal can cover a hundred twenty miles? A computer can easily detect this signal and abort further time travel, with plenty of time to spare."

With this question answered, Knight moved on, bringing the colonel fully up to speed on what had happened at Lake Las Vegas. Vargas was skeptical of the story's veracity until Knight spoke about octa-nitro-cubane. This struck a chord.

Vargas himself had begun this program, and he knew the destructive potential of this explosive. When he had first heard of the devastation at Lake Las Vegas, octa-nitro-cubane had come to mind. He had discounted it immediately, but only because he knew it was impossible to make. Despite going to heroic lengths, his people had only managed to produce an amount of this substance so minuscule it could only be seen under the most powerful of microscopes.

But time travel duplication explained how this minute amount could have been amplified. And the chemist who ran the octa-nitro-cubane lab, Dr. Bob Botchie, had been very close to Lee Cargill, had worked for him on an earlier project. Vargas wouldn't be surprised to learn that Cargill had convinced Botchie to give him a fraction of his microscopic supply under the table, without breathing a word about it to anyone.

Knight's story was ringing true. He could still be a raving madman, but everything he said held together well, and he seemed measured and rational.

Vargas noted absently that Rourk continued to hold a gun on him, but this had been going on for so long that Vargas barely noticed he was there. He wasn't even sure if Rourk could speak. The man had become nothing more than a mute statue that blended in with the scenery.

"Why did you split off from Cargill in the first place?" asked Vargas.

"He got power hungry," said Knight. "I'm a lot more capable than he is. Which makes me a threat. He wanted me out. Basically it was, 'Thanks for the invention, Edgar, but I'm not sharing my kingdom.' He tried to have me killed, but failed. And not by much."

"How did he explain your absence from the team?"

"He convinced President Janney that I was out of control. A tyrant in the making. A war monger who had branched out on his own." He shook his head in disgust. "Cargill killed *thousands* at Lake Las Vegas. Just to get to me. He used a machine gun to kill a fly. So who's the one out of control? I'll leave that for you to decide."

"So Janney and Cargill were behind the fake story that was spread about your death?"

"That's right."

"How did Cargill miss you at Lake Las Vegas?"

"I left the island just before the attack," said Knight. "Cargill didn't know it."

"So it was just luck?"

"That's right."

The discussion continued for almost twenty minutes, at which point the truck came to a final stop on a narrow, private road. Knight threw open the door and all three men exited.

The road bordered a field that continued on for many acres, perfectly level but currently fallow. Twenty yards behind them, a red farmhouse could be seen, kept in such good condition it could have been removed from a three-dimensional painting.

"So this is your farm?" said Vargas.

Knight nodded.

"What's it growing? Dirt?"

"Apparently," replied Knight with a shrug. "Used to grow something else, but I never bothered to find out what. I guess we're between growing seasons. I didn't care. The owner was motivated to sell, and I was motivated to buy. Through intermediaries, I've acquired massive land holdings across the United States and around the world."

He paused. "When I travel, I don't like to stay at hotels."

Vargas glanced back at the trailer and Knight's makeshift bedroom inside, and rolled his eyes. "No kidding," he muttered.

A moment later he and Knight were joined by the truck's driver and *another* identical twin, who had been awaiting their arrival. Vargas studied the three matching henchmen with great interest. "Is this your demonstration of time travel?" he asked Knight. "Three of a kind?"

The inventor smiled. "No. Not conclusive enough. You might think I went to the trouble to get identical triplets to fool you."

"Identical triplets? I didn't know there was such a thing."

"There is. Very rare, but possible. These three aren't triplets, but I don't want you to have any doubt. You already know Jack Rourk," he said, pointing to the man who was *still* holding a gun on him. "And this," continued Knight, gesturing toward the driver, "is Jack Rourk. Finally," he added, shifting his gaze to the newcomer, "let me introduce you to Jack Rourk."

"Is this all of him?" asked Vargas.

"Not quite. There are five altogether. The other two are performing duties elsewhere. I wouldn't usually produce any copies of a man like Jack, but I've been a little shorthanded since Lake Las Vegas. And Jack is very talented, and very loyal. And he works well with himselves."

"Is that supposed to be time travel humor?" said Vargas, his expression much closer to a scowl than a smile.

"Apparently not," replied Knight.

Vargas's eye narrowed. "So how many more copies of *you* are out there?"

"Only one Edgar Knight, I'm afraid."

"Why is that?"

"Too many cooks spoil the broth. You can only have a single brain, a single CEO. Multiple limbs are okay, like Rourk, but only one of me is allowed."

"I see," said Vargas, who seemed satisfied by this answer. "So how long until your *actual* demonstration?" he asked. "And do I get to choose which object you send back?"

"You're not getting this, are you?" said Knight. "I'm not sending an object back. I'm sending *you*."

Vargas's eyes widened, but he otherwise retained a stoic expression.

"No proof is more convincing," continued Knight. "Forty-five millionths of a second. When you arrive in the past, it'll be like a trip down memory lane," he added with a grin.

"Your time machine is in the back of the trailer," said Vargas, "isn't it?"

"Very good."

"But it's above ground," said Vargas. "Won't something that goes back in time end up a few feet too high?"

"No. Objects don't end up inside solid matter, and they don't end up in mid-air, either, for reasons that aren't entirely clear. Has to do with gravity."

"So you can time travel from an airplane?"

Knight shook his head. "We tried. The time machine has to be closer than about seventeen feet to the ground or it won't work."

"It's all so . . . arbitrary," said Vargas.

"It only seems that way," said Knight. "Once we have a full understanding of the underlying laws of nature, it will all make sense. That's why Nathan Wexler's work is so important. Not just for extending the distance we can travel back in time to a half-second. It will help us derive a universal theory to explain this, to manipulate it."

Knight paused for a moment and then continued. "At one time the motion of the planets in our solar system seemed arbitrary. Then Kepler came along with his laws of planetary motion. Newton followed with his laws of gravitation, improving upon Kepler, allowing us to precisely explain what we were seeing and to predict the future. All except for the planet Mercury, whose orbit was slightly different than Newton's equations predicted. Then Einstein came along. His work, which gave us a better understanding of gravity, was able to precisely explain why Mercury's orbit was off. That's how science works."

"You can skip the history lessons," said Vargas bluntly. "I'd like to remain focused on the present." He arched an eyebrow. "And what you have in mind for the future."

"Good," said Knight. "Then let's get right to it."

He and the gun-toting version of Jack Rourk climbed back into the trailer and then motioned for the colonel to do the same.

Once Vargas had joined them, Knight peeled adhesive from a flat piece of black plastic, the size of a nickel, and stuck it on Vargas's shirt. "The sensor I was telling you about," he explained. "It will communicate directly with the time machine once you land. The time machine has its own sensors that will detect you and abort a second firing, but it's better to have redundancy."

Knight gestured for his guest to enter the device that filled the back ten feet of the trailer. "There's a comm system inside," he explained. "So we can communicate without shouting."

Vargas entered the transparent Plexiglas compartment and closed the airtight door behind him, his expression skeptical. Talk about unimpressive. The device didn't just look low-tech, it looked *no*-tech. Where were the spinning vortices, lights, and space-distorting visuals he had come to expect from time travel movies?

"Stand on the small X in the center," said Knight, manipulating the computer on his small table. "Time travel will commence in exactly two minutes."

Knight began to exit the vehicle.

"Where are you going?" asked Vargas.

"Two of the Jacks and I will be greeting you when you arrive back in time." He gestured to the third Jack Rourk, still in the trailer, still holding his gun, although at least now that Vargas was behind Plexiglas, the weapon was down at his side. "This Jack will make sure you don't get lonely in there."

Saying this, Knight exited the trailer, not waiting for a response.

Vargas remained glued to the small white X in the middle of the Plexiglas chamber, feeling like an idiot. There was no way this could really work. The contraption just seemed too simple.

After a period of time, a computer voice filled the small chamber. "Time travel commencing in ten . . . nine . . . eight . . . seven . . . six . . . "

Vargas braced himself for whatever was to come. He had asked Knight questions about the *how* of time travel. Perhaps he should have asked about its safety, its effect on the human body. He supposed he was about to find out.

". . . one . . . zero," said the computer, and before the final number had even fully registered Vargas was standing on dirt, with Edgar Knight and two Jack Rourks just a few yards away. There was no disorientation, no visual distortion, no sick feeling in the pit of his stomach.

One instant he was in the truck, the next he was here. *Unbelievable.*

"Welcome to the past," said Knight. "If you need help understanding our ancient version of English, let me know," he added wryly.

"This isn't about time travel at all," said Vargas. "It's about teleportation."

"It's mostly about *duplication*," Knight corrected. "Which is great on its own, but a negative when it comes to teleportation. Let me show you what your dislocation in space has wrought."

Knight led the group the fifty-eight feet back to the truck, where Jack Rourk had already escorted Colonel Hank Vargas back out of the trailer and to the ground.

"Holy shit!" said the Vargas who had just exited the vehicle as he watched his double and Knight approach. "I thought it had failed," he said to Knight when they arrived. "I thought you were playing me for a fool."

"That's because it *did* fail. The *you* it worked on is right beside me. Once it worked on him, it failed to work on you."

Both versions of Vargas considered this statement in silence.

"Go ahead and talk to each other," said Knight. "Ask each other questions. Whatever it takes to convince yourselves that the man you're looking at is as much *you* as you are. That he knows everything about your past that you do. Your deepest, darkest secrets. Your most forbidden desires. I'll wait."

"No need," said both men in unison. "I'm convinced already."

Both were taken aback as they realized they had issued identical responses, further underscoring that they weren't just identical in appearance.

"That's great to hear," said Knight, removing a silenced gun from a hidden holster and firing without an instant's hesitation. He pulled the trigger twice in rapid succession, and the Vargas who had not traveled through time fell to the soil, his blood adding further nutrients to the fallow ground.

"*What the fuck?*" shouted Hank Vargas, taken completely by surprise. "Are you out of your mind?"

"Don't tell me you got attached to him already?" said Knight. "You only just met."

"Why?" said Vargas. He knew Knight was dangerous and cold-blooded, but even he hadn't guessed the man could kill with such ruthless, emotionless efficiency, even given that the victim had been a duplicate.

"The *why* should be obvious. I only need one of you. And *you* only need one of you. Unless you wanted to share your life and your paycheck with him. I made an exception for Jack, but we can't have any freelancing Hank Vargas's running around. Besides, I want you to feel special."

Knight returned the gun to its holster. "I can't say I didn't enjoy that," he added with a cruel smile. "When you were my boss, you could be a real asshole." An air of menace came over his features. "No offense."

"None taken," spat Vargas, his guard now fully up where it belonged. Knight had acted friendly and had lulled him to sleep. He wouldn't be lulled again.

"I'm disappointed by your lack of backbone," said Knight. "Duplicates are expendable. The time machine giveth, and you and I taketh away. If you're going to be joining me, you need to toughen up."

Vargas's expression darkened further. *Be careful what you wish for*, he thought, but aloud he said, "I'll make sure my toughness never comes into question again."

32

Knight escorted Vargas into the farmhouse along with all three Rourks, who stood guard as unobtrusively as before, just beyond the family room where he and Vargas took up residence.

Knight sat on a red leather sofa and gestured for Vargas to sit in a matching recliner across from him. He had paid extra to buy the farm fully furnished, but this was for convenience only. This was the first time he had actually seen the inside of the farmhouse, and he hated it, both the furniture and décor.

Knight was the future. This ugly piece of Americana was the rural past, decorated by someone whose tacky tastes could only appeal to the idiotic brood he had left behind at a young age.

The family room walls were lined with an alternating pattern of chickens and roosters, in yellows and reds, which he found hard to believe. Didn't farmers get enough of the real thing to leave these unappealing fowl off of the wallpaper?

Knight shook his head and turned to face his guest. He was well pleased by how things were going so far. He had tried to get into Vargas's head by killing the man's double, and he was certain he had succeeded. He needed Vargas to respect him. To know that he was deadly serious. To never doubt his resolve, his threats, or the lengths he was prepared to go to get what he wanted.

"So why am I here, Edgar?" said the colonel. "You mentioned us working together. How? Why do you need me?"

"To help me achieve my goals."

"I'm listening."

"I have a plan to get you inside Q5."

Vargas considered. "For what purpose?"

"First, revenge. Admittedly, the more petty and irrational of my goals. I know intellectually that completing my grand vision takes precedence, and that this is relatively unimportant. Emotionally, it's another story. Cargill and the Bonnie-and-Clyde couple responsible for the attack on Lake Las Vegas, Aaron Blake and Jenna Morrison, need to suffer. They outmaneuvered me. I can't let that stand."

"Outmaneuvered you?" repeated Vargas in disbelief. "Their Op *failed*. They hit everything *but* the target."

"Only because I got lucky," replied Knight. He wasn't sure why he didn't tell Vargas that he had been a backup copy, and that Cargill's attack *had* succeeded in killing Knight One. Pride? An instinct to never disclose more than was necessary? It was unclear. "Cargill doesn't know he missed me, by the way, and he can never be told."

Vargas nodded. "So you want revenge," he said. "I get that. But what's this grand vision you spoke of?"

"I plan to transform the world. Lift it to new heights. Dramatically improve the human condition."

Vargas smirked. "No, seriously," he said, "what are your goals?"

"I've never been more serious. *These* are my goals."

Vargas's smirk vanished, replaced by a look of incredulity. "And how do you intend to do all this?" he asked. "By releasing your time travel technology to the world?"

"No. Far too dangerous. I want to *control* the world's morons, not *arm* them. I want to unite the countries of the world under a single global government. With me at the helm." He raised his eyebrows. "And with you as my second-in-command."

Vargas shook his head and frowned deeply. "Can't be done. Not even with your time travel tech."

"I agree," said Knight evenly. "Not this moment it can't. But very soon. Because if I can get my hands on Wexler's work, increase my range to a hundred twenty miles, no world leader will be safe from me. From my organization. After that, the way forward is clear, the chances of success, regardless of how wildly improbable my end goals sound to you at the moment, are extremely high."

"Even then it can't be done," countered Vargas. "It's absurd. One private citizen taking on the collective might of the entire globe? Even *you* can't manage that."

Knight sighed and began to massage his forehead. Was there no one who had any vision other than him? Vargas's daring military thinking in the weapons realm had impressed him, but the colonel's inability to see the big picture now was highly disappointing.

Knight already possessed the brilliance of a god, but he needed to develop the patience of one, as well.

He took a deep breath and launched into a lengthy description of what he had in mind. He explained how he had duplicated the greatest minds of the time, creating his Brain Trust, and the breathtaking advances they had made. How time travel could create unlimited wealth. How he could use this wealth to buy a small mercenary army, describing the one he had begun to put together that had been largely destroyed at Lake Las Vegas, despite this disclosure tarnishing an earlier assertion that Cargill had killed only innocents when he had attacked.

"And as you've seen," he told the colonel, "with a time machine, I can turn a small, handpicked group of mercenaries into the largest army the world has ever seen. I can borrow thousands of copies of each soldier from forty-five microseconds in his future."

"Is this what you intend to do?" asked Vargas.

"Not at all. I bring it up just to emphasize that I can do as much as I need to do with the human resources I have." He smiled. "I'm my own force multiplier."

Knight went on to explain why he wouldn't need an army to accomplish his goals. With the ability to teleport a hundred twenty miles, he could easily demonstrate to world leaders that they would never be safe from him, would never be beyond his reach. He could seduce them with unlimited wealth and power, and threaten them with physical harm, a potent combination.

Initially, all he would ask was for leaders to push to create a joint cooperative body, similar to the UN, but broader, and one contemplating greater trade and military cooperation. A European Union with far more countries, even if a majority of the public in a given leader's country was against such a move.

He would reward leaders who pushed for this world body, and punish those who refused. He would spread wealth to rig elections, and see to it that this new world body had success after success. He would use time travel and other advanced technology to destroy terrorist regimes, and wipe out dictators and their governments, making sure all credit for such victories accrued to the world body.

The early president of this emerging worldwide government would be elected by the body itself, but Knight would be the one pulling the president's strings, and in due course would come out of the shadows to take the reins of power himself.

By having this governing body cleanse the world community of rogue nations and weed out Jihadists with unprecedented thoroughness and finality, and by channeling unprecedented wealth, prosperity, and Brain Trust technology through this group, the idea of a worldwide government would become celebrated, heralded as something long overdue. The group could accrue legitimate governing power, slowly and inexorably, under cover of world leaders and the media—all of whom Knight would control.

Ultimately, the recipe for world government wasn't that complicated, if you had the means to produce the ingredients. Rid the world of the cancer of dictatorships and terrorist states. Spread unlimited wealth. Usher in a new age of peace. Control leaders and information flow. Mix liberally. Then, add in mountains of sugar—or tenderize with an iron fist—as needed.

It wouldn't happen overnight, but Knight was certain he could achieve his goals within ten years, turning the globe into what was essentially a magnified version of the US, except without term limits for the president. Not the *United States of America*, but rather the *United Countries of the World*. Just as with individual states in America, every country would have a certain level of autonomy, but would be under the enumerated powers of the central authority.

And Knight would be above it all. The perfect ruler. A man possessing both a love of knowledge and a keen intelligence. Plato's *philosopher king*.

Vargas still didn't seem entirely convinced that this would work, but Knight could tell he was now taking the idea much more seriously.

The strategy Knight laid out was good, as far as it went, but he left out a few key elements to ensure maximum palatability. He purposely failed to mention that he would wipe out those with inferior intelligence in favor of millions of geniuses, whom he would duplicate to fill the void, a substantial upgrade for the species.

Knight knew better than that. Anything that smacked of eugenics would be rejected immediately as being Hitlerian, a bridge too far, even by those who should have known better. He had no doubt that even Vargas, a man who treated his people like slaves, whipping them to create ever harsher weapons capable of mutilating millions, would be appalled by eugenics.

Hitler had given this idea too bad of a name for it to ever recover. But the difference between Knight and Hitler was that Hitler had gotten it backwards. Ironically, he had killed off the exact wrong group, the group that had the most to offer Germany—possibly due to jealousy over this very fact.

Knight, on the other hand, respected only genius, not caring what god a man foolishly preferred to believe in. Not caring if he preferred to wear a silly beanie on his head rather than a symbol of a man being tortured to death around his neck.

Had Einstein not felt forced to leave Germany because he was Jewish, he would not have lent his genius to America's Manhattan Project, along with seven other key Jewish contributors who had fled Europe, including John von Neumann, Edward Teller, and Leo Szilard. All in all, twenty-seven Jews assisted in the creation of the atom bomb—including *seven* future Nobel Laureates—and the likes of J. Robert Oppenheimer and Richard Feynman.

Had Hitler not been obsessed with killing Jews, Germany could well have developed the atom bomb first, winning the war.

When *Knight* thinned the human herd, he would do it right. He would thin the most feeble-minded, and cultivate the geniuses—not thin geniuses and cultivate psychopaths as Hitler had done.

Eugenics wasn't the only motive Knight concealed from his guest. From his perch atop the world, after duplicating multiple copies of the greatest collection of geniuses in history, he would push this group to extend the human lifespan and eventually conquer death itself.

That was a new endgame for him, one he had come upon while waiting inside his Wyoming mansion to be put to death. Right now,

Knight could produce thousands of copies of himself, have all the backups he needed, but they would all eventually age and die, at essentially the same rate that he did.

But this would no longer be true when he was done reshaping the world, when he had finished pushing the boundaries of human genius.

But this part of his strategy wasn't something he was about to disclose.

"What do you think?" asked Knight when he had finished outlining the sanitized version of his plan. "Still say it can't be done?"

"You've certainly thought it through," admitted Vargas. "But even if it *is* possible, why would you want to do it? How much power and wealth does anyone *need*? I didn't think anyone could be more ambitious than me, but I see now how wrong I was. Given your time travel technology, you could amass more wealth and power than anyone in history. *Without* going to any of this trouble. Or taking on any of this risk."

"It isn't about wealth and power," said Knight, and this much was true. It was about control. It was about ridding the human species of terrorists and ignoramuses, and elevating genius so he could live forever.

"What *is* it about, then?" pressed Vargas.

"It's about me raising the species to undreamed of heights. At the risk of being immodest, I'm the only one who can do it. It will be my gift to the world. And even though you think it's too grandiose, not worth the trouble, you'll get to ride my coattails."

"Just to be clear," said Vargas, "you make it seem as though this transformation of society will be bloodless. I assure you, the truth is *much* different. To make this a reality, you'll have to wipe out large groups, and scores of individual players, who are neither terrorists nor dictators."

Knight eyed him with interest. "Do you have a problem with that?" he asked.

"I'd be your number two man?"

"Yes. I can't govern the world alone. You'd basically be the president of any number of countries, among other duties."

Vargas considered. "Then no," he said finally. "I don't have a problem with that. What's a little bloodshed in the grand scheme of things?" He paused. "Of course, all of this depends on what you want me to do. I'm assuming it isn't a suicide mission."

"Far from it," said Knight.

"You began this by saying you thought you could get me into Q5."

"There is some risk that my plan won't work, but I think the odds are very good."

Vargas nodded. "I assume my contribution will be to bring Nathan Wexler's work back out. To enable you to extend your teleportation reach."

"And help me shut down Q5 behind you."

"By shut down, you mean . . . "

"Destroy them. Completely. And any personnel or technology that could be used to reconstitute them."

"Why?" asked the colonel.

"Because they have the same tech I do. They're the only ones who can stop me. When Cargill and Q5 are gone, the path won't be easy, but it will be clear."

"And you'll also get that revenge thing sorted out, won't you?" pointed out Vargas.

"Icing on the cake," said Knight, flashing a predatory smile. He leaned forward. "What about it, Colonel? If you agree to join me, I'll require you to do exactly as I tell you. I'll demand absolute loyalty. But the rewards will be almost beyond comprehension."

He paused to let this sink in. "So," he finished, staring deeply into Vargas's eyes, "are you in?"

There was a long silence as Vargas weighed his decision. Finally, a smile spread slowly across his face. "Absolutely," he said enthusiastically. "You came to the right man."

33

Hank Vargas took a bathroom break while Knight sent one of the Rourk trio to pick up sandwiches and an assortment of beverages.

When Rourk returned, twenty minutes later, the five men ate a hasty lunch and resumed proceedings, with each of the two principals now holding ice-cold bottles of water.

"So what is your plan for getting me inside Q5?" asked Vargas.

Knight laid it out for him in great detail over almost thirty minutes. When this discussion ended, Vargas nodded enthusiastically. "I think it'll work," he said. "I'll *make* it work," he added.

"You'd better," said Knight. "We won't get a second chance."

"Let me get back to my office to prepare. Organize my thoughts."

"Sure," said Knight. "But we need to take care of one more thing before you leave."

Vargas raised his eyebrows.

"I know you don't share my goals," said Knight. "Too visionary. Too grandiose. I get that. Regardless, I'm also certain that you'd love to get your hands on my tech. Take the easy route to wealth and power you spoke about."

"You're worried that I'll turn on you?"

"In a word, *yes*."

"You have the knowledge of time travel and the passwords to make it happen. I can't get anywhere without you. I'm more than content to be your number two."

Knight laughed. "You forget that I *know* you. That I've worked with you. You've never struck me as the kind of man who's content being anything other than number one. And an extreme alpha number one, at that. Which is good. I'd have no use for you otherwise. But I still need to take precautions. If I don't, once you're inside Cheyenne Mountain, you'll be able to do whatever the fuck you want."

"I am content being number two," said Vargas, "because that's what I am now. My boss is Kate Johnson, Secretary of Defense. And I don't respect this bitch one bit. If I can handle playing second fiddle to *her*, following you won't be a problem. If you can pull this off, being *your* second-in-command will bring me far more power than I could ever get on my own. What can I do to convince you that I'm all-in? That I won't cross you?"

"I'm so glad you asked," said Knight. He pulled a titanium capsule from his pocket and placed it in the palm of his hand. "See this?"

"Barely," said Vargas, squinting at the silver capsule in Knight's hand, about half the size of an extended-release cold capsule. "What is it?"

"It's a very sophisticated, computerized poison delivery system. There are two very tiny compartments inside. One contains a toxin so lethal that even this tiny amount is enough to kill a man ten times over. The other contains an agent that can nullify the toxin."

"There is no such poison delivery system," said Vargas. "I've been in charge of black weapons programs now for years. I'd know if such a thing existed."

"There is *now*," said Vargas. "A little trick my Brain Trust cooked up."

The colonel's eyes narrowed. "And you've confirmed it works?"

"Perfectly."

Vargas shook his head adamantly. "If you think I'm going to let that anywhere near me, you're out of your fucking mind."

"Do you consider having it implanted in your skull, *near you*?"

Vargas rose to his full height with a menacing intensity, and all three Rourks made a point of extending guns in his direction. He visibly relaxed his posture, so he no longer looked like a predator poised to strike, and they relaxed their aggressive postures in turn.

"So here is how I envision this working," continued Knight calmly. "I implant this in your skull. Very easy to do, with almost no pain and no aftereffects. Not only does it have a computer onboard, it has a receiver that my Brain Trust cooked up. One that picks up signals, even through lead walls. Even inside Cheyenne Mountain," he added pointedly. "It will be set to release the toxin into your brain every

Sunday at midnight, Eastern Standard Time. Unless I send a signal telling it to abort. If you're as loyal as you say, I'll reset it every week, in plenty of time, and you'll have nothing to worry about. Cross me, and you'll at least have the chance to say Sunday prayers one last time before you go."

"Not a chance," snapped Vargas.

"Why not?" said Knight. "You tell me you'll be loyal. That you won't cross me. So prove it. This is just an insurance policy, one I'll never have to cash in, right?"

"Just because I know I won't cross you," said Vargas, "still doesn't mean I'll let you stick a goddamned time bomb in my head."

"I'm afraid that's the deal. Non-negotiable. You'll never get a better one in a thousand life-times. Take it or leave it. I should also point out that this won't be a threat to you forever. Once we've taken out Q5 and set things in motion, I expect us to be operating mostly out of different locations. And you'll have earned my trust. At that time, I'll issue the order to open the partition between compartments so the toxin is neutralized. I'd remove the device entirely, but once it's in, it's tamper proof. So much so that even I can't remove it."

"Your word that you'll eventually neutralize it doesn't change a thing," said Vargas. "It's not going to happen. I won't let any man keep a sword at my throat. What if this tech malfunctions? I'm supposed to just trust it? What if you die in a car accident? Or get drunk and forget to send the kill code? Or lose your fucking mind?"

The unmistakable sound of helicopter blades whipping through the air could be heard off in the distance, swiftly growing louder. "Hold that thought," said Knight. "This is my ride."

"Your ride?"

"Good timing, actually, since we seem to be at something of an impasse. The helo will be landing any minute behind the house. I have some matters I need to attend to for a few hours. So while I'm gone, I want you to think through everything we've talked about. Think about what I've shown you. *You've traveled through time.* Think about that! Think about what I'm offering."

"Even if I agreed to your implant, how do I know you won't kill me once I've done what you want?"

"You don't. But you have my word. Even if you weren't critical to my plans, you have an impressive skill set, one that can be very useful to me. Special forces. Considerable combat experience. Black Ops experience. Well connected. And I can't do this alone. I'm fresh out of top lieutenants after Cargill's attack. You succeed, and you're the last person on Earth I'd kill."

"And if I refuse to have that thing implanted?"

"Then I have no use for you," said Knight in disdain, raising his voice to be heard over the growing din of the helicopter as it landed twenty feet away from the farmhouse. "You're free to go back to your life and pretend this meeting never took place. I'll find another way. But you'll always know that you turned your back on the ultimate opportunity."

Knight walked to the door and turned back. "Give it two hours of steady thought," he shouted, "and we can talk more when I return. I know you'll make the right decision," he added as he exited the farmhouse.

Minutes later Vargas heard the helo fly off, carrying the most dangerous man on Earth to an unknown destination, and leaving him with much to ponder.

34

As Blake cut through the pitch-black night on a motorcycle, continuing his recon activities, he felt very much like a field mouse inside a hawk sanctuary. Even though China and America were not at war, anytime an operative engaged in clandestine operations in another country, he had to consider himself behind enemy lines. But this was usually more metaphorical than real.

Not this time.

Blake decided he would have been safer had he been an American spy hiding in Nazi Germany during the Second World War.

Blake pulled the motorcycle to the north and left the road he had been on, canceling his contact's night-vision feature as he did. His second night in the backwoods of China was cold, dark, and moonless. While he could use his contact to drive without headlights on any paved roads that he was forced to take, this wasn't possible while riding over rough terrain. This was a perilous activity even with the headlights on full, and he had come close to wiping out on several occasions.

He had been lucky that Zhang had made such an excellent choice in motorcycles. The bike had plenty of horsepower but was whisper quiet, incorporating noise-reduction technology that had only become available earlier in the year. It was also a crossover, designed for both street and off-road usage, as capable when tearing through woods and rough terrain as the best mountain bikes.

He made his way to the top of a wooded hill and pulled out his binoculars for the fourth time that night, his last, not bothering to dismount from the bike. He cursed to himself once again as more helicopters came into view off in the distance, adding to the many he had already seen, moving in tight circles, slowly, methodically, *inexorably*.

Just great. A perfect addition to the roadblocks that continued to sprout up like weeds.

The roadblocks from the first night hadn't been dismantled. They had been *expanded*. It was a nightmare.

His recon indicated that the roadblocks formed a large noose, and he was near one of the noose's boundaries. So far the helos had started beyond this boundary and were making their way outward, in case he had made it through. Smart. If he had escaped the initial perimeter, the helos might spot him. And if he hadn't, if he was still trapped within the perimeter—which he was—they had all the time in the world to constrict the snare until he was theirs.

This operation was sucking up a huge amount of manpower. Not only that, but it was disruptive to the entire area, no doubt causing a precipitous rise in the anxiety levels of the local citizenry and causing a public relations black eye. Blake could only imagine the panic he would see in rural America, say in the middle of Iowa, if the military set up roadblocks at every exit and manned them with soldiers sporting automatic weapons. The Chinese government and military were less concerned about public perception than the American government would be, but the actions he was witnessing would still only be made as a last resort.

With this level of commitment from the Chinese military, it was only a matter of time before the walls finished closing in around him. He wasn't just a spy behind enemy lines. He was a spy trapped behind the lines of an enemy who was willing to use an *army* to find him. Worse, he was a spy saddled with a massive eighteen-wheeler that he couldn't leave, one he had covered in duplicated tree branches to help disguise it from above, but which made mobility and concealment as difficult as possible.

He decided that this must be why something that was hard to find was referred to as a *needle* in a haystack. Apparently, a *Mack truck* in a haystack wasn't as much of a challenge.

Why were they so keen to find him? While he was an enigma, and there had been a brutal gang war at the airport, this shouldn't have been enough. Not for the measures they were taking.

But how could they know about his real mission and the purpose of the kettles? Only two men on Earth knew about this, so there was zero chance of a leak.

What was going on?

Whatever it was, one thing had become clear: his chances of survival, let alone success, were rapidly diminishing.

35

Colonel Hank Vargas clenched his fists, seething, as Knight exited the room.

Shit! Shit! Shit!

This had gone both better and worse than he could ever have imagined.

Time travel? Who could have possibly guessed *that*? Guessed both its limitations and the stunning possibilities it opened up *despite* these limitations?

Now what?

Knight was lying, there was no question about that. There was no way he'd let Vargas go free if he refused to cooperate. He would know too much. Knight would never allow him to live.

Knight hoped Vargas would acquiesce to the implantable capsule on his own, but if he didn't, he wouldn't be given a choice.

Vargas considered his options. Escape would be easy, despite three armed Jack Rourks guarding him. If he blinked in a certain sequence, the smart contact lens he had put in his right eye that morning would signal his ring to forcibly expel a hideous odor, one that would have the Rourks vomiting all over themselves, making it surprisingly difficult for them to aim a gun.

He had taken a pill before leaving that left him temporarily immune to the smell, but he had experienced it during a test run a month before, and it somehow overwhelmed the revulsion centers of the brain in ways that even its creators couldn't have predicted. He shuddered just thinking about what a horrible, debilitating experience it had been,

Another blink pattern would trigger Vargas's hat to flash as brightly as a stun grenade, temporarily blinding his three adversaries. But why risk one of them getting off a lucky shot while blind?

Instead, if he chose to escape, he would take door number three, the blink pattern that would trigger the release of a sonic blast from his belt so powerful it would kill all three Rourks. In fact, it would kill everyone within a room twice this size.

This was the reason it was still experimental. The scientists involved were working on a way to make it less lethal. Unconsciousness would be ideal, in case the user had allies in the room with him. It was only even usable in its current form because the device's inventors had managed to make the deadly acoustic waveform emanate outward from the belt in a highly directional three-hundred-sixty-degree circle, making it weak enough at its point of origin to spare the man wearing it. Even so, Vargas would be deaf for several minutes and feel like he *wanted* to die.

But was escape his only option? The more he thought about it, the more convinced he became that it was. He couldn't let Knight booby trap his skull under any circumstances. It was as simple as that.

So he would take out the three Rourks and lie in wait for Knight to return, killing him when he did. He had no other choice.

Vargas took a deep breath and walked closer to his three guards, who were spread along the wall that contained the room's only exit. He blinked twice, paused, and then blinked twice again, bracing himself for a shriek that would be at a pitch he couldn't hear, but which would drill through his ears and into his brain, incapacitating him and killing the three Rourks.

Nothing happened.

No sonic wave. No unhearable acoustic blast mowing down all in the room like they were blades of grass. No massive headache and urge to puke his brains out onto the floor.

He tried three more times to activate the device, and failed each time. It was still in the prototype stage, but he had seen the reports, and it had only failed once out of hundreds of tests.

He sighed. This was a very bad break. He would have to go with the vomit-inducing smell. He might be temporarily immune from it, but when the three Rourks heaved the contents of their stomachs onto the floor, he wouldn't be immune from *this* smell. And he'd have to relieve one of them of their gun while it was happening, a messy endeavor at best.

Vargas shook his head in disgust and executed the simple blink sequence that would activate the stench bomb.

Again, nothing happened.

It couldn't be. The odds against both devices failing were astronomical. And based on the results of rigorous testing, the chances that the electronics in the contact lens had failed were even smaller.

Unless the devices *hadn't* failed.

Unless Knight had detected his lens, knew what it could do, and had used Brain Trust technology to make sure it couldn't issue any remote commands to trigger his hidden weapons. When Vargas's hat also failed, he was certain this was the case.

Maybe Knight *was* as brilliant as he thought he was, after all. So much for the easy way out.

Vargas knew he was partly to blame for this disaster. There were versions of these hidden weapons that could be activated by hand. These wouldn't have required receipt of a signal from his contact lens, nor would they have given off a detectable electronic signature. But he hadn't brought them. Next time he would be smarter. If there was a next time.

His only chance now was to be bold. He would have to take a significant risk with his life. It was either this or allow Knight to put a deadly capsule in his head. Just because his odds of survival had plummeted didn't change his decision.

Time for plan B.

He began to walk toward the door. "It's been fun, guys," he said to the three Rourks, "but I really need to go."

All three laughed at the same time, in the same way, and extended their weapons. "Sorry, but we can't let you do that," they all said at once.

"Okay," he snapped in annoyance. "I'm not going to listen to you dickheads in stereo. You, in the middle," he said, pointing. "You're going to do the talking for the three stooges from now on."

"We don't take orders from you," said the Jack Rourk in the middle, while the other two remained silent, doing exactly what he had instructed.

"Here's what's going to happen," said Vargas. "I'm going to walk out that door. And you aren't going to stop me. Why? Because you've heard how critical I am to your boss's plans. Indispensable. Kill me and he'll never get what he wants."

"He said you were free to leave if you chose not to help him," noted the man in the middle. "You're hardly indispensable."

"We both know he was lying. If I choose not to go forward, he'll *force* that capsule on me. I'm too important to his plans. But if you really don't think he was lying, then it shouldn't trouble you to let me leave. I hereby announce that I choose not to help him. Now get the fuck out of my way."

The Rourks glanced at each other in confusion.

"If you believe he was telling the truth about letting me walk," continued Vargas, "no reason to stand in my way now."

"You aren't going *anywhere*," said the spokesman Vargas had designated.

"Which means you *do* believe Knight was lying. If this is the case, then we're back to me being indispensable to him. So are you really going to shoot me? Or maim me? You heard his plan to get me into Q5. You think if you give me a bullet wound to explain away, this will help my chances? I'll make the decision even easier for you: wound me and I'll kill *myself*."

When the Rourks remained silent, Vargas shook his head in contempt. "Let me spell it out for you in terms that even you can understand," he said. "Try to stop me, and your boss's plans are fucked."

"Same thing will happen if we let you leave," said middle Rourk.

Vargas shook his head again. "No. I'll still be alive, and Knight will be able to find me. If he really is as formidable as he claims, I can't stop him from capturing me and putting me to work."

Vargas walked briskly forward, giving them as little time as possible to think their way through this riddle. They each returned their guns to their holsters at the same time, and drew closer together to physically block his path, just as Vargas hoped they would.

He pretended to stumble as he neared the middle Rourk, barreling toward him so the man had no other choice but to catch him and break his fall. The moment Rourk did, Vargas pulled the man's gun from its holster and put multiple shots through his torso in the direction of the Rourk on the left, the bullets managing to penetrate the first Rourk and embed themselves in the second. The Rourk on the right reacted immediately, pulling his own gun, but Vargas spun the dead middle Rourk into his gun hand, defecting his shot, and then put several bullets through the last Rourk's head.

Satisfied, he surveyed the three identical bodies, all gushing blood on the hardwood floor of the farmhouse. He put an additional bullet into each of their heads, just to be sure, and calmly glided to the door. Once out of the room, he would plan the perfect ambush for when Knight returned. Knight would be dead before he even knew what hit him.

Vargas certainly couldn't let him return to this room. Even if he removed the three bodies, he wouldn't have time to clean the blood spatter that now decorated the walls along with the chickens and roosters.

Vargas threw open the door and stepped through.

"Freeze!" screamed Edgar Knight, shoving an assault rifle against Vargas's temple. "Drop it!"

Vargas swallowed hard and released the gun, which made a loud thud as it hit the hardwood floor.

"Back up!" shouted Knight. "Now!"

Vargas blew out a breath and did as he was told. "I think you might have missed your helicopter ride," he said.

"It was just a decoy," said Knight.

"Yeah, no shit," said Vargas in frustration.

36

"Very impressive, Colonel," said Knight in admiration. "I knew you had a reputation as being capable in the field, but I had no idea. When I worked with you, you were just an asshole and a bureaucrat."

"So this was nothing but a setup?" said the colonel in disgust. "Just to see what I would do?"

"You're also quicker on the uptake than I expected," said Knight. "Yes. I was curious to see how you would play this. And I took the liberty of deactivating all of your weapons. You have some nice toys, but I know what your scientists have been working on, and expected you might bring a few with you."

"I still don't see the point."

"I put you in a bind, and I wanted to see what you'd do about it. A little test. I wondered if you'd really believe I'd let you walk if you refused to have the capsule implanted. If you did, I'd have no further use for you, since you'd be too stupid to pull this off, anyway."

Vargas glared at him but didn't reply.

"I monitored your contact lens," continued Knight, "and was happy to see you at least tried to set off your weapons. That answered one question. The next question was, what would you do when your toys didn't work? I had no idea, really. I just wanted to see if you'd roll over, deciding you had no way out. Of course you aren't going to let me put something in your fucking head. Who could blame you? I always knew I'd have to do that against your will. But I wondered if you would try to escape, even without any weapons. From what I've read about you, I thought you might have a chance, even against three armed men who were all well trained."

"Happy?" barked Vargas.

"Extremely," said Knight. "I was watching on my phone and listening through a comm. The Rourks didn't know I was just outside the door. Just like you, they thought I had flown off in the helo." He shook his head in wonder. "The logic you used on them was brilliant. I couldn't have done better myself. And you killed them all so quickly, and left the room so decisively, if I'd have waited another few seconds to pocket my phone and raise my gun, you would have killed me too."

"I'm so glad you're impressed," growled Vargas.

"*More* than impressed," said Knight. "I take back what I said about your lack of backbone."

He gestured to the three dead men on the floor. "And thanks for saving me the trouble of killing them," he added. "I let them hear every word of our conversation. If they were smart, they would have realized I couldn't let them live after that—especially because I have two more copies of Jack Rourk elsewhere."

"While you were entertaining yourself," snapped Vargas, "did you consider what would have happened if I *hadn't* been so effective? What if I tried to escape without reminding them I'm indispensable? What if they had killed me, your ticket into Q5? How could you possibly take that risk?"

Knight shook his head. "I didn't. I programmed my time machine to make *two* extra copies of you. When it detected the first in the field, it changed polarity and sent the second fifty-eight feet away into the farmhouse. I didn't choose to stop the truck where I did by accident. I measured the distance to the farmhouse beforehand. I had a colleague inside who knocked the third you out with a dart gun and dragged you to a room upstairs."

"So you got to conduct your little experiment on me without any risk at all."

"That's right. If you were killed, I'd just wake the other you and start all over." Knight shrugged. "Since you not only survived, you *impressed*, the extra copy of you is now . . . redundant. I'll have him disposed of momentarily."

There was a long silence as Vargas considered just how easily Knight had outsmarted him at every turn. "So now what?" he asked finally.

"Now we go forward as planned. I'm more excited than ever about making you my second-in-command. Which should give you great confidence that I'll keep you alive. For this to work, you'll have to be able to think on your feet. After what you've just shown me, I'm confident you won't have any trouble. I think we're going to make a great team."

"I don't doubt it," said Vargas. "Does this mean that you'll forgo the damn capsule?"

Knight laughed. "Are you kidding? Now I need it more than ever. You're more impressive than I thought. Far too dangerous to be left on your own recognizance."

"Don't do this, Edgar," said the colonel. "We're alike, you and I. Only you're more ambitious than I am, and more capable. But we both want to tame the world. Bend it to our will. We're both unafraid of killing if necessary to make this happen. And I've come around to your way of thinking. Really. History only remembers big deeds. I'm ready to embrace the old adage, 'Kill one man and you're a murderer. Kill millions of men, and you're a conqueror.'"

"Are you saying you're ready to become a conqueror with me? Willing to kill millions of men?"

"Only if we have to. But yes. If that's what it takes to end terrorism and dictatorships forever, it would be worth it."

"You know that's not the entire quote," said Knight. "It's, 'Kill one man and you're a murderer. Kill millions of men, and you're a conqueror. Kill them *all*, and you're a *god*.'"

"Good thing you don't aspire to become a god, then," said Vargas.

Knight laughed. "No, no. Only a conqueror. And only if I have to. A bloodless coup is still the goal."

"Good," said Vargas. "Then we couldn't be more on the same page. You can trust me. No need to implant your capsule."

Knight removed a dart gun from a pocket and shot Vargas point-blank in the stomach. "Good to know," he said as the colonel faded into unconsciousness.

37

Hank Vargas opened his eyes and tried to shake the fog from his mind. He was in his own room, lying on his own bed, so why did something feel wrong? As his head continued to clear, he realized what was troubling him.

He was fully clothed. For a man who had slept in his underwear for decades, this was alarming, especially because he had no idea why this would be.

In one quick burst his meeting with Knight came flooding back to him, along with a memory of the dart in his gut that had ended it.

Vargas could feel a slight, throbbing pain just behind his right ear. *Son of a bitch!* he thought as he threw open the blinds, flooding the room with morning light. After his eyes adjusted he examined the site of the throbbing in his bathroom mirror. Sure enough, a small, round bandage was affixed to his head just above the ear. He lifted the bandage to reveal what appeared to be a small hole that had been bored into his lower skull, very near his brain stem. His ear was ringing just a bit, as well, but relatively free of pain, as promised.

Vargas cursed again. The bastard had really done it. He considered for a moment that it might be a bluff, that Knight might have just stabbed him with a horse needle, but knowing the man he decided this was wishful thinking.

The colonel removed his phone from an end table and checked a prominent text that was still showing on the screen, from Edgar Knight, instructing Vargas to call him when he woke up.

"Sorry about the implant thing," said Knight when he answered, his holographic image appearing in front of the colonel. "I really will reset it each week with plenty of time to spare."

Vargas fumed, but decided it wouldn't pay to lash out. "How do I know it's really there?" he asked.

"Sounds like you don't trust me," said Knight in amusement. "I can't help but be hurt."

"Go fuck yourself."

Knight laughed. "You know, with time travel duplication, I really could. But I think I'll pass." He paused. "Look, Hank, I know I implanted this against your will. But we're partners now. And this is just an insurance policy. Now that it's in place, why would I lie to you? I'm excited to have you as my right-hand man."

"That's because you don't have a time bomb in your head."

"That's a little dramatic," said Knight, "but I get your point. And I promise you that you'll get over this. You said you wanted to join me. If this is true, you have nothing to worry about."

"I do want to join you," said Vargas. "I *have*. And if I was certain I could trust you, the implant *wouldn't* bother me."

"Good, then it won't bother you for long. You'll soon realize I'm sane, a good boss, and a man of my word. As a first step, you're welcome to get a skull X-ray to confirm the capsule's presence. Just be sure that when the doctor spots it, he doesn't try to take it out. That would be very bad," he added pointedly. "But if you're going to confirm it, do this in a hurry. I want you to set up your meeting yesterday, if possible."

"Understood," said Vargas.

"Your phone was already untraceable and unhackable," continued Knight, "but—while you were out—I added some features to make it even more so. I also added the Brain Trust invention I mentioned to you that will ensure you get good cell reception, even inside Cheyenne Mountain, without having to piggyback on the base's Wi-Fi."

"While I was *out*?" said Vargas. "You make it sound like I was at dinner, enjoying lobster bisque, while you graciously upgraded my phone."

"Okay. While you were on your ass, knocked unconscious against your will. Better?"

"Yes. Since we'll be working as a team for a long time to come, you should know I like my medicine straight, without any sugarcoating."

"Good. That's how I prefer to deliver it," said Knight. He paused. "I trust you'll be spending some quality time preparing for this upcoming meeting, thinking through your approach."

"Of course."

"Including thinking through possible curve balls you might get thrown."

"I said I'd be prepared!" snapped the colonel. "I know what's riding on this. Cargill's days are numbered."

"*Lee's* days are numbered," corrected Knight. "Remember, you're pretending you were his mentor, so use his first name—like you were best friends."

"Of course."

"Good," said Knight. "Let me add one last thing. For this to work you have to establish trust—and at least a little rapport. So be friendly and respectful. *Charming* even. Whatever you do, you can't be arrogant and condescending. You can't be argumentative and caustic. In short, be yourself . . . only the opposite."

"Fuck you!" spat Vargas.

"Perfect," said Knight. "Keep behaving exactly like this. Only the opposite."

38

"My name is Colonel Hank Vargas, and I need to meet with the president as soon as possible."

"I've never heard of a Colonel Hank Vargas," snapped B. Joseph Kotrich, suddenly sorry he had taken the audio-only call. Kotrich was President Janney's chief of staff and the ultimate gatekeeper. "Who are you? How did you get this number?"

Before Vargas could formulate an answer, Kotrich continued. "You know what, I don't care who you are. If you really are a colonel, then go through the chain of command. When the Secretary of Defense asks me to schedule a meeting between you and the president, I'll be happy to do it."

"You haven't heard of me," hissed Vargas, "because I'm high up in Black Operations. You're not *supposed* to have heard of me, shit for brains. And the fact that I *do* have your number tells you I'm connected and someone to take seriously. But Janney knows who I am. So check with him. Trust me, he'll take the meeting."

"Chain of command, asshole," said Kotrich.

"Can't. The purpose of the meeting is too sensitive. Too secret. Not even the SecDef knows what this is about. But Janney does. Don't tell him about this call and he'll have your head."

"Is that a threat?" snapped Kotrich.

"No shit!" said Vargas. "Look," he continued, deciding to take another tack, "if this wasn't of the utmost importance, I wouldn't be this persistent about it. I know this is unusual. But I can't overstate the stakes here."

There was a long pause. "Okay," said Kotrich finally, "but you'd better be on the level. I'm meeting with the president in an hour. I'll give him your name and tell him you want a meeting. But if he doesn't know what this is about, I'll have your superiors cover you in so much shit, you'll never smell fresh air again."

"Tell him I need an hour of his time, but that I'll settle for forty-five millionths of a second. Those exact words. Repeat them."

"What the hell is that supposed to mean?"

"It's an inside joke. It will mean something to Janney. Tell him these exact words."

"If you and the president shared inside jokes, I'd know who you were, and you'd have met with him before."

"If you tell him exactly what I just said, and he doesn't want to meet with me, you can have me busted down to a fucking private, okay? Now please repeat it for me, so I know you have it."

"If he doesn't know what this is about," said Kotrich, "I'll do worse than have you busted down in rank. I'll have you sent for psychiatric evaluation. With a recommendation of having you stripped of all duties and committed to an asylum."

"Fine," said Vargas without hesitation. "Now can you repeat what I said?" he asked for the third time.

"I've got it," said the chief of staff. "You want an hour meeting with the president. But forty-five milliseconds will do."

"*Micro*seconds!" corrected Vargas. "Milliseconds are only thousandths of a second. I said *millionths*. But don't use either one so there is no mistake. Just say forty-five *millionths* of a second. Okay? Then call me back and tell me when and where we're meeting."

Kotrich shook his head in disbelief. "Sure," he said cynically. "When men are knocking at your door with a straight jacket, don't say I didn't warn you."

* * *

Just under three hours later chief of staff B. Joseph Kotrich contacted Vargas. "All right, *Colonel*, you're in," he began, in such a way that it was clear that when he said colonel, he meant asshole.

Kotrich was a man of order and rules. He didn't appreciate calls out of the blue from arrogant jackasses bypassing their command structure, making demands and threats, and calling him names. "The president will meet with you at a private home he maintains in the area in one hour. I'll text you the address."

"Private home?" said Vargas. "The president doesn't have any homes in the area."

"You aren't the only one with secrets, Colonel," said Kotrich. "He'll meet with you, but he doesn't want you seen. And he doesn't want you logging in to the White House. Cheer up. I'd imagine a cockroach like you likes the idea of staying in the darkness."

Vargas ignored this attempt to provoke him. "Tell the president I'll see him in an hour," he said, hanging up before Kotrich could reply.

39

President Alex Janney looked smaller in person. Thinner and older too. Apparently, makeup and a television camera were his friends. Not that he looked frail. He still had a handsome but affable face and black hair, almost certainly from a bottle, as was Vargas's own. And he still exuded the power one would expect from the leader of the free world.

Just not quite as much as he did on a screen.

The president sat behind a massive lacquered desk that looked like it was hacked from a tree of gargantuan diameter, with the tree's rings still present, advertising the desk's authenticity. Four men had met Vargas at the entry foyer, frisking him thoroughly, and putting him through metal detectors and other sensors, even knowing to look for prototype weaponry that he might be concealing. Someone had done their homework.

Janney looked Vargas up and down like he was under a microscope. The colonel sat with his hands folded neatly and tried to maintain a relaxed, friendly expression, taking Knight's advice to heart. He had rehearsed enough to actually feel somewhat relaxed, even given all the lies he was about to tell.

"Thanks for meeting with me so quickly, Mr. President," he heard himself say. "It's an honor."

"Yeah, cut the bullshit," snapped Janney. "You got my attention with forty-five millionths of a second. Unusually specific. Suggesting you think it might mean something. So what is it that you think you know?"

"*Everything*," responded Vargas. "Q5's been busy. I'm here because I'm worried that *you* might not know what they're really up to."

"What *I* know," said Janney, "is that I had Cargill and his group removed from your authority a while ago. And no one is more adamant, more crazy paranoid, about secrecy than Cargill. In this case, for very good reason. Which is why he insisted he be spun off in the first place. So how could you know the first thing about Q5?"

"Because Lee changed his mind," replied Vargas. "At least when it came to me. I was his mentor, and there were times he needed someone senior to use as a sounding board. Someone he trusted. So he told me all about time travel. Duplication. Teleportation."

Janney's eyes widened slightly as Vargas said these words. The president still hadn't brought himself to totally believe Vargas knew what this was all about, despite his reference to forty-five millionths of a second, but it was impossible to harbor a doubt any longer.

"Mentor?" said the president in disbelief. "Someone he trusted? He told me just the opposite. When Knight discovered this tech, he and Cargill bypassed the chain of command and came straight to me. Cargill insisted Q5 be separated from the pack, removed from your grip. He said you were overbearing and arrogant, the last person he could trust with this technology. He said you had a history of being overzealous with your use of force."

Vargas pretended to look hurt. He had war gamed this conversation at length. He had no idea what Cargill might have told the president when he had wrested Q5 from Vargas's leadership, but he knew enough to plan out a response in case Cargill had trashed him.

"That's painful to hear," he began. "I'm not going to lie," he added, which, by itself, was the biggest lie of all. "Lee and I were very close. He must have wanted to get a promotion, run the group himself, and thought disparaging me might do the trick." He shook his head sadly. "And it worked. But later, he must have realized he needed my help."

Vargas sighed. "I guess I shouldn't be surprised that he'd stab me in the back. The race to climb the career ladder can be a full-contact sport."

Janney shook his head in disgust. "You're kidding, right? I don't even think *you* believe what you're saying—like you're reciting lines, and badly. You and I both know he didn't make up his accusations from whole cloth. After his plea to make Q5 its own island, I studied your file. You're smart and impressive. Quite accomplished. But Cargill was right. No question in my mind that you were overly . . . enthusiastic with your use of drone strikes and missiles when you were in charge of these programs. And you were a strong advocate of advanced interrogation methods on prisoners."

"That was long ago," said Vargas. "Under an administration that expected this kind of . . . aggressiveness. Since then, I've been nothing but judicious in my actions. Which is why I was put in the position I'm in now in the first place. How I've passed the psych evaluations with flying colors."

"This is also true," acknowledged Janney. "Which is why—while I agreed with Cargill about burying Q5 even deeper in secrecy and removing it from your control—I didn't have you fired."

"And I've never given you any reason to regret that decision," said Vargas. "If you've checked my record since my more . . . overzealous days . . . you'll see that I've been very measured in my management of our country's black weapons programs. But getting back to the topic at hand, you should know that Lee and I discussed the proper use of force on many occasions over the past few years. I know he doesn't believe what he told you about me. He did this for reasons of his own."

"I've known and worked with Cargill ever since he came to me to ask to be spun off," said the president. "Kate and I have discussed you and your programs," he added, referring to his Secretary of Defense, "but you and I have never met in person before. So why should I believe you over him? And even if he lied about you to get control of Q5, why should I care?"

Vargas blew out a long breath. "If I'm lying, how would I know about time travel? About 45.15 microseconds and fifty-eight feet?"

Vargas could tell this gave the president pause. "I don't know," replied Janney. "But there are others in the know within Q5. There are plenty of people who could have leaked, other than him."

"Even if you refuse to believe I got my information from Lee, himself, that doesn't change what I know. Or its importance. It doesn't change why I thought it was critical that we meet."

"Oh?" said Janney, raising his eyebrows. "And why is that?"

"Did Lee tell you he killed Knight at Lake Las Vegas?"

Janney blinked rapidly in confusion. "No, because he *didn't* kill him. Edgar Knight killed *himself*. While tampering with time travel."

Wow, thought Vargas. Even Knight hadn't anticipated that Cargill would lie about being responsible for the explosion. "Is that really what he told you?" asked Vargas in dismay.

Janney nodded. "You're saying it isn't entirely true?"

"*Entirely true?* Mr. President. No. I'm saying *none* of it is true. I'm saying there are so many things wrong with this statement, it's hard to know where to even begin."

"Are you going to tell me what *is* true?" snapped Janney. "Or just play word games?"

"The explosion had nothing to do with time travel. As you know, the energy for time travel is spent entirely on pushing something back through time. Time travel itself can't cause an explosion. But Lee can. And he did in this case."

"Ridiculous," said the president. "Why would he do that? The explosion killed thousands. Apparently, there is a way that time travel *can* result in an explosion. The experts tell me what happened at Lake Las Vegas wasn't caused by any conventional explosive. They would have seen traces. Not that they hadn't already guessed this was the case from the magnitude of the blast. So it must have been caused by Knight changing up the protocols."

"There's another explanation, sir," said Vargas. "It was caused by an experimental explosive. One being developed by one of my labs. Octa-nitro-cubane. Chemists can only make amounts so small, they're harmless, but Lee can amplify it using time travel. My people analyzed some of the slag from ground zero and found its signature. One that your people wouldn't know to look for. There is no doubt this is the explosive Lee used. And again, only he could produce the quantities that were used."

The president's eyes narrowed as he considered this claim.

"That's why I came to you," continued Vargas. "I've been worried about Lee for some time now. But when I learned he had done this, I knew he was completely off the reservation. Much too dangerous to be allowed to continue to run Q5."

Janney studied the visitor across from him for several long seconds. "So you're telling me that Cargill wanted Knight dead so badly he took it upon himself to kill thousands of people? Without getting a green light from me?"

Vargas shook his head sadly. "No. It's worse than that, Mr. President. I'm telling you he annihilated Lake Las Vegas, and everyone working there, for entirely unknown reasons. For reasons having nothing to do with Knight."

Janney shook his head adamantly. "If he did this—and I'm not saying he did—he did it to kill Knight. He saw him as the ultimate threat. He couldn't possibly have a greater motive."

"He must have," said Vargas.

"How can you say that with such certainty?"

"Because Knight was long dead at the time of the strike," said Vargas. "And Lee knew it. Not dead as in the false story you and Lee spread around, dead. But dead for real. Six months ago. I killed him myself, after Lee begged for my help. I tracked him down using prototype tech from one of my labs and killed him. You were right about Knight being Lee's Holy Grail."

"Impossible," said Janney. "Cargill has reported on Knight's activities several times recently."

"Just shows he has a good imagination. Like telling you that Knight killed himself on that man-made little island. Knight wasn't even alive at the time. And he was never on this island, even when he was alive. Lee destroyed it for reasons of his own, causing massive loss of life."

Vargas had never seen the president this rattled. Normally putting on an unflappable air, he now looked as if he had just been punched in the gut. "Assuming this is true," said Janney, "did Cargill tell you anything that might explain these actions?"

"Not a thing," replied the colonel. "He cut off all communications with me over a month ago. My people only found the unmistakable signature of octa-nitro-cubane yesterday. Which is when I decided I had to come to you. I was sure you hadn't been in on this attack. And judging from the lies that Lee has fed you, he's more than just off the reservation. He's possibly out of his mind."

Janney shook his head. "He was as rational as ever when I spoke with him recently," he pointed out. "There must be another explanation."

"Then we need to find it quickly, Mr. President. Because you can't have a loose cannon wielding more power than anyone on the planet. Now that his teleportation range has been extended to a hundred twenty miles, no one is safe. Not even you, sir."

"A hundred twenty miles?" whispered Janney. "What are you talking about?"

"You know, Nathan Wexler's work? Extending time travel to almost half a second. During which time the Earth moves about a hundred twenty miles."

"It's true that Cargill was hot after Wexler's work," said Janney, "but only because Wexler had developed the theoretical underpinnings of time travel. Cargill thought this would improve the process. But he never mentioned anything about going further back in time. He told me forty-five microseconds was the limit."

"It was before Wexler," said the colonel. "But now Lee can move in such huge jumps that nothing is safe from him, not even the White House."

Vargas paused to let this sink in. "I think the world of Lee Cargill," he continued softly. "But I'm a patriot, and he's become too dangerous to leave in place. I think you'll agree that he has to be stopped."

The president didn't respond.

Vargas shook his head. "But stopping him won't be easy," he continued. "Try to fire him, and you might set off a powder keg. Marshal the forces at your command to remove him and they'd have no chance, unless you told them what they were up against—which you can't do. I would argue that you have to find a way to take care of this in-house."

"So what would you recommend?"

"Let me investigate him. He's been working with virtually no real oversight for a long time now. So let me bring you overwhelming evidence that everything I say is true. If it is, we can't haul him in front of a Congressional committee. We can't imprison him for mass murder, or even abuse of power. He knows too much. So you'll need to be the judge and jury. I can help with the execution part. It's the only way to defuse this."

"And I suppose you would replace him at the helm?"

"Q5 *was* originally in my camp, so why not return it there? And I'm one of the few who knows its secrets. So yes, I believe I'd be an excellent choice to replace him. I'm a reformed man, as you know. I only want to preserve the peace. So I'd run the group the way Lee is *supposed* to be running it." Vargas shrugged. "But put Mother Teresa in charge if it makes you feel better. After I take him out, you can choose whoever you want."

"Assuming you can really bring me unimpeachable evidence of all you say," said Janney.

"Of course."

"We're done here," said Janney. "For now. I have a lot to think about. I want you back here tomorrow morning at ten."

"Yes, sir, Mr. President," said Vargas. "I'll be here."

40

Lee Cargill took a deep breath and answered the call, which was unexpected, to say the least. When the computer-generated holographic image of the president materialized in front of him, this marked the only time Janney had ever called him out of the blue.

"Good evening, Mr. President," he said, bringing his mind to full alertness for the curve balls that were certain to be thrown at him any minute. Their relationship over the years had been strictly business. This wasn't a social call, and the president couldn't care any less about how he was doing, or the weather in Colorado, or in making any other small talk. "What can I do for you, sir?"

"Are you familiar with something called octa-nitro-cubane?"

"Yes," said Cargill, as internal alarm sirens began to scream. "It's the most potent non-nuclear explosive ever discovered. Theoretically. But making even microscopic amounts is prohibitively expensive and time-consuming."

"Right. This being said, it's come to my attention, through certain channels, that the residue of this chemical, its signature, was found at Lake Las Vegas. I was wondering if you knew anything about this?"

The president tried to act casual, almost disinterested, but Cargill was certain that Janney was studying his body language like an election day exit poll. "Are you concerned that some other global power has found a way to make this explosive in quantity?" asked Cargill.

The president stared into Cargill's eyes for several long seconds. "This is one worry, yes," he replied finally.

"Well, rest easy, Mr. President," said Cargill with a smile. "It's a hoax. Whoever told your people they found its signature was lying. It has no signature, before or after it explodes. It's a chemical structure thing that's over my head, but I'm sure this is true. So true, that it isn't even *theoretically* possible to identify it as the culprit after an explosion. Assuming you could produce enough of it to matter in the first place."

Janney's eyes narrowed. "You're absolutely certain about this?"

"Absolutely. Pick a top chemist of your choice and ask him or her. I guarantee what I've told you will be confirmed."

The president nodded slowly, and his mind was clearly racing. "Even if it leaves no signature," said Janney, "in your mind, would an octa-nitro-cubane explosion resemble the one that occurred in Lake Las Vegas?"

"It might," said Cargill. "The explosion was so fierce, it was the first explosive I suspected after it happened. But, like I told you, we found lots of dark energy residue there, a clear indication that Knight unleashed it accidentally."

"Had you seen or spoken to him in the months prior to his death?"

Cargill shrugged, once again keenly aware that the president was a hawk with its eyes on a rodent. Somehow, Janney had come to suspect that he was lying about Lake Las Vegas. "I hadn't, no," he replied. "But several new members of my team did. Just a few weeks ago, in fact."

"Which members?"

"Jenna Morrison, Aaron Blake, Nathan Wexler, and Dan Walsh."

"Would you mind if I spoke to them about this interaction? I'd like to know what Knight was like at the time."

"Can I ask why, Mr. President?"

"Just to satisfy a personal curiosity about his last days."

Cargill sighed. "I'd prefer that you didn't, sir," he said.

It wouldn't be a disaster if Janney did speak with them, but Cargill would have to school them in how to answer, so they wouldn't reveal information he had withheld from the president, or contradict one of the lies he had told him. "I'd prefer that they be allowed to move on, sir," said Cargill, "forgetting that Knight ever existed. But you're the president, sir, so you certainly don't need my permission. If you want to speak with them, I'll make this happen."

The president stared deeply into Cargill's virtual eyes once again. "No, I think I'm good for now. But I'll likely be calling you again very soon. I'm contemplating certain changes."

"Changes, Mr. President?"

"Yes. I'll let you know."

41

The meeting began a few minutes before ten, with Hank Vargas once again inside a secret home the president maintained to keep his business off the record. The colonel sat facing Alex Janney, as before, with only a gargantuan tree-desk between them.

"I did some thinking about what we discussed," said Janney. "And some research." He raised his eyebrows. "Turns out there is no way known to science to tell for sure if octa-nitro-cubane was used to cause an explosion."

"Who told you that, Mr. President?" asked Vargas, fighting to keep a calm expression.

"Your own people," replied Janney. "The ones who are working on it. So you were lying to me about that, weren't you?"

Vargas swallowed hard. Janney was nobody's fool, despite what his political enemies would like the public to believe. "Yes, but only about being able to detect its signature. This was the explosive used, and it was Lee who used it. The head scientist in my octa-nitro-cubane group, Bob Botchie, gave a minute amount of this to Lee, who amplified it. I overheard a conversation that makes me certain. I just couldn't find any evidence I could bring to you."

"So you made up the explosive signature bit in case I wasn't in the mood to take your word for it."

"I'm sorry, Mr. President. I know what I know. Again, the only lie was about *how* I knew. Everything I said about Lee is true."

"But it shows you're willing to lie to me. It calls your veracity into question."

Vargas lowered his eyes. "Yes. And if this mistake means that you ignore my warnings and let Lee proceed unchecked, then it will end up being one of the most costly mistakes in history. I'm begging you,

Mr. President. Even if you no longer trust me to take back the reins of Q5, find someone you do trust to check out what I've told you."

The president paused, and Vargas could tell this plea had the desired effect. By showing such a readiness to step aside, it made his accusations more believable, since this wasn't about him gaining more power.

"There are also four people in Q5 who had recent interactions with Knight," said Janney. "Well after the time you told me you killed him."

"I have no explanation for that, sir," said Vargas. "I know I killed him. They are either lying, or they were fooled by an impostor."

"Is it possible he sent himself back in time—made a copy?"

"Possible, but given Knight's personality, it's more likely that these four you're speaking about were fooled."

"I also did additional checking up on you," said Janney, changing gears abruptly yet again. "The word I'm getting is that you're a hard-ass who is hated by many of your people. But Kate Johnson vouched for you. She says you're extremely competent, and that your track record in your position has been good. She understands why others— I didn't specifically name Lee Cargill—think you're too hawkish, but she has found you stable and reasonable. She's impressed with how quickly you follow orders, and that you haven't taken advantage of the power your position affords."

He paused. "Do you have anything to add to this analysis, Colonel?"

"Only that you've trusted me with America's most advanced weapons programs for years. You know full well that I've never abused this trust. That I've never advocated to use one of the powerful weapons under my control in anger. I've never disobeyed an order, as Secretary Johnson has told you."

The president remained silent for almost three full minutes, not caring that the man in his office was forced to wait while he made complex mental calculations.

"You've lied to me, Hank. Maybe it was for the right reasons. Maybe not. But now I don't trust you enough to let you take over Q5. First, you may be lying about Cargill, in which case he should remain in power. Even if you aren't, you need to re-earn my trust before I'd be willing to let you have sole control of a tech that, in the wrong hands, can become a more potent weapon than all of your other programs combined."

Vargas considered jumping in to make his case further, but resisted, sensing somehow that Janney wasn't finished, and remaining silent was the better bet.

"But I have a feeling Cargill has been lying to me also. And if *you're* right, he can't be trusted to stay the head of Q5. So how to get to the bottom of this? My options are limited. The pool of people who know that time travel exists is very small, and I need to keep it that way. With a secret this big, every person you tell increases the risk that it will leak out into the public exponentially. So I can't unleash an investigative team to look into your accusations. Cargill would get wind of it. And I can't send some random player inside Q5. This would raise suspicions, also."

Janney sighed. "The only real option I have is to send *you* in. You already know about time travel and were once his boss. He won't like it, but I can make a case for it that won't set off his internal alarms. So I'm going to have you reintroduced to Q5. But not as Lee's boss, as his equal. Co-leaders of the group, if you will. He doesn't trust you. You don't trust him. You'll serve as checks on each other's power. I'm sure he'll be trying to prove that you're an out-of-control war monger who can't be trusted. You'll be trying to prove the same about him. You'll have one month to bring me evidence to back up your claims about him. Evidence that he's taken thousands of lives for no apparent reason, didn't get permission from me, and then lied about it afterwards."

He paused. "Bring me evidence and I'll make a decision as to whether we need your skills as an executioner. If you're right, and you continue to show yourself competent and trustworthy, I'll consider putting you in charge. Consider. I may also pull you and put a Tibetan monk in the position. We'll have to see."

The colonel nodded. "Understood, sir."

Vargas had shown he possessed intimate knowledge of time travel, Lee Cargill, and Q5. He had made accusations that had the ring of truth, since many *were* true. He had thought that this combination would shock the president enough to make him easily manipulated. But Janney had proven more astute than Knight had guessed, and his instincts had proven quite sharp.

Still, while Knight had hoped this strategy would put Vargas back in charge of Q5 entirely, the colonel was certain Knight would settle for having a puppet inside who was the co-equal of Cargill. More than settle. He would be ecstatic. Vargas was in. Given how dodgy this attempt had proven to be, Knight would count his blessings.

"Thank you, Mr. President," said Vargas. "Lee has become unstable and represents an unparalleled danger to the globe. I'm going to prove that to you, sir. You won't regret this."

"We'll see," said Janney grimly. "Just know that if it turns out that what you've said about Cargill isn't true, you *will* regret it. I can promise you that."

PART 5

"There is a fifth dimension beyond that which is known to man. It is a dimension as vast as space and as timeless as infinity. It is the middle ground between light and shadow, between science and superstition, and it lies between the pit of man's fears and the summit of his knowledge."

—Rod Serling, excerpted from *The Twilight Zone*, opening narration, season one

"You're traveling through another dimension, a dimension not only of sight and sound but of mind."

—Rod Serling, opening narration, season two (and perhaps the better known version)

42

Major Long He's pulse was racing. He hadn't been this charged up in many years. Even so, he managed to maintain an outer expression of absolute calm as he waited for twenty soldiers to spread out through the dark woods in a giant circle, a human net. This net would ensure that the man at its center couldn't possibly escape, even if he was able to overcome Long and the four trained commandos who would venture to the center of the net, spider-like, to neutralize the prey they would find there.

Prey that was not immobilized by sticky spider silk, but rather asleep under a massive truck covered in branches—just as helpless as a trapped insect, but without the struggling.

It was surreal. Twenty-five soldiers in total, each with night-vision gear attached to their faces. All there to contain one man, who had somehow found a way to squirrel an eighteen-wheeler into the woods, a hundred yards away from the nearest, unpaved road, like he was David Copperfield.

Remarkable. Copperfield had made the Statue of Liberty disappear, but this was obviously sleight of hand. But whoever this man was, *he* had navigated a semi into a woods while only plowing down a half-dozen or so small trees in the process. Now *this* was truly magical.

But his magic had run out.

One of Long's underlings had spotted this mystery man off in the distance just ninety minutes earlier, shortly after night had fallen. The man had been standing, a state-of-the-art motorcycle between his legs and an equally state-of-the-art pair of night-vision binoculars glued to his eyes, scouting one of the roadblocks Colonel Li had ordered.

This didn't mean he was the man they were looking for. His features couldn't be deciphered in the night, and it was possible he was a local, concerned about the military's sudden interest in his neighborhood. Or more likely, part of China's criminal element, whose smuggling and other activities were being hampered by roadblocks that had stubbornly persisted now for several days and nights, slowing traffic to a crawl as soldiers waved each vehicle through.

Still, the sighting of this man was the most promising development so far, and Long spared no time or resources following up.

And now it had been confirmed beyond a shadow of a doubt: This was the man they'd been after. The presence of the truck in the woods had sealed it, which, even from a distance and in the dark, was visibly scarred by bullet wounds. They were finally on the verge of learning who this Caucasian was, and what this was all about.

When the twenty soldiers silently finished creating their human circle, each stationing themselves approximately twenty meters from the truck, Long signaled to the four commandos beside him to begin closing in.

The major moved forward with them, creeping quietly toward the supine man beneath the truck, under cover of darkness. Each of the five moved more slowly, more deliberately, than a sloth, picking their steps one at a time, carefully studying the neon green night-vision depiction of the forest floor to ensure they wouldn't step on branches, twigs, or other debris that would give their presence away.

Each commando was armed with a QBZ-95X assault rifle. The 95X was a recent improvement on the Chinese designed QBZ-95. Light and compact due to its polymer construction, it nevertheless possessed an innovative recoil buffer system that made it the most controllable sub-machine gun anywhere in the world.

For this mission, however, these rifles were slung over shoulders, and handguns were drawn instead. Non-lethal force was the order of the day.

Long ignored the many bats now visible in his night-vision field, winging jerkily through the air overhead as they hunted insect prey. They weren't the only hunters out this night.

The forest suddenly exploded in sound and fury.

A dozen deafening concussive blasts shook trees and men alike. Blinding light exploded into the night like a supernova.

Long was nearly thrown from his feet and one of the commandos beside him lost his footing and slammed into a tree trunk. Many hundreds of bats for kilometers around lost their ability to echo-locate, and several crashed into trees of their own.

Despite his disorientation, Long knew immediately that these were nothing more than flash bang grenades, designed to deafen and blind, especially effective against night-vision equipment. The man they were after wasn't as sound asleep as he had appeared to be, somehow managing to blow a string of stun grenades in a circle around him.

But his strategy wouldn't work. Not this time. Long's preparations had been thorough, despite having been made on the fly. He had scanned the area for explosive signatures before moving in, and had only found those indicative of stun grenades. So the major had equipped his team with night vision that automatically blocked sudden, massive increases in light, and comms that did the same when it came to sound.

The moment the stun grenades exploded the man they were after jumped to his feet, expecting Long and his men to be blind, deaf, and disoriented: fish in a barrel. He raised a gun and prepared to shoot his way through a gauntlet of soldiers he thought were now helpless.

"Freeze!" shouted Long in English. The major fired a shot that grazed the man's shoulder, making it clear that his vision was still perfect.

"You're surrounded!" screamed Long. "Twenty-five soldiers with assault rifles who can all still see you. Hand's up!" he demanded. "You have no chance!"

The man still in Long's sights glanced at his shoulder, where a thin stream of blood was leaking from the superficial wound, and came to a quick decision. He threw his hands high over his head. "Don't shoot!" he shouted back. "I surrender."

43

The major instructed the soldiers to remove their night-vision equipment while one of his men set up a generator connected to six huge banks of portable floodlights to illuminate the truck and a broad swath of woods. Nocturnal animals that had fled the area after the flash-bangs had been triggered were hit with a second burst of daylight, this one proving stubbornly persistent.

With this complete, Long had two of his men disarm the prisoner and affix zip ties to his wrists and ankles.

Long wasn't sure what he had expected, but he wasn't impressed by the fugitive's physical appearance. "What's your name?" he demanded.

The man glared at him and gritted his teeth. "You first," he growled.

"Okay," said Long. "Why not? I'm Major Long He." He gestured toward the prisoner, indicating that it was now his turn.

The short Caucasian actually smiled. "My name isn't really important," he replied. "But why don't you call me Blake. If this doesn't work, I'll answer to whatever name you choose."

Long considered. This sounded like a first name, and wasn't likely to be his real one, anyway. Still, while having a real name would help if he could find it in their databases, it wasn't worth fighting for. Not when there was so much other information that was.

"Understand this," said Long icily, "from now on, *I* decide what's important and what isn't." He paused. "But for now, *Blake*, I'll play along. We're going to be spending a lot of time together while you tell me everything you know."

Long nodded toward the truck. "But first, it's time to get a look inside."

He issued orders to two men, who peeled the trailer's door open and set another powerful portable light inside. Long's heart skipped a beat as he saw the refrigerator strapped at the very back of the long compartment, near the cab.

This was the mother lode. Colonel Li would be ecstatic.

The mission was officially over. At least the capture part.

The *interrogation* part, however, had only just begun.

The major noted the extensive coating of dried blood on the floor of the trailer and the large swath of blood spatter on the stainless steel appliance. "What happened in here?" he asked.

Blake shrugged. "Are you talking about the red?" he said innocently. "I think it's a bold design choice on Sub-Zero's part. Stainless steel can be a bit sterile."

Li turned to the two men now inside the trailer and gestured toward the refrigerator. "Open it!" he commanded in Chinese.

"I wouldn't do that if I were you," said Blake, shaking his head as though he were dealing with an idiot. When Long didn't immediately belay his order, Blake's tone became more urgent, and more demanding. "They can't open that!" he shouted, sounding panicked. "Tell them!"

Long wasn't used to taking orders from prisoners, but in this case he made an exception, as Li's warning about the destructive potential of dark energy came to the fore of his consciousness. He countermanded his order, and the soldiers who had been approaching the stainless steel appliance stopped in their tracks.

Blake blew out a sigh of relief.

Long turned back to his prisoner. "So you speak Chinese?" he said.

"Not a word," said Blake. "What you ordered was obvious."

"So why shouldn't I open your steel box?" asked the major.

"Because it's been booby trapped," replied Blake. He brought the fingers of both hands together and then, to the extent allowed by the zip ties, abruptly spread them apart. "Boom," he whispered.

The major studied his prisoner for several long seconds, taking his measure. "I swept the area with sensors," he said. "No trace of any explosives."

"Because the one I used doesn't *have* a signature," insisted Blake. "Trust me when I tell you that if you open that refrigerator, we'll have to finish this conversation in the afterlife."

Long studied his prisoner. "Okay," he said after a long pause. "We can keep it closed. For now. But you need to tell me what it is. And what's inside of it."

Blake smiled. "Of course. It's a refrigerator. And inside: a dozen eggs and some skim milk."

"Keep trying to be funny and see how long you live."

"Tough audience," said the prisoner. "Here's the deal, if you arrange for us to speak privately, I think our conversation can be more . . . interesting."

Long considered. Being alone with this man might not be good for his health, even though he appeared harmless and was bound, but the possible reward was well worth the minimal risk. And the prisoner knew that escape was impossible.

A few minutes later both he and Blake were inside the trailer. The major remained standing, a gun in his hand, while the prisoner sat with his back against a side wall of the vehicle, avoiding a slick of blood nearby. The door was closed, leaving them alone with each other and a refrigerator. Twenty-four armed soldiers waited just outside the compartment's only exit, eliminating any chance of escape.

"Okay, Blake, it's just the two of us now. So tell me what's in that refrigerator. Who you are. And what you're doing in China."

"I'll tell you everything you want to know. But I have three conditions."

"Conditions!" barked Long. "You forget that *you're* the prisoner, and I have the gun. Believe me, you'll tell me everything you know, willingly or not."

"Even if this is true, why not do this the easy way? I've conducted interrogations before. It's a dream to have a cooperative prisoner, rather than one you have to coerce. You get better quality information that way. Unless you get off on coercion."

"Get off?" said Long questioningly.

"Sorry. It means, unless you enjoy torture."

"I don't. But I also won't agree to any *conditions*."

"Really?" said Blake innocently. "You haven't even heard them yet."

Long studied him for several seconds. "Okay," he said finally. "Tell me."

"One, I see that you haven't contacted your commander yet. Does he know you found your man?"

Long shook his head. "Not yet. I was about to inform him."

"Don't," said Blake simply. "Wait until we're through here. Who knows, you might learn something that will change your mind about the situation. You can always tell him in an hour or two."

"And your second condition?"

"Tell me why you've been so eager to find me. What is it you know? Or *think* you do? Why would you possibly think my cargo is anything other than what it appears to be?"

"Go on," said Long.

"The last condition is that you order your men to get the hell out of here. The explosive I mentioned is unstable. It could remain inert for a thousand years, or it could blow any second."

The major couldn't help but be insulted by this request. If this man thought he was really stupid enough to fall for something this patently ridiculous, he was about to learn otherwise. "If it blows," he said, "then *you* will die, also. Yet you didn't ask me to remove *you* from its presence. You expect me to believe that you want to protect my men, but not yourself? That you're only looking out for their welfare?"

"You think I'm asking for this so I can overpower you and escape?"

"Yes."

"I'd have no chance. Even with your men gone. I know it's hard to believe, but I really want them to clear out so I don't risk innocent lives. I've done enough of that. I have no beef with any of you."

"No beef?"

"It means that you and your men are not my enemies," said Blake. "Even though it might look that way to you. I don't want anyone hurt. These men have parents and siblings who love them. Many have wives and children who depend on them."

"I don't know what you're trying to accomplish by pretending to be concerned for my men," said Long. "But they will remain where they are. They know the risks of military service."

Blake glared at him in contempt. "You've got me where you want me," he said in desperation, extending his bound hands to underscore the point. "Why risk lives that don't need to be risked?" he pleaded.

Long shook his head. "I'll agree to your first two conditions," he said, "but not your last. Your choice. You can decide this is good enough and cooperate. Or we can do this another way."

Blake was seething, but after a few seconds he nodded his agreement. "Okay," he said, visibly trying to depressurize. "We have an agreement. Tell me why you've been so desperate to find me, and I'll tell you everything you want to know."

The major eyed the prisoner skeptically, but decided to go forward. "We have an initiative to study dark energy," he began, certain Blake would know what this was. "A few months ago, one of our scientists developed a dark energy detector."

Blake's eyes lit up like a sun. "So you *do* know my device taps into dark energy," he said excitedly. "But you don't know anything else about it. Which explains the lengths you've taken to find me. I don't blame you. My intel sources were sure China hadn't developed a detector, and I know there haven't been any leaks on my end, so I couldn't see how you would know. But it was the only way to explain your . . . heightened . . . interest."

Long was pleasantly surprised. The prisoner had said he would willingly tell the truth, but the major hadn't really believed him. Until now. Until the man hadn't bothered to deny that his device tapped the dark energy field. He seemed more delighted than upset at Long's revelation, as though it had cleared up a mystery but was of no further import. Almost as if he was relieved.

"So you admit your steel box has a connection to dark energy?" said the major.

"Absolutely," said Blake. He narrowed his eyes in confusion. "Wait a minute. If you have a detector, how is it that it took you so long to find me?"

The major considered if he should continue to answer Blake's questions. Why not? His prisoner wasn't going anywhere, and he seemed to be cooperating. Long didn't want to do anything that might jeopardize this.

"The sensor array was very near the Beijing airport," explained the major. "It only has a range of about ten kilometers or so, but it detected dark energy when you landed."

"So once I flew out of range, your detector became useless."

"Not quite. We've managed to outfit a few helicopters with smaller versions to aid in our search. One is about eighty miles north of here right now, in fact, and slowly working its way south. In another three or four hours, it would have found you, even if we hadn't."

Blake's eyes widened excitedly and the wheels in his head appeared to be spinning. "Thank you, Major Long. You've been very helpful."

"Now it's *your* turn," said the Chinese major. "What is that device? And what are you doing in China?"

"I'm really sorry," said Blake. "About everything." The prisoner sounded absolutely sincere, even anguished. "But I have to go back on my word. Not even my own president knows what I'm doing here, so I'm afraid I can't tell you."

Long's features hardened. He would make Blake pay for betraying his own agreement.

"I feel sick about this," continued the prisoner. "But I did try to spare your men. Their deaths are partly on you."

Their deaths? What was that supposed to mean?

And then, right on cue, all hell broke loose outside.

44

A second Aaron Blake stood quietly inside the nested kettles, clutching an assault rifle. He had been there for hours, bored out of his mind until his duplicate had joined him in the trailer with a Chinese major in tow.

After this, he had all the entertainment he could want. Video and audio streamed to his contact lens and comm from a tiny camera embedded on the outside of the fake Sub-Zero, and he had watched the scene unfold with all the intensity of a Peeping Tom.

The other Blake had been pushed against one wall of the trailer, where he had slid to the floor. His wrists and ankles were bound with zip-ties and the major hovered over him, a gun in his hand. "Okay, Blake," said his captor, "it's just the two of us now. So tell me what's in that refrigerator. Who you are. And what you're doing in China."

"I'll tell you everything you want to know. But I have three conditions."

"Conditions!" said the major. "You forget that *you're* the prisoner, and I have the gun. Believe me, you'll tell me everything you know, willingly or not."

The Blake in the kettle observed the unfolding discussion and couldn't help but admire his duplicate's performance. His other self was masterful, manipulating his captor with all the skill of a virtuoso.

Earlier that day, Blake had been forced to make a hard choice. He needed to know what he was up against, no matter what the personal cost. You couldn't win a game if you didn't know its rules. Besides, the Chinese forces would close in soon enough. So he would make sure they did so on *his* terms. He would allow himself to be ambushed and interrogated, getting the info he needed in return.

Just before sundown, he had made a single copy of himself. He had stayed inside the truck while his duplicate ventured out to use himself as bait, purposely allowing himself to be seen. The Blake left behind had rigged a number of flash-bang grenades to detonate on his duplicate's command when he returned. Their use would ensure the Chinese wouldn't suspect he had *wanted* to be captured. He had felt certain the men after him would be competent enough to withstand some pesky stun grenades, and this confidence had been borne out.

Now, those who had captured him were in for the surprise of their lives. They couldn't possibly guess there were now two of him, with one tucked away inside a weapon of mass duplication, able to provide as many reinforcements as needed.

So Blake had waited for his double under the truck to be captured. He had pre-programmed the inner kettle, K-2, to send him fifty-eight feet away. The time travel would commence on his mark, and would abort after K-2 detected the number of copies he would specify just before issuing this command.

And now the act had almost played itself out, with the captured Blake playing his part to perfection. They could have taken out the major and his team at any time, but they needed to accomplish a few things before they did.

First, the captured Blake needed to learn if the major had informed his superiors that he might have found him, or had decided to wait until he confirmed he had the right man. If Blake was lucky enough that the latter was true, he needed to freeze the major from doing so until it was too late.

Second, he needed to learn what the Chinese military knew. Why they had put so much manpower into finding him. Finally, he hoped to spare as many of the soldiers as possible from what was to come.

His double had managed to accomplish two of these goals, but the third was not to be. Not that this was the prisoner's fault. No task was trickier than convincing a major to send his force away, no matter what the argument, especially when the argument came from the most wanted operative in all of China.

The Blake waiting inside the kettle felt a profound sadness when it became clear the major wouldn't budge on this issue, and he could see the Blake in the trailer was having his own trouble choking down this reality.

The Blake in the kettle also knew his twin was feeling a profound anger. An anger directed at himself.

Fighting terrorists had been so simple, although he hadn't appreciated this at the time. *Decisions* were simple. Clear cut. The terrorists dedicated their lives to killing anyone and everyone who didn't subscribe to their radical views. The need to kill them was unambiguous. Kill or be killed.

But much of the killing Blake was now doing was *anything* but clear cut.

He was being forced to weigh lives against each other like they were so much dirt. To make ethical decisions so complex they made calculus look like *addition*. And to kill innocents he would rather do anything but kill, including himself, who was now destined to die over and over and over again.

Blake prepared his automatic rifle for action and spread his legs slightly apart, crouching in a ready position. The other Blake had done all he could, gotten all the information he could.

The time to act had come at last, as Blake listened to his duplicate apologize to the major for the coming deaths of his men.

"K-2," he whispered. "I want ten copies." He took a deep breath and made sure his grip on the weapon was firm. "Mark!"

45

One moment Blake was crouching inside a kettle and the next he was standing on dirt, surrounded by clusters of trees and fellow Aaron Blakes. As far as the ten Blakes were concerned, all had arrived where they were simultaneously, as the local universe reset each time a new copy arrived and moved forward from there.

Up until an instant earlier they were one man, so each knew precisely what to do without need of communication or coordination. When the Blake still in the kettle sent a "go" command through their comms, they would move in. The other Blake in the trailer, the one who had been escorted there by Major Long, was the only version without a comm or contact lens, since he had removed and hidden these items in preparation for being captured.

The *go* command came seconds after the ten duplicates arrived in the past. Blake had planned out the attack in his head, which meant it was in *all* of their heads. The two closest to the truck rushed in toward the concentration of Chinese soldiers, showing themselves and opening fire, their weapons set on semi-automatic, allowing them to get off shots in rapid succession but preventing them from spitting out more than a single round per trigger pull.

Had they set their weapons to fully automatic, they could have made bloody Swiss cheese of all twenty-four soldiers, congregated as they were, pumping hundreds of rounds through their bodies before they could even raise their weapons, before they even realized they were under siege. But this uncontrolled spray of fire would risk further damage to the truck, which was already hanging on by a thread.

The soldiers were caught napping, certain that no force could outflank them, which in a sane universe was true. Even with weapons on semi-automatic, it was a *massacre*. The two Blakes found nothing but easy targets, shooting one helpless man and then the next, only needing a slight adjustment of their aim in between. It was a first-person video game come to life, and the two Blakes were in a fierce battle to determine who would set the high score.

Eleven Chinese soldiers fell in the initial flurry of death before any of the others managed to regroup and return fire. When the return fire did come, it was fully automatic, and both Blakes were torn to shreds, blood splattering into the crisp night air from every square foot of their bodies.

As soon as the first two Blakes were down, and the attention of all remaining soldiers was focused in one direction, two more Blakes emerged from behind them. These two picked off eight more Chinese soldiers before they, too, were taken out.

The next pair of Blakes finished the job, although not before the last soldier standing managed to spray them with automatic fire just before he fell, killing them both. Even so, all twenty-four Chinese had now been cut down, while four Blakes remained, untouched. The shooting on the Blakes' part had been so precise that the flood lamps still bathed the woods in light, and the truck remained unscathed.

The Blakes still alive wasted no time pumping additional holes in the Chinese corpses sprawled across the forest floor, making certain that every last one was well and truly dead.

Finally, the last bullet spent, a deafening hush came over the woods. No bats, crickets, or even breeze-swept leaves dared to make a single sound, as if stunned into silence by the carnage they had witnessed.

It was the ultimate bloodbath. The woods had become a charnel house, with thirty men dead, most horribly disfigured, and many lying across each other like cordwood, a scene gorier than anything out of a big-budget Hollywood slaughter-fest. Blood slickened the forest floor and painted nearby leaves and branches alike.

"Report!" ordered the Blake who had hidden inside the kettle after he was certain the firing had ceased.

"All hostiles down," reported four voices in his comm at the same time.

Seconds later the door to the back of the truck slid open to reveal the two Blakes inside. The moment he had given the *go* command, the Blake in the kettle had come out firing, killing the major as he was spinning around and drawing his weapon.

Six Blakes were now alive, but that wouldn't be true for long. Only one was destined to complete the mission, and even he would die soon thereafter as the kettle exploded inside Kim's bedroom.

All six remembered the thought process Blake had undergone when there had only been one of him, knowing he was about to produce many, condemning them to death.

Was this an absolute necessity? he had asked himself. Why *couldn't* a handful of surviving Blakes be allowed to go on living?

After all, he loved a challenge, living dangerously, pitting his skills against a merciless world to try to stay alive. The duplicates would know that the Blake back in the States held title to his name and life. So they could use their cunning to try to escape from China. They could find a tropical island somewhere to settle down, changing their identities. They wouldn't have to die. They'd only have to disappear from the grid and forge a new life outside of America.

But as tempting as this was, Blake had realized it wasn't possible. The risk was too great. What if three or four of the duplicates were killed? Four Caucasians in China of the exact same build. The authorities would soon connect the dots and realize they were identical, down to their scars and the cavities in their teeth, which even identical twins wouldn't share. This would raise too many questions. The Chinese would spend extraordinary resources getting to the bottom of it, hunting for other Blakes around the world, digging with the manpower and persistence that only China could manage, and possibly discovering the Blake in America along the way.

And what if one of the Blakes was captured? They would all go to heroic lengths not to be taken alive, but there were no guarantees. Even though Blake was confident a copy of him would never talk, there was no telling what experimental drugs or methods the Chinese might use to force information from him. Information like the existence of Q5. The reality of time travel.

In the final analysis, there was no way out. Allowing multiple Blakes to live was not an option. Many more Blakes, each as human as the original, would be forced to condemn themselves to death in service to the greater cause.

Blake had learned what he needed to know to possibly get his mission back on track. But the cost had been very high.

And not just to the Chinese soldiers he had slaughtered.

46

"Report," said Blake as he sped through the night on a motorcycle that had been sent back through time. A split-second younger version of the bike was still back at the truck.

"No sign of any activity," replied one of the Blakes at the site of the massacre, who had been designated as the liaison to the one now traveling.

"Excellent," said Blake as he hurtled northward as quickly as he could. If additional soldiers hadn't heard the flash-bangs and gunfire and sent reinforcements by now, they never would. Even so, the Blake who had been stationed within the kettle had returned to his position there, just in case.

"We've stacked all of the dead bodies together," reported the liaison, "combing the woods nearby for any human . . . debris . . . we might have missed. We've plotted out the best path for the truck to take to get back to the road, and marked it with floods, which we'll turn on when it's ready to leave."

"Good work," said Blake. "Thanks. I'll call in with updates as soon as I have them."

He ended the call and increased the speed of the bike even further. "K-1," he said to the kettle supercomputer, still tied into his comm, "how much longer until I reach the truck stop?"

"At your average speed, sixteen more minutes."

Blake frowned. Still plenty of time—if everything went right. But if he was stopped, or had trouble carrying out the next phase of the mission, it would be a different story. And if Long had lied about the helo that was slowly coming this way, the mission would go down in flames. Not that the major had any reason to lie, but it was always a possibility.

Fourteen minutes later Blake arrived at the truck stop K-1 had directed him to. It was clean and looked to be fairly new, with an extensive parking area, eight fueling stations, a restaurant, and a facility with fifteen showers. Dozens of semis were parked in the lot, with dozens more refueling at one of the many islands.

There were more than eight million semis in China. Eight million. And all Blake needed was one of them.

He abandoned his motorcycle and helmet and carefully hid behind a parked truck near the restaurant's exit.

Less than five minutes later a short truck driver approached Blake's position on his way out to the lot. The trucker was dressed in a black T-shirt and baseball cap, with the same Chinese lettering on both, *Grand Panda Trucking*, which K-1 displayed on Blake's contact lens in English.

Blake drew his phone from a pocket and slipped out from behind the truck as the man passed, following him as quietly as a shadow. K-1 had programmed the phone to his specifications, so it would speak one of the Chinese phrases he had pre-programmed in each time he hit a circular icon on the screen.

"Excuse me," said Blake pleasantly to the man in English, now only five feet ahead.

The man wheeled around, startled, unaware that anyone had been nearby.

When the trucker completed his turn, Blake pressed the circular icon on his phone. "Make a sound and you're dead!" said the phone in Chinese, like the evil son of Siri and Cortana. Blake pointed a gun at the trucker's chest at the same time.

The man's eyes widened, but he heeded the warning the phone had given, and remained silent.

Blake pressed the icon a second time. "Give me your keys and lead me to your truck," said the phone. "Cooperate and you won't get hurt. Cross me and you'll die very painfully."

Once again, Blake was keenly aware that this was an innocent man, and was sickened by what he was doing. At least this was a positive sign. The moment something like this no longer troubled him was the moment he had truly become a monster.

The trucker's breath seemed to catch in his throat. His eyes darted wildly, desperate to identify a source of rescue, without success. Blake extended his gun and pressed the circular icon on his phone one last time. "Move!" it demanded. "Now!"

The trucker swallowed hard and then turned around and continued his journey, with Blake so close behind they were almost touching. Four minutes later they arrived at the man's truck, parked among dozens of others in the poorly lit lot.

"Thank you," said Blake pleasantly in English when they reached their destination. This said, he slammed the butt of his gun savagely into the man's skull, knocking him to the ground. He confirmed that the trucker still had a pulse and then slowly, with herculean effort, pulled the trucker's dead weight into the passenger side of the large cab.

"I'm sorry," he whispered, removing the trucker's hat and placing it on his own head to disguise his Caucasian hair.

Blake pulled out of the truck stop and headed due north. Three miles later he passed through another of the ubiquitous woodland areas and pulled off the road, dragging the unconscious driver into the woods and forcing a pill down his throat. The poor trucker would awaken eight hours later, sore but well rested. Most importantly, he would come out of this alive.

Which is more than Blake could say for himself.

He opened the back of the trailer and climbed inside. Fortunately, the trucker must have already made a delivery, as one fourth of the trailer nearest the door was empty. The remainder of the large compartment was stuffed to the gills with wooden pallets, stacked high with colorful running shoes, at least as evidenced by the pictures on the outside of the boxes.

Blake positioned himself at the exact center of the empty space within the trailer. "K-1," he called out. "Can I assume you're still reading me?"

"Loud and clear," responded the supercomputer, still inside the semi he had left in the woods.

"Good. Do you have my precise GPS coordinates?"

"Yes."

"I need you to send K-2 back into the past. Can you arrange the settings and time interval to land it precisely where I'm standing?"

"Negative," replied the supercomputer after the briefest of pauses. "You're in between 45.15 microsecond intervals."

"Understood," said Blake. He peeled off the adhesive on a nickel-sized sensor, activated it, and stuck it to the floor by his feet. "Are you reading the sensor I just activated and placed nearby?"

"I am."

"Good. Track this sensor as it moves, and name it the *bull's-eye*."

"Done," said K-1.

"Good. I'm in the back end of a semi-tractor-trailer. I will take two steps in the direction the vehicle is facing, so you can determine its heading." He took two small steps forward. "Was this sufficient?"

"Yes."

"If I moved the truck forward, in the direction of my steps, how far would I have to go for you to be able to land K-2 on the bull's-eye?"

"Twenty-two feet, five inches," replied K-1.

"Good. I'm going to get in the cab and start the truck. Then I'll begin inching it forward. Tell me when I've arrived in a position that will allow you to place K-2 where I've specified."

Blake proceeded as he had outlined, until K-1 called a halt. Less than a minute later Blake confirmed that a copy of the inner kettle had materialized inside the trailer, a perfect shot from forty-five miles away.

Blake returned to the cab and continued on his original heading. After driving another twelve miles, he was rewarded for his efforts by the sound of a slow-moving helicopter approaching his position from the north. One not only traveling at a snail's pace, but progressing through a moving window of tight circles, an obvious search pattern.

Blake allowed himself a smile as the helo abruptly changed course to come closer to his position, and then followed his truck from a discreet distance thereafter.

"Sense anything interesting?" he said aloud to the aircraft.

Had the helo made it farther south and detected the dark energy signature of the truck in the woods, the mission would have been over. But Blake had managed to throw this dog the very bone it was after, just in time.

He could only imagine the frenzy the Chinese who were after him must now be in, hastily accumulating enough force to subdue him, even if he tried to use the heavy truck as a weapon. He wondered how long it would take for the military to strike. He put the over/under at a half-hour, and placed his own bet on the under.

Sure enough, twenty-four minutes later, dozens of cars, military trucks, and helicopters appeared out of nowhere, with impressive co-ordination, surrounding him on all sides as well as from above. Four of the helos were armed with machine guns and missiles.

"*Stop and you won't be harmed,*" boomed a voice in English at an incredible decibel level, emanating from an unknown source.

Blake sighed and slowly rolled to a stop.

"Good news," he reported to the Blake handling communications back at the original truck. "I'm about fifty-seven miles north of your position, and the Chinese have taken the bait."

He now had little doubt the plan would work exactly as he had laid it out in his head. The Chinese were looking for him and a Sub-Zero refrigerator with a dark energy signature, and they had now found both.

They could never guess that both he and the refrigerator were capable of being fruitful and multiplying.

Now that the Chinese had their prize, Blake would be astonished if the roadblocks at all critical arteries weren't disbanded within the hour.

"Outstanding," said his liaison, although his enthusiasm was somewhat diminished by the fact that this success would hasten his own death. "I'll let the others know."

Blake ended the communication and watched the scene outside of his window in fascination. Dozens of armed soldiers were making their way slowly to the cab from all directions.

He knew exactly how this would play out. Once he was captured and bound, and brought to a detention facility, a professional inter-rogator would be assigned to him. Blake would lead this man on a wild goose chase for as long as he could. Tease him that the answers he was looking for were right around the corner.

Then, as soon as Blake decided that relatively few people were within range of the kettle, he would command its detonation, which would kill him and turn the kettle into slag.

Another Blake was even now setting off on a motorcycle to check the status of the roadblocks. As soon as they were confirmed down, the Blake who was now inside the kettle in the original truck would emerge to continue his journey to the Chinese-Korean border. All other Blakes would gather near the wall of corpses they had built.

Once the semi was forty or fifty miles away, the Blake who was driving would order K-1 to teleport a copy of the inner kettle as close to this wall of corpses—and his still-living brethren—as possible, triggering its onboard octa-nitro-cubane and vaporizing all.

He forced himself not to think about how close he and his numerous alter egos were to death. He had volunteered for this mission, after all, and had known he wouldn't come out alive.

Blake took a deep breath, opened the cab door, and jumped to the pavement, his hands high over his head. "Okay," he said unnecessarily. "I surrender."

A wry smile came over his face. "But are you sure you brought enough men?" he added, rolling his eyes.

47

Nathan Wexler and Jenna Morrison strolled together along a honeycombed maze of corridors, working their way to the conference room assigned to Q5, where the unparalleled physicist would finally discuss the fifth dimension in terms he hoped a layman like Blake would understand. Not that the material was easy to get one's mind around, even without introducing the brutal mathematics that caused searing migraine headaches in even the world's most accomplished mathematicians and physicists. But he hoped his presentation would at least provide a glimmer of the possibilities.

Provided he could keep his feet on the ground long enough to get through the preliminary discussions. Not easy to do given the considerable progress he had made coming up with a time travel suppressor, already. Even less easy to do considering he had extended this work in an unexpected direction, potentially solving one of the biggest mysteries in all of cosmology, and opening up possibilities both terrifying and magnificent.

His plan was to wait until the end to share this discovery with the group, but he was so flush with excitement he thought he might levitate to the ceiling and blurt it out at any moment in a fit of giddy enthusiasm. He had to remind himself that while the potential discovery was looking promising, it was still only a theory. More work needed to be done to confirm it beyond a shadow of a doubt.

But if he *was* able to confirm it, it would be extraordinary. Revolutionary. Arguably the greatest discovery in all of human history. It would shake society to its very core—if he could ever disclose it, that is.

Wexler couldn't imagine being much happier than he was at this moment. Working on momentous projects with people he admired, and Jenna by his side. And say what you might about Edgar Knight's motives and ethics, his brilliance could not be questioned. He had managed to prove out Wexler's theories in the real world through intuition and force of will alone.

Wexler's only complaint was with his surroundings. If not for the camaraderie and intellectual stimulation, he was sure he would be going absolutely batty, living with no direct sunlight and in claustrophobic conditions only a mole rat could love. The Cheyenne Mountain bunker complex was undeniably remarkable, but mankind had evolved to live in the great outdoors, not inside a mountain.

When they arrived at the conference room, Wexler took a seat at the head of the table and tested his computer to be sure he could send his primitive visuals to the main monitor above him. Before long the rest of the senior management team arrived, but the four invited members of Q5's Inner Circle not on assignment elsewhere appeared to be no-shows.

The Inner Circle was now under Blake's purview. Its members knew about time travel and Q5's goals, but weren't formally members of the senior management team. They played the roles of operations management, security, and muscle, as needed.

Each member was bright, talented, highly trained, and deadly. Knight and his men had recently killed a number of them, severely thinning out their ranks, and Q5 was still stinging from these losses.

Cargill rose from his chair as soon as the last of the senior management team arrived. "Sorry, Nathan," he began, "but I need to share something with you, Daniel, and Jenna before we begin. News that can't wait."

His troubled expression made it clear that this particular news was anything but good. "As you all know, Q5 was originally designated a black weapons program. In the beginning, I reported to a Colonel Hank Vargas. When Edgar made his breakthrough discoveries, we were able to get President Janney to agree to pull us away from this group and give us total autonomy."

"Right," said Jenna. "We remember the story. You were convinced this Colonel Vargas was a real-life Dr. Strangelove."

Cargill nodded. "That's right. But this argument alone didn't convince the president."

"Then what did?" asked Jenna.

"The security and privacy arguments," replied Cargill. "The more people in the loop, the more likely you get a leak. I'm pretty sure the likelihood goes up exponentially with every person added.

"Don't get me wrong," he continued, "Janney did take my concerns about Hank Vargas seriously. He trusted my instincts about the man, but only to a certain extent. He thought some of my accusations were overblown. In the end, he did agree to do what we asked, but he didn't fire Vargas as I had strongly recommended."

Cargill blew out a long breath. "The reason I bring this up is that three hours ago I was informed by a written order from the president that I will no longer be the sole head of Q5. Vargas and I will be co-equals. The president himself briefed the colonel on the history of time travel and our activities."

Allen and Blake were already aware of this bombshell, but the three members who weren't all expressed shock and outrage at the same time, and all shouted questions that overlapped each other.

Cargill waited for the buzz to die down and then continued. "The president called me a few days ago with some strange questions, which had me worried. He must have already been contemplating this change at the time. Q5 won't be folded back under black weapons command, so no one other than Vargas will need to be read in. We'll continue to be autonomous, and the colonel will continue to spend most of his time in his prior position. But he will also be co-commander of this group."

"I'm not military," said Wexler, "but even I know that this is untenable. No organization can operate effectively with two heads."

"I agree," said Cargill. "The president wrote the order, and seemed to go out of his way to add extra language to rationalize this move. He tried his best to spin it in a positive light, and make it clear that I still have his full support." He shook his head and frowned. "But I don't believe that for a second. And I see this as an initial move only. The end-game is to remove me entirely, with Vargas as my replacement."

"How can you be sure of that?" said Tini.

"I've lost Janney's confidence," replied Cargill, "but he doesn't want to spook me. He wants this to be a staged coup."

Cargill shook his head, more annoyed with himself than the president. "I can't blame him for losing trust. I haven't been straight with him, and I did a poor job of lying to cover up what happened at Lake Las Vegas. He turned out to be more astute than I gave him credit for. I brought this on myself."

Jenna was visibly distraught. "He can't do that," she insisted. "If he gets rid of you, he gets rid of all of us. You've built a great team here. We aren't about to work for anyone else, especially not someone with Vargas's reputation. He'll see time travel only as a weapon, while we're trying to see this as everything *but* a weapon."

"Thanks, Jenna," replied Cargill. "I appreciate your loyalty. But let's hope it doesn't come to that. I agree, we can't let Vargas take over. We can't even let him know our innermost secrets—which not even the president knows. But we aren't out of options yet. There's still time to get a read on the situation and convince Janney to reverse course."

"So when does this change go into effect?" asked Wexler.

"Vargas is scheduled to arrive here in a little over two hours," replied Allen.

Wexler was taken aback. "That soon?" he said. "Then why are we having this meeting?"

Cargill smiled tiredly. "We might as well," he replied. "There's nothing more we can do right now other than wait and see how this begins to play out. Besides, I have no doubt your presentation will be fascinating. It'll get our minds off our troubles for a while."

"Not to mention," added Blake, "that if you were to cancel now, I'd just have to keep badgering you about it until you went mad."

Cargill arched an eyebrow. "You also hinted to me this morning that you had some surprise revelations to make at the end of your lecture. We should learn what these are *before* Colonel Vargas arrives."

"Just so all of you know," said Blake, "we aren't sitting on our hands. I've asked Joe O'Bannon and Tom TenBrink to prepare for Vargas's visit."

Wexler nodded thoughtfully. These were two of the four Inner Circle no-shows. It was all beginning to make sense. "I notice that

Chris Entwistle and Eric Beal aren't here either," he said. "Are they involved?"

Blake shook his head. "No. They had to rush off for an important mission. Sorry about that. I guess I've managed to order a good chunk of your audience somewhere else."

"Not at all," said the physicist. "As I said, I'm just surprised Lee didn't cancel this meeting entirely."

Jenna eyed Blake. "You say that Joe and Tom are preparing for Vargas's visit," she said. "How?"

"They're shoring up our personal and electronic security," he replied. "Making sure none of us are surprised. Making sure the colonel can't learn anything we don't want him to learn."

"He already has," noted Tini, "in spades."

Blake frowned. "Unfortunately, this is true. I should say, making sure he can't learn anything *else* we don't want him to know. It's the best we can do at this point. O'Bannon and TenBrink are also preparing the colonel's quarters. And arranging for a tour and demonstration that Lee will be giving him."

"After he meets all of you, of course," said Cargill. "When he does, be cordial and outwardly welcoming. I'll get him out of your hair as soon as I can."

Wexler exchanged a worried glance with Jenna. She had marshaled the team toward a laudable goal, and the group's productivity and morale were extraordinary.

Until now.

This shake-up threatened to ruin everything they were building, everything they were striving toward. Wexler couldn't see how this could possibly have a good outcome.

Yet he wasn't about to underestimate the members of Q5. Cargill had managed to survive Knight's bloody coup. He had withstood Knight's betrayal, and the betrayals of the men Knight had taken with him, as well as those he had left behind as moles. Cargill had prevailed in the struggle to get to Wexler's discovery first. And finally, the head of Q5 and this team had found a way to rescue Wexler from Lake Las Vegas in the face of impossible odds.

Cargill had shown himself to be clever and resourceful, and that was *before* Aaron Blake was in the picture. Wexler had seen Blake in action at Lake Las Vegas, and he was now the last man on Earth Wexler would ever bet against.

So it wasn't time to panic yet. Wexler would put his faith in this team. And he would begin taking precautions of his own. He would make sure that all traces of his work, the few electronic versions that existed, could be erased remotely, on his command.

Q5 employed a number of brilliant physicists, but only he and Tini were well versed enough in the exotic physics and mathematics involved in his theory to fully understand it, and to recreate sixty-eight pages of dense mathematics. And as long as they kept his work bottled up, it would remain that way.

So Wexler would rely on those with a better knowledge of how to repel the soft invasion that Colonel Hank Vargas represented. But if they failed, he would do everything in his power to limit the scope and scale of the technology, hampering those who might seek to use it as the ultimate weapon.

48

"The fifth dimension," began Nathan Wexler, now standing at the head of the table to address his seated colleagues, "sounds pretty exotic. Magical. And in many ways, it is. But most laypeople have no idea how to describe what it really is, what it really means."

"Tell me about it," said Blake.

The corners of Wexler's mouth turned up into the hint of a smile. "The first clue, that many people overlook, is the word *dimension*. This really says it all. It's as simple, and as complicated, as that. There are three spatial dimensions with which we are all familiar. We live in a world of length, width, and height. And time is considered the fourth dimension. Why? Because, while I can communicate the position of any object in our universe by giving you three spatial coordinates, positions change with time, so I need to give you a *time* coordinate as well. It isn't enough for me to tell you to meet me at the coffee shop at the intersection of Oak and Maple streets, on the second floor. I need to tell you *when* to be there also."

Wexler was pleased to note that grim and anxious expressions had already disappeared, replaced by expressions of thoughtfulness and curiosity. Perhaps his presentation would take minds off the coming storm, after all.

"So when I say the fifth dimension," continued Wexler, "I really mean the fourth *spatial* dimension. It's only the fifth if you count the non-spatial dimension of time."

"I'm with you so far," said Blake. "But you just said there were only *three* spatial dimensions. So how does a fourth have any meaning?"

Jenna and Joe Allen nodded, agreeing with Blake's logic.

"That's the crux of the matter, isn't it?" said Wexler. "Let's examine this from another angle. A dimension is something you can measure, but it's also useful to think of it as a direction you can move in. The first dimension is a line. It has length, but not width or height. If you're a train on a north/south track, your options for movement are severely limited. Forwards or backwards. That's it. North or south, on a very narrow strip."

Wexler paused to let this sink in.

"The second dimension is a square—a flat surface," he continued. "Length and width, but no height. But going from the first dimension to the second gives you a universe of options for movement that you didn't have before. Now you can travel north, south, east, west, or any angle in between. Instead of only being able to explore a narrow train track running across America, you can explore any point on the entire continent."

"Assuming the continent is entirely flat," said Jenna.

"Correct," replied Wexler. "So let's move on to the third dimension. Moving from the second to the third gives you another universe of possibilities. Now you're in a cube. You can go side to side, back and forth, and up and down. And anywhere in between. Driving in your futuristic car that can transform into both a helicopter and a magic drill, you aren't just limited to exploring every point on the continent. You can explore every point above it, and every point below it."

He paused. "Any questions?"

When none were forthcoming, Wexler continued. "So to go from the first spatial dimension to the second, you have to go side to side. And from the second to the third, up and down. So what direction would you have to travel in to go from the third dimension to the fourth?"

He waited a few seconds. "Jenna?" he said, putting the spotlight on the woman he loved.

She was so deep in concentration he wasn't sure she heard the question, but she came out of her trance and shook her head in amusement. "Very cute, Nathan. There isn't any such direction. You've covered them all. It doesn't exist."

Wexler smiled. "Don't be so sure," he said. "Just because we can't perceive it, or even imagine it, doesn't mean it isn't there. We're very limited beings. Imagine an intelligent sea creature living near a thermal vent way down in the black, murky depths of the ocean. It would perceive the ocean to be its entire universe. It couldn't possibly know that there was another universe above the surface, one with physics more bizarre than it could ever envision. Do you think such a sea creature could ever comprehend or imagine fire, even if fire was described to it in great detail?"

Wexler didn't wait for a response. "But the situation we may find ourselves in is worse than that. There are radio waves traveling through us right now, transmitting music, talk shows, and phone conversations, but we have no way to perceive them. Not without a phone or a radio. If you were from a primitive culture and I told you the voices coming from the box in your hand didn't originate there, and asked you to point to where you thought they came from, where would you point?"

There were thoughtful nods around the table as his point struck home.

"Microwaves heat up your food," he continued, "but you can't see them. Show a primitive a glass of cold water coming to a boil inside a microwave, and then ask him what's doing the heating. You can't blame him if he answers, *magic*, especially when he discovers that the walls of the magic box and everything inside of it—*except* the water—are cool to the touch.

"And there are mysteries that confound even modern civilization. Take the discovery of dark matter. Something we know is there based on its effect on other matter, but which we can't see or detect in any way. And the list goes on. We're incapable of perceiving things that are extremely small, or of comprehending things that are extremely large."

Wexler paused for almost fifteen seconds to allow his audience to ponder these limitations of human perception.

"One last example," he said finally. "We know that an atom is more than 99.999 percent dead space. An atom's nucleus is like a marble in the center of an empty football stadium. Yet we aren't equipped to see any gaps in atoms or in matter. We see and feel objects as being solid, even though they aren't. If I asked you to point to the ninety-nine percent empty space left by the many atoms that comprise my face, where would you point?"

Blake nodded, and a smile crept over his face. "Jenna told me you had a way of making complex subjects fascinating and understandable," he said. "Now I can see what she means."

"Thanks," said Wexler, obviously pleased. "I just hope that this was sufficient to make my point."

"More than sufficient," said Allen. "You're saying that just because we can't point to, or even imagine, a direction that isn't north/south, east/west, or up/down—or anything in between—doesn't mean it can't exist."

"That's right," said Wexler. "But even if we can't visualize the fourth spatial dimension, there are still ways we can understand some of its properties. Understand how beings living there would interact with poor humans who can only sense three dimensions. One of the most useful thought experiments comes to us from a book written by an English schoolmaster, Edwin Abbott, in 1884. A book called *Flatland*.

"Abbott figured the best way to understand how bizarre, how incomprehensible, fifth-dimensional beings would appear to us," continued Wexler, "is to think about how bizarre and incomprehensible *we* would appear to beings living in *lower* dimensions. So he imagined a kingdom that existed in a universe with only one dimension, which he called *Lineland*. And one that existed in a universe with only two dimensions, which he called *Flatland*. In Lineland, of course, there would be no degrees of freedom at all. Inhabitants would be line segments, and they could never get past each other, never change their order."

He touched his computer, and an image appeared on the conference room monitor above his head.

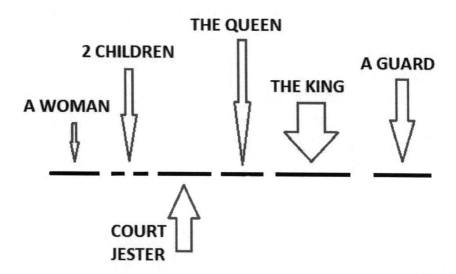

"This is a partial recreation of Abbott's depiction of Lineland. Notice that if you're the king, you're stuck between the queen and a guard for your entire life."

He paused. "Now imagine that this line stretches on forever. Imagine further that there's a line parallel to it, separated from Lineland by a trillionth of an inch. As tantalizingly close as this line is, the beings on Lineland would be unable to perceive it. They would never know it was there, despite it being as large as their own universe. And they would never be able to bridge this gap and go for a visit."

The physicist raised his eyebrows. "A two-dimensional being, on the other hand, would not only see the other line, but could easily travel to it."

"So it's a parallel universe," mumbled Blake to himself, deep in thought. "Literally."

Wexler nodded. "So let's move on to Flatland," he said. "This is the more important land to get us thinking about how we would interact with the fourth spatial dimension. Imagine the universe as a table-top, a slice of our three-dimensional universe cut infinitesimally thin. The inhabitants of this world, Flatland, can't perceive up and down, no matter how hard they try. They just aren't wired for it. Something a millimeter over their head is forever imperceptible to them. Ask them to point to where the mystical "up" from a higher dimension might be, and they can't do it. Just like we can't do it. The up and down is there, they just can't perceive or imagine it."

He paused. "So what would life be like for beings in this universe?" Wexler brought up another simplified image on the monitor.

"Here are two Flatlanders," he said. "Notice that they have much more room to maneuver than Linelanders. But what do *they* see when they look at each other?"

Jenna's eyes widened as she considered this question. "Lines," she answered in surprise.

"Very good," said Wexler. "From above, we can see that they're circular. But *they* can't. If you place a quarter on a table and lower your eyes to the table's edge, so you're on the same plane as the quarter, you can demonstrate this to yourself. All you'll be able to see is a line made by the edge of the quarter."

He paused. "Now imagine the Linelanders have sensors capable of perceiving 2-D shapes the way we can. If I shoved a pointy ice-cream cone from the third dimension through their world, what would their eyes see? And what would their sensors see?"

He gestured to Blake. "Aaron."

"Their eyes would see a point appear," he replied slowly, thinking it through, "as the bottom tip of the cone first touched their world. This would then become a line as the wider part of the cone passed through. A line that would keep growing until it finally disappeared."

"And their sensors?" asked Wexler.

"Their sensors would first detect a single point, as before," replied Blake. "And then circles of increasing size. Finally, the large circle would disappear as the cone finished passing through."

"Sounds like a mess," said Wexler in amusement. "Sensors say one thing, eyes say another. Things morphing into different shapes, appearing and disappearing in a way that to Flatlanders would surely seem random. But as miraculous, as inexplicable, as these bizarre results would be to them, they couldn't be more straightforward to us."

"Which is why you always blame the fifth dimension for all the bizarre results we see with time travel," said Cargill. "All the results that seem impossible and random."

"Exactly," said the physicist. "And someone with decades of mathematical training, capable of grasping higher dimensional mathematics, might eventually be able to make sense of it all. Understand precisely why the rules are the way they are. But even without this training, I'm hoping my introduction at least gives you a sense as to how higher dimensions can lead to head-scratching results."

"It does," said Blake. "Thank you."

"And this is only the beginning of the thought experiments you can do," said Wexler. "Imagine if there was a line between two Flatlanders. They could no longer see each other. But as three-dimensional beings peering down from above, we could see them both. Not only that, we could see *inside* of them. We could reach down and pull out their insides, without breaking their skin."

He threw up another image on the screen.

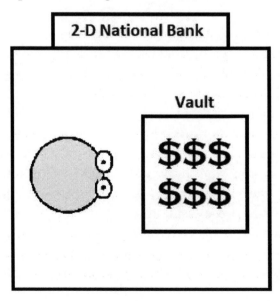

"Wow, Nathan," said Daniel Tini wryly, "fancy graphics aren't your strong suit."

Wexler laughed. "You don't think there's a computer animation job waiting for me at Pixar?"

Tini shook his head in amusement.

"I like using basic images," explained Wexler. "The simpler the better in my book."

"If simple is your goal," said Jenna with a twinkle in her eye, "then you've achieved perfection."

"Thanks," he replied. "I think."

He pointed to the image he had just displayed above his head. "Here we have a Flatland bank. The Flatlander shown is blocked from the money, just as surely as we'd be blocked by a vault on our own world. And he can't see how much money is inside, if any. But looking down from above, *we* can. Not only that, we can reach inside and *take* the money without any trouble."

"So things that are enclosed in one dimension, impenetrable, can be wide open in another," said Jenna.

"That's right," replied Wexler. "Basically, we'd seem omniscient and omnipotent to the poor Flatlanders. We could say hello, and our voices would seem to come from nowhere. We could reach down, pick up this Flatlander, lift him through a dimension his mind isn't capable of recognizing, and plop him down inside the vault. To him, it would seem that he had teleported through an impenetrable barrier."

Blake nodded. "So by analogy, a fifth-dimensional being could reach inside of us and remove one of our kidneys without breaking any skin. Could enter a bank vault like it offered no protection. Could seem to be a disembodied voice. Could materialize anywhere, and disappear from anywhere."

"Yes," replied Wexler. "It's possible that God is a fifth-dimensional being. Or maybe more correctly, any being living in a fifth dimension would seem like a god to us. As far as teleportation through space goes, dimensions can be curled up. Imagine you're a 1-D creature living on a strand of DNA. DNA is supercoiled, like a string you keep twisting until the twists begin to twist on themselves, and then twist on themselves again. This supercoiling is nature's way of fitting three billion base pairs of DNA inside a microscopic cell. If you uncoiled the DNA in a single cell and stretched it out, it would be over six feet long. To put this on a scale easier to understand, if a human cell were twelve inches long, the DNA strand inside of it, when uncoiled, would extend for *fifty-six miles.*

"If you're a Linelander," he continued after a brief pause, "only capable of perceiving the first dimension as it curls through the second and third, you'd have to travel all fifty-six miles along this super-coiled spaghetti to get from one end to another."

He arched an eyebrow. "If you're *me,* on the other hand, you'd realize the beginning and end of the supercoiled DNA rope are just twelve inches away from each other. I'd just have to take a single short step to bridge this gap. To Linelanders, I'd disappear at the starting line and reappear, fifty-six miles away, in an instant."

"Which is what teleportation would seem like to us," said Cargill.

Wexler nodded. "These are just simple analogies," he said. "I'm leaving out a multitude of complexities. But these are the basic concepts of how some of the things we're trying to accomplish should be possible."

"Wow," said Blake. "My head hurts, as promised. But some of this is actually making sense to me. Well done."

Everyone around the table, whose expressions had been spellbound, seconded this praise, except for Tini, who knew the subject matter almost as well as his colleague.

"Thanks," said Wexler. "But as I mentioned, this was just the warm-up act. If you really want your mind to be blown, stay tuned. Once I provide just a little more background, I can move on and share a preliminary finding I've made. One that I haven't told anyone about, including Daniel or Jenna. One that, if true, will turn out to be the most consequential discovery in all of human history."

This extraordinary statement hit the room like a cyclone.

"Is that all?" said Cargill wryly, regaining his voice and his sense of humor after several seconds of stunned silence. "And here I thought you might have discovered something important."

49

All those seated around the conference room table stared at Nathan Wexler with unbridled anticipation. Had anyone else made such a bold claim, he or she would have been thought insane, or at least met with disbelief. Not this man. This was a man known to be modest and unassuming, to downplay his breathtaking discoveries—not a man given to hyperbole.

"Before I share the punchline," began Wexler, "there is some additional background you need to know. The good news is that this pertains to a time travel suppressor field, our number one priority, so it's absolutely relevant."

"To say we're all ears doesn't even begin to cover it," said Cargill.

"My work on discovering a way to suppress time travel is going very well," said Wexler. "Much better than I thought. I'm now confident I can come up with a solution, and soon. Even better, since time travel is a fifth-dimensional effect, I should be able to block it in that dimension."

"Is that a good thing?" asked Blake.

"Very good. Blocking time travel across a large area will require a tremendous amount of dark energy. By doing this beyond our three-dimensional universe, the suppressor field will have virtually no effect on us. I'll be sharing the mathematics of the situation with Daniel later today, but I did prepare a few images to give you an idea of how you might block an effect in another dimension."

"Are your graphics as sophisticated as the last batch?" said Jenna impishly.

"I *wish*," replied Wexler, managing to keep a straight face.

Laughter broke out around the table.

"I'd love to give you an example of the true situation," said the physicist, "as it applies to time travel. But I can't. If higher dimensional analysis is tricky, trying to do this and fold *time travel* in at the same time is beyond treacherous. So I have to use a simple, imperfect substitute."

"Which is?" said Jenna.

"Vision," he replied. "Eyesight."

Saying this, he sent an image to the screen overhead.

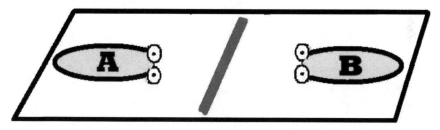

"Here are two flatlanders," he said. "*A* and *B*. *A* can't see *B* because there is a barrier blocking his view."

Wexler paused. "Now let's suppose that a Flatland version of Edgar Knight—hopefully not a psychopath this time—invents a device that can bring the third dimension into play. He's able to place a mirror overhead," he said, bringing up another simple graphic, "capable of reflecting *B's* image to *A's* eyes, so *A* can now see him."

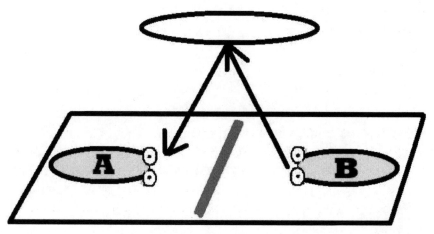

"*A* would have no awareness of the mirror," said Wexler, "or anything above his head, for that matter. To him, it would seem like he was seeing through a wall. Now, if you wanted to block this effect, *suppress* it, if you will, you could do this in the third dimension. Like so," he finished, bringing up the last of his image collection.

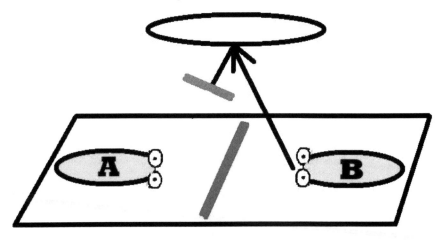

"Suddenly the magic trick won't work," he said. "But *A* has no idea why it's now blocked when it wasn't before. The disruption occurs in a dimension he can't sense, and doesn't impact his world in the least."

"Okay," said Cargill slowly. "Sounds like you have a good plan of attack worked out for our kettle suppressor. But this can't be the breakthrough you were talking about."

"No, this is just important background," replied Wexler. "As I said, an imperfect example. I told you such a suppressor would have virtually no impact on our universe. The key word is *virtually.* With the real suppressor I envision—which is much more complicated than in this example—the impact wouldn't be zero. It would be exceedingly small, but not quite zero. I calculated it out. The good news is that if we built a suppressor capable of blocking time travel across the entire globe, the impact would be so negligible that our sensors could barely detect it. If we were to suppress time travel on a planetary scale, the math suggests space-time would be distorted around the suppressor a minuscule amount, resulting in a slight interference to solar photons passing by."

Wexler paused, shook his head, and erupted into a delighted grin. A grin that looked like it might never go away. "It was then that I had a wild thought," he said, looking like a five-year-old who had fallen onto a mountain of chocolate. "I thought about a flickering star over a thousand light-years away. One formally designated KIC 8462852."

Daniel Tini jolted to attention, almost coming out of his chair. His eyes widened and his mind was clearly racing. "Tabby's Star?" he whispered as if he had just been injected with pure adrenaline.

Wexler nodded.

"No *fricking way!*" he shouted. "You calculated the effect a suppressor would have on our universe if it was vastly scaled up, didn't you? You examined it at galactic scales?"

"I did," gushed Wexler.

"Can you two slow down," said Jenna, "and bring the rest of us along for the ride."

"Sorry," said Wexler sheepishly. "Should have known Daniel would connect the dots right away. Does Tabby's Star ring a bell for any of you?"

He surveyed the room and saw nothing but blank stares.

"I've been doing a lot of talking," he said. "Daniel, do you suppose you could bring them up to speed?"

"Of course," replied Tini, whose enthusiasm now matched that of his fellow physicist. He paused in thought, deciding how best to begin. "The Kepler Space Telescope has been looking for planets around distant stars since 2009," he said. "Not just looking for them, but finding them. Thousands of them. The method for doing this is fairly simple. It just stares, unblinkingly, at 156,000 stars, and measures their brightness."

Tini paused. "You may be asking, why measure the brightness of a star if you're looking for a planet? The answer is that distant planets don't give off nearly enough light for a telescope to see. But if a planet is orbiting a star, once each orbit, it will come between the star and Kepler's sensors. When it does, the star will appear to dim—just a touch."

Blake nodded thoughtfully. "So if a Kepler way out in deep space were watching our sun," he said, "it would appear to dim every three hundred sixty-five days as the Earth blocked it."

"Exactly," said Tini. "Our sun would dim by a tiny fraction of one percent. This dimming, and its repetition at precise intervals of time, would tell Kepler the size of our planet, and the duration of its year."

There were nods all around, indicating Tini's audience was still with him.

"In 2015," continued the physicist, "a woman named Tabby Boyajian was studying data from Kepler and noticed a star dimming in impossible ways, about thirteen hundred light-years away."

"Which explains why you called it Tabby's Star," noted Jenna.

"It's also been called the WTF Star," said Tini. "The official story is that WTF comes from Boyajian's paper, which she wrote with forty-eight other authors, entitled *KIC 8462852: Where's the Flux.*" He paused. "Where's the flux—*WTF.* Get it?"

"That's the formal story," added Wexler. "But believe me, when people use these initials, they're thinking about the other meaning of WTF. A sentiment that has never been more appropriate."

"When you say it dims in impossible ways," asked Blake, "what does that mean?"

"It means Kepler has observed a dip in the star's brightness of over twenty percent!" replied the physicist excitedly. "Over the course of just a few days. That's one hell of a flicker. Twenty percent! First it detected a dimming of almost fifteen percent, and a few years later over *twenty.* A planet the size of Jupiter would only cause a dip of about *one* percent. And Tabby's Star has exhibited other, frequent, dips in brightness smaller than these. And they are all non-periodic! There is no way these observations are due to an orbiting planet. And no other star ever observed behaves even remotely in this way."

"So what *is* responsible?" asked Allen.

"Cosmologists have come up with any number of theories to try to explain it," said Tini. "But they've all failed. No theory has yet been able to account for all the bizarre observations," he added.

Tini faced his physicist colleague and raised his eyebrows. "Until now. Right, Nathan?"

Eyes widened around the table as the others finally realized why the two physicists had been so excited.

"You're kidding me," said Jenna for the entire gathering.

"It's a preliminary finding," said Wexler modestly. "I don't want to get ahead of myself. But when I thought of Tabby's Star, I decided to extend the math. It was a wild hunch, but worth exploring. As I said, suppressing time travel on a planetary scale only creates a negligible effect. But it turns out, if you were to set up a suppressor near Tabby's Star so ridiculously powerful that it blocked time travel in a radius of roughly nine hundred light-years—creating a time-travel-free sphere with a volume of over three billion cubic light years—you'd see *precisely* what we've been seeing. The exact, seemingly random series of dimming events.

"The fifth-dimensional math here is thornier than ever," he continued, "and I need to refine the calculations to be sure I didn't miss anything. But if I didn't, the conclusions are clear. An alien version of Jenna Morrison, within an alien version of Q5, must have long ago decided that suppression of time travel was a good thing. Such a good thing, in fact, that this civilization blocked it in an unimaginably vast swath of interstellar space, covering many millions of stars."

"Unbelievable!" said Jenna. "I'm not sure where to even begin to process that. This is absolute evidence, not just of alien life and intelligence, but a civilization with next-level engineering capabilities."

"It's also evidence that by making a suppressor a primary goal of our group," said Wexler, "you put us on the right track. It looks like we're now following in the footsteps of a galactic civilization."

"But how are they using this suppressor field?" said Blake. "Does it have gaps, like we envisioned, where time travel is permissible?"

"It might," said Wexler. "There's no way to tell for sure. If there are gaps in the field, they'd be a very small fraction of the total. They'd affect the brightness of Tabby's Star, but not enough so that we could tell the difference from the baseline. Not with Kepler's current capabilities."

"So they might have implemented Jenna's exact plan," said Blake. "In fact, I'd be stunned if they didn't. They'd have to have solved the problems Jenna is looking into now. How to control access. How to ensure time travel is used responsibly. And *who* should control access."

"Maybe they went the AI route," said Tini.

"I'm not sure what you mean," said Jenna. "Are you suggesting they created an AI to police time travel permissible sectors within their suppressor field?"

"Yes, exactly," replied Tini. "They'd certainly be advanced enough to create an AI that would be benevolent and up to the task."

"There is a troubling aspect to this," said Wexler. "When we start thinking about the policing of this suppressor field, we need to tuck another question into the back of our minds. Namely, is our use of time travel attracting attention from this galactic civilization?" He raised an eyebrow. "If we don't choose to control time travel, will they control it for us?"

Tini whistled. "So this new discovery of yours," he said, "along with being magnificent, humbling, awe-inspiring, and a hundred other superlatives, is also a bit terrifying."

"What you said about this being the most consequential discovery in history is absolutely true," said Cargill. "I never doubted your judgment on that, but this is even bigger than I'd imagined. This will change how humanity thinks about its place in the cosmos forever."

Wexler shook his head. "Not if we can't disclose it," he said. "Which we can't. At least not yet. We'd have to first disclose time travel, along with my theoretical work. Our proof of this alien civilization is dependent on very sophisticated math pertaining to suppressing time travel in another dimension. Without disclosing *everything*, there is no way to prove that the dimming pattern of Tabby's Star is anything but random."

"So another earth-shattering discovery we have to keep bottled up," said Blake.

"For now," said Jenna. "But this gives us even more incentive to get our own suppressor up and running. To figure out how to manage a world with time travel in it. Once we do, we can disclose this also, and Nathan can get his twenty-seven Nobel prizes."

"I'd settle for just being able to live on the Earth's surface," said Nathan with a grin. "Being able to get out from under a mountain— literally—would be reward enough."

Cargill returned his smile. "It's a deal. If you'll work on teleportation, interstellar travel, a time travel suppressor field, and on proving the existence of an advanced galactic civilization," he said, ticking these off on his fingers, "I'll work on getting us an above-ground headquarters."

Jenna laughed. "Well, that seems fair," she said, rolling her eyes.

50

Cargill was forced to leave the conference room while the group was still engaged in discussion to prepare for his imminent meeting with Hank Vargas. Talk about a letdown. He had gone from a mind-blowing meeting at which Nathan Wexler had disclosed wonders unlike anything he had ever contemplated, revealed the existence of a powerful galactic civilization, to having to deal with the ultimate asshole.

Falling from paradise into a steaming pile of horse manure was the only comparison that came to mind. It was utterly jarring, and made him resent the presence of the colonel even more than he otherwise would have.

His only saving grace was that he had heard from the Aaron Blake overseas just before Wexler's meeting had begun. Blake had escaped China and was well on his way to his final position in North Korea, against all odds. He had been nursing a wounded semi he couldn't abandon, hiding with it in the woods, and surrounded by a determined swarm of Chinese military who saw him as priority number one. And the walls had been closing in.

So *of course* he had managed to extricate himself.

Nothing Blake accomplished in the field could surprise him anymore. To be honest, even the Aaron Blake in Cheyenne Mountain was surprised he had made it out, and no one knew Aaron Blake's capabilities better than he did.

Blake was having to proceed slowly and carefully, by cover of night, due to the condition of his truck, but he was working his way toward his planned destination even now, and would be in place before too long.

Cargill's days in power might be numbered, but at least he had the pleasure of knowing that Kim Jong-un's were too.

Now, almost two hours since he had left the conference room, Cargill was at his office desk, facing the handsome, leering face of Colonel Hank Vargas seated across from him. Vargas looked around the office and nodded. "Not bad, Lee," he said. "Given how limited the real estate is down here, this isn't too cramped of a workspace."

"I'm glad you like it," said Cargill, struggling to stay pleasant. "The best part is that with no windows," he added dryly, "you're never distracted by sunlight, trees, or birds."

Vargas smiled and studied the ceiling, which was eight feet up but had been left to look like a natural part of a cave. "They do make sure you know where you are," he noted. "As if anyone down here could forget."

Cargill nodded, wondering when the colonel would dispense with the small talk.

"The tour and demonstration were remarkable, Lee," continued Vargas. "Not that I doubted the president's word. But time travel teleportation and duplication need to be seen to be believed. The implications are immense. When I saw an exact duplicate of my wallet appear fifty-eight feet away, knowing how the trick was being done, well, that was pretty special."

"That it is."

"Your team seems impressive also. Very much on the chilly side," he noted, raising his eyebrows, "but not any more than I expected."

"Let's cut to the chase, Hank," said Cargill abruptly, having finally lost his patience. "What are you doing here?"

A slow smile came over the colonel's face. "Look, Lee, this wasn't *my* doing," he lied. "Janney contacted *me*. It wasn't my idea to have your group split from my organization in the first place, and this wasn't my idea either. Although I think I know why the president did it. And why he chose me."

"Enlighten me then."

"I got the sense he's lost trust in you. He quizzed me pretty extensively about the devastation at Lake Las Vegas, and about an experimental explosive one of my groups is working on. I believe he thinks more happened at Lake Las Vegas than you've let on."

"Uh-huh," said Cargill evenly. "Go on."

"So he made us co-commanders," said Vargas. "I'm sure you're wondering what the fuck that means."

"Couldn't have said it better myself."

"It means he doesn't want you removed. And he doesn't want more people to know about Q5. I'll spend some time with this group, but mostly I'll be running my other groups. I think he assigned me to the ridiculous title of co-commander so he doesn't have all his Q5 eggs in one basket. Since the group was originally under me, and he trusts me with all black weapons programs in the country, I was the obvious choice. He wants someone else to have the Q5 command codes and know where your secrets are hidden. Including the plans for how to construct your teapots."

"*Kettles*," spat Cargill, suspecting the colonel had made this mistake on purpose.

"Right," said Vargas with an insincere smile. "I hadn't heard the term until I got here. But the point is, Janney wants someone else in the chain of command, largely living outside of this group, as an insurance policy. He wants vital knowledge spread out. In case you decide to freelance, maybe. Follow in Knight's footsteps. Or in case you drop dead from a heart attack."

"*Am I* going to die of a heart attack, Hank?"

"What's that supposed to mean?"

"Don't play stupid. You're many things, but stupid isn't one of them."

"Look, Lee, this is not a coup. Janney doesn't want you removed. I'll be mostly out of your hair. This was always your group. I was your boss, but this was your fiefdom. Now, I'm not even your boss."

"Yeah, we're co-equals," said Cargill bitterly. "I get that. What a brilliant idea to ensure failure."

Vargas actually laughed. "I agree. It's the dumbest management idea of all time. If it were real. But we share leadership in name only. You're still running this group. These are *your* people. I've seen the kind of loyalty you command. We both know that even if Janney put me on top your team would never follow me. They might pay me lip service, but they'd do what you told them behind the scenes. Am I right?"

Cargill ignored the question. "So what do *you* want, Hank? I've worked for you before. I know you have ideas of your own for how technology should be used. Ideas sure to conflict with mine. Are you telling me you *aren't* going to try to mold this organization into your likeness? That you plan to just step aside?"

"In this case, yes. I'm here because the president asked me to be. But I have no agenda of my own. Really."

"*Bullshit!*" snapped Cargill. "I *know* you, Hank. You've never found a weapons system you thought was powerful *enough*. But this one is. Finally, something that lives up to your standards. And you're just going to forget you saw it? Become Janney's insurance policy and leave us alone? You can't expect me to believe that."

"I don't care *what* you believe!" snapped Vargas. "And I don't appreciate the implication that I'm lying. Again, I didn't lobby for this position. Janney contacted me out of the blue. Yes, I'll be sure to give the team my input. And you'd better believe you'll be sharing all of your secrets with me so I can fulfill my duty to serve as Janney's insurance policy. But what impact do you think I can have on Q5 as a co-commander—in name only? With a team we both know is loyal to *you*? I'd love to hear what you think I can do."

Cargill fumed but didn't respond.

"And you're forgetting the buck stops with Janney anyway. So even if I could compel Q5 to do something they won't like—like shoving a kettle up your pasty white ass—the president would have to sign off on it."

A long silence settled over the office.

"Okay," said Cargill finally. "I'm skeptical that you've suddenly changed stripes, but I guess time will tell. If you operate as you claim, we'll get along just fine. I have no problem with spreading some of our eggs to a different basket. It isn't necessary, since I don't plan on going rogue—or dropping dead," he added pointedly, "but I get why Janney might want to take this precaution." His eyes narrowed and he glared at his guest in contempt. "But if you do have a hidden agenda, Hank, I'm going to find it."

Cargill rose and opened his office door. "Let me show you to your quarters," he said, making it clear the meeting was over.

Vargas rose and faced him, their eyes locked in a staring contest.

"Last thing," said Cargill, "let me make this crystal clear. If you try to stab me in the back, or wrest control of this organization from me, I promise that you'll regret it."

"Is that a threat?" said Vargas.

"What do *you* think?" said Cargill icily.

51

"Colonel Vargas," said Knight with enthusiasm, answering the call on the first ring. "How nice to hear from you. How was your first twenty-four hours inside the mountain?"

"This phone better be as untraceable as you say," said Vargas, sitting on the small bed in his Cheyenne Mountain quarters.

"Relax. It's even *more* untraceable than I say. My Brain Trust did amazing work. Before Cargill blew them all up, of course. Notice how clear the reception is. That's through a mountain. *Without* piggybacking on Cheyenne's signal."

"Sunday isn't far away," said Vargas. "Have you reset your poison capsule? You wouldn't want to accidentally kill your only mole within Q5."

"Don't worry. I reset it last night. Just forget it's there. You're really becoming a *head case* about this."

"Not funny, asshole!"

"Is that any way to talk to your boss?" said Knight in amusement. "Seriously, though, you have to relax. I won't forget to reset it. It's going to be with you for a while. If you're this high-strung about it, you'll die of stress at a young age."

"Yeah, *stress* isn't what I'm worried about dying from. You're sure the capsule was able to receive your signal in here?"

"Positive. Like I said, it contains advanced tech that allows it to pick up signals anywhere. And an onboard computer that sends me a confirmation that the stand-down order was received. You're good to go. So enough of this. I need you to give me a full report."

"I got the tour and the demonstration," said Vargas. "I met the team. Cargill doesn't trust me."

"Yeah, who could have seen that coming?" said Knight sarcastically. "The important thing is, did you get Wexler's work? Cargill can be as suspicious of you as he wants, but you are co-captain of his team now. He can't deny you the passwords to the family jewels."

"No, he gave me passwords without a fight. Only they weren't the real passwords. I used them once I was alone in my quarters. They opened up the information vault—thousands of files. Everything I looked at checked out as being legitimate. Except for Wexler's work. Pages and pages of complex mathematics that look like hieroglyphics. Only it wasn't Wexler's work."

"How could you possibly know that?" said Knight.

"Because I copied sections of the hieroglyphics and ran them through an online plagiarism program. The work is an exact copy of a doctoral dissertation on some esoteric aspect of higher dimensional mathematics, published in a scientific journal called *Acta Mathematica*. A dissertation not written by Nathan Wexler."

"I have to give Cargill credit," said Knight. "It was a nice effort. Since you're not trained to recognize Wexler's work, why not substitute something else that looks the part?" He paused. "And I have to give you credit also, Hank. I would have known it was a fake, but running it through a plagiarism program was smart."

"I assume the blueprints for how to construct a time travel device are fake also," said Vargas.

"I have no doubt."

"The problem is," said the colonel, "that Cargill has boxed me in. If I complain that Wexler's work isn't the real thing, he'll get more suspicious, and push back even harder. Because if I weren't in here working for you, this is the last of Q5's files I'd ever open. Why would I? I'd look at files pertaining to security, operations, plans and goals, personnel, and a dozen other things—which I could actually comprehend—before opening that one. And even if I did open it, why would I go to so much trouble to verify it?"

"You're right," said Knight. "But I didn't expect Cargill to give up his biggest secrets just like that. It was worth a try, but I thought it would probably fail."

"And when did you want to share this suspicion with me?"

"Not to worry," said Knight. "I have a Plan B. One that will get me the science I want, and also the revenge. There's more than one way to skin a cat. This way will just be a little bit . . . messier."

52

"The semi's in place and well concealed," reported Blake. "I'm about eighty-five miles from Kim's palace in Hyangsan. I can have the injections ready to go in minutes. I'm positioned so that I'm an exact interval of forty-five microseconds away from the center of his bedroom according to the GPS coordinates and blueprints I was given."

"Outstanding!" said Cargill into his phone. "Same type of wooded hiding spot as in China?"

"Yes. But without roadblocks. And without a Chinese army with dark energy detectors."

"So you think you can remain hidden for a while if you had to?"

"If I had to, yes. I'm in a wilderness area even more uninhabited than the one I chose in China. It's daylight here, so the first window of opportunity won't come about for twelve to fourteen hours. I'll be ready to go as soon as I get a green light."

"Good. Intel suggests that Kim will be spending his nights there for at least the next week. But I hope to pull the trigger sooner rather than later."

"Understood," said Blake. "How's your Vargas problem coming along?"

"Hard to say. We're working on a solution now. Don't worry about us. You have more than enough on your plate as it is. But there has been one change of plan. I'd like you to accompany Kim to the Swedish embassy, and be part of the team that delivers him to America."

"Are you implying what I think you're implying?"

"Yes," replied Cargill. "This is no longer a suicide mission."

"Isn't this stepping even farther out onto that slippery slope? What happened to the Lee Cargill who existed before I joined up? At first you refused to duplicate a human—under any circumstances. Then you came to support duplication if it was for the right cause, and as long as the duplicates were eliminated soon after their appearance. And now this? Are you seriously contemplating keeping one around indefinitely?"

"More than contemplating."

"What happened?"

"*You* happened," said Cargill. "You're a good man, Aaron. One I've come to admire. You're also very special. Only a few of you were supposed to die on this mission. But to complete it, you've sacrificed twelve of you already. No one should have to stand on ground they know will be vaporized and just let it happen. But your duplicates did. If ever someone deserved to come out of a suicide mission alive, it's you."

"That won't bring back the others," said Blake. "And one version of me will still be left behind in the woods, and another in Kim's quarters. Both will need to die."

"I'm well aware," replied Cargill. "But it will ensure one of you survives with most of the memories and experiences of all of you. Like an uninterrupted thread running through your stay in the Far East." He paused. "Just so you aren't too shocked, I want this for practical reasons also. You continue to show just how formidable you are. You also know about time travel and support our goals. I could use a thousand like you. But I'll settle for two."

"I assume my stay of execution is conditional," said Blake.

"No strings attached. I could try, but we both know it wouldn't matter. If you want to live, I can't stop you. And I wouldn't want to. You've always been guided by your own principles. I would hope that if you decided to survive, you'd agree to change identity. To let the Blake back here continue to be the one and only Blake."

"Of course," came the reply. "That much was understood."

"Good," said Cargill. "After this, you can carve out any life you choose for yourself. With a grateful Q5 providing all the assistance you want, financial or otherwise. My hope is that you'll make yourself available to take on missions for us if the need arises."

"Did you run this by the me in Cheyenne Mountain?"

"I did. He predicted that you'd welcome the chance to stay alive. But that if I didn't specifically order you to accompany Kim to America, you'd suicide as planned. He also told me that you'd change identities to get out of his way, whether I suggested it or not."

"And with respect to tackling additional missions for you?" said Blake.

"He predicted you'd be all-in. He tells me he only feels truly alive when under fire. He's an adrenaline junkie who loves a challenge. He's been trying to fight it, but says that, under the circumstances, you would choose to embrace it." Cargill shrugged. "But who knows? You aren't the same person anymore. Your experiences have diverged."

Blake laughed. "Not by that much they haven't. He's right on every particular. I'll deliver Kim as you ask. After that, I'll step aside and take another identity. And I'd welcome the chance to help carry out your most challenging future missions. Beats the hell out of ending this thread, as you call it, in an explosion in Kim's bedroom."

"That's great to hear," said Cargill. "Thanks, Aaron."

"No thanks are needed," came the reply. "I had resigned myself to dying for the cause. Living for the cause is a hell of a lot better."

53

Hank Vargas's eyes slowly fluttered open and he struggled to bring them into focus.

He was in the same clothing he had been in when he retired to his Cheyenne Mountain sleeping quarters an unknown length of time ago, but he was no longer there, or on a bed. Instead, he was seated on a heavy steel chair with his ankles bound close together with zip ties, and his wrists bound the same way behind the back of the chair. Several thick strips of silver duct tape were glued firmly over his mouth.

The colonel found himself alone in the center of a large, well-lit room, about twenty-five yards on a side, with a low, unfinished granite ceiling. This was the room in which time travel had been demonstrated to him, when his wallet had been beamed fifty-eight feet away.

He had pretended to be amazed. And he truly had been. It was just that after Knight's more outrageous demonstration of the effect, a teleported wallet didn't get him as excited as would normally be the case for the completely uninitiated.

Vargas's right eye was throbbing, and while he could still see, it had surely suffered minor trauma. As his mind became more awake, the nature of this trauma became clear: someone had removed the smart contact from his eye, probably just pinching it off with their fingers, and not doing a particularly delicate job of it. He felt tenderness in a small spot on his back, as well, as if someone had stabbed him viciously with a horse needle, or had shot him with a tranquilizer dart, which was more likely. He slept on his stomach, so his back would be an easy target.

All of this added up to Lee Cargill. Who else? Even if Vargas imagined there was a rogue element in one of the other groups housed within Cheyenne Mountain, only Cargill would know that he was wearing a smart contact lens capable of activating hidden weapons with a pattern of blinks.

Sure enough, seconds later, just as his mind returned to full wakefulness and alert, Cargill entered the room, with Blake and Allen in tow. Cargill walked over to where Vargas was bound and ripped the duct tape from his mouth.

The colonel fought to stay calm. "Can't say I love your initiation rites, Lee," he said. "Do all new members of Q5 get hazed like this?"

Cargill smiled wearily and shook his head. "No, Hank. You're special."

"What the fuck is this about?" demanded Vargas. "Have you lost your mind? The president wants me to share command with you. Yet I went out of my way to assure you the group is still yours. And this is the thanks I get?"

"Yeah, I've already ordered your medal," said Cargill. "Should arrive any day."

Vargas ignored the sarcasm. "I didn't say backing off from command was heroic, Lee. I was just trying to make a peace offering. So why assume I'm an enemy?"

"Because I don't trust a word you say," replied Cargill. He motioned to Allen, who walked around the colonel's chair and took up a position behind him. Vargas struggled to turn his head to see what he was up to, but failed.

"So what now?" snapped Vargas. "Are you going to kill me? Yeah, that won't make Janney more suspicious of you. Big mistake."

"I'm touched that you're looking out for me," said Cargill. "But why don't you let me worry about that."

Vargas shot upward, intending to lift the steel chair he was tied to and use it as a bludgeon to wipe the smirk from Cargill's face.

But the chair had other ideas. It was somehow firmly affixed to the floor, and he was lucky his attempt didn't tear muscles in his legs or damage his bound wrists.

Seconds after his body slammed back into the chair, he felt a sharp stabbing pain in his arm.

As he was trying to process what had happened, Allen reappeared in front of him holding an empty syringe, whose contents had no doubt just been emptied into his arm.

"What did you inject me with, you piece of shit!"

No one replied. Blake and Allen both studied him with great interest while Cargill checked his watch.

"Relax, Hank," said Cargill. "Take deep breaths. Let's pause our conversation for a few minutes."

"*What was in that syringe?*" shouted Vargas.

"That's the opposite of relaxing," noted Cargill calmly. "Another word and I'll duct tape your mouth shut again. Your choice."

Vargas's mind raced. There was no question he and Cargill were slated to be antagonists, but he hadn't expected a move like *this*. He had been assigned by the president, and had done nothing to threaten this man or his team. Nothing yet.

Cargill must have seen through Vargas's assurances, clearly enough to make a bold, reckless move from which he would never recover, whether he let Vargas live or not. Either way, Cargill had to know that Janney's suspicions would now be confirmed, and the president would seek out an immediate, permanent solution to make sure that a rogue wasn't in charge of the most powerful technology in history.

Vargas had always liked Cargill—as much as he allowed himself to like any of the men under his command. He had trusted Cargill where he had never trusted Knight. Knight was a narcissist and borderline psychopath. Brilliant, but uncontrollable.

Cargill was also brilliant—in his own way. Absent Knight's corrosive influence, Cargill's people tended to be fiercely loyal to him. And he had a genius for assembling teams that were astonishingly productive and cohesive. Unlike Knight, however, Cargill had always been straight-laced, more a Boy Scout than a ruthless dictator capable of calling any play to advance the ball, regardless of the ethics or consequences.

But based on what Knight had told him, and what he was now witnessing, Cargill had changed dramatically.

The longer Vargas sat in silence, reflecting, the more he regretted the current turn of events. He liked Lee Cargill. He liked all three of these men. A lot. Admired them even. Wanted to be closer to them. He realized he was willing to do anything to gain their acceptance, make them happy. So why were they doing this to him?

Cargill checked his watch and smiled. "Congratulations, Colonel," he said at last. "You're still alive. If you were going to drop dead, this would have happened several minutes ago."

"What was in that syringe?" repeated Vargas. But this time he said it calmly, without a hint of malice.

"I removed your contact lens, as I'm sure you know," said Cargill, ignoring the question. "But this didn't disarm the weapons you have hidden. Can they be activated in other ways?"

"Yes, I made sure to bring newer versions that can be activated manually if the contact lens is confiscated or fails. But I need my hands. To be honest, when you first came in the room, my plan was to wait a while and then ask you to untie me to pee. Once you did, I planned to trigger one or more of them manually."

"Good to know," said Blake. "So where are your booby traps and weapons hidden?"

"In my belt and watch," replied Vargas helpfully.

Cargill considered. "That makes sense," he said. "Explains why you were sleeping in your clothes." He nodded at Allen who removed these items from the prisoner and set them well beyond his reach.

"Why did I just share all that with you?" asked the colonel.

"You couldn't help yourself," replied Cargill.

Shit, thought Vargas feebly as he realized what was happening to him. He knew he should have been far more outraged, but his concern was more academic than actual. He trusted that his friend had done the right thing. "You injected me with T-4," he said aloud, "didn't you?"

"Developed by one of your own teams," replied Cargill. "As you know, if you're among the half who can tolerate it, and survive past the first minute or two, you're home free."

Vargas nodded. He didn't know all the intricacies of the development of this chemical, but he knew the basics. The research team responsible had studied how both truth serums and oxytocin affected the brain, and created a potent drug that substantially amplified and intensified the effects these chemicals brought about. Oxytocin was a hormone that acted as a neurotransmitter in the brain, with powerful effects on human behavior. It was released when a woman breastfed to promote a strong emotional bond with her baby. Its level increased in both men and women after a hug, kiss, or orgasm. It was thought to play a significant role in pair-bonding. Thought to increase empathy, trust, love, and generosity.

No wonder he had suddenly realized how much he admired the men in the room with him. How much he trusted them. How much he wanted their approval. No wonder his rage was now gone, replaced by a desire to please.

The drug was extraordinarily effective. It managed to take the edge off, to reorient a subject, but without dulling their intellect. He could carry on as coherent a discussion as ever, only with an irresistible desire to please and tell the truth. Even knowing that his trust in these men was false, was drug-induced, Vargas realized he didn't care. He still couldn't stop himself from revealing anything they wanted to know.

"Didn't you take a big gamble using T-4?" said Vargas, genuinely concerned for the welfare of his friend Lee. "What if it had killed me?"

"A risk we were prepared to take," replied Cargill. "And a necessity. Since I know how much of a ruthless, hawkish, lying asshole you are, the bigger risk would be not learning what you're really up to." He leaned in toward the colonel. "So now that you're being cooperative, let me ask again, why did Janney send you here?"

"Because I came to him and told him you had gone off the reservation. That you were probably mad. That you had destroyed Lake Las Vegas for absolutely no reason, using octa-nitro-cubane. And that you and I remained close after Q5 split off, and that you had told me all about time travel."

"What?" said Cargill. "I thought Janney summoned *you*."

Vargas shook his head. "I arranged for the first meeting. I practically forced it on him."

"And you knew about time travel *before* the meeting?" said Blake. "Correct."

"How?" said Cargill. "Who told you?"

"Edgar Knight."

"How long ago was this?" asked Cargill, stunned.

"Less than a week ago."

"You must have the timing wrong," said Joe Allen. "Knight was already dead at that point."

Vargas shrugged. "For a dead man, he sounded very healthy when I spoke to him last night."

54

Cargill felt the room spinning around him and he reflexively put a hand on Blake's shoulder to steady himself.

Knight was alive?

Impossible. He couldn't have survived. He was at Lake Las Vegas. Nathan Wexler had confirmed as much when Blake had teleported him out of there. Which left only one possibility.

There was now no doubt that they had made the right choice in interrogating Vargas, and in using T-4. It had paid off even better than they had thought it would. He, Allen, and Blake had discussed this move at length, and all had agreed. O'Bannon and TenBrink had done a masterful job of paving the way, preparing Vargas's quarters to perfection. Not only had they made sure that his lock could be readily defeated, but had seen to it that this could be done, and the door opened, without making a sound.

"Did Knight tell you there had been more than one of him?" asked Cargill.

Vargas shook his head. "No, just the opposite. After I had seen multiple copies of one of his men, I asked him point-blank if there were more copies of *him*. He told me no. That you could have many arms, but you could only have a single brain." The colonel paused in thought. "He also told me he wasn't at Lake Las Vegas when you attacked."

"He was lying," said Cargill. "He was there all right. Which means he did have extra copies of himself generated. I didn't think he'd ever allow that."

"Why don't we back up," suggested Blake. "Start at the beginning." He nodded at the prisoner. "Why don't you tell us when you first spoke to Knight. And under what circumstances."

Vargas proceeded to do just this, thoroughly and precisely.

He described how Knight had brought him to his farm in Maryland, at gunpoint, and the events that had unfolded there. He didn't leave out that Knight had demonstrated time travel by sending him back in time, and then ruthlessly killing his double in front of him, or the three copies of Jack Rourk he had dispatched.

The mention of Jack Rourk brought scowls to all three interrogators. This man was once a trusted member of Q5's Inner Circle, but had become one of Knight's moles. He had shot another member of the Inner Circle, Mark Argent, on Palomar Mountain, in cold blood, so he could get a copy of Wexler's work he had thought Blake was carrying.

But Blake had gotten the better of him, wounding him and ending up with his phone. Then he had tricked him in such a way that he was made to look the fool in front of Knight, humiliating him.

The colonel went on to detail the titanium capsule Knight wanted implanted in his head, and how Knight had pretended to leave the farm, drawing Vargas out and outsmarting him, not watering this down in the least. Even if he were to tell this story to a trusted confidant, he probably wouldn't have admitted that Knight ultimately knocked him out and implanted a time-bomb in his head against his will.

The disclosure left no doubt of two things: Edgar Knight was alive. And T-4 was an interrogator's dream, if only it didn't kill half the subjects before they could talk.

Vargas also detailed Knight's goals and plans for the future. Knight wanted to get his hands on Wexler's work, on his fabled half-second time travel capability. He wanted to extract revenge on Q5 for attacking his headquarters as they had. And he wanted to bring about a global hegemony, with him sitting on the throne, dramatically reshaping the world. In exchange for Vargas's help, Knight had promised to make him the number two man in his new world order.

"So where do things stand now?" asked Cargill when he had finished. "You managed to convince President Janney to send you here. But you learned I wasn't about to give you Wexler's work. So what's the plan going forward?"

"*My* plan or Knight's plan?"

"Aren't they one and the same?" asked Blake.

Vargas shook his head vigorously. "Not at all. Although, now that I think so highly of you, I'd never think of carrying mine out."

"Why don't you tell us what your plan *was*," said Cargill, rolling his eyes. "As of last night. But tell us about Knight's plan before you do."

"Of course," said Vargas helpfully. "Originally, he hoped you'd give me a legitimate password, so he could get Wexler's work the easy way. Now that he knows this won't happen, Plan B is for me to deliver the entire management team into his hands. He'll then force Nathan Wexler or Daniel Tini to recreate Wexler's breakthrough from scratch. He's convinced these are the only two physicists on the team capable of doing it. Then he plans to kill the rest of the team and destroy all time travel technical specs, so that Q5 can never rise again. Meaning he'll be the only one left who can wield time travel."

"Sure," said Cargill. "Leaving the world defenseless against him."

"Exactly," said the colonel. "But before Q5 is destroyed, he wants to torture and kill the three people he believes were responsible for the attack on his Lake Las Vegas headquarters."

"And who does he think that is?" asked Cargill.

"You, Aaron Blake, and Jenna Morrison."

Blake frowned. "Surprisingly accurate," he noted.

"Is that his entire plan?" asked Cargill.

"In the near term, yes. You already know his long-range plans, which haven't changed."

"And *your* plan?" asked Blake. "You know, as of last night?"

"I planned to destroy Q5 and kill its key players myself, including the three of you. But instead of forcing Wexler and Tini to reveal how to extend time travel to a half second, they'd be the *first* ones I'd kill. I also planned to kill Edgar Knight and purge all time travel technology from the face of the planet."

Cargill blinked in confusion. "Didn't you just tell us that Knight has a booby trap in your head? If he dies, you die."

Vargas sighed. "I was as good as dead when he implanted the capsule. It's only a matter of time. A year at the outset. But even if this weren't true, I'd be willing to sacrifice my life to stop him."

"To stop him?" said Cargill in disbelief. This had to be total bullshit. Except that it *couldn't* be. The T-4 was working too well. "Why would you want to do that?"

"When I realized just how dangerous time travel is, how it could be used as the ultimate weapon, I knew it had to be stopped. Knight's wild, psychopathic ambition to transform the world to his twisted ideal is horrific. But even if Knight were a pacifist, my plan would have been to kill you and bury this tech, no matter what the cost. It's too powerful a weapon to be allowed to exist."

"What?" said Cargill, as if he was certain his ears had failed him. "Too powerful a weapon? No weapon has ever been powerful *enough* for you. You're more hawkish than Knight. So how can what you say possibly be true?"

"I *was* hawkish," replied Vargas. "Many years ago. I did some terrible things in the name of defending our national interests. But as time passed, I saw too many wars, too much bloodshed. And for what? Over the years, I lost too many friends, saw too many good men die."

The colonel shrugged. "So I changed," he continued. "Had an epiphany. I became horrified by the nature of humanity. Convinced that we had to find a way to uncock the gun we were holding to our own head. So I maneuvered to be put in charge of black weapons. So I could control things from the inside."

Cargill had never been more stunned, never more at a loss for words. He couldn't believe what he was hearing. He glanced at this watch, confirming that the T-4 wouldn't wear off for several hours. "Control things, how?" he asked.

"Let me back up for a moment," said Vargas. "To get my current position, I had to appear appropriately hawkish. This isn't a job you give to a dove. Once I was in, I began to shift as many projects and resources as I could from offensive applications to defensive. Not that I'm a pacifist. I still make sure we stay ahead of the enemy. I still support weapons we can give our men and women in the field to enhance their battlefield effectiveness. Relatively small stuff that can save individual lives. Powered exoskeletons, smart contact lenses, sonic weapons, and so on. But I killed off all WMD programs, and the worst of what was left. Because once we develop these weapons, it's only a matter of time before others do too. So we haven't gained an advantage, we've just brought our species that much closer to the brink."

"Who are you trying to kid?" said Cargill. "I was in your organization. You never found a weapons program you *didn't* support. You green-lighted all of them."

"Did I?" replied Vargas. "Don't focus on what I *said* I supported. What I pretended to push for. Focus on what actually ended up seeing the light of day. I couldn't *say* I wanted to end WMD or other large-scale, high-impact weapons programs because I felt they were too horrible to be used. I'd be removed from my position. So I did the opposite. I killed off these programs claiming they weren't horrible *enough*. You just accused me of this yourself. I earned a reputation as a tyrant and a warmonger, but I killed off programs without anyone knowing that this was my goal from the beginning. And through it all, I kept my job."

Cargill's eyes widened as memories of his time under Vargas came rushing back. The colonel was exactly right. This is what *had* happened.

Vargas had never been satisfied with the destructive potential of the worst weapons being worked on. He insisted they not be deployed until they were improved in impossible ways, or he killed the programs outright for not meeting his lethality goals.

And Cargill had fallen for it like everyone else. Cargill had met plenty of wolves in sheep's clothing. But he had never once considered that Vargas might be the opposite: a sheep in *wolf's* clothing. It was stunning.

"Your behavior was all a ruse," whispered Cargill. "It's obvious now. So of course you'd want to shut time travel down, too, no matter what it took. You want to stop Knight as much as we do."

"That's right. And to stop *you*, also. To end the threat of this capability once and for all. I planned to act when I had you both in my sights, so to speak."

"What did you and Knight discuss last night?" asked Allen.

"I told him about the dummy file you'd given me access to. The one you made up to look like Wexler's theory."

"Speaking of that," said Cargill, "how did you know it wasn't real? You've never said. I wouldn't think higher dimensional mathematics was bathroom reading material for you."

Vargas explained how he had run the file through a plagiarism program.

A broad smile came over Cargill's face. "This is just incredible," he said to his prisoner. "So it turns out we're of exact like mind when it comes to weapons, you and I. You're of exact like mind with our entire management team. And you're clever enough to kill weapons programs in such a way that no one suspects your true position on them. And clever enough to check advanced math that you have no hope of understanding. An hour ago I thought you were the world's biggest asshole, and now I have nothing but admiration for you. And I haven't even been drugged with T-4."

Vargas smiled and was clearly quite pleased.

"So Knight wants you to deliver us to him on a silver platter," said Cargill. "How?"

"By either finding dirt on you, or framing you. Either way. He's tasked me with continuing to trace out where the secrets are kept, so I can do a thorough job of burying Q5 and its tech for good."

"Which is what you planned to do on your own, anyway," said Cargill.

"Right. Once I find dirt, or manufacture it, I'm supposed to take it to Janney and get him to lure the entire senior management team out of Cheyenne Mountain."

"Lure us out, how?" asked Cargill.

Vargas shrugged. "Any pretense would do. The president would just have to make it sound innocent so you wouldn't raise your guard. He could simply tell you he wants to meet the newcomers on your team. He's never met Aaron, Jenna, Daniel, or Nathan, so this request wouldn't be too suspicious."

"And knowing when we're traveling to meet with Janney," said Cargill, "you can divert us into Knight's hands. Delivering everyone he wants. Danial and Nathan for information. Aaron, Jenna, and me for revenge."

"Exactly. He's thinking of framing you further from there. The president won't know you were diverted by force. He'll think you fled. That you went rogue and convinced the entire team to go with you. Knight can have a few key people killed in a way that makes you look responsible, to make it worse. When Janney learns that all traces of the recipe for time travel are gone, you'll get blamed for that as well."

"An impressive strategy," admitted Blake. "I assume *your* plan was to carry this out exactly as Knight wanted, but instead of just killing us, you'd kill him at the same time."

"Yes. And myself also, since this has become something I can't avoid. Not if I want to stop him."

Cargill nodded thoughtfully. "Suppose I could demonstrate to you that our team shares your principles. Unambiguously. Not when you're drugged and have to trust me, but convince you when you're stone-cold sober. Demonstrate to you that we've been working to-ward peaceful uses of this technology, and fighting to keep it out of the hands of people who would use it as a weapon—which we *thought* included you. If I could prove this to you, would you join us?"

"No question about it," said Vargas.

"Well, you are still under the influence of T-4," noted Allen.

"I'm aware," said the colonel. "But I've shared my philosophy, and you know I can't lie. If you really can convince me your philosophy is the same, why *wouldn't* I be willing to join forces? Why wouldn't I be *eager* to join forces?"

Cargill exchanged glances with Blake and Allen. This couldn't have worked out better. With Vargas in their camp, and knowing Knight's plan, they could turn the tables. They could let Knight think he was getting the drop on them while the reverse was true. Then they could interrogate *him* instead of the other way around. Learn how many duplicates of himself he had made, and where they were kept. Put down this cockroach a second time, but this time do it right, make it final.

"How do you feel about killing someone in their sleep, Aaron?" asked Cargill.

Blake sighed. "It's better than killing someone who can see it coming," he replied. "I'll take care of it right away."

"Thanks," replied Cargill.

A second version of Hank Vargas was even now in his quarters, sleeping soundly. They had broken in earlier, hit Vargas with a tranquilizer dart, and then taken him to a kettle, where they had made a single copy. They had returned the original to bed, with an extra dose of knockout drug to keep him sleeping for another six hours, and awakened the copy in the room they were now in, bound and gagged.

If the injection of T-4 had killed the copy, they would repeat the exercise the next night, this time attempting a different kind of interrogation. In this way, they could learn what they were up against and kill the duplicate each time, leaving Vargas to awaken, none the wiser.

None of them could have guessed that the duplicate would become their ally. Given this, it made more sense to kill the original instead, and keep the conversation going.

Cargill turned to Blake. "Don't dispose of the body like we planned," he said. "Just seal him in a body bag, making sure it can't leak any odors, and leave him locked in his quarters. We can dispose of him later. Since *this* Hank Vargas will still be alive and active," he said, gesturing to the prisoner that Joe Allen was now freeing, "no one will be knocking down his door looking for him."

"Roger that," said Blake.

Cargill took a deep breath. Everything was finally breaking their way. But he was spinning too many plates. He wouldn't get any sleep for a long time. First, he needed to spend hours getting Vargas fully up to speed and providing absolute proof of his own sincerity.

Then it was time to call the president.

55

President Alex Janney stared at Linda Cosgrove across his magnificent desk and shook his head in contempt. "I didn't invite you to the Oval Office to listen to excuses," he said. "If you can't control your own coalition, than maybe you shouldn't be Speaker of the House."

Speaker Cosgrove shot him an easy smile, unperturbed. "So why *did* you invite me?" she asked. "To make threats?"

Janney sighed. "Apparently not successful ones."

"Look," said the Speaker, "the founders purposely designed our government so that passing legislation isn't easy. Trying to get Congress to pull in one direction is worse than herding cats. It's herding self-interested, narcissistic, opportunistic cats. Who only care about getting reelected, no matter how much they pretend to care about their constituencies."

"The founders may have wanted checks and balances, Linda," said Janney, "but they have to be rolling in their graves at our inability to agree on *anything*. And they weren't the ones who decided the idiots in the Office of Budget and Management should control important legislation."

Janney was about to go on when a small screen affixed to the desk in front of him came to life and large words began to scroll across it.

Lee Cargill called in and is holding, began the message. *Says he can't overstate the urgency of speaking with you. Says he needs an hour, at minimum.*

Janney cursed under his breath. Goddammit!

The government was too big, his responsibilities too great. Too great for him, too great for a thousand men. It was a constant swim against the current. Try to move forward, be proactive, and a hurricane or earthquake, a missile test or successful terrorist attack, could divert him for days or weeks. Sometimes it seemed that the job entailed little more than reacting to one crisis after another.

He was tempted to have his assistant tell Cargill to go pound sand, but knew he couldn't. Not given the tech the man controlled, and the fact that he had just sent Vargas inside to rattle his cage. Apparently, this had worked only too well.

The president told Linda Cosgrove that something had come up, apologized, and promised to reschedule. The Speaker looked miffed, and who could blame her? The idea was to light a fire under her ass, not piss her off for no reason.

Minutes later a computer-generated holographic image of Cargill appeared across Janney's desk, at the very location the Speaker had just vacated.

"You do know that I have a job of my own, right?" snapped Janney the moment Cargill appeared. "I just blew off Linda Cosgrove for this. What do you want?"

"I'll get right to it, Mr. President," said Cargill, bleary-eyed and looking like he had the weight of the world on his shoulders. "It's time for full disclosure. There's a lot I haven't shared with you. That ends now."

"Haven't *shared* with me?" said Janney. "Or do you mean there's a lot you've been *lying* to me about?"

"I had my reasons for what I did. Which I'll tell you while I set the record straight. But I hope you'll at least appreciate that I didn't mislead you for personal gain or for power. I did it for what I deemed important security reasons, and for the good of humanity as a whole."

"Do you know how self-important even *saying* something like this sounds?" said Janney.

"What can I tell you?" replied Cargill. "We both know time travel has the power to transform civilization. Sounds like hyperbole, but if anything, it's understatement. But I have a lot to cover, so I'll get right to it. If, when I'm done, you think I'm a liability and want me gone, I'll leave willingly. If you think I should be executed, I won't put up a fight. I just ask you to keep an open mind."

"Go on," said the president, who couldn't help but be intrigued, especially by the word *executed*.

"First, I have a duplicate of my best operative, Aaron Blake, hiding in North Korea, standing by. If you give him the green light, he can teleport into Kim Jong-un's palace, kidnap one copy of Kim, and leave another in place. And he can poison the one left in power so he'll only live another three or four days."

Janney stared at the image across from him in disbelief. "Where do I even begin to unpack that statement?" he said.

"I'll provide all of the background you need."

"This is much worse than just misleading me!" snapped Janney. "You set up an Op to remove a dangerous foreign leader without my authorization. Who do you think you are?"

"I don't blame you for being angry," said Cargill. "But I only put Blake in place, nothing more. Given the tools that time travel gives me, I figured getting him in place was so dead simple I wouldn't need your authorization. I'd only need that to *proceed* with the Op."

Janney considered. "Even if I buy this, you stretched your authority past its limits, and you know it. But go on. Did getting him in place turn out to be as easy as you thought?"

Cargill grimaced for just an instant before a neutral expression returned to his face. "Not quite," he said. "But easy enough. He's there and ready, after all."

"Okay," said the president. "So what other background do I need?"

"First," began Cargill, "you need to know why Knight and I pursued Nathan Wexler's work so zealously. I told you it was an important theory that could help advance what we're doing. But it was more than that, and I knew it. It was work that would allow us to increase the distance traveled through time to almost half a second."

Janney's eyes widened. "Are you saying you can do this right now?"

Cargill nodded.

"And you've *kept* it from me?" said Janney. His surprise was faked, since Vargas had filled him in, but his outrage was very real.

"I'm afraid so, Mr. President."

"How does that translate into teleportation distance?" asked Janney, already knowing the answer.

"The Earth moves about a hundred twenty miles in half a second."

"And you didn't deem this important enough for me to know?"

Cargill lowered his eyes. "I'm sorry, sir. But we both know the immense power and possibilities that fifty-eight feet gives us. So what about almost *eleven thousand times* this distance? If one is tempted to use time travel as a weapon when an object can be lobbed fifty-eight feet into enemy territory, how tempting is a hundred twenty miles?"

He paused. "I had to ask myself what you would do if I told you. Would this be enough power to finally seduce you into pursuing the technology's military applications? You and I see eye to eye for the most part, but absolute power corrupts. I've already become corrupted. I'm making duplicates of people, something I vowed to never do. I'm using the tech for military applications, like abducting Kim. I couldn't be sure what you would do once you pondered the potential of a half-second. And neither could you. So I chose to shield you from the possible corrupting power of this discovery."

"To *shield* me?" barked the president. "You aren't my parent, Lee, and this isn't your call. And a lie is a lie."

As far as motives went, this wasn't the worst Janney had ever heard. *If* it was true. But the result was more power concentrated in Cargill's hands.

"You're right," said Cargill. "But there were other considerations, other ways you might react. You could panic, realizing how vulnerable America would be if this ever got into the wrong hands. Realizing how vulnerable *you* are, personally. If this technology can capture Kim, it can certainly bypass the Secret Service. Any concerns you had about me would be greatly amplified, because you would know that I could reach you effortlessly, wherever you were. You would know you could never be safe from me."

"Is that a veiled threat?"

"Not at all. If I wanted to threaten you with physical harm—since you'd be powerless to stop me—I'd have already done it."

Janney stared into his guest's holographic eyes for several seconds and then nodded. "Go on."

"So you could have seen the half-second breakthrough as an irresistible weapon. Or you could have seen it as too big a danger, and shut it down. At the time, Knight was still at large. If I disclosed this to you, you might decide to mothball the program, leaving Knight as the only one with the keys. I couldn't risk that."

"So you had no confidence that I'd make the right decision," said Janney, insulted. "Either I'd embrace the added power too much, or fear it too much. You know there's a middle ground, right? The one you think *you've* been taking, I presume."

"I'm sorry, Mr. President. I trust your judgment. But even if there was a five percent chance you would fall on either side of this fence, I didn't want to risk it. But it's worth the risk now."

"What changed?"

"Nathan Wexler has come up with a theory of how to suppress time travel. More than a theory. Late last night, he actually perfected a crude, working prototype. Right now it can block a kettle from firing, but he hopes that one day he'll be able to protect a *destination* from incoming travelers. A destination like the White House. Create conditions in the fifth dimension that will make the White House seem like the inside of a mountain, rejecting any deliveries from the near future. You would no longer be vulnerable, and we could protect all of our important installations."

"But this is only theory at this point?"

"Yes, and it's a much tougher problem than blocking time travel at the source. But I would never underestimate Nathan Wexler. Just the kettle suppressor is a major game-changer. The group's been discussing ways we can implement these suppressors so we can eventually share this tech with the world. I can tell you more about this later, but the bottom line is that the landscape has shifted dramatically."

Janney shook his head. This was an understatement. The capabilities and issues Cargill was raising were each worthy of months and years of deep thought. And the man wasn't finished. Cargill wasn't forcing him to drink from a fire hose, he was forcing him to drink from *Victoria Falls* while standing at the bottom with his mouth open, looking up.

"With this as background," continued Cargill, "let me return to Blake in North Korea and outline the plan."

Cargill did this as succinctly as possible. When he finished, he said, "I need a go/no-go decision, Mr. President. We'll never have an opportunity like this again. The *world* will never have an opportunity like this again."

"If I give the green light, then what?"

"Kim's palace in Hyangsan is out of teleportation range of South Korea. But Blake can teleport himself and Kim to Pyongyang. The Swedish Embassy there has agreed to let two of our men inside, and empty a large room for us—no questions asked. I chose Chris Entwistle and Eric Beal of our Inner Circle. Both are ex-special forces, and both have considerable experience conducting interrogations. They'll smuggle Blake and Kim to South Korea. From there, we'll have our fastest jet take them wherever you'd like. But wherever Kim ends up, we'll need a number of duplicates so we can try various means of interrogation."

"Which is why you want *your* men in charge," said Janney.

"Exactly. The interrogators have to already know about time travel."

"Where would you take him?" asked the president.

"We could bring him here to Cheyenne Mountain," offered Cargill. "Or we could land him anywhere you want. Camp David is another option. We'd just have to move a kettle there. But we'd have to do it quickly. After the palace explodes, the Kim Jong-un we leave in North Korea will have his hands full purging his government. Three or four days later, he'll die, plunging the country into greater chaos. At that point, we'll need to be prepared to go in and nullify the threat once and for all based on the intel we get from our version of the man. Right at the moment of maximum confusion and vulnerability."

Janney paused for several seconds in thought. "If this really is our chance to end this crisis," he said, "we'll need to do it right. I'd need my Secretary of Defense and the Chairman of the Joint Chiefs on board. I'm the Commander in Chief, but having their full support will be critical. And there's no way I'll get this support unless they're absolutely convinced that our intel is rock solid, that we've identified every last landmine."

"Then show them that you've captured Kim Jong-un."

"While the other one is still alive in North Korea?" said Janney.

"Tell them he isn't. It's just North Korea refusing to acknowledge reality. Tell them we kidnapped him from his own country, and any reports that he's still in North Korea are false. Once they realize we really have Kim, they'll get on board in a hurry."

"With questions I can't answer unless I disclose time travel."

"Sure you can," said Cargill. "Just tell them you authorized a daring secret mission to grab him. Tell them you sent in SEAL Team 6, but you won't disclose operational details. This is your prerogative as president. Sure, they won't like it, and they'll still have questions, but they aren't going to look a gift Kim Jong-un in the mouth, regardless of how he fell into their lap."

"How much time before you need a decision?"

Cargill checked his watch. "A little under two hours."

Janney hit a button on his desk. "Cancel my meetings for the next three hours," he said to his assistant, not waiting for a response.

"Okay," he said, turning back to Cargill. "Let's keep going. You've lied to me. Repeatedly. About matters big and small. So why should I trust what you're telling me about the North Korean situation? If this fails and innocents are killed by the remnants of Kim's regime, I'll be crucified."

"It won't fail," said Cargill.

"Before I decide, what else haven't you told me about?"

Cargill sighed. "I haven't told you about what happened at Lake Las Vegas. What I told you was a lie. But so was what *Vargas* told you. It's time you knew the truth."

"How do you know what Vargas told me?"

"I'll get to that in a minute. First, let me start with Lake Las Vegas, which was where Knight had established his headquarters."

Cargill told him about seizing the chance to take out Knight once and for all. About using Aaron Blake and Jenna Morrison as bait, arming them with undetectable bombs and waiting for Knight to reel them in. Not knowing in advance where Knight would take them risked that innocents would become collateral damage, but Cargill had made the call that they had no other choice.

He spent a few minutes describing what factors he had weighed when making this decision, and the ethics of impossible choices, using Truman's decision to drop the Bomb as one example.

Janney found his arguments more persuasive than he thought he would. Cargill managed to get across the immensity of the issues involved, and sounded genuinely sickened by his own decision. Janney had always found him to be a brilliant organizer and idealist. Events may have changed him, but few men could have withstood the demands of power any better.

The president wasn't sure what decision he would have made. Part of him was relieved that Cargill had taken this into his own hands. In Truman's heart of hearts, would he have been relieved if the decision to drop the bomb on Japan had been made for him? If a rogue general had ordered this without consulting Truman, would he have been doing the president a favor?

"I can't blame you if you condemn me for this act," finished Cargill. "I've condemned myself. I'd just ask you to give it more thought before you decide if it was justified or not."

"I will," said the president.

"Thank you," said Cargill. He shook his head miserably. "But it gets even more tragic. While we did kill Knight on the island, we've learned that he generated at least one duplicate beforehand."

"What?" snapped Janney. "You told me he'd never allow a copy of himself."

"I was wrong. And at least one version of him survived our attack."

"Are you positive?"

"Yes. At least one of him is out there. Maybe more." Cargill shook his head in disgust. "Who do you think sent Hank Vargas to meet with you in the first place?" he said.

56

Cargill thought the discussion was going relatively well, although there was no way to know for sure. The president was reeling from all he was saying—understandably so—but seemed to be keeping an open mind.

Cargill went on to explain the current state of play, beginning with the interrogation they had conducted on a duplicate of the colonel, and how they had become the unlikeliest of allies.

This surprised Janney as much as anything. "So Hank Vargas," he said, "the man you warned me was one of the most dangerous men alive—the man you said couldn't be trusted—turns out to share your philosophy almost exactly."

"Yeah, I know. You couldn't make this up."

"I'll want to speak with him for a few minutes, without you present, when this is done."

"Of course, Mr. President," replied Cargill. "For as long as you'd like."

He went on to describe how Knight had recruited Vargas, and the grand vision he had shared. "And this is just the tip of the iceberg," said Cargill. "Knight must have decided that some aspects of his plan were too ugly to even share with the colonel. Ask Vargas how big of a danger he thinks Knight represents. He'll second what I've been saying. With Knight's ability to wield time travel, the risk he poses justifies extreme measures to stop him."

"Except that the extreme measures *you* used," said the president pointedly, "*didn't* stop him."

Cargill scowled. "No, they didn't," he said. "But we did set him back. Way back. He lost his headquarters and most of his followers."

"Yet he still managed to manipulate me into putting Vargas into your camp."

"Underscoring further just how big of a danger he represents," said Cargill. "Look, Mr. President, now that you're up to speed, there are two important decisions I'm asking you to make. First, we're poised to end the North Korean threat. We can capture Kim and leave a copy of him in place at the same time. We just need your say-so. In my view, the reward is huge and the risk small."

"And the other decision?" asked Janney.

"Now that Vargas is in our camp, we can use him to take out Knight. We can pretend to fall for Knight's plan to capture us, and turn the tables. I'm skeptical that he's had the chance to set up an additional duplicate of himself, but if we capture him, we can know for sure. If he *has* made another duplicate, we can learn where he is and eliminate him too. I'd like your support for this effort, as well."

Janney paused in thought. "Let's tackle the North Korean question first," he said. "You know that every Op is risky, no matter how straightforward on paper. I think you're underestimating the risk here."

Cargill shook his head. "Trust me, Mr. President. Aaron Blake won't fail you. I'm not sure he knows *how* to fail."

The president closed his eyes for an extended period, inhaling and exhaling deeply several times, as though trying to achieve some Zen-like meditative state.

"Okay," said Janney finally. "Tell Blake he has his green light. Give him my private number and tell him I'm on call for anything he needs. Have your three colleagues bring Kim to Camp David as fast as possible. I'll make sure a section of the retreat is cordoned off and secured, and that they can move Kim there without anyone seeing him."

"Thank you, Mr. President," said Cargill. "You won't regret this. I'll coordinate with you so that you have a kettle in place when they arrive."

"Good," said Janney. "With respect to your strategy to stop Knight, you have a green light there as well. Assuming, of course, that when I speak with Colonel Vargas, he backs up what you've been telling me."

"He will, sir."

"Then you'll have my blessing to proceed as you think best. But this time get it right. Make sure you kill him, *and* his copies."

"We will," said Cargill firmly.

"Good. But just because I've sided with you on these two decisions, don't think this is over. You lied to me repeatedly. Not about little things, but about enormous things. You killed thousands without any authorization. You took the law into your own hands."

"I understand, sir," said Cargill. "And I am guilty of these charges. My only hope is that you come to appreciate my motives and believe I'm still the best man to run the show. Making sure you're never left out of the loop again," he hastened to add.

"If you bring me Kim Jong-un, and we're able to defuse North Korea's strike capabilities, I'll consider *not* hanging you. After that, we'll have to see about keeping you on in your current role."

"Understood," said Cargill somberly. "And thank you, sir."

57

Aaron Blake took a deep breath and prepared to split into two men once again. One would capture and also slowly poison the most dangerous, unpredictable tyrant in the world, and one would add to the growing list of Blakes who would give their lives for the cause, flashing out of existence in a massive octa-nitro-cubane fireball.

Challenging, important work for one. Death to the other. It hardly seemed fair.

Cargill had just informed him he had finally come clean with the president, who had personally authorized the mission and who would no doubt take full credit for its success—as he should. Cargill and Q5 were desperate to remain in the shadows, anyway, and this momentous military victory would translate into a massive political victory. It was hard to imagine this wouldn't put the president in a more forgiving mood when it came to Cargill's many transgressions.

Nothing succeeded like success.

For several nights now, with nothing to do but wait for the order to complete his mission, Blake had used the night-vision capability of his lens to admire a magnificent pair of large owls who had nested in the crook of a thick branch almost directly overhead. Even though night vision turned them a fluorescent green, it couldn't take away their simple majesty.

At the moment, the female was manning the nest, but Blake knew from experience that the male would be returning soon to share a meal.

"K-1," said Blake aloud, "I need to modify my orders."

Blake quickly relayed new instructions to the kettle supercomputer. The original plan had been for K-1 to send K-2, with him inside, into Kim's bedroom. Once K-1 detected K-2 arriving at the palace, it would abort further time travel, and detonate immediately.

The new plan was nearly identical. Only this time, K-1 would wait a single minute before detonation.

Once K-1 acknowledged its new marching orders, Blake stepped into the nested kettles, made sure K-2's video and audio were sending data to his lens, so that he could observe the environment outside of the kettle when he landed, and prepared his weapons and syringes. This completed, he mentally rehearsed the steps he planned to take one last time. He had pantomimed these steps dozens of times over the past twenty-four hours, leaving as little to chance as possible.

"Mark!" he called out, giving the order to time jump.

Nothing happened.

Shit! he thought, feeling ill in the pit of his stomach. He must have been the copy left behind. Just as this realization came, K-1 confirmed that he and the inner kettle had arrived from the future— eighty miles away. Hopefully, the GPS coordinates he had been given were accurate, and his double was even now emerging from the kettle inside Kim's bedroom.

Blake walked briskly to the edge of the open trailer, looked up at the trees, and drew his handgun. The night was dark, but his lens could readily see that the male owl had now returned, and he and his mate were both minding their nest.

Blake allowed himself to admire their magnificence once again, but only for a few seconds. He then pointed his gun in their direction and fired off multiple shots. Both owls darted into the air and climbed, and other wildlife scattered through the air or undergrowth, desperate to get away from the violent eruption of sound.

Blake only wished he could run as well, fleeing the violent eruption soon to come, one that would bring much more than merely sound.

He followed the owls as they flew out of sight and experienced a single moment of contentment before the reality of the situation returned.

It was a feeble gesture. He had killed scores of innocents. He was beyond redemption. Saving a few owls and other forest creatures wouldn't make up for what he had done, wouldn't make any difference in the scheme of things.

But it would make all the difference in the world to these two owls, he told himself.

He closed his eyes. He had but seconds to live. Every survival instinct in his body begged him to sprint from the scene and save himself, but he managed to find the force of will to hold himself in place and await his fate.

This was going to truly suck. At least he wouldn't feel any pain. He would be torn to pieces before he knew what hit him. One instant a living, thinking man, filled with hopes and aspirations and visions of a future.

And the next . . . nothingness.

It would happen so quickly he'd have no way to sense it before it was over, no chance to brace himself for dissolution.

Had he left K-1's original orders alone, he would have been duplicated and annihilated at the same time, and wouldn't have had to face the agony of waiting for death to come.

This was the far greater torture.

He just hoped the owls appreciated it.

This was his last thought as the kettle turned into a shrapnel-filled fireball that snuffed out his consciousness at a speed faster than sound.

* * *

Blake and the inner kettle arrived at the foot of Kim Jong-un's massive bed, and video and audio feeds began coming to him immediately. He exited the kettle a moment later, deciding the coast was clear.

The room was dim, but there was still enough light for him to see without the use of night vision.

He took in the scene with practiced efficiency. Kim's people were starving, but his bedroom was as enormous and well-appointed as the finest palaces of history. The room sported the finest Persian carpets thrown over gleaming marble flooring. Two ivory statues of lions, with jewel-encrusted ivory platforms on their backs, served as end tables on either side of the bed, a thumb in the eye to those around the world trying to save the elephant from extinction.

The room had a single entrance, a heavy steel door, hermetically sealed, half as thick as the doors that protected Cheyenne Mountain from a nuclear strike. Sensors in the kettle reported to Blake's lens that the walls were also steel, covered in plaster on the outside, but thick enough that a tank couldn't make it through them.

Fortunately, this wasn't an issue for a time traveler.

Kim was sprawled out on the bed, naked, doughy, and repulsive. Two naked young girls, perhaps seventeen, were lying beside him. All three appeared to be unconscious. Empty bottles of wine were strewn about the bed haphazardly, along with empty lobster husks and half-empty steel containers filled with melted butter. The scene had all the trappings of a drunken orgy that Caligula might have envied.

Blake exited the kettle and approached the North Korean leader, one of the most recognizable figures in the world. The bed smelled of alcohol, butter, flatulence, and sex, which only added to the surreal nature of the experience.

The man was certainly living down to every low expectation one could have of him. Blake had no doubt he could blow a trumpet in Kim's ear without causing him to stir. But the two girls were another story. They could be in drunken comas, sober but asleep, or even fully awake and only faking sleep. There was no way for him to know.

He desperately wanted to wake them. Scream at them to run. Force them to flee the palace as fast as they could, and get out of harm's way.

But he couldn't risk that they would alert others on their way out. He couldn't risk delaying his mission until they cleared the blast zone—if they were even able to run. And when they were questioned later, he couldn't have them babbling about a stainless steel refrigerator and a strange Caucasian who had somehow joined them in the room.

Bile rose in his throat as he raised a silenced gun and put a bullet into each of their heads.

He cursed to himself as a wave of self-loathing swept over him.

Who knew how long these girls had been suffering, forced to perform whatever sexual acts Kim demanded. Who knew how many nights they had been degraded without any ability to protest, their lives in constant jeopardy from the whims of a cruel dictator who fancied himself divine.

But instead of rescuing them as they deserved, he had ended their lives.

It was an irony only Satan could appreciate. The Blake he had left behind was going out of his way to save two owls and other woodland wildlife. Meanwhile, here *he* was murdering two helpless young women whose only crime was having been physically appealing to North Korea's supreme leader.

Blake's eyes burned with hatred as he neared Kim's unconscious form, and it was all he could do not to tear the dictator's head off with his bare hands. Instead, he injected the pudgy leader with a sedative and worked to shove his rotund, dead-weight body into a pair of pants, unable to keep a permanent expression of disgust from his face, having been forced to see something he would never be able to un-see.

He had been notified before he had made the jump that Chris Entwistle and Eric Beal were waiting for him in the Swedish Embassy, in a large room whose GPS coordinates he had been given. He had K-2 establish communications with these men and wrestled Kim's lifeless bulk into the kettle, having to hug the man's bare torso to do so, suddenly wishing he had taken the time to cover it with a shirt. Or a flamethrower.

"Sending Kim to you now," he said to his two colleagues in Pyongyang, seconds before he had K-2 send the dictator the precise duration of time that would land him near the center of the room they were in.

"Holy shit!" said Beal after a brief pause, obviating the need for Blake to ask if K-2 had been on target. "It's really him! *Unbelievable.*"

"And he looks like an even bigger buffoon in person," chimed in Entwistle.

Blake didn't respond. Instead, he injected the Kim still in the kettle with a slow-acting poison and sent him a hundred yards away from the palace. Finally, he pulled the Kim who remained in the kettle to the floor of the room, entered the kettle, and sent himself back in time to join his two colleagues inside the Swedish embassy.

The moment he materialized there, the kettle in Kim's bedroom exploded, obliterating the palace in Hyangsan and creating a massive fireball that was clearly visible for miles.

And inside Kim's bedroom, yet another Blake was turned to paste, along with a crazed dictator and the dead bodies of two lovely young girls.

* * *

"Welcome to the party," said Entwistle when Blake popped into existence.

"Congratulations, Aaron," said Beal, nodding toward the man who was stretched out on the floor. "You did it. Kim Jong-un in the flesh."

"Yeah, *a lot* of flesh," said Entwistle. "A half-dressed asshole who reeks of alcohol. Why am I not surprised?"

"Yeah, half-dressed *now*," said Blake. "He wasn't that way when I found him."

The faces of both of Blake's colleagues twisted up into expressions of absolute disgust. "They don't pay you enough for this, Aaron," said Beal.

Blake laughed. "You can say that again."

"Are you ready?" asked Entwistle.

"What's the plan?" said Blake. "Lee assured me you had one, but didn't elaborate."

Just as he said this his eyes came upon an odd contraption in the room that had to be a kettle. It was only big enough to contain one man at a time, and was mounted on a motorized chassis. One glance at the room's doorframe made it clear to Blake that it had been carefully designed with these dimensions in mind, so that it could be driven through the door with almost no room to spare.

"Let me guess," he added. "We're going to teleport out."

Beal winced. "We aren't happy about it, either," he said. "Lee realized that after the palace exploded, North Korea would be locked down tight as a drum. Smuggling Kim out would be dicey at best."

"I knew that much," said Blake. "But I thought he knew of some slick underground railroad-type system to get to South Korea."

"Not so much," said Beal. "I don't think he wanted to tell you that you'd have to die another time to get out of here." He frowned. "I'm not thrilled about it, either. I don't suppose experience makes it any easier."

"I don't have any experience," said Blake. "I've never had to face certain death before. You'd have to ask my deceased brethren."

"Right," said Beal. "Dumb question."

"So what is the plan?" asked Blake. "I can't believe we're prepared to blow up the embassy."

"We're not," replied Beal. "The kettle is set to teleport the three of us, one at a time, onto a runway at Camp Casey, a US army base in Daegu City, South Korea."

"Daegu City?" said Blake, raising his eyebrows.

"It's forty miles north of Seoul," explained Beal. "The three of us left behind will shove Kim in the kettle and send him to the versions of us on the runway."

"And then what?" said Blake.

"We have a large helo just outside," replied Entwistle. "We can use a remote to drive the kettle out of the building and onto the helo. The three of us will join the kettle inside and climb as quickly as we can, with the goal of flying to an unpopulated area."

"No doubt attracting the immediate attention of North Korean authorities," said Blake, "who will tell us the city is in lockdown and demand that we land."

"We'll land, all right," said Beal miserably. "But after we blow the tiny explosive charge inside the kettle, there won't be much of us or the helo left to find."

Blake shuddered. "Now I forgive Cargill for not telling me the plan earlier," he said. "I wish I didn't know now."

"It really is the only way to be sure we get out," said Entwistle.

"I know," said Blake. "What about the versions of us who end up on the runway? Where will they be going?"

"Our final destination is inside Catoctin Mountain Park," said Beal. "The jet will land nearby and we'll helicopter in."

"Catoctin Mountain Park?" said Blake. "I'm not familiar."

"Camp David," said Beal. "President Janney will be waiting for us there."

58

Colonel Li Ming sat in a dark room in silence. In the days of cellphones and comms and AI assistants, Li found it critical to spend quality time alone in thought, without any possibility of interruption.

And no situation he had encountered in his career was more worthy of thought than this one.

After finally catching the man they were after, they had brought him to a nearby detention facility, which had promptly exploded, leaving no trace of the man, and reducing his cargo to tiny scraps of mangled metal. The force of the explosion was extraordinary. Unheard of.

Except that it wasn't.

It was almost identical in power and scale to the one that had created a crater at a private airport in Shenyang. Almost identical to one that had leveled more than an acre of forest about eighty kilometers from where the man had been captured, a location Li learned had been the destination of Major Long He and twenty-four men who had gone missing.

And the same tiny scraps of stainless steel had been found at both locations.

DEI Director Chang had inspected the sites of these explosions and was convinced they weren't due to dark energy, although he wouldn't rule it out entirely. But one more similarity became clear: whatever explosive had been used left no clue as to its identity.

Then, not five hours earlier, Kim Jong-un's palace in Hyangsan had exploded. According to Li's intelligence sources, Kim had been far enough away from the palace that he had survived, but he had been so drunk he had no idea how he came to be there, or what had tipped him off to leave.

Which is not how Kim reported it in the statement he had made on national television two hours earlier. In yet another rewrite of history, Kim explained that he had seen something suspicious in the wee hours of the night outside the palace grounds and had gone out to investigate, his uncanny, godlike instincts serving him well yet again. Two men in a truck had fled when he approached, and while he was giving chase, the palace had exploded behind him.

Kim had nothing to say about a helicopter that had exploded fifteen minutes later near Pyongyang.

Like the three explosions in China, Colonel Li's operatives had confirmed that the two in North Korea hadn't left a signature, either.

Whoever was behind this had revealed two technologies with potentially game changing effects. An unknown type of explosive, and even more troubling, a device that could tap into the dark energy field.

These advances almost had to have stemmed from America, from its black laboratories, which were better funded than any in the world, including China's. Also, the man they had captured spoke English, and appeared to be a native American, as well.

And he was now their only real lead. They had to learn who he was. His past. What organization he was representing.

But this was much easier said than done. Had he escaped, they could have at least hoped to get lucky with facial recognition in the weeks and months ahead. But now they weren't looking for a living man, they were looking to reconstruct the history of a life, having precious few clues and without any remains of his body to go on.

Despite these obstacles, Li was certain he could convince his superiors to make learning this man's identity one of China's highest military priorities. This was a man who had entered their country with mysterious cargo, and who had left nothing but death and havoc in his wake.

Li had no doubt that he would ultimately get whatever resources he asked for to aid in his search.

His people had already tried to match the images they had of this man to online photos, but had failed. The Caucasian's explosives had left no signature, and *he* had left no Internet footprint, unheard of in this day and age. Once again, a measure of the sophistication of the people behind him, who had managed the miraculous feat of scrubbing his life from the Web.

Even if Li's people had found a remnant of the Caucasian's past, this would only be the beginning. Anything they were likely to find online wouldn't point to who he had been working for, how he happened to be traveling with a refrigerator that gave off a dark energy signature, and what, exactly, he had been doing in China.

But so far, they hadn't found a single thread to even begin pulling on.

No matter, Li decided. He had no doubt he would find a path. Eventually. He was nothing if not patient, nothing if not persistent, and he had the vast resources of a mighty nation at his disposal.

He would learn who this man was, and what he had been up to.

It was only a matter of time.

PART 6

"Double, double, toil and trouble;
Fire burn, and caldron bubble."

—Shakespeare (Macbeth)

59

Colonel Hank Vargas sat on the edge of the bed in his Cheyenne Mountain quarters and tried not to reflect on the body bag underneath it. Sharing one's quarters with a corpse was creepy enough, but this was especially the case when you and the corpse were one and the same.

He felt a strange temptation to unzip the bag and experience the surreal oddity of gazing at his own remains, without needing an out-of-body experience to do it.

He shook his head. What was he thinking? Forgetting how macabre it would be for just a moment, once opened, the bag would no longer contain any smell that might have developed, turning his small quarters into a noxious hell.

Not that he wouldn't be joining his two deceased duplicates in actual, biblical hell before too long. As much as he kept trying to push his impending death from his mind, it kept resurfacing.

He was terrified of death. Worse, he felt he had so much life left in him, so much to accomplish. He had been overzealous with drone strikes earlier in his career, and had vowed to spend the rest of his life making amends. He just never realized how short this period of time would end up being.

But he had seen scores of younger men, friends, die in battle, die for what they believed in. How was this any different? He had let Knight get the better of him, had let him implant a booby trap in his head. At that point he was already dead.

But he now had the chance to do more good in his death throes than he could have done in decades more of life. And at least he had witnessed the miracle of time travel, of duplication and teleportation, and gotten a glimpse into the possibilities science had opened up, thorny as they were.

And he would die knowing the technology was in good hands. Cargill was exactly the man he had thought he was. He hadn't met that often with Cargill and Knight when they were in his group, simply because dark energy was such a pie-in-the-sky concept he didn't take it seriously. In his view, it wasn't a weapons program he had to kill, because it already had no chance of success.

Who knew?

But his instincts about both men had turned out to be right—even more than he could have guessed. Cargill was a much better man even than he had thought, and Knight far worse.

But Knight wouldn't be on the stage for long, either. The man had outsmarted Vargas and had most likely ended his existence, but Vargas was about to return the favor.

He still had some hope of survival. Cargill had sworn to him that saving his life would be their highest priority. Once they had Knight in custody, there was a fifty percent chance he would survive T-4. If he did, they could get the command that would open the partition inside the titanium capsule in the colonel's skull, nullifying the poison. Even if T-4 killed Knight rather than loosening his tongue, they could work to get a duplicate Knight to reveal the information they needed to save Vargas's life in other ways.

For now, the colonel knew he had to put all of this from his mind. He needed to be sharp.

Vargas placed a call to Knight, reporting that he had things well in hand, and that President Janney had read the incriminating material he had found on Cargill, which showed that Cargill had been responsible for Lake Las Vegas and could teleport more than a hundred miles.

"Did he buy it?" asked Knight.

"What do you mean?" said Vargas. "The evidence I found was real, not manufactured. So of course he bought it."

"And was he as furious as you would expect?"

"More. You have no idea. I thought he might fly out here and kill Cargill himself. So when I recommended he find a pretense to lure Cargill and his senior management team out of their Cheyenne Mountain stronghold, he agreed enthusiastically."

"Great work, Colonel. When and where?"

"We're all leaving at ten tomorrow morning in a Pave Hawk helicopter. Two pilots from the Cheyenne Mountain Air Force Station will fly us to meet with the president at Fort Riley in Kansas."

"Janney won't really be there, right?"

"Correct. Once we arrive, he's agreed that I should take Cargill aside, in private, and see to it that he's relieved of command—with extreme prejudice. Janney will then call in to the group and explain that Cargill will be staying at the base, taking on a new assignment, and that Janney will select someone to replace him as head of Q5 as soon as he can."

"You couldn't convince the president to put you in charge?"

"I tried," said Vargas. "He said he wasn't ready to commit, but that I was still under consideration. Who knows, he still might decide I'm the right man."

"He won't," said Knight. "If he was going to choose you, he would have done so right away. He doesn't trust you, either. In his mind, you fulfilled your role. You proved Cargill was off the reservation and got rid of him. He'll say thanks and push you back out of Q5."

"I'm not convinced of that," said Vargas.

"Don't worry about it," replied Knight. "It's just as well. We'll go through with the original plan and intercept the Q5 management team on their way to Fort Riley. Then I can make sure they get the payback they deserve, and get Wexler's work from him or Daniel Tini."

"Wouldn't it be easier to torture the correct passwords out of Cargill?"

"No. I know the bastard too well. He always sets up two passwords. One opens the files. One wipes them out beyond any possibility of reconstruction. Even if I got him to give me a password, I couldn't trust it wasn't the one that would kill the information. I'm better off breaking the scientists. And I'll know if the work they provide to me is real or not. If 45.15 microseconds falls logically out of the postulates and equations, it's the real thing."

"Understood."

"Why Fort Riley?" asked Knight.

"Why does it matter? You told me to get the president to draw them away from the protection of Cheyenne Mountain. And away from their toys."

"Just a strange location for the president to be," said Knight. "Or at least *pretend* to be. Especially since it's public knowledge that he's at Camp David, and plans to be there for an indefinite period of time. I don't want them getting suspicious."

"It was Janney's idea. Cargill knows that the president would never ask the entire Q5 management team to the White House. They'd all have to log in, and it's too public. So the president told Cargill he wanted to meet with them as part of two days of secret meetings he'll be holding with all key Black Ops groups. At Fort Riley, away from the press pool and any prying eyes.

"As far as Camp David goes," continued Vargas, "he told Cargill this was part of the ruse. By publicly announcing a stay at his retreat, he can steal away for two days of meetings while the press continues to believe he's still at Camp David, being reclusive. By making it seem like Q5 is just one of many groups being summoned, part of a black projects review, this won't raise any red flags. I think it's a solid strategy."

"I agree," said Knight. "I guess Janney is more astute than he seems."

"He would have to be," said Vargas in amusement. He paused. "So how do you want to go about intercepting them?"

"Tell me more about these Pave Hawks," said Knight.

"Part of an aging fleet. Being replaced. Used by special forces groups for insertions and search and rescue missions. The one we'll be taking has been deweaponized. Good speed and range. Crew of four, including two pilots, and with enough room for a combat-equipped squad of eleven. For this trip, though, it will just be two pilots and the seven of us."

"Can you get the command codes for the one you'll be taking?"

"No question about it," said Vargas. "There's very little military information I can't access. Why?"

"With the codes, I'll be able to take over the aircraft remotely, and kill all communications, including cell phones."

"Impossible. The autopilot has been specifically upgraded to prevent this kind of thing."

"I know," said Knight smugly. "The scientist who came up with the upgrade was one of the many members of my Brain Trust. She was a pain in the ass, but by having one copy of her tortured to death in front of the other, she became cooperative. She created some nice technology to seize control. Again, demonstrating the benefit of being able to peel off duplicates of high-IQ scientists."

"And you're *certain* you can do this?"

"Positive," replied Knight. "But I need some time to flesh out a plan. Why don't you get me the codes while I do some thinking. I'll call you when I've finished."

Twenty minutes later Vargas texted the requested codes, and just under an hour later, Knight called back. "I've worked this through," he said. "Here's the plan: Bring a gas mask with you when you leave tomorrow. Hide it in a rucksack or in your clothing so you can access it quickly. After I take control of your helo, I'll divert it to a location near Loveland, Colorado, which is about a hundred and thirty miles north of Cheyenne Mountain. I'll place a number of drones at the landing site. The instant the helo touches down and a door opens, I'll have them shoot in some gas canisters. Very potent and fast-acting. So after landing, open a door and hold your breath. Then put on the mask. The rest of your fellow passengers will be out in seconds."

"Got it," said Vargas.

"I'll have a pickup truck parked right next to the landing coordinates. One with an eight-foot bed and a vinyl cover you can roll up over it. The cab will be tinted so no one can see inside."

"Let me guess," said Vargas. "You want me to lay Cargill and the team out in the back of the pickup and seal them inside. Turn the pickup's bed into a steel coffin."

"It had better *not* be a coffin," said Knight. "You'll need to be sure they're getting enough air to survive. I can't get Wexler's breakthrough from corpses."

"Of course," said Vargas. "Speaking of which, what happens to the pilots? I'm not comfortable killing helpless men who have nothing to do with this."

"No need," said Knight. "If they aren't given a reversal agent, they'll be out for eighteen hours. Just leave them." He paused. "As for you and your Q5 cargo," he continued, "the keys to the pickup will be on the front seat. You'll need to drive to where a four-lane tunnel cuts through a mountain, about thirty minutes away. I've chosen this carefully. The tunnel doesn't get much traffic, and doesn't have any cameras inside. I'll send you directions."

"I don't understand."

"Once you're close to the tunnel, I'll have my men drive two vehicles inside. One will be the same pickup that you're driving. The other will be the semi you were in during our first meeting, except with the time machine and furniture removed. They'll move in just before you get there, timing it so they disrupt the flow of traffic as little as possible. When you enter the tunnel, stay to the right. I'll make sure the semi is parked with its trailer door open and a ramp extended. Drive inside very slowly."

Vargas shook his head, not understanding why any of this was necessary. "Are you sure it will fit?"

"Yes!" said Knight emphatically. "You think I'd leave that to chance? You'll have nine inches of clearance on either side."

"Why such an elaborate plan?" asked Vargas. "No one has any reason to believe the helo isn't going to Fort Riley. So no one will be following it after you take control. And the pilots will be out for eighteen hours, as you said."

"And when the Q5 team never arrives at Fort Riley?" said Knight.

Vargas considered. "Yeah, I see your point," he said. "When they fail to show, Janney will be moving heaven and earth to find out what happened to them. He'll have his people pull transponder data, satellite footage, and street camera footage."

"Exactly. And when they track the helo to Loveland, the satellite history will show you moving them to the pickup."

"Right," said Vargas. "Go on."

"While you're pulling the pickup truck into the back of the semi," continued Knight, "one of my men will be driving out of the other side of the tunnel in the same pickup. The intelligence people Janney tasks with finding the Q5 team will be tracing *its* path, thinking it's the one you drove into the tunnel."

"I assume you've made sure it has the same license plate number as mine."

"What about *same pickup* don't you understand?" snapped Knight. "Same pickup, same plates, same tires. It will *be* the pickup you're driving—just forty-five millionths of a second older."

"Understood," replied the colonel. "I didn't know you had a time machine big enough to do that."

"Now you do," said Knight simply. "Once you've driven into the trailer," he continued, "my men will pull the ramp back inside, close you in, and get the hell out of the tunnel. The faster we get out of there and stop disrupting traffic, the better."

"Your men?" said Vargas. "Does that mean two more Jack Rourks?"

"No it doesn't," said Knight irritably. "I'm down to one of him, which is how I prefer it. I haven't just been waiting around for your calls. I've been recruiting scores of mercenaries, rebuilding my security team. I can copy however many men I need, but having individual soldiers is a lot less conspicuous. Good mercs aren't hard to recruit when you've done it before and money is no object."

"So what happens after we're all sealed up in the trailer?"

"Unroll the cover of the pickup so our guests get plenty of air. The driver will exit the tunnel and proceed to a secluded area a few miles away, where he'll have a car parked. He'll give you the keys to the semi and take off. Then it's your turn to drive. I'll call you with directions to where I'll be waiting for you. It might take you three or four hours to get there, but none of your passengers will awaken. Just in case, I'll have cameras inside the trailer to monitor them, and a variety of sensors and suppressors, as well, so they can't be tracked using their phones. Or any other method, for that matter."

"I assume I'll be driving in the opposite direction from the decoy pickup truck," said Vargas.

"Correct. Not that it really matters. They won't be paying any attention to the semi."

"How do you know I can drive a semi?" asked Vargas.

"They train you special forces guys up right," replied Knight. "Although I'd imagine you're rusty."

"I'm sure it will come back to me," said Vargas. He paused. "Congratulations, Edgar. Your plan is brilliant."

"Of course it is," replied Knight, seemingly unaware of the arrogance of this response.

* * *

Minutes later, Vargas was inside a Cheyenne Mountain conference room, laying out Knight's plan to the Q5 team.

"Impressive," said Blake when the colonel had finished. "As much as I hate to give him any credit, he's an excellent strategist."

"I'm not thrilled that we'll all have to be knocked out," said Cargill.

"I don't blame you," said Vargas. "But at least when you come to, we'll have Knight in custody. That should make it a little easier to stomach."

"Why won't he tell you where he'll be until you're driving the semi?" asked Jenna.

Vargas shrugged. "He's a cautious man. But I'll contact the strike team as soon as I know. And since we're forewarned about the pickup ruse, we can also have the semi we end up in followed, just for good measure."

"Can I bring weapons?" asked Blake. "I can't see why I would need them, but I'd feel better having them. Knight isn't a man to underestimate."

Vargas considered. "*You* can, Aaron, but no one else. Remember, we're supposed to be flying to meet with the president. It's totally within character for you to be packing, even knowing the Secret Service will be disarming you. I'm sure you'd feel naked if you weren't. But it would be out of character for the rest of us. At this point, even for me."

"I'd like to also wear that smart contact lens you brought here?" said Blake. "Along with a few of the hidden weapons it can activate? Just in case."

"That's out," said Vargas, shaking his head vigorously. "For any of us. That contact is the first thing he'll be looking for. "

Blake sighed. "Yeah. I suppose so."

"Okay," said Cargill. "Let's make this happen."

"Just one further point," said Vargas. "Be sure that none of you brace yourselves for the incoming gas when the helo door is about to open. You can't give away that you know it's coming. Knight will be watching."

Cargill nodded. "The president is busy at Camp David, but later tonight I'll brief him on this. Thank you, Hank. This is coming together beautifully."

"Glad we ended up on the same side," said the colonel.

Cargill nodded. "Me too."

After a pause, Cargill turned to Allen and Blake. "Since we'll all be out cold, I'd like to recommend to the president that Tom TenBrink command the operation to capture Knight, with Joe O'Bannon his second-in-command. What do you think?"

"I think those are excellent choices," replied Allen.

"I agree," said Blake.

"Hank?" asked Cargill.

"Weren't these the two men who tampered with my quarters so you could abduct me?"

"They're very versatile," replied Cargill with a smile.

Vargas laughed. "Apparently so," he said. "Other than this fine work, I'm not familiar enough with them to weigh in. But I trust your judgment."

"Good," said the head of Q5, "then it's settled. "I'll ask them to join us."

Within five minutes, both had arrived in the conference room, and Vargas repeated the briefing a second time. When TenBrink and O'Bannon were up to speed and the discussion had died out, Cargill declared this part of the meeting over.

"But before we disband," he added, "there is one more thing I'd like to share. Something Aaron and I have been keeping to ourselves for some time now. You've all heard the news about the attempted assassination of Kim Jong-un. How his palace was destroyed, and how he happened to be outside of it at the time."

Everyone in the room nodded.

"Well, there's more to this than meets the eye. Much more. So let me tell you what really happened in North Korea. And the real reason the president is at Camp David right now, along with three of our people."

60

Loading six unconscious bodies into the back of a pickup was a more strenuous endeavor than Vargas had anticipated, but he finally managed it. Knight had chosen his landing site well, and there was no one around to observe the colonel loading his disturbing cargo, like a psychopathic mass murderer on a weekend bender.

So far, all had gone according to plan. Knight had taken control of the helo very soon after it was out of sight of the base, and locked the doors in place. Even so, the pilots had launched into a frenzy of activity, going to great lengths to repel the remote hijacking. When this proved impossible, they came up with a daring plan to shape a charge to blow a door off the helo so all could escape using parachutes.

Vargas had been tempted to come clean, to tell the pilots that they *wanted* to be hijacked, but Cargill wouldn't allow it. They should have known that Air Force pilots who had flown in hotbeds around the world wouldn't take something like this lying down. Not until Vargas was finally forced to order them to do just this, much to their disgust.

Superior officers often seemed like incompetent buffoons to those below them. Sometimes this was because they *were* incompetent buffoons. But other times it was because they were privy to the bigger picture, and their underlings were not.

Vargas drove the pickup truck to the tunnel Knight had specified, and entered. Traffic was light, and he was able to pull into the back of the semi without anyone observing. A few cars entered before the semi began moving again, and honked their displeasure at having to suddenly switch lanes to avoid hitting a stationary eighteen-wheeler, inexplicably deciding to park on a road with no shoulder.

Before Vargas knew it, the trailer stopped in an abandoned parking lot, and he peeled open the door and took over driving duties.

The moment he started up the truck, he got a call from Edgar Knight, who no doubt had cameras inside the cab as well as the trailer.

Knight's voice was ecstatic. "That went off just as I drew it up," he said. "You did it, Hank! You wormed your way into Q5 and pulled these bastards back out."

"Just remember my contributions," said Vargas. "And how instrumental this is to your plans. I've held up my end of the bargain . . . " he added, leaving the sentence hanging.

"And I'll hold up mine," said Knight on cue. "Have no fear, after this success, you're more valuable to me as a second than ever."

"Good," said Vargas. "So where am I going?"

"I'm inside the main farmhouse on the Chester Moreland Pivot Farm in Nebraska," said Knight, "which I recently acquired. You know how much I love farming," he added wryly.

"What the hell is a *pivot farm?*" asked Vargas.

"Has something to do with how the irrigation is done, I think," said Vargas. "The important thing is that I've sent the driving directions to your phone. Like I said before, you should be here in three or four hours. I'll be waiting."

"Roger that," said the colonel, ending the connection.

Vargas drove in silence for ten minutes before stopping at a gas station to use the facilities. He entered the bathroom, well away from any prying eyes and ears Knight might have inside the cab, and removed a second cellphone from his pocket.

He dialed a number that allowed him to communicate with Joe O'Bannon and Tom TenBrink, whom Janney had put in command as Cargill had recommended.

"Thought you might be calling in," said TenBrink when Vargas announced himself. "We've been watching you from the sky. Just to be sure we have the right semi, can you confirm that you just stopped at a Shell gas station on Elk Mountain Road."

"That's right," said Vargas. "And I have Knight's location," he added triumphantly. "He's inside the main farmhouse at the Chester Moreland Pivot Farm in Nebraska."

Vargas paused to text them the address. "I'm three hours and twenty minutes out. When do you think you'll be able to commence a strike?"

"We can mobilize our forces there fairly quickly," replied TenBrink. "After that, timing will depend on the situation on the ground." He paused. "That being said," he added, "we'll be shooting for two hours from now."

"Understood," said Vargas.

"Enjoy your drive, Colonel," said TenBrink. "The second we have him, we'll alert you and send a helo to your position. By the time you and your sleeping cargo make it back to Cheyenne Mountain, Knight will be wrapped up with a bow."

"Roger that," said Vargas. "Happy hunting."

61

Blake was as charged up as he had ever been. As if dodging a death sentence in North Korea hadn't been exhilarating enough, the past few days had been as exciting, as consequential, as any he had ever experienced.

Spending his days and nights nestled inside the presidential retreat wasn't too bad, either.

FDR had established the mountain retreat in 1942, situated on two hundred wooded acres of scenic land, sixty-two miles from Washington DC. Since this time, Camp David had been designated for the sole use of whichever president was in power, much like the White House. Originally named Shangri-La, Eisenhower had changed it to Camp David to honor his father. Regardless, since it was technically a military installation, its official name was the Naval Support Facility Thurmont, and it was staffed and guarded by a combination of Naval, Marine, and Secret Service personnel.

While Blake had been given the full run of the retreat by the president, he had spent much of his time inside a labyrinthian series of offices and meeting rooms underground, which had never been disclosed to the public.

But *where* he was staying was much less mind-blowing than *who* he was staying with.

Along with Eric Beal and Chris Entwistle, who were in charge of interrogating the North Korean leader, the only people other than Blake allowed in the bowels of the retreat—the only people to know that Kim Jong-un was imprisoned there—were the president, his Secretary of Defense, Kate Johnson, and the Chairman of the Joint Chiefs of Staff, General Gary Herman.

Heady company, indeed. And Johnson and Herman had no idea a kettle was now also housed under Camp David, nor that there was more than one Kim Jong-un being interrogated there.

Blake and the president had hit it off famously, and he had spent many hours with the man, both during meals and in working sessions with Secretary Johnson and General Herman. Janney had introduced Blake simply as the man behind Kim's capture, but had made it clear Blake was under orders not to divulge anything else about his mission or team, even to them.

The progress of the interrogation had been stunning, especially during the past few days. Cargill had sent a supply of T-4 along with the kettle, but their first attempt to use it had killed Kim within seconds. Even so, Blake had realized they were in a unique position to experiment with its dosing.

Without access to a kettle, experimentation was impossible. If the first dose killed a subject, there could be no testing of a different dose. But the ability to make endless duplicates of a subject made it possible to search for a dose that wasn't too potent, killing the subject, or too weak, rendering the serum useless. One that was just right: the Goldilocks dose.

While Blake took responsibility for this testing, Entwistle and Beal interrogated multiple Kims using other methods. If one Kim gave up information, they would go after the same information with another Kim from a different angle. If the information was bogus, the other Kim would often tell a different lie. Only if three Kims independently provided the same intel would they become convinced it was true. All intel was checked in the field, whenever possible, using all available resources, including the re-tasking of satellites to take hard looks at coordinates where Kim indicated missile launchers were hidden.

Then, even better news broke out. After two days, and twenty-six dead Kim Jong-uns, Blake succeeded in his quest. It turned out that there was no single dose of T-4 that would work. The first six doses Blake had tried all killed the Korean tyrant. When Blake finally found a dilution just under the threshold of lethality, it was completely ineffective.

Only when Blake had gotten more creative did the breakthrough occur. After considerable further experimentation, he discovered that if the highest non-lethal dose was administered once an hour over a four-hour period, Kim's tongue would finally become unstuck, and he would spill his guts for two to three hours before finally dying. At this point, another Kim would already be in the process of being dosed, and would soon get his two or three hours on stage.

Because of this success, they were able to obtain intel from the North Korean leader that was more comprehensive than they had dared to hope was possible. Whatever else one might say about the man, Blake found his knowledge of his own weapons and their positioning to be encyclopedic. Since everything that could be checked out, did check out, Secretary Johnson and General Herman developed great confidence in the information, even without knowing exactly how it had been wrung from Kim Jong-un.

Meanwhile, the situation in North Korea was deteriorating by the hour. The country was in utter turmoil, and intel reports from the region couldn't begin to keep up, no matter how rapidly they were updated. The Kim in power, whom Johnson and Herman had been told was an impostor, was livid about the loss of his favorite palace and the attempt on his life, and was shaking things up, just as Cargill had predicted.

No head was safe from the chopping block. Kim had already had hundreds of men and women in his government put to death, and no one knew who might be next. Blake wondered what would happen first. Would Kim drop dead from the poison in his veins, which was due to happen any time? Or, given the immense fear and desperation his purge was creating in his followers, would he be assassinated before this occurred?

While it appeared as if North Korea would tear itself up without any further outside intervention, Janney was relishing the chance to help this collapse along and relieve the country of its ability to unleash weapons of mass destruction. Now that the multi-pronged strike on North Korea was imminent, the president had been in one planning session after another with his Secretary of Defense and Chairman of the Joint Chiefs. They had tied in generals, admirals, and intelligence personnel via secure videoconferencing to plan the attack, which would include missile strikes, fighter-jet sorties, and the deployment of hundreds of teams of special forces commandos on the ground.

And Blake had a front-row seat to it all.

Not only that, but a front-row seat to the mission to capture Knight, which was also underway. The president had just received a report that Knight's location was now known, and Tom TenBrink was marshaling forces to end the threat that he posed, as well. This time, not only killing Knight, but making sure that he *stayed* dead.

Kim Jong-un's regime and Edgar Knight would both be taken down within days of each other, possibly *hours*. To a soldier like Blake, there was no satisfaction greater than taking part in a historic mission to subdue America's greatest enemies. And here he was, witness to two missions that were each even more historic, more consequential, than the mission that had taken out Osama Bin Laden.

For a man like Blake, this was a hundred Super Bowl Sundays tied into one.

62

Captain Tom TenBrink had considerable experience on special forces missions, and had even commanded several, but nothing of the scope and importance of this mission. His Inner Circle colleague, Joe O'Bannon, had also been in the special forces, achieving the rank of lieutenant before being handpicked to join Q5.

But this mission was well beyond the scope of anything either man had ever done, or even been part of. It blended together eight special forces teams into one massive team, ready for anything.

Well, almost anything. With time travel thrown into the mix, possibilities emerged that none on these teams had encountered, or even imagined.

TenBrink stood next to O'Bannon and a special forces major, Joe Lazear, in an open field four miles beyond the outer boundary of the Chester Moreland Pivot Farm, on a site they had chosen from satellite footage to become their staging area. Several men were now stationed around the perimeter of the field to ensure no one would stumble on them, a veritable special forces army preparing for battle on an empty tract of wilderness in the heart of Nebraska.

Major Lazear had considerable experience directing multidisciplinary teams and, by rights, should have been in command. He wasn't simply because he didn't have knowledge of either Edgar Knight or time travel. If duplication or teleportation reared their ugly heads, only TenBrink and O'Bannon would know what was happening.

TenBrink studied the satellite feed on his tablet computer yet again. Nothing had changed. The video continued to show nine mercenaries, armed with assault rifles, patrolling the perimeter of the main house, leaving no doubt that Knight was inside. The satellite imagery was much more impressive than any available to civilians, with respect to both sharpness and magnification. The video footage could well have been shot from an overhanging tree, for all anyone could tell.

"We now have four F-22 Raptors in the air," said Joe Lazear. "They're flying in formation as if on a training mission. In addition, six Apache helicopters are now airborne. Any or all of these aircraft can reach Knight within minutes. Before we proceed, though, I recommend we do further recon with a few drones. The satellite imagery is excellent, but it can't get the angle to peer through windows. The drones can, from as far as a mile out. This will give us a better read on what's going on inside."

TenBrink considered. "We can't take that risk," he said. "Knight has no idea we know where he is. We need to keep it that way."

"Understood," said Major Lazear. "But there's no way he'll spot the drones. No sensors can detect their presence from a mile out."

"You don't know Edgar Knight," said TenBrink. "He has access to some very advanced tech. Just because *we* can't do something doesn't mean *he* can't. We need to err on the side of paranoia."

"Can I ask who this guy is?" said Lazear. "And what this is all about? I was contacted by President Janney himself on this. Directly. So I know the priority of this mission is off the charts high."

"What did the president tell you?" asked O'Bannon.

"Just that I was to follow Captain TenBrink's and your orders to the letter. Without hesitation. That a man named Edgar Knight was the target, and needed to be taken alive, at all costs. That I was authorized to draw on unlimited military resources and to use any weapon in our arsenal, including missiles, if need be. Even on American soil. And that I could never tell anyone about this mission."

TenBrink winced. "Yeah, sorry about keeping you in the dark, but I really can't add anything to what you've been told. But back to the task at hand, I won't risk trying to get a look inside the farmhouse. So, based solely on what we're seeing *outside*, Major, what are your recommendations?"

Lazear paused in thought. "I can get a dozen snipers in range of the guards within twenty minutes," he said. "We should be able to take them all out simultaneously. Then we can move in and show

Knight the full extent of what he's up against. Order him to basically come out with his hands raised."

"We can't do that either," said TenBrink. "It could backfire."

"Normally, I'd agree," said the major. "A cornered rat could come out firing rather than surrender. But our force will be overwhelming. Staggering. And he doesn't have any innocents to use as human shields. Imagine staring out a window at an Apache helicopter at point-blank range, with its massive machine gun pointed right at you. Not to mention multiple Hellfire missiles with thermobaric warheads. Now multiply this by six. Then add in four Raptors in formation roaring across your field of view for good measure."

Lazear paused to let this imagery sink in. "Trust me, no man can face even a single Apache helicopter at short range without being intimidated. And by *intimidated*, I mean without soiling his pants. I don't care what tech Knight has, he won't stand a chance. He'll know that."

TenBrink sighed. This was true, as long as Knight wasn't able to materialize grenades inside the helos when they were fifty-eight feet away. "Sorry, Major," he said. "I know it's hard to plan an Op when you haven't been fully briefed. But this man could be more formidable than anything you've ever come up against. So we need to take him off the field first—then take out the men guarding the house."

"How would you propose we do that?" asked the major.

"Since we can't kill him," said TenBrink, "we need to knock him out."

O'Bannon nodded. "We could hit the inside of that farmhouse with enough gas to knock out a herd of elephants. But we'd need to do it quickly, before Knight could prepare—or retaliate."

Lazear considered. "We have missiles that we can fire from drones, with a range of five miles. Missiles that are tiny, but also very fast, and very accurate. We could fire enough of these missiles to deliver a gas-canister payload through every window in the farmhouse, upstairs and down. He would have little warning, if any at all. If he did spot them streaking in across his farm, he'd think they were armed with explosives, so he wouldn't be diving for a gas mask."

"You have a gas in mind that won't kill him, no matter how much he inhales?" asked O'Bannon.

"Yes."

"Perfect," said TenBrink. "Let's do it."

Lazear made a call to set things in motion. Several minutes later he paused his conversation and turned to his temporary commander. "We can commence the attack in an hour," he said. "Is this acceptable?"

TenBrink swiped his tablet to check on Vargas's progress, bringing up another screen. Satellites showed the truck was now only ninety-five miles away. "Make it forty-five minutes," he said to the major. An hour should still give them plenty of cushion, but TenBrink wanted to capture Knight before Vargas and his Q5 cargo got anywhere near him.

"Roger that," said Lazear. He spoke for another minute into the phone and then ended the connection. "Forty-five minutes will be tight," he reported, "but they'll do their best."

"Now that this is being readied," said O'Bannon, "we need to plan out the rest. Assuming we knock out Knight and whoever else is inside that farmhouse, we'll still need to go in and get him. Which means taking out the nine men outside. And they'll be diving for cover the moment the missiles hit, so snipers won't work."

"What about moving in from the ground?" said TenBrink.

Lazear shook his head. "This farm is mostly open space." He consulted his tablet once again. "We'd have little cover on any approach," he continued. "A few silos, some large tractors, a storage shed, and a few large mounds of what Google tells me are harvested Sugar Beets."

"Lack of cover isn't our only problem," said O'Bannon. "Who knows what landmines Knight has in store for us? Including actual, literal, landmines." He turned to the major. "I say we use the intimidation strategy you wanted to use on Knight. Give his men a close encounter with a half-dozen angry Apaches and see if they don't want to surrender."

"Agreed," said TenBrink.

"Good," said Joe Lazear. "Looks like we have a plan."

"Almost," said TenBrink wearily, imagining Knight or one of his mercs inside a kettle, able to send in unlimited reinforcements. "We have to alert everyone involved that if they see two or more hostiles suddenly seem to appear from out of nowhere, who look identical, they need to sound an alarm. If this happens, we'll need to call an immediate retreat and hit that farmhouse with everything we have."

"Two or more hostiles who look identical?" repeated Lazear in disbelief. "Who appear out of nowhere? Are you serious?"

"Just make this clear to our forces!" snapped TenBrink. "No matter how crazy it sounds. Just make sure if this happens we reduce that farmhouse to ash."

"Roger that," said the major, declining to question the order further. "I'm sure you're aware that if it comes to this, we'll have failed to take Knight alive."

"Let's hope it doesn't come to this, then," said TenBrink. "But we have to be—"

He stopped in mid-sentence. A screaming whistling noise was growing in pitch and intensity with shocking speed, causing his breath to catch in his throat and his heart to accelerate, even before he fully comprehended what he was hearing. The sound created a visceral dread that he had never felt outside of his worst nightmares.

Suddenly, TenBrink realized what it was. He had never heard a low-altitude missile streak through the sky above him at almost a thousand miles per hour, but he knew instinctively that this is what he was hearing now.

He glanced at his tablet computer just in time to see multiple missiles converge on the farmhouse. Not small missiles with gas warheads, but full-scale missiles used in war zones. The farmhouse erupted into a towering fireball, and the mercs patrolling outside burst into flame and then disintegrated an instant later as the heat spread. At the same time this scene was playing on his tablet, TenBrink could see and hear the aftermath of the strike himself, even four miles away from it.

"*What the hell happened?*" he screamed. "Who fired on that farmhouse?"

"It wasn't us!" shouted Lazear a few seconds later, listening to his comm and consulting his tablet. "All of our birds still have their full missile compliments."

"Who could it be, then?" demanded TenBrink. "And how did they—"

"*Incoming!*" interrupted Lazear, shrieking this warning to everyone in the large clearing. "One missile, tracking this way! Run!" he added, taking his own advice.

Everyone began sprinting to safety, but the warning had come too late. The missile struck on the northernmost border of the staging area, where most of the special forces soldiers were congregated. The explosion and fire wiped out a dozen of them and wounded and disfigured a dozen more, turning the tranquil clearing into a raging hell.

O'Bannon, TenBrink, and Lazear had been lucky enough to be on the southernmost border of the clearing, and escaped with only hearing loss and the equivalent of severe sunburns from the heat.

"No other missiles detected!" shouted Lazear. "We're working to learn their origin and how they slipped past our defenses. Medical personnel are being flown here now."

TenBrink heard these shouted words, but only just, as his ears wouldn't stop ringing.

How had this happened? Who could be responsible? It had to have been someone who wanted Knight dead, and who had also known about their Op, as evidenced by the last missile to fall.

If there was a new player in the game, TenBrink needed to figure out who this might be. And he needed to figure it out in a hurry.

63

Hank Vargas noted the incoming call from Tom TenBrink with satisfaction. This could only be good news. TenBrink knew the cab was bugged, and would never call unless he had Knight tied up like a rodeo steer.

"Vargas here," he answered cheerfully.

"Knight is dead!" shouted TenBrink, just short of hysterical. The sound of incoming helicopters and total pandemonium could be heard in the background. "Someone took out the farmhouse with multiple missiles. They also sent one to hit us at the staging area."

Vargas's eyes widened. *What the hell!* He struggled for breath, as if he had just been sucker punched in the gut.

He needed to pull over and find out how this had happened.

A sniper round streaked in from a bluff overlooking the road, punching two holes the size of nickels in the cab's side windows, the second a foot in front of Vargas's head. If he hadn't just hit the brakes to begin pulling over, the second hole would have been drilled through his ears.

Vargas ducked down as two more bullets whistled through the cab, one missing, and one grazing his shoulder. A moment later the large tire on the passenger's side of the cab erupted into rubber shrapnel, creating a heart-stopping explosion of sound, and Vargas slammed on the brakes, wrestling the lilting and unstable vehicle to a stop, the trailer fishtailing across three lanes.

"I'm under fire!" he yelled at a phone that was no longer in his hand. Not waiting for a response, he opened the door and launched himself to the road, keeping the trailer between himself and the shooter.

More shots rang out, this time from the opposite direction. While several penetrated the trailer, none came close to his position. Vargas spotted three shooters emerging from a sparse woods on the side he was on, too distant to achieve accuracy but closing fast, each face hidden by a black ski mask.

He was unarmed and surrounded, so running was out of the question.

Unfortunately, surrender didn't appear to be an option, either.

Vargas rushed to the back of the trailer and threw open the door as a shot grazed his thigh, drawing more blood. He climbed inside and retrieved a gun from the sleeping Aaron Blake, and then jumped back to the pavement again, firing at the approaching trio.

He managed to hit one of the hostiles in the arm before a bullet from another finally penetrated his right shoulder, making further shooting impossible.

In Vargas's last moments of consciousness, he realized he wasn't upset that he would die here. The poison capsule in his head was scheduled to kill him soon enough, anyway. He was upset that the Op had failed, and that he would now never get to see the look on Knight's face when he realized Vargas had betrayed him.

But this thought was fleeting as bullet after bullet found its mark, and he was jerked about like a puppet having a seizure before falling dead to the pavement, gushing blood from at least six gaping wounds.

Seconds later the three shooters were joined by the initial sniper, who had traveled there from his position on the opposite bluff. He nodded at them and they quickly retreated back to the trees, concentrating on getting away from the scene now that their work was completed.

The sniper wasted no time climbing into the trailer and surveying the six bodies lying prone in the pickup's long bed. Then, satisfied that they were all accounted for, he produced an automatic weapon, pointed it at the helpless sleepers, and depressed the trigger.

64

Aaron Blake's phone rang and he fished it out of his pocket with great interest. Only a handful of people in the world had this number, and he was currently with most of them at Camp David.

When he saw that it was Tom TenBrink on the line, he allowed his spirits to soar in celebration. They must have captured Knight. They were halfway home.

Still, TenBrink shouldn't be calling him. He had been ignoring Blake as he should, reporting directly to the president.

Cargill had informed the senior management team and Inner Circle that a second Blake was alive, and had described Blake's exploits in China, North Korea, and now Camp David. But this second Blake had insisted Cargill include a prohibition against anyone from Q5 reaching out to him. He had known that choosing to survive the mission in North Korea had come at a cost. Maintaining relationships with members of the team wouldn't be fair to either of the Blakes. The Blake still at Cheyenne Mountain deserved to be the one and only, keeping sole possession of his identity and his relationships. And the second Blake, forced to take on a new identity and new life, would be better served with a clean break from those who seemed like family to him.

Only Cargill would stay in touch, and then only to help him resettle and feed him missions from time to time.

Clearly, TenBrink hadn't been able to help himself. He knew full well how important the capture of Knight would be to the Blake at Camp David, and didn't want him to hear about it secondhand from the president.

It was hard to be upset with Tom TenBrink when his motives were so good. Still, Blake would have to remind him that he found it too painful to have emotional connections to his old life, and they needed to sever all ties for the sake of his mental health. "You shouldn't be calling me, Tom," he said as he answered the call. "No matter how good the news."

"The news *isn't* good!" said TenBrink emphatically, his voice reflecting considerable trauma. "The Op was a cluster fuck! The farmhouse Knight was in was annihilated! He's dead, Aaron! A flea couldn't have survived. The team we had ready to go in suffered numerous casualties."

TenBrink paused, as if unable to bring himself to continue. "And *they're* dead, too," he finally whispered in horror. "All of them."

"Slow down, Tom. What happened? *Who's* dead?"

"Cargill and the entire team."

Blake's throat constricted. "No!" he pleaded. "That can't be true! It's impossible. The president just told me they were unconscious in the back of a pickup, and weren't anywhere near Knight's farm."

"That's true. But they were killed inside the pickup. Minutes after Knight and the farmhouse went up in flames. By multiple gunmen. We have footage from satellites and several motorists. I'll send it to you. Three gunmen murdered Vargas, and a fourth opened fire on the rest while they were still out cold. I've sent men to the site to get human eyes on the scene and to verify that they're dead. But the footage leaves no doubt."

The room whipped around Blake's head, and he struggled to retain his balance.

He couldn't bring himself to believe it. This was supposed to be the team's finest hour. The country's finest hour. How could this have happened? "Who did this?" he mumbled, almost too dazed to speak.

"It was coordinated, so whoever killed Knight also killed our people. The gunmen were all wearing black ski masks. At this moment, we have no idea. But we need you back at Cheyenne Mountain immediately!"

"What?" said Blake stupidly, still reeling.

"Lee told us not to contact you. But he also said that if our Blake was killed, he'd call you in to resume your identity and take your twin's place on the team. Well, our Blake is *dead*, Aaron! So we need you back. And since Cargill and Allen are dead also, guess what, you're the highest-ranking surviving member of senior management. Which makes you the new head of Q5."

"No," mumbled Blake. "I won't do it. What's the point? How can I come back to Q5 knowing that the rest of the team is gone?"

"Snap out of it, Aaron!" shouted TenBrink. "I'm supposed to be the one who is shell-shocked here. You'll forge another team. Rebuild. Lee says he gave all members of the senior management team elaborate instructions on how to retrieve his password, in case he was killed. The password that will give the bearer a full set of keys to the kingdom, full access to the technology. But retrieval has to be done on-site, and requires the passing of a battery of biometric tests."

When Blake didn't respond immediately, TenBrink's intensity increased even more. "Come on, Aaron!" he thundered. "We can't let Knight win! You have to rebuild Q5!"

"But Knight *didn't* win," noted Blake, his mind finally beginning to peek through the fog. "He's dead, too. I'm not sure who won here, but it wasn't Knight, and it wasn't us."

"Are you coming back?"

Blake nodded woodenly. "Yes. I'll take a helo to the fastest military jet in the area. I'll be with you in a few hours. In the meantime, send everything you have on the mission and what happened. Satellite footage, reports from the ground, all communications, and so on. Everything. And I want us to be in communication while I'm flying. We need to learn who's behind this. Immediately."

"I couldn't agree more," said TenBrink, visibly relieved. "And *thank you*. I'll begin sending footage and reports your way now," he added, signing off, leaving Blake to suffer in silence.

Blake had lost friends before on the battlefield. But nothing had ever hit him as hard as this. This loss was *devastating*. He had witnessed carnage so horrific it would make a surgeon or butcher puke, and hadn't once felt even a hint of nausea. But he found the thought of losing his Q5 colleagues so powerful that he was now fighting back vomit.

He loved this team. All had good souls. Lee Cargill was a brilliant manager of people and a master strategist. Nathan Wexler was a *god*, the Einstein of his generation. His loss was incalculable.

And yet Blake's mind kept returning to Jenna Morrison. Only when he thought of *her* lying dead in the back of a pickup truck did his stomach threaten to release its contents onto the floor.

Had he been in *love* with her?

It hardly seemed possible. And yet, his reaction to her death left no doubt.

He *had* been. He just hadn't let himself realize how he felt until now. He had suppressed his true feelings because there was no point. She had been engaged to a man he admired, who treated her the way she deserved, whom she had met long before Blake had come into the picture.

As he realized how he had really felt about this extraordinary woman, the emotional floodgates crashed open even wider, making the pain he was feeling almost unbearable.

Without warning, tears began to slide down his cheeks, a wholly unfamiliar sensation.

It was the first time Blake had been forced to tears since he was a young boy.

PART 7

Duplicity (Noun)

- Deceitfulness in speech or conduct; double-dealing. Synonyms: deceit, deception, fraud, guile, trickery.

- The state or quality of having two elements or parts; being twofold or double.

  —Dictionary.com

65

Cargill's eyes shot open and he gasped, as though a shot of pure adrenaline had been injected into him.

He saw a syringe moving away from his arm. Perhaps it had been.

His eyes drifted upward to take in the scene, and Edgar Knight's face swam into view. Cargill threw out his hands to seize the man's neck and choke him to death, which almost pulled his arms from their sockets as they refused to carry out his commands. His wrists and arms were locked in place, tied to the side of his chair with zip ties, and the chair had been firmly affixed to the floor.

Standard Knight arrangements.

"Glad you're with us," said Knight. "I revived you last, so I could begin the moment you were conscious."

To his left, affixed to another chair, was Hank Vargas, and on the far wall, the rest of the management team, not only bound like he and Vargas had been, but gagged with duct tape. All were conscious, except for Blake, who Cargill's eyes settled upon, trying to confirm that his chest was still rising and falling.

"Don't worry," said Knight, as if reading his mind, "he's still alive. I just chose not to revive him."

"Why not?" asked Cargill.

"The things his duplicate managed to accomplish at Lake Las Vegas shouldn't have been possible. So I studied his past. Turns out he's accomplished a number of miraculous feats in his career. But it's a lot harder to create miracles when you're unconscious. Security is being upgraded at this site even as we speak. When it's finished, I'll wake him. Even then, I'll make sure he's so immobilized he can't even twitch."

"And the duct tape?" asked Cargill.

"We don't want any interruptions. It's better to keep this initial reunion cozy and intimate, don't you think? I revived Hank just a few seconds before you."

Cargill took in his surroundings. To all appearances he was in a great room in a mansion, a room that flowed from the family room, which they were now in, to the kitchen, without interruption. The ceilings of both rooms soared eighteen feet high. The floor was a beautiful white marble with veins of gray, matching a marble-topped island in the kitchen that was so expansive it was the size of an actual island. He was facing a twenty-foot long sliding glass door that could be hidden within the wall on either side, creating a wide indoor/outdoor opening looking out at nearby mountains.

"Where are we?" demanded Cargill.

"You don't sound happy to see me," said Knight, pretending to be hurt. "And after all the trouble I've taken to reunite you with your trusted friend and colleague."

"You *were* trusted," said Cargill evenly. "Right up until you decided to freelance, leaving a string of bodies and moles behind."

"I see you don't forgive easily," said Knight with a grin. "No wonder you never married."

"What is this about, Edgar?" demanded Vargas. "I delivered Q5 as promised. So why am I a prisoner?"

Knight laughed in delight. "Hank, it's so bold of you to pretend you've been wronged, so audacious, I can't help but be impressed. You plan to fuck me over, and then, when you awaken in an unknown situation with me on top, you pretend that this is how you intended it all along. Even though you don't have the first clue as to how you got here. That takes balls, even for you."

"What are you talking about?" said Vargas.

"All will be revealed in due course," said Knight. "I'm enjoying this too much to rush it. Like old times, isn't it? Me, my boss, and my boss's boss." He glared at Cargill. "Although I'm mostly interested in you, Lee."

"I'm flattered," said Cargill. "And good for you," he added, making a show of pulling at his restraints. "You've finally figured out a way to get me to listen to your demented crap."

"Are you really going to complain about a few restraints?" said Knight in amusement. "You should be thanking me. Look around," he added, gesturing to the twenty-foot-long disappearing sliding glass door. "This isn't bad, as far as prisons go. A room and a view fit for a king. I was a prisoner here myself for a while."

Cargill didn't respond, but looked decidedly skeptical.

"But don't let the view fool you," continued Knight. "You're here to receive some serious payback. I have to hand it to you, Lee. You outsmarted me at Lake Las Vegas. You and your Bonnie-and-Clyde duo over there," he added, gesturing toward Aaron Blake and Jenna Morrison immobilized against the wall. "Apparently, even the dullest among us can have a lucky inspiration that can best the smartest among us."

Knight turned to Vargas and shook his head. "And yes," he added, "they did kill a version of me at Lake Las Vegas. I was a duplicate, being stored in this very residence, under house arrest. I couldn't even venture to the other buildings in this complex. I lied to you when I said their attack had failed, Hank. It didn't. Which is why I'm so pissed off. As if it isn't galling enough to be outsmarted by a talentless hack like Lee, he almost won. For good. If I hadn't had the foresight to keep a duplicate off-site, he would have."

"Now who doesn't forgive easily?" said Cargill. "Good thing you aren't married. Not that you wouldn't eat your wife and children before too long, anyway."

"Is that the wittiest response you've got?" said Knight. "I was hoping you'd be more entertaining. But no matter, you'll provide entertainment, one way or another. I have a lot planned for you and your Lake Las Vegas accomplices. First I'm going to torture you. Then I'm going to kill you."

He studied the colonel. "By rights I should be giving *you* the same treatment, Hank. But since you failed so miserably, and allowed me to get the upper hand, I'll give you a clean death."

Knight rose from his chair and surveyed the prisoners against the back wall. "And while I may keep the rest of you around for a few months, at some point I'm going to have to kill everyone but Nathan Wexler. I'd prefer to keep some of you on indefinitely, but I can't take the chance that you'd eventually find a way to escape. You all have knowledge that could make my life more difficult. Dr. Wexler, of course, is priceless. Irreplaceable. So he's safe."

Knight removed a gun and walked over to the wall of hostages. "But this is too big of a crowd to manage," he said. "And I want to send a message about the importance of being cooperative."

Without warning Knight depressed the trigger four times, putting two rounds each into the helpless seated figures of Joe Allen and Daniel Tini, who both died instantly. Blake was in between these two men, but he was unconscious, blissfully unaware of this heinous act. Jenna and Wexler both shouted in horror, but their screams were almost entirely muffled by the tape over their mouths.

"You think that's going to help you earn respect?" barked Cargill. "You think you're softening us up?"

"Yes," said Knight simply, returning to his seat and ignoring the dead bodies and shocked prisoners now behind him. "I can make threats all day long, but until I demonstrate I'm not squeamish about carrying them out, they're toothless. This will ensure I get maximum cooperation going forward."

"This will do the *opposite*," said Cargill. "Maybe you're the *dumb* one in your family," he added, knowing that no insult would sting Knight more. "We already know to take your threats seriously. You think this savage act will intimidate us? Make us more pliable? It will only *strengthen* our resolve to resist you. This is just a barbaric reminder of your true colors. That while you pretend to be rational and claim that you only want the best for humanity, you're just as ruthless as all the Hitlers and Stalins before you."

"I have my reasons for everything I do," said Knight defiantly. "Even when I take revenge on you, I'll be sure to have my top mercs involved, so they get to witness the penalty for crossing me."

"So the crazed butcher thing is just an act?" said Cargill in disdain. "You're just playing a calculated game of chess, and not getting any sick enjoyment from your sadism? No one is buying it, Edgar. You don't torture people unless you *like* it."

"I know it looks that way at a micro level," said Knight. "But if you could see the big picture, put my actions into context, you'd understand. Just like I'm sure you can put your own actions at Lake Las Vegas into context. I just killed two people to serve the bigger picture. How many thousands did you kill, Lee?"

Cargill was struggling to remain calm, but this was a shot to his metaphorical balls, and his upper lip curled into a snarl. "Rationalize all you want," he spat. "But our actions couldn't be more different. I'm a starving man who hunts for food. You're a well-fed man who hunts for *pleasure*."

Knight shook his head in disgust. "I've forgotten just how self-righteous you can be. A neat trick coming from a mass murderer."

"And I've forgotten just how self-delusional you can be!" spat Cargill.

Knight sighed. "I know I'm wasting my breath," he said. "And I know we've been down this path before. But I intend to transform the world in a way that will increase global happiness and prosperity to undreamed of levels. Having a strong leader in control isn't always bad. Were the people of Iraq better off with, or without, Saddam Hussein? Almost everyone would say they were better off *with*. He ruled with an iron fist, but he established order in an unruly part of the world. He left no room for religious zealots bent on terrorism and dedicated to the death of all non-believers. How many times has America made the mistake of removing a dictator in the Middle East, only to make things worse?"

"We aren't talking about the Middle East," said Cargill. "And even if we were, you aren't talking about removing dictators in regions that have grown accustomed to them. You're talking about inserting ones in regions that have grown accustomed to freedom."

"Admittedly, this analogy isn't ideal," said Knight. "But I have no plans to be a dictator. In areas where a firm hand is needed, I will supply it. But in most parts of the world, I'll run things with a velvet glove. I'll do everything to foster growth, prosperity, and freedom. Worldwide peace will be a given. All terrorism and fundamentalism will be rooted out and destroyed. No taxation will be necessary, because of the riches time travel will bring. I'll reduce regulations, so entrepreneurs aren't buried under red tape. I'll institute a system of justice across the globe that will be tough but fair, based on our own concept of *innocent until proven guilty*."

As usual, Cargill couldn't help but find Knight's vision of paradise appealing. If one didn't focus on the millions who would have to die to achieve it, and if one believed he could be trusted to be the benevolent ruler he described. But even if his vision could be accomplished without bloodshed, and even if Knight ruled like a saint, Cargill was against it.

Freedom was messy. Humans were messy. No one man should have this kind of power, not even a saint. And Knight was the opposite of this. He was a butcher sure to let the power go to his head, sure to become a tyrant bent on imposing his twisted will on the world no matter what the cost in human lives.

"Most importantly," continued Knight, "I'll rid the world of those at the lower end of the intelligence spectrum. Enrich it with duplicates of mankind's greatest geniuses. Plato reasoned that only a philosopher could make a just ruler. A man not dedicated to greed and power and possessions, but a man with a great intellect, dedicated to the never-ending pursuit of knowledge, of understanding, and most importantly, wisdom."

"Beautiful words coming from a man who just slaughtered two people in cold blood," said Cargill, "and then moved on without a care. We all know your position, and we've all rejected it. But I see now that you're spouting off this insanity more for your sake than ours. You need to keep deluding yourself that you're the hero of your own story rather than the villain."

"You know," said Knight, "I almost want to keep you alive, just to show you the amazing future I'll bring about. Almost. But it's clear that no matter how compelling my arguments, you'll never see things my way."

"Here's a tip," said Cargill. "If you want someone to subscribe to your vision of utopia, don't gun down two innocent men just for shock value before you start spouting it."

"I don't know, Lee. The two I killed were your closest associates and friends, and it hasn't affected you a bit. I don't sense you mourning their loss in the least. Maybe you're colder than I am."

Cargill shook his head. "If you had only killed Joe, I might have bought it. But you killed Daniel. He's one of only two men who can recreate Wexler's theory. You'd never make the mistake of killing him until you're certain you have what you want."

"Meaning?" said Knight.

"Meaning you've made a copy of each of us," said Cargill. "It's obvious. I'm sure you plan to make an extra copy any time you kill one of us. So you never run out. If you wanted me to believe I had lost my friends forever, you wouldn't have killed Daniel, and you wouldn't have insisted that *all* of us are condemned to death. Because if you're keeping Nathan alive, you're also keeping Jenna alive. You know she's your best means of controlling him."

Knight nodded. "Maybe you aren't quite as stupid as I thought."

"Look, Edgar," said Hank Vargas, "I've tried to stay out of this. Let you and Lee . . . catch up. But it's time you told me what's going on. Where did you get this insane idea that I'm not on your side? The last I knew I was in the back of the semi, in the tunnel. Then I woke up here. Why did you change the plan? And why have you turned on me? I did everything you asked."

"Enough!" shouted Knight, openly showing anger for the first time. "This is annoyingly thick-headed, Hank, even coming from you. I know you and Lee teamed up against me. You turned out to be a huge disappointment. A closet pacifist? Makes me want to puke. You came across as such a pure hawk. It was a brilliant deception, I have to admit. Had me fooled, and that isn't easy. I really did want you as my second. None of that was a lie."

Cargill's mind raced, but try as he might, he couldn't figure out how Knight had known they were working together. The only way was if they were betrayed by Vargas, but he was in the same boat as the rest of them.

"Can't figure it out, Lee?" taunted Knight, as if reading his mind. "Good. You got the better of me in Lake Las Vegas, and now I'm returning the favor. Order is restored. The gifted once again come out ahead of the incompetent."

"Is this gloating the torture you were talking about?" said Cargill. "Because it's very effective. Are you going to tell us how we came to be here, or are you going to bore us to death?"

Knight laughed. "I really do miss you, Lee. I may keep a copy of you alive forever, after all, just to amuse myself. Hank told you about how I knocked him out and performed some very minor surgery on him, right? How I implanted a titanium capsule with some poison inside, which needed to be reset each week?"

"He told me."

"I *know* he told you," replied Knight smugly. "Because I know *everything* he told you. The titanium capsule wasn't the only thing I implanted. While he was out, I took the liberty of putting a listening device in his head also. Whenever he called me, it squirted its data to his phone and on to me, without him knowing. Hope that wasn't too much of an invasion of privacy, Hank."

Vargas and Cargill exchanged horrified glances.

"What's the matter, Lee?" said Knight. "You look ill. I mean, this has gotta hurt, right? And it should. I can't tell you how much it hurt me to hear your exchange with the colonel during his interrogation. It made me queasy. Learning that he was sabotaging weapons programs was so disappointing. And listening while you two became soul mates was utterly sickening."

"If you were listening in," said Cargill, "then you knew we were having your semi tracked when it left the tunnel. How did you elude the trackers?"

"The plan I shared with Hank was accurate up until the time he and the pickup were enclosed in my semi. But after that, not so much. The colonel thought my plan was brilliant, but he didn't know the half of it. I converted the entire trailer into a time machine. Had another semi parked fifty-eight feet away, just outside the tunnel. I sent all of you and the pickup into the past, into the other eighteen-wheeler, where I had Hank gassed, so you could all get some shut-eye together." He shrugged. "Then I called the other version of Hank Vargas and told him I was on a farm in Nebraska."

There was a long silence in the room as the four still-conscious prisoners worked through the implications of this deception.

"Where are we really?" said Vargas, breaking the spell.

"In Wyoming. At a complex that will become my new headquarters. Like I said, I'm having security enhanced right now. And I'll need to have a large office complex built to go along with the mansion, guesthouses, and warehouses on-site. But it won't be long until this headquarters is every bit the equal of the one I had in Lake Las Vegas."

"So while our people were staking out a farm that you weren't at," said Cargill, "and following the wrong semi, you had us brought here."

"That's right," said Knight proudly. "But there's so much more to it than that. I made it look like I was in the farmhouse. I had nine recently hired mercs patrol outside, just for show. And you're going to love this: I sent in missiles to destroy the farmhouse, and take out some of your strike team, as well."

Cargill whitened. "Why?" he demanded. "You had already won! What was the point? Another demonstration of what a rational, caring ruler you'd make?" he added venomously.

"That's why you don't have any of your soldiers in this room with you now," said Vargas. "You didn't want them to know how callously you set up and killed nine of their colleagues, just because you needed some expendable props."

"This is true," admitted Knight. "Might make them think I'm less than a model employer."

"Where did you get *missiles*?" demanded Vargas.

"I had a lot of goodies stored at warehouses here, for a rainy day. I just need one of something, and I can make all I need. I improved the missile I acquired using Brain Trust innovations."

Cargill looked horrified. "So you've arranged for Janney and everyone else to think you're dead," he said. "They'll stop looking for you. And they'll have no idea who sent the missiles."

"Very good, Lee. That's right. Seems like you just answered your own question about what the point to this was. Not only am I back off the radar, they'll be tilting at windmills trying to figure out what phantom third party is behind this. I've now gotten them off my tail, and ensured they'll begin chasing their own tails."

Knight raised his eyebrows. "And I had some mercenaries take out your duplicates in the semi, too. This makes it look like the phantom third party behind the missiles has it in for both of us. Even better, Lee, because of this massacre, Janney thinks you and your team are dead. So there's no one out there looking for *you*, either. I could parade you through Times Square and no one would pay attention. You and your team will be written off, and Q5 will die. Exactly what I wanted."

Knight seemed to relish the look of absolute horror on his rival's face. "I know you came out on the losing side this time," he said, "but you can't tell me you aren't impressed."

"Yeah, as soon as I get out of here," snapped Cargill, "I'll nominate you for psychopath of the year award."

"We both know you're never leaving."

"And we both know you're never getting Nathan's work," replied Cargill. "I don't care what kind of coercion you try. He and Daniel know how important it is, what you'd be able to do with it. And you've just reminded everyone that your assurances of being a benevolent philosopher king are worthless. That you're more Hitler than Gandhi."

Knight smiled. "You're forgetting something, Lee. Something important."

Cargill searched his mind but had no idea what Knight was getting at.

"Give up?" asked Knight.

"Just tell me, you fucking prick!" said Cargill.

"You seem strangely irritable, Lee. You really need to work on that. Here's what you're missing. The listening device in Hank's head didn't just pick up that you and he were teaming up. I learned something else. I learned about a wonder drug, a truth serum called T-4. It might take me a day or two, but I'm working on a plan to get my hands on a small supply. Thanks for revealing its existence. Between you, Nathan, and Daniel, I'm sure one of you will have the courtesy of not dying after I inject it."

He shrugged. "And if you all do, well . . . that's okay too. Like you so wisely noted, I'll have made more of you."

The room fell silent. Cargill knew Knight was pausing to let him stew, to let him marinate in the full realization of just how badly he had lost.

And he had. Completely. The team was helpless, and no one even knew they were still alive, let alone in a complex in Wyoming.

There was little reason now to believe Knight wouldn't accomplish all of his sick goals. What could stop him? He had beaten Cargill and Q5 when he was crippled. Just how formidable would he become with a few years to build his resources? And especially with the ability to teleport over a hundred miles?

And it was Cargill's fault. He should have realized that Knight would do something like implant a listening device in Vargas's skull. Just because this wasn't possible with any current technology, and Vargas had passed a routine screen for bugs, wasn't a good enough excuse.

He should have known better. By copying the world's best inventors and geniuses and putting them to work, Knight had too many aces up his sleeve. While Cargill was trying to be a Boy Scout, refusing to follow suit, Knight was developing capabilities far surpassing Q5's, at least outside of the realm of time travel. He had managed to take control of a military helicopter, plant a working bug in a man's skull, and upgrade missiles so they could evade US defenses. God only knew what else he could do.

Cargill should have taken greater pains to consider the many advances Knight's Brain Trust might have made. He had been too shortsighted.

And now the entire world would pay for his self-righteousness, and for his failure of imagination.

66

Blake awoke with a start and gasped. Where was he?

A self-satisfied face came into view holding a syringe, which had no doubt been used to blast him out of his gas-induced slumber. A face that he recognized, but couldn't immediately place.

Blake's hands were stretched above his head and zip tied together to a steel ring. His ankles were bound as well. And he no longer felt the reassuring presence of his gun.

He was inside what looked to be a rec room within a mansion, complete with a small bathroom in the corner. A regulation-sized pool table and sectional sofa had been pushed into the opposite corner of the huge room, crammed there to provide as much floor space as possible, and hundred-inch monitors adorned each wall. Three guards stood near the distant door with automatic weapons slung across their chests, while the man who had injected Blake remained only a few feet away.

Nearby, the entire Q5 team was out cold, laid out on the hardwood floor with their wrists bound together with zip ties.

"Hello, Blake," said his nearest captor. "Remember me?"

Blake's eyes narrowed in thought. Without warning, the man launched an iron fist into his unprepared stomach, a painful sucker punch that scored a direct hit on his solar plexus, driving all breath from his lungs. Blake's body reflexively tried to double-over from the blow, but his bonds held firm and prevented this from occurring. He gasped like a fish out of water, and couldn't draw in any air for so long he thought he might black out. Finally, just in the nick of time, his diaphragm recovered and he managed to suck in a breath.

"I asked you a question," said his captor calmly. "Do you remember me?"

Upon hearing his voice a second time, Blake finally placed him. It was Jack Rourk. The man who had once been a trusted member of Q5 before revealing himself to be one of Knight's moles. Blake had tricked him on Palomar Mountain, escaping and wounding the man in the process. "Should I?" replied Blake dismissively, suspecting this answer would get under Rourk's skin.

Rourk drove another fist into his gut. This time Blake was just able to tighten his stomach in time, keeping the air in his lungs, but not preventing an explosion of pain as the blow struck the precise muscle group it had before.

"How about now?" said Rourk.

Blake winced and waited for the intensity of the pain to subside. Perhaps getting under Rourk's skin on purpose wasn't as good an idea as he had thought. "Yeah, I remember you, you piece of shit!" he replied. "I remember the last time we met. You had me at gunpoint then, also. Do you remember how *that* worked out for you?"

"You got lucky, asshole. But your luck has run out. And this time, *you're* going to do the suffering."

"Is that why you revived me early?" said Blake. "To settle a score?"

"No shit, genius."

"If I got so lucky on Palomar Mountain," said Blake, "why do you need to beat on me while I'm hogtied? I'm not asking for a fair fight, but how about at least cutting me loose from this wall? I'll still be wrist and ankle cuffed, and you still have three other armed men in the room."

"You got lucky," said Rourk, "but that doesn't mean you're not good. Why take any chances I don't have to? Besides, I'm not interested in making you comfortable. I'm interested in the opposite."

"Where are we?" said Blake.

"Why should I tell you?"

"Come on, Jack. Don't you want to rub salt in my wound? Explain to me just how screwed I really am?"

Rourk actually smiled. "You do make a good point," he said. "You're in a guesthouse. Guest mansion, really. Almost nine thousand square feet. Within a complex in Wyoming that Knight is turning into his full-fledged headquarters. The last place you or your team will ever see. I guess your plan didn't work out too well, did it? Knight knew all about it. He knew you teamed up with Vargas."

Rourk went on to give a quick summary of what had happened, including how they had been teleported into another truck in the tunnel, the destruction of a decoy farmhouse in Nebraska, and the murders of their duplicates in the original semi.

Blake's breath caught in his throat as he listened. How could he have known Vargas would have a bug inside his head? Especially since no such technology was known to exist.

And yet he *should* have known. It was his job to consider all possibilities, even the most unlikely, and he had failed.

And now everything could be lost. Their lives were the least of it. If Knight finally won this battle with Q5 there would be no check on his power, little to stop him from achieving his warped goals. The world would be at his mercy.

And mercy wasn't one of Knight's strong suits.

Blake gritted his teeth and ratcheted up his resolve. They hadn't lost yet. The odds weren't great, but they weren't zero, either. He had made a last-minute preparation that just might turn the tide. He had borrowed the belt they had taken from Vargas. After the T-4-assisted interrogation, Blake had made it a point to learn about the new weapons the colonel had brought to the table. Vargas had vetoed letting Blake wear a smart contact lens, because Knight could detect it visually, and his sensors could detect its electronic signature.

But the belt didn't need the contact lens for activation. Blake could manually activate it by squeezing both sides of the buckle toward each other, producing a three-hundred-sixty-degree sonic blast that would kill everyone in the room except him. It could only be fired once, but this should be plenty.

Since the sonic weapon, while dormant, didn't give off an electronic signature and couldn't be detected by sensors of any kind, it was highly unlikely to be discovered. Even so, he was taking a risk, no matter how small. Knight had cameras inside the semi, and if he could tell on sight that the belt was more than it seemed, it would blow the mission. There was no reason for Blake to have such a weapon if he really thought he was going to an innocent meeting with the president.

He had concluded that the chances of the belt being discovered were so remote it was worth bringing along, but he had refrained from telling the team, just in case Cargill decided to veto this precaution.

"So now you know just how *fucked* you are," said Rourk cheerfully after finishing his narrative. He smiled. "You know, I am glad I decided to share that with you. Thanks."

"Why isn't Knight here?" said Blake. "To rub in his victory. To revive Nathan Wexler and try to learn his secrets."

"Because all of you are duplicates."

"Yeah, you told me," said Blake. "He teleported us out of the original semi."

"That's not what I mean. He duplicated you *again* when you arrived here. You're just backups. The other versions are in the main house with Knight right now, having a little chat. Except for the other version of you. He's there, too, but still unconscious."

"Lucky him," muttered Blake.

"You got that right," said Rourk. "I'm guessing you'll be with me in this guesthouse for some time. It will serve as a prison for Q5 duplicates for weeks, or even months. This residence, and the entire complex, is getting a security upgrade right now. In another four or five hours, an AI will be able to distinguish between those who belong here and those who don't, and deploy lasers to stop anyone who doesn't. Not that the place won't always be crawling with human security personnel, but automation just adds an extra layer."

"Security personnel?" said Blake derisively. "You mean mercenaries? The soldier equivalent of whores?"

Rourk shook his head. "I mean soldiers who have chosen to align themselves with the future," he replied, ignoring the pointed barb. "You backups will be imprisoned in this guesthouse while Knight does his thing with your duplicates. If any are killed in the process, one of you will eventually replace them. But not before another copy is deposited here, on deck."

"Yeah," said Blake in disgust. "I get it. We're backups so the originals can be expendable. Like you, right Jack? How many copies of you have been killed off? I know Vargas got three of you by himself."

Rourk shrugged. "So what?"

"So what?" repeated Blake in dismay. "Do you know what Knight's reaction was after Vargas killed a trio of Jack Rourks on a farm in Maryland? I do. The colonel told me. Knight *thanked* him for saving him the trouble of killing you."

"Why the fuck do I care how many copies of me are killed? I'm still here. These others mean nothing to me."

"They should. Because Knight doesn't give a shit about anyone's life but his own. It isn't just duplicates he's willing to kill without blinking. You told me Knight blew up the farmhouse in Nebraska he pretended to be in. So how many of his mercenary hires did he kill there?"

"What are you talking about? None."

"Are you really that stupid?" said Blake. "You think anyone would buy that he was in the farmhouse without at least a handful of men patrolling the perimeter? Men he sent there knowing they'd be sacrificed to throw others off his trail."

"It's not going to work, Blake. I've been with him since the beginning. The other soldiers in this room are almost as senior as I am. I know some of his new hires are expendable. But not us. He only trusts his top people with knowledge of time travel, and most of these were at Lake Las Vegas when it was wiped out. So Knight sees the four of us as the *opposite* of expendable."

"Keep telling yourself that," said Blake in disgust.

He frowned deeply. He was getting nowhere. Rourk couldn't be rattled, and as long as his hands were tied above his head, his belt was useless.

But he couldn't let Knight win. And when the security was fully installed in four or five hours, his window of opportunity could well be closed forever. If ever there was a time for an act of desperation, this was it.

Blake's stomach turned as he realized what he would have to do. The course he was being forced to take was uglier than any man should ever have to contemplate. He was so tired of duplicates and death and impossible choices.

But here he was again.

He needed to kill everyone in this room the moment he had the chance. Which meant killing those who had become more than colleagues, more than family. No matter what, he would have to be certain he killed the backup versions of Cargill, Wexler, and Tini, the three men who could be coerced or drugged into giving Knight the information he needed in order to become unstoppable.

Ideally, after he carried out this despicable act, he would make his way to the main mansion and find a way to kill Knight and get the team out of this. But this was a long shot, at best. He would make the attempt, but if this looked to be impossible, he would be forced to go down a much darker road. He'd be forced to eliminate the Cargill, Wexler, and Tini he found in the main mansion—now the only living copies of these men—extinguishing their minds from the universe forever.

Having to kill his friends—*twice*—to prevent Knight from getting the vital information inside of their heads was too horrible for words.

At least the duplicates in the room with him now had been asleep when they were brought into this frame of time. At least they would perish without having ever been conscious. But according to Rourk, the original versions still with Knight *had* been revived—all except for him.

Even so, he would likely have no other choice but to kill them anyway.

The stakes were too high to do anything else.

67

Blake was considering his options when another fist slammed into his jaw. Rourk shot him a cruel smile. "You didn't think this was going to be all talk, did you?"

Blake's jaw throbbed painfully. "Very impressive," he said. "You can batter a helpless prisoner. But before you continue to dazzle us all with your toughness, how about letting me use the bathroom? Or do you, *literally*, want to beat the shit out of me?"

Before Rourk could answer, one of his three colleagues approached with a sour expression on his pockmarked face. He was tall, ugly, and bulging with muscles that suggested many years of heavy steroid use. "We're beginning to lose patience over here, Jack," he said. "Time to inject this guy with a knockout drug. We need to get out of here and help install the sensors and lasers."

"Give me a break, Ajax. We have plenty of time. We only have to test the system when the grunts have finished."

"That's not what Knight told us," replied the newcomer.

Blake watched the exchange with great interest. The musclehead was called Ajax, a name made famous in Greek mythology. Ajax had been a Greek warrior, one depicted as tall, strong, and fearless, who had played a pivotal role in the Trojan War. Blake thought the ape in front of him looked too stupid to have chosen the name on purpose, but it was impossible to know for sure. In any case, Blake could sense coming friction between the two men. Perhaps he could find a way to help this along.

"Rank has its privileges," said Rourk. "And this is one of them. So why don't you guys just relax for a while longer. We have hours to spare." He nodded toward Blake. "I've owed this prick for a while now. I *need* this."

"You *need* this?" said Ajax incredulously.

"That's right."

"Okay, Jack. I'm glad you put it that way. Because I'm thinking it's time for me to take care of *my* needs."

He walked back to the other side of the room, reached into a bag, and removed a roll of silver duct tape and one of a number of filled syringes. He then returned to where Jenna Morrison was lying on her back on the floor. He tore off two short lengths of tape and affixed them over Jenna's mouth, and then knelt down beside her, extending the syringe toward her arm.

"What are you doing?" barked Rourk.

"I'm reviving the girl. You get your jollies your way, and I'll get them mine."

"What are you talking about?" said Rourk.

"What do you *think* I'm talking about? I'm going to fuck her brains out, that's what I'm talking about."

"Right now?" said Rourk in dismay.

"Not here," said Ajax. "But yes. You have needs, Jack. Well, so do I. And you're right. We do have a few hours to spare. And it's not like we don't have any bedrooms around here." He turned to his two colleagues still standing against the back wall. "You guys want in?" he asked.

"Only if you're willing to take sloppy seconds," said the taller of the two. "Because I'm sure as hell not."

The man beside him nodded his agreement.

"Not a chance," said Ajax. "Sorry I offered."

Blake had fought to keep it together, but something inside of him snapped. His mind was on fire. He yanked at his restraints like a wild animal, desperate to get his hands on the man named Ajax, a more visceral reaction than any he had ever had. "You touch her, assface, and I'll—"

"And you'll what?" interrupted Ajax, drawing a gun and pointing it at Blake's forehead. "I know exactly what you'll do! You'll shut your fucking mouth! One more word and I'll knock you out cold. One more word! This is a private discussion between me and Jack."

Blake's face curled up into a feral snarl, and he choked back the threats he was desperate to make. He couldn't take the chance that

Ajax really would knock him out. If he was unconscious until after the automated security was in place, all hope was lost.

Ajax returned his gun to its holster and gazed at Jenna like a starving man eyeing a steak.

"I can't let you do this," said Rourk.

"You aren't *letting* me do shit!" replied the musclehead, sticking the needle in Jenna's arm and pushing the plunger home.

Whatever reversal agent was in the syringe acted almost instantly. Jenna gasped awake, her eyes bulging as she took in her surroundings.

"I don't answer to you, Jack!" continued Ajax. "Do you know how long it's been since I've been laid? This is bullshit. How many times since we began working for Knight has he refused to let us leave a compound like this for days, or even *weeks*? He promised in these cases he'd bring in enough pussy for everyone—to make up for it. All he'd have to do is bring in one hot chick and make as many duplicates as needed. How hard is that? But he hasn't. I'm as loyal as the next guy, but I didn't sign on to be a fucking priest."

"We all want to get laid," said Rourk. "And Knight did say he'd take care of it. But you need to keep your dick in your pants a while longer. You heard what he said about these prisoners."

"I did hear. Did you? He said our job was to make sure they didn't escape and they weren't harmed. Period. Did you hear him say, don't fuck anyone? And *he* brought her here. Might as well bring a girl to a male prison. What does he expect?" Ajax shook his head. "And he said not to hurt them. What do you think *you've* been doing, Jack? So who's not following orders? I'll tie this bitch to the bedposts so she can't resist, so I won't have to hurt her."

Rourk still looked unconvinced.

"You know what else Knight told us?" said Ajax. He nodded toward Blake. "He told us *this* man was too dangerous to revive until the upgrades were in place. And yet me and the boys were willing to help stand guard while you got some revenge. So don't lecture me, asshole! Besides, why do *you* care if I fuck her?"

Ajax pulled Jenna to a standing position, daring Rourk to object further.

Rourk shrugged, indicating his surrender. "Just make sure you bring her back in one piece."

As the two men spoke, Jenna continued to shout into the duct tape, her muffled words indecipherable. Her eyes were wide, horrified—*pleading*.

Ajax pushed her ahead as he made his way from the room. Just as they approached the door, Jenna tried to resist, and he slammed her into the wall with considerable force. "Be smart, sweetheart. Don't make me be rougher than I need to be."

As the two were leaving the room, Blake went emotionally berserk. He had experienced bloodlust in the heat of battle many times, but never like this. He felt a primal, mindless desire to rip out Ajax's jugular with his teeth.

He would be protective of any woman in Jenna's situation. But this was different. It was a mindless rage of such magnitude that it stripped him of all rationality. Given she was a duplicate, he had been prepared to kill her in her sleep if he had to. But he would not stand for *this*. Duplicate or no duplicate, he would not allow her to be violated by this ape, no matter what he had to do to prevent it.

A whisper of clarity made it through the rage that was consuming his mind.

He was in love with Jenna Morrison. He suddenly saw it, clear as day.

His eyes widened as the floodgates of his true feelings were torn open.

He was in love with her. It was the only way to explain his reaction. He had suppressed his feelings, but it was now obvious. He could never have her, since Nathan Wexler had come first, but that didn't change how he felt.

"*Hold on, Jenna,*" he mouthed silently, closing his eyes and breathing deeply to calm himself.

If he wanted to have any hope of saving her, of saving anyone, he needed to let go of his rage and let the creative mind that had served him so well regain control.

68

Blake continued taking deep breaths. He was panicked, out of his mind with rage and a desperation to kill Ajax, but he couldn't show any of this. If he did, Rourk would delight in drilling at this nerve and wasting precious time.

And time was something Blake couldn't spare.

"Glad that's over," said Blake casually, as if complaining about a noisy car alarm that had finally been shut off. "So how about that bathroom break I was asking about before we got interrupted?"

"That's all you have to say? No ranting and raving about what's happening to the girl? I thought you might blow a blood vessel when he took her out of here."

"Would ranting and raving help?" asked Blake.

"You know it wouldn't."

"Exactly. So what's the point of me getting excited? But there is a point to me using the bathroom."

Rourk shook his head in amusement. "You're back to the bathroom again? Really? How many movies have I seen where a prisoner escapes after being cut loose to pee? Twenty? Fifty? You really think I'll fall for that?"

"This isn't a movie, Jack. Are you saying that no prisoner has ever needed to use a bathroom without it being a ploy? In all of human history? Come on. I've been gassed, revived, and hit in the gut several times. My insides aren't handling it well. I'm telling you, if I don't get to the bathroom in a few minutes, pee is the least of our worries. I might be wearing what comes out, but *you* won't be able to get away from the smell. Don't say I didn't warn you."

Rourk stared into Blake's eyes, searching for deception.

"You're still thinking about it?" said Blake. "Seriously? My wrists and ankles will still be cuffed. You still have two guys in here with assault rifles. You think I'm going to take you out and then waddle over there and kick their asses? Good to know you have so much respect for my abilities."

Rourk bent over and removed a combat knife sheathed inside his right pant leg near the ankle. "You have five minutes!" he snapped, reaching up and cutting Blake's hands loose from the ring above his head.

Blake let out an audible sigh of relief as his arms fell down to his stomach, his muscles sore from maintaining a reach for so long, even though he had let the zip ties take most of the weight. "Thank you," he said as he began taking tiny penguin steps toward the bathroom.

After he had traveled ten feet and could feel blood flow returning to his hands, he braced himself mentally and squeezed both sides of his belt buckle as hard as he could.

There was no sound, but something stabbed at his brain like an ice pick, delivering a searing headache and a wave of nausea like nothing he had ever felt. The pain and disorientation were so severe that he barely noticed that Rourk and his two colleagues had collapsed to the floor.

Blake joined them on the floor seconds later as a wall of dizziness hit him like the shock wave of a nuclear blast. He managed to fight off vomit, but only because his stomach was empty.

The room spun around him like an amusement park ride and his ears continued to ring, his hearing temporarily lost. He closed his eyes to shut off the spinning room and tried to rise to his hands and knees, falling back to the floor twice before his inner ear recovered enough for him to manage it.

Mercifully, his searing headache, hearing loss, nausea, and dizziness continued to subside with every second that passed, and he was soon able to take a survey of the room. Everyone who had been inside was now dead, including his five colleagues. Blood was slowly leaking from the ears of each victim and onto the nearby floor.

The loss of his friends by his own hand, no matter how necessary, was devastating, but he couldn't allow this to slow him down. He forced them from his thoughts and crawled to Rourk's body, removing the combat knife from its sheath and using it to sever the zip ties.

The acoustic effect had now worn off enough that he could move with almost half of his normal agility, and he was improving quickly. He tried Rourk's cell phone, but it couldn't reach anyone outside of the complex. Knight didn't trust his own people, and had blocked all signals from leaving, just like he had done at his Lake Las Vegas headquarters.

Blake conducted a hasty search of the fallen guards. Each had multiple weapons, but he was ecstatic when he found a single gun with a silencer among them. He took this, a spare magazine, and Rourk's combat knife. He declined to take an automatic rifle. If he were to use an unsilenced weapon, especially this one, he would bring every soldier within the compound running.

Blake entered the hallway with the silenced gun in one hand and a combat knife in the other. He threw open the door of the first room he came to and entered, gun extended. It was empty, but just as he was about to wheel back around, in the epitome of bad timing, a merc rounded the corner of the hallway. "Freeze!" said the man, rushing forward and shoving the barrel of his gun between Blake's shoulder blades.

Blake held up his hands, quickly flipping the combat knife so the blade was hidden behind his left forearm. "I surrender," he said, letting the gun turn in his right hand so it was upside down. He then made a show of tossing it to the floor.

The instant he did, knowing the merc's attention would be drawn to his falling gun, he dropped to a crouch and spun around, driving the combat knife into the man's heart, all the way to its hilt.

Without missing a beat, Blake rose to his full height and grabbed the handle of the buried knife to help him drag the merc into the room, shutting him just inside its entrance.

Blake surveyed his surroundings and quickly made his way to the front stairs, checking rooms one by one as he did, moving with more haste than was wise. He was frantic, driven to find Jenna before it was too late.

Two mercenaries were against one wall of the third room he opened, installing a steel box that most likely contained a computer and laser. He put one silenced round into each of their heads instead of his usual two, intent on saving ammunition.

When he reached the entry staircase another hired gun was working on an electronic panel at the massive front door, which Blake guessed was an AI-controlled locking mechanism. Blake desperately wanted to put the soldier down and move on, but leaving a body where it was so likely to be found was too reckless, even in his current state of haste.

Blake was skilled enough to sneak up on a man across a forest floor strewn with twigs, leaves, and pinecones, so approaching soundlessly across smooth marble was no challenge at all.

"Say a word and you die," he whispered when he and his gun were within five feet of the man. "Do what I say and you live. Your choice."

The man raised his hands in silence, indicating his decision.

Blake opened the door to the coat closet nearby. "Get inside!" he ordered under his breath. "Now!"

The moment the merc entered the closet, Blake shot him in the head and lowered him to the ground, closing the door behind him.

He raced up the stairs and threw open the first door he came to at the top of the landing, gun extended.

It was Jenna! On the bed. *He had found her.*

His heart began beating like a snare drum as he took in the scene. But what he was seeing was so unexpected that he had to blink and look again to be sure it was real.

The scene didn't change. He hadn't imagined it. It *was* real. His heart began to throttle back as quickly as it had accelerated. She was safe.

More than safe.

Ajax was on the floor at one side of the small bed, gushing blood from multiple gouges on his head and face, unconscious or dead. A heavy brass lamp was lying beside him, now as dented and disfigured as Ajax's head.

Jenna Morrison was on the bed, tied spread-eagle on her back, save for one hand that Ajax must have been in the process of tying when she had clocked him with the lamp. After the first blow, she must have pressed her advantage in a berserker rage, crashing the lamp into her would-be rapist in rapid-fire fashion until he had become dead weight, and then pushing him off the bed.

She was now in the process of sawing through the zip tie binding her other hand to the bed, using a sharp piece of the light bulb that had shattered upon contact.

"Jenna, thank God!" said Blake, rushing over to her and bending down to give her a quick hug, unable to stop himself.

"Aaron?" she said in relief, dropping the glass shard and putting her one free arm around him.

A single tear escaped from Blake's right eye as he rose, which he quickly wiped away before she could see it. He sawed at her remaining bonds with the combat knife while she rebuttoned her blouse. Ajax must have decided he couldn't wait until her last hand was tied down to begin removing this garment.

A fatal mistake.

Blake gazed at Jenna and tried to keep a love-struck expression from his face. Not easy to do now that his true feelings had made themselves known, and after she once again proved just how remarkable she really was.

"How did you turn into such a badass?" he said.

"I was panicked at first," she replied. "But then I just asked myself, WWABD. You know, What Would Aaron Blake Do?"

He laughed. "Well, next time, if I'm going to go to the trouble of rescuing you, the least you could do is pretend to need rescuing."

"Sorry about that, Aaron," she responded with an impish smile. "As much as I wanted to stay helpless so you could play the hero, you *were* a little late."

"In my defense," said Blake, so relieved that he couldn't stop smiling, "I tried really hard to get here sooner."

"What took you so long?" said Jenna.

"Bad traffic," he replied with a grin. "I guess I should have used the carpool lane."

69

Jenna Morrison exited the guesthouse and began walking toward the main mansion, fifty yards away, as though she was out for a casual stroll.

"Freeze!" said one of two armed men who rushed toward her from behind an outcropping of trees. "Hands up!"

Jenna jumped like a coiled spring. "Okay, okay," she blurted out, raising her hands and looking nearly petrified with fear. "Don't point those . . . *things* at me. *Please*. What did I do?"

The mercs glanced at each other in confusion. "What did you do?" one of the men repeated in disbelief. "The better question is, how the hell did you escape?"

"Escape?" she said. "I don't understand. Put down your guns and we can talk about it," she added, as though speaking to two mental patients who were terribly misguided.

"Come on," said the second merc, "don't pretend you aren't one of the prisoners that Knight was keeping inside."

"Prisoners?" said Jenna. "Have you guys been drinking? I was hired by a guy named Ajax. You know, to show him a good time. That guy's into some kinky shit. All I know is that I did my job, and now I'm leaving. If you don't believe me, go inside and ask him."

The two men lowered their guns, trying to decide what to make of her, when bullet holes appeared in both of their foreheads and they collapsed to the lawn.

Jenna took a deep breath while Blake rushed to her side, still holding a silenced gun. "That was brilliant," he said. "You have nerves of steel."

"Not really," said Jenna. "I just have confidence in *you*."

Blake smiled. He had made certain that no more hostiles remained alive in the guesthouse, but he thought it likely that a few men were watching the front door. Jenna had courageously agreed to play the role of a hunting dog, flushing out the quail for him to shoot.

It couldn't have worked any better.

The only difference was that he would never hurt a helpless quail.

"Now what?" whispered Jenna.

"Give me a minute to think," he replied.

He sighed. Jenna knew very little of what was happening. He had told her it was complicated, and couldn't spare the time to fill her in until later. She didn't know she was a duplicate, or anything that Rourk had told him.

And she didn't know that if he wasn't able to capture or kill Knight cleanly, he would have to turn against his own, including the man she was about to marry.

He first had to attempt a rescue, but there was no way she was coming with him. He would not put her life in jeopardy, under any circumstances.

"Knight is blocking all signals out of this area," he said after only a few seconds had passed, "making cell phones useless. No calls, text, or Internet."

"Like he did at Lake Las Vegas?" said Jenna.

"Exactly." Blake pointed due south of the main residence, to a small warehouse. "Rourk told me the suppressor is housed in there," he lied.

He took a deep breath. He hated lying to her, but if he didn't tell her a convincing story, she would insist on joining him. "I'm going to destroy it," he said. "Restore communications so we can call in the Calvary. But it will be heavily guarded. I won't be able to take it out without advertising my presence. So I need you to stay here. Go back to the room Ajax took you to, get his phone, and find a good place in the house to hide. Keep trying to call Tom TenBrink or Joe O'Bannon. If I'm successful, you'll be able to get through. They can track your phone, and they'll know what to do."

"What about the rest of the team?" asked Jenna, referring to the duplicates who were next to her in the rec room when she had awakened.

Blake looked sick as an image of his dead colleagues flashed into his mind, but he caught himself before she noticed. "Leave them alone for now," he said. "The room they're in is the first one any guards who enter the house will check. For now, the team is safer unconscious. And *you're* safer not being anywhere near that room. They'll be fine."

"You're sure about that?" she asked.

"Positive," he replied. "Trust me," he added, the words tasting bitter as they left his mouth.

Jenna shook her head. "I hate this plan," she said. "It makes sense for everyone but you. If they really will be on you as soon as you destroy the suppressor, I can't let you do this."

Blake forced a smile. "You know better than that, Jenna. I'm not so easy to kill. But if it does come to that, you know there's another me out there. The one sent to North Korea. I wish I had time to explain, but this is a risk I have to take."

"Now go!" he added emphatically. "I need to know you're safely hidden, so if I am forced to sacrifice myself, it isn't for nothing."

Jenna nodded solemnly, and her eyes moistened. She leaned over and kissed him on the cheek. "Good luck, Aaron. You know how much you mean to me."

"I feel the same," he said simply, wishing he could say more, but not wanting to make this messier than it already was. "Stay safe, Jenna Morrison. I'll be back soon."

70

Knight stared intently at his former boss. "I want you to know, Lee, I'm going to miss you when you're gone. We do share some important history. You were the first person, other than me, to learn that time itself could be breached, and how the universe chose to handle this situation."

"That's beautiful, Edgar," spat Hank Vargas. "But do you know what will happen when *you're* gone? The entire world will celebrate. Ding-dong, the dick is dead."

"Are you trying to piss me off on purpose?" said Knight icily. "Lee and I were having a moment and you ruined it. Not to mention that you're worthless. So no more talking, okay?"

Knight opened a cabinet, removed a roll of duct tape, and gagged Vargas's mouth, so he joined Jenna and her fiancé as mute observers. Just as he finished, two of his soldiers entered the room, shoving Aaron Blake in front of them, his wrists zip tied together behind his back. He was bleeding from bullet wounds in his thigh and upper arm and looked like he had just fought the armies of hell.

Knight's eyes widened in shock.

"Sorry to interrupt," said one of the mercs, "but he was inside this house, working his way here, when we captured him."

Knight glanced at the unconscious Blake still gagged against the far wall, his hands tied to either side of a chair, and then back at the newcomer. "This isn't possible," he whispered.

"If you say so," said Blake.

"What happened?" Knight asked one of the two guards. "Give me the short version."

"He escaped," said the mercenary. "Once we recaptured him, I sent Jake to check out the guesthouse. Everyone there was dead. Not just our people, but the prisoners too. Not a single survivor. This guy also killed two men who had been patrolling outside. Then he killed five of our men in *this* residence before we were able to stop him."

Knight bared his teeth like a feral animal, furious. "Is that *idiot*, Jack Rourk, one of the casualties?"

"He is."

"Good!" spat Knight. "I told that jackass not to revive this man under any circumstances. Given his track record, we were lucky you stopped him before he reached this room. Any idea how he did it?"

"None," replied the shorter merc. "But Jake reported that everyone in the room had blood leaking from their ears."

Knight's eyes narrowed in thought. "Remove his belt," he said suddenly as he realized what must have happened. "And his too," he added, gesturing toward the other Blake in the room, who was still unconscious.

The shorter merc did as requested and handed the two identical belts to Knight, who inspected them carefully.

"Well done," he said to Blake. "I didn't realize Vargas's sonic weapon could be triggered manually. I thought checking for smart contacts was enough."

"You thought wrong," said Blake simply.

Knight shrugged. "Just a minor setback," he said. "I'll make another copy of your friends and I'll be back where I started."

"Except for the scores of mercs I just took out," said Blake. "You're running pretty thin on them all of a sudden."

"I'll hire more," said Knight, unconcerned. "In the meanwhile, I'll copy the few who are left to take the place of those you killed. Be up to strength almost before you finish dying."

He stared at the mountains through the large slider for several seconds, and then turned back to face Blake and his two escorts. "Craig," he said to the taller of the mercs, "take a few men and go back to the guesthouse. I want it scoured with a fine-tooth comb. You're looking for possible booby traps, indications he might have something more planned, and clues as to how he got the drop on so many of our people after using the belt. I don't trust him. I also want to learn how he operates, what makes him so good at his job."

"Understood," said Craig.

Knight turned back to Blake. "Thanks for stopping by," he said. "As fun as this has been, I'm afraid I have others matters to attend to, and I already have one of you."

He gestured to the sole remaining soldier, who still had a gun pressed into Blake's back. "Take him outside and kill him," he ordered. "I don't care where. I just don't want another dead body in here. Speaking of which," he added, nodding toward the bodies of Daniel Tini and Joe Allen. "When you're done with him, grab someone else and get rid of these two."

"I'm not going anywhere," said Blake calmly. "Tell him to back off, or I'll kill everyone in this room."

Knight laughed. "You're the fucking energizer bunny, you know that? You never stop. You're shot up, bleeding on my floor, and you act like you're ready to run a marathon. But this time you're bluffing. You're all out of belts."

"The belt only works once, anyway," said Blake. "So instead, I thought I'd bring back an old classic." He slowly turned so that his back was to Knight for just a moment, just long enough for him to see the ring Blake held between his thumb and forefinger.

Knight's smile vanished. "Back away as he said," he ordered his only remaining soldier. "In fact, leave us. I'll let you know when I want you back."

"Good choice," said Blake as the merc left the room. "The colonel told us you knew about Jenna and what she was able to do with her little ring at Lake Las Vegas. What is it with octa-nitro-cubane and rings? They seem to go together like peanut butter and jelly. I give this a good squeeze and we all die."

"I'm not buying it," said Knight. "You fascinate me, so I've made it a point to study your past. You have a reputation for being able to create and sell complex bluffs on the fly. You're smart, inventive, and ballsy. Your only flaw is that you're on the wrong side of this. In any event, I know you're bluffing."

"Am I?" said Blake. "Since you were listening in to the colonel, I assume you heard when he prepped us for this mission. Do you remember me asking about weapons? About the smart contact? Remember me saying it would be a mistake to underestimate you?

I wasn't just saying that. If I haven't learned that lesson by now, I'm incapable of learning. I had no idea what inventions your duplicates might have cooked up that you could throw at us. So I brought the belt without telling anyone. If I did that, is it really a stretch to believe that I also prepared this ring—just in case?"

Knight tried to remain impassive, but an unmistakable flicker of doubt crossed his face. "I still think you're bluffing," he said. "But even if you aren't, you're forgetting something. You killed the duplicates I made of your friends. So if you blow this residence, you and your Q5 colleagues are gone—for good."

He raised his eyebrows. "But I'm not," he added. "There's another copy of me off-site. So go ahead and kill us all. Make Q5 extinct. You'll just make it that much easier for my duplicate when he takes over."

Blake smiled. "Now who's bluffing?" he said. "You're a control freak. So it isn't as simple as making a duplicate of yourself. You have to find a way to contain him until he's needed. I don't think you've had time to set this up."

"Trigger your ring and you'll learn otherwise," hissed Knight. "Oh wait," he added smugly, "no you won't. Because you and your team will be blown to bits."

"We both know that even if you *have* set up a duplicate of yourself, you can't let me do this. This room contains the only living versions of Cargill, Wexler, and Tini. If they die, you'll never get at Wexler's work. You'll never understand the theory behind your invention. Never extend its reach beyond fifty-eight feet."

Blake paused to let this sink in. "The *last* thing I want to do is trigger this ring," he added. "But believe me, I will if I have to."

Knight paused for several seconds. "Okay," he said, "just to humor you, what are you proposing?"

"That you take your remaining men and walk away in peace."

"So I don't get Wexler's work, and the Q5 team goes free? I don't think so."

"It's the best I can offer. This way, you still have a chance of getting at his work in the future. If I blow us up, it won't matter if you have a thousand duplicates ready to take your place, that chance goes away forever."

"If I do this, Q5 has the advantage. You can already go back almost half a second. And now you'll know I'm alive and coming for you. You'll be on guard."

Blake shrugged. "You'll still have your Brain Trust inventions and your creativity. I thought you were the greatest talent the world has ever known. Don't tell me you're doubting your ability to beat us."

Knight stared at him for what seemed like eternity. "No deal," he said finally. He extended his gun toward Blake. "Instead, I'm calling your bluff. Go ahead. Trigger your ring. Do your worst."

After a brief pause, Knight smiled. "I didn't think so," he said, pulling the trigger three times in quick succession. Blake fell to the floor, dead before he landed.

"I guess the mess in here is going to get worse before it gets better," said Knight, quite pleased with himself.

71

Cargill's face fell as his last shred of hope fled his body like air from a popped balloon.

Knight eyed his rival, more self-satisfied than ever. "Even you didn't know he was bluffing, did you?"

"Of course I knew. I just didn't know if you would fall for it or not."

"Bullshit!" said Knight.

"How did *you* know he was bluffing?"

Knight shook his head. "I didn't. I just have bigger balls than you. I'm just better at playing high-stakes poker."

"Yeah, psychopaths usually are," said Cargill.

Knight was about to respond when his phone buzzed. He touched an icon on the screen and a holographic image of the mercenary named Craig materialized in front of him. Craig explained that there had been one survivor at the guesthouse, after all. Jake had failed to realize the girl wasn't among the bodies in the rec room, and they had found her hiding in a closet. She had shot the first man who had stumbled upon her before they were finally able to subdue her.

"Here's what I want you to do," said Knight. "Frisk her and scan her for hidden weapons. When you're through, bring her here."

Almost seven minutes later, Craig arrived, pushing Jenna into the room at gunpoint.

"No!" she whispered as she nearly tripped over Blake's corpse still on the floor. A tear slid down her face as she gazed in horror at his bullet-riddled body. She dropped to her knees and tried to check for his pulse, even though her hands were bound together.

"Don't bother," said Knight. "He's gone."

"You son of a bitch!" she screamed.

She was about to continue when she took in the room for the first time and further words froze in her mouth. Lee Cargill and Hank Vargas were on one side of the room, and against the back wall were all of her other colleagues, including Aaron Blake and another Jenna Morrison. Daniel Tini and Joe Allen were both dead, and Blake looked alive but unconscious.

"I don't understand," she said, rising to her feet. "You made duplicates of us?"

"I made duplicates of *them*," said Knight, waving his hand to encompass the entire room. "But as you know, original versus duplicate is a somewhat arbitrary designation. Luck of the draw." His eyes narrowed. "You mean you had no idea you were a copy? Blake didn't tell you?"

She shook her head.

"Interesting," he said, not sure what to make of this. "I had you brought to me," he continued, "because I want to learn how Blake got as far as he did. And if he cooked up anything else. So I want you to tell me what happened. What he said to you. Every detail."

"And I want you to shove a flaming poker up your ass," she replied. "But we can't always get what we want."

Knight shook his head in amusement. "You're already so much more entertaining than Lee and Hank here," he said. "But make no mistake, in this case, I *am* going to get what I want. You're going to tell me one way or another. So why not do this the easy way?"

Knight's phone buzzed again, and seconds later a holographic image of yet another soldier appeared in front of him. Knight shot him a withering glare. "*What is it?*" he snapped.

"A guy on a dirt bike just drove up to a group of us," the merc said. "I have no idea how he and the bike even got on the grounds. But he was waving a white flag, so we didn't shoot him."

"Who is he?" said Knight.

"Says he's Aaron Blake, and insists we bring him to you."

Knight's eyes widened. "Show me?" he said.

The merc adjusted his phone so that another holographic imagine now appeared in the room. It was Blake, all right. There could be no doubt.

Knight looked rattled, even more so than he had when the other Blake was threatening to turn the mansion into a crater. "Frisk him thoroughly," he ordered. "Remove his belt and any rings or other jewelry. Manually check him for a contact lens, and wand him with every sensor we have. Then bind his wrists behind his back and bring him here."

"Roger that," said the merc, ending the call.

Knight turned to Cargill. "How is there a third Blake?" he demanded. "And what is he doing here?"

"I don't know, Edgar," said Cargill with a smile. "Don't tell me you lost count of how many of him you made."

"What happened to your vow of never duplicating anyone?" demanded Knight. "You made an exception for the Lake Las Vegas Op, but I would have bet my life that was a special circumstance."

"If only you *had* bet your life," said Cargill. "I changed my mind, Edgar. Turns out that you can never have too many Aaron Blakes. There's plenty more where this one came from."

"No more conversation," said Knight, glaring at his former boss. "I need to think."

There was an extended silence in the room until the prisoner finally arrived, bound as Knight had specified. The soldier who brought him pushed him forward until he was next to Jenna and his identical twin, dead on the floor.

"You can leave now," said Knight to the soldier, who promptly did so.

Blake took in the room with practiced efficiency. The entire team was present, including two duplicates of himself—one dead and one unconscious—a murdered Daniel Tini and Joe Allen, and both a seated and standing Jenna Morrison. His eyes returned to Knight. "Looks like you've been busy."

"We're all that's left," said Jenna hurriedly beside him. "He made other duplicates but—"

"Not another word!" thundered Knight. "One more syllable and I'll shoot you in the leg and let you bleed out."

Jenna glared at him with the intensity of a supernova, but remained silent.

Knight took a calming breath and turned his attention back to Blake. "You're just full of surprises, aren't you?" he said, shaking his head. "How many times do I have to kill you?"

Blake smiled. "We ask ourselves the same thing about you."

"Why are you here?" demanded Knight. "Eager to share the fate of your double on the floor there?"

"Good guess," said Blake, "but no. I'm here to make a deal."

"Here from where?"

"Turns out Q5 keeps an extra of me, just for rainy days," replied Blake. "Sorry it took me so long to get here," he added, addressing his Q5 colleagues.

"How did you find me?" asked Knight.

"You know that truck my friends were in? The one heading to a farm in Nebraska? Well, I'm not going to lie, I was pretty upset when I learned they were butchered. So I flew to the site myself to inspect it, to try to find out who was responsible. I've been told I'm a very talented commando. But I think you know I quit the military to become a private detective, because I believe I'm a better detective than I am a soldier. I believe I'm especially good at coming up with an exhaustive list of scenarios that might explain a crime—no matter how unlikely."

"And one of your scenarios was that I was behind it all, right?" said Knight.

"Yes. It was about the sixth one I considered. You did a great job of making it look like a mysterious third party was responsible. And for you to be behind it, you'd have to know we teamed up with the colonel. I couldn't see how this was possible, but I decided to accept it as a premise and go from there. Assuming you did know we were coming, I considered possible steps you might have taken to throw us off the scent."

"Let me guess," said Knight. "Once you suspected I used time travel duplication to play a shell game, you had satellites check to see if there were any trucks within fifty-eight feet of the tunnel when the colonel drove his pickup inside?"

"Very good," said Blake. "Maybe you should have been a detective yourself. There was one truck parked outside of the tunnel at exactly this distance. Imagine that. The satellites had no trouble tracking it."

"So if you knew I was here," asked Knight, "why not a surprise attack? You could have entered a time machine fifty miles from here and flooded the zone with a thousand copies of yourself."

"I wasn't sure exactly where you were within your compound. Even if I knew, I wouldn't make scores of other selves, knowing that all of them would have to die. Besides, if I attacked, you could use members of the team as hostages."

"I can still use them as hostages."

"But now there's no need. I'm your prisoner."

"So what deal are you proposing?"

"Take your men and leave. We'll let you go in peace. Call this round a draw, and live to fight another day."

"And if I decline?"

"Lose-lose," said Blake, "we all die here." He arched an eyebrow. "Go ahead, I know you want to ask, *me and what army*, right?"

Knight sighed. "I already know the answer. The United States Army. You brought them with, didn't you?"

"As a matter of fact, I did."

"Shit!" said Knight miserably. "I see it now. You asked to be taken to me so your allies watching the satellite feed would know my exact position within the compound."

"Very good," taunted Blake. He nodded toward one of the three large monitors in the room, which displayed a digital clock in its lower left corner. "How accurate does that keep time?" he asked.

"To the second," replied Knight.

"Excellent. So in just under two minutes, all the fighter jets and combat helos that we planned to use on that farm in Nebraska will make their presence known. I wanted to give myself some time to explain the situation before they arrived here. They can be pretty intimidating. Once the Apache combat helos arrive and hover outside, watch the clock. The next time the minute digit changes, we'll have exactly ten minutes left, to the second. If they don't hear from me by then, they'll hit us with everything they've got. So I suggest you unblock cell phone reception so it can reach beyond this complex and let me contact them. Tell them you've agreed to my terms. I'll stay on the line while you leave here. They won't touch you."

"Déjà vu all over again, huh Edgar?" taunted Cargill. "It's the exact same deal the other Blake offered. Only this time he's not bluffing."

Blake raised his eyebrows. "Really?" he said, glancing at his fallen duplicate. "And here I thought I was being original."

A furious wave of noise began to penetrate the closed sliding glass door, growing louder by the second, as low-flying helicopters and higher-flying fighter jets all streaked toward Knight's complex.

Less than a minute later, the Apaches all arrived, ringing the complex and hovering in place. Every inch of this helicopter had been built to be predatory, lethal, and it showed. The presence of even a single one was the epitome of menacing, but bunches of them together could evoke terror in the bravest of men.

Blake raised his voice to be heard over the powerful din. "Right on time," he said, gesturing toward the digital clock. The seconds were counting up from forty-three. "As I mentioned," he continued after waiting until the number reached sixty, "you now have exactly ten minutes. I have no doubt that your men are already fleeing. Even assuming they're loyal, when you come face-to-face with this much air power, it's every man for himself. But don't worry, we'll be letting them go in peace."

Knight walked closer to the slider and looked out, just as four Raptors screamed by, seemingly close enough to touch. Their massive engines were so powerful that the entire mansion shook as they passed.

He then eyed the helicopters, still in place, for an extended period of time, as if making a calculation.

"You're now down to *nine* minutes," announced Blake, as the minute digit on the clock changed from a three to a four.

Knight snapped out of his reverie and a scowl came over his face. "Go for it," he hissed. "Kill everyone in this room. It won't matter. I've already made copies of Wexler and Tini, which my newly freed duplicate will be able to interrogate."

"Based on what Jenna was trying to tell me," said Blake, "I doubt they're still alive. But even if they are, it doesn't matter. The satellites have been watching. And no one has left the premises since my colleagues arrived. So any duplicates you might have made are still on the grounds somewhere. If you let the deadline pass, the military has orders to blow this entire complex into the stone age, allowing no one to survive, duplicates or otherwise. And then they'll do seismology to be sure they didn't miss any hiding underground."

Knight's face became a mask of hatred as he finally realized he had no way out. "Even if I did what you asked," he said bitterly, "you won't just let me leave here."

"I'm a man of my word," said Blake. "If you walk away, you won't be touched."

Knight shook his head. "Bullshit!" he spat. "No matter how honorable you are, the stakes are too high. You'd be a fool to let me waltz out of here, and I know you aren't that. And you're right, when my duplicate takes over, he can't have Wexler's work lost forever."

He paused in thought. "So here's what I'm going to do," he continued. "I'm going to kill Lee, Hank, and Jenna in front of you. Both Jennas. You'll get to see your friends die, and know they'll be gone forever. Then I'm going to kill *you*. After that I'm going to go outside so your people don't attack the mansion, making sure Nathan Wexler survives. Then I'm going to kill myself in front of them. This will unleash my duplicate, who will inherit a world in which Q5 has been decimated. My successor can then redouble efforts to get at Wexler's work."

Knight raised his gun and pointed it at Blake's forehead. "How does that sound, *Detective*? I'll bet you didn't see *that* coming."

Blake sighed. "Have you checked the time?"

Knight glanced at the digital clock. "Only two and a half minutes have passed," he said. "Which still gives me more than seven minutes to kill you and everyone else who's expendable. Plenty of time."

Blake kept his eyes on the clock and smiled. "You forgot one thing."

"And what is that?" asked Knight.

"Give it some thought," said Blake. "You'll figure it out."

Knight paused for several seconds and finally shook his head. "You're stalling."

"You're just saying that because you're stumped."

"Tell me or don't tell me," said Knight dismissively. "Either way, you have seconds to live."

"Okay," said Blake. "I'll tell you. You forgot that I'm a better strategist than you. I predicted this is exactly where we'd end up. I wanted to give you at least a chance to surrender, but I doubted you would."

He paused for several long seconds, staring at Knight but carefully minding the clock in his peripheral vision.

"So I lied," he continued finally. "My personal air force out there doesn't have orders to destroy this compound, after all. The attack is designed to take you alive. And I lied about the timing of the attack. I said ten minutes, but it's really a lot shorter than that. So I guess I *was* trying to stall. Right up until the *actual* attack, which is scheduled to happen . . . *now*," he finished triumphantly, as the number of minutes displayed on the clock rose by one yet again.

Before he even finished the sentence several gas canisters crashed through the slider, shattering it into thousands of pieces. The canisters bounced off the floor and hit the back wall, releasing a thick, billowing cloud of knockout gas that rapidly filled the room.

Blake, armed with knowledge of what was about to happen, managed to hold his breath, delaying the inevitable by a minute or two, but everyone else in the room lost consciousness almost immediately.

To Knight's credit, he assimilated the situation with remarkable speed, and a moment before he would otherwise have passed out, he pressed the barrel of his gun to the side of his head and pulled the trigger.

PART 8

"I've got too much time on my hands
It's ticking away with my sanity
I've got too much time on my hands
It's hard to believe such a calamity
I've got too much time on my hands
And it's ticking away, ticking away from me"

—Styx, *Too Much Time on my Hands*

72

Lee Cargill touched his phone and the virtual presence of the Commander in Chief now appeared to be sitting across from him in his temporary Cheyenne Mountain headquarters.

The only question was if Cargill's *job* would be equally temporary. Or even his freedom.

Janney appeared exhausted but in good spirits. And why not? The action he had ordered in North Korea could not have gone better. The US now had control of all WMD in this country, and basically all other means North Korea could use to attack its own population or any other.

In the media and around the world this strike was being called one of the boldest in military history, and was an event of such historic and geopolitical importance that it was one of the few that weren't completely politicized in America, the reaction not breaking cleanly along Democrat and Republican party lines.

Still, the president was widely praised in some circles and vilified in others. Yes, the action had been flawless, as finely tuned as an expensive Swiss watch, but it was also seen as extraordinarily reckless. The attack had succeeded beyond anyone's wildest imagination, but Janney couldn't have been sure of this. What if the results hadn't been so good? Was it really okay to have a president capable of making a move this risky? One who put millions of lives at risk on a plan that needed considerable luck to work.

At least this was the general consensus.

Unfortunately, Janney couldn't disclose that the US had captured Kim Jong-un well before the attack, nor that a modified dosing regimen of T-4 had given the military all the intel it needed.

But even those who complained of the president's recklessness couldn't help but give him the highest marks for execution. The decision itself could be criticized, but the results were beyond reproach. There were only a handful of casualties on the US side, and little loss of life in North Korea or damage to the country's nonmilitary infrastructure. The timing and precision had been nothing short of stunning.

America had propped up a leader to replace Kim, by all accounts a perfect choice. This was a man who had been in Kim's government until just a month earlier, when he had defected to the West. A man who had shown his passion to defeat all that Kim stood for, to reverse North Korea's pursuit of weapons and its aggressive posture so that it would no longer be a pariah nation, and to focus on strengthening its economy so its people could thrive rather than starve.

"Sorry it's taken me so long to arrange this call," said Janney.

"Not at all," said Cargill. It had only been five days since the events in Knight's Wyoming mansion. Hours after Cargill had regained consciousness, Kim Jong-un had finally died from the poison Blake had injected, and the US military had launched its campaign. "Given how busy you've been, I just appreciate that you're taking the time now."

The president's expression grew somber. "Before I continue, Lee, I want to tell you how sorry I am for your losses."

"Thank you, sir," said Cargill, his eyes reflecting a deep pain. "Daniel Tini and Joe Allen were good men. They served their country well. More importantly, they played a big role in helping to pave the way for a better future for humanity. One day, their contributions will be widely recognized."

"And Hank Vargas?"

Cargill shook his head solemnly. "I'm afraid we lost him too. We did everything we could to disarm the titanium capsule, but we failed. At least he died a hero. He was a man I despised for many years, and he turned out to be a man I greatly admired. He could have gone along with Knight and stayed alive. Could have been the second most powerful man on Earth. But he sacrificed his own life for what he thought was right."

"We've lost a lot of good people since Nathan Wexler's work first emerged," said Janney. "But like you said, one day the world will honor the historical contributions they made. I intend to see to that. And this will include Hank Vargas."

"Thank you, sir," said Cargill.

The president sighed and then proceeded to get down to business. "I know you've been trying to cover up the mess Knight left behind," he said. "How's that coming?"

"Better than expected," replied Cargill. "I can't take much credit. The North Korean action has completely dominated news coverage since you went in. There have been stories about missiles rumored to have hit a farmhouse in Nebraska, but these stories have been getting very little play. We've reported that the incident in question was a fertilizer fire and that anyone who suggests otherwise is a conspiracy nut. The harder story to kill is the one involving four gunmen who massacred seven people on a highway. People who were in the back of a pickup truck at the time. Which itself was in the back of an eighteen-wheeler. Not the kind of story you see every day."

"Or ever," said Janney.

"Fortunately, we were able to take over jurisdiction of the investigation right away. Once we feed the media a false narrative of what happened, this should eventually die out."

"I don't know," said Janney. "You'll need some serious creativity to explain away a story this bizarre. I look forward to learning what you come up with."

"Yeah, me too," said Cargill with a grin. He paused. "If I may ask, sir," he added in a more serious tone, "how goes the fallout from your actions in North Korea?"

"Reaction has been very favorable on the whole, as I'm sure you know from the news. But even if this had been terrible politics, we neutralized a longstanding threat that was building to the point of no return. So even if the political consequences had been strongly negative, it wouldn't have mattered. I know that's hard to believe coming from a politician," he added wryly.

"I'm just glad it was so successful."

"Amen to that. And we owe it to you, Lee. And to Aaron Blake."

"We set it up," said Cargill, "but there have been presidents in the past who wouldn't have risked going forward, even given these favorable circumstances. And it wasn't my neck in the guillotine if this had somehow backfired."

"That's very generous of you, Lee, but I know where the credit really belongs. Regardless, countries around the world are breathing a huge sigh of relief." Janney frowned. "Well, at least most of them. Our chief rivals on the world stage are denouncing us, as you'd expect. As you've probably heard, China has publicly expressed outrage. They've condemned what they call our illegal aggression. But our sources in Beijing tell me that it's a different story in private. Even the Politburo is relieved that Kim has been nullified. They haven't been sure they could control him now for some time. And they're in awe of our military action. It was more thorough and precise than they could have managed, and they have no idea how we could possibly have had better intel on North Korea than they did."

"Good," said Cargill with a smile. "It never hurts to keep them guessing."

Janney's face took on a more serious expression, an indication that the time for small talk had ended. "Let me get to the reason for this call, Lee."

Cargill braced himself and nodded for the president to continue.

"I've decided to keep you on as head of Q5," said Janney, getting to the punchline immediately. "That doesn't mean I condone your actions," he hastened to add. "But I've read your recent report, and I agree with the direction you're proposing to take the group. And you did deliver Kim Jong-un."

The president's expression darkened. "You've also violated my trust," he said gravely. "*Repeatedly*. And while you handled your considerable power as ethically as anyone could have—for the most part—you're also responsible for Lake Las Vegas."

Cargill nodded, a haunted look in his eye.

"But I can't say for certain this wasn't warranted," continued Janney. "We've never faced a threat like Knight, a man capable of whipping up an instant army of unlimited size—among many other capabilities. Most of the people you killed were part of Knight's team. That doesn't mean they deserved to die, but given the threat he posed, who knows? It could have been the right call."

"Thank you for giving me the benefit of the doubt, sir," said Cargill.

"I almost didn't," said Janney, "but Aaron Blake tipped the scales. I got to know him at Camp David, and I came to like and respect him a great deal. He thinks very highly of you. He has absolute faith that you're a good man, with a fully developed conscience. He told me he would follow you to the ends of the Earth. Anyone who inspires that kind of loyalty in a man like Aaron gets my vote to head Q5."

"Thank you for sharing this, Mr. President," said Cargill earnestly. "It means a lot to know I have this kind of support from someone like him. He was my third-in-command," he added. "With Joe Allen gone, he'll become my second." He paused. "Well, the Aaron *here* will—not the one who was with you at Camp David."

"Right," said Janney. "*That* Aaron has agreed to conduct select Ops for Q5."

"Exactly."

"Good," said Janney. "Even though you'll retain your post, Lee, it goes without saying that you're on thin ice. No more rogue operations in Nevada or North Korea. In fact, *nothing* significant happens from now on without my knowledge and buy-in. Understood?"

"Perfectly, sir."

"I also want a hands-on role. I want to be video-conferenced in for important internal meetings. My time is limited, but I've been a fool. Q5 is history changing, history *making*. It isn't just one of a hundred similar groups—it's the *only* group. Interstellar travel, teleportation. And if you really are able to suppress the time travel effect, unlimited wealth. How did I ever think anything on my schedule was even *close* to this important?"

"I don't know, sir," said Cargill, "but I welcome your participation. Really. I didn't trust you before only because I thought the stakes were too high to trust you. But circumstances forced me to come clean, and I couldn't be happier that I did."

"Good," said Janney. "I'm glad we're finally on the same page. But let me get back to Edgar Knight," he said. "Your report says he claimed to have another duplicate ready to rise from his ashes. Do you think this is true?"

"Hard to say. We found a titanium capsule in his head. The same one he implanted in the colonel. He admitted to being trapped in the mansion at some point. We think that when we killed his predecessor, he was freed to take over."

"Why such an elaborate setup?" asked the president.

"He doesn't like sharing power, even with a duplicate. We don't think he had the time or resources to recreate this setup before we killed him."

"So you think he was bluffing?"

"We hope so," said Cargill. "But we have no choice but to assume he's still out there. We'll stay on guard and do everything we can to find him."

"Why would he kill himself if he *didn't* have a backup?"

"He was facing capture," said Cargill, "which he knew would be followed by execution. Maybe he didn't want to give us the satisfaction of beating him again. Maybe he couldn't live with that—literally. By killing himself, we'd be likely to believe he does have a duplicate ready. Without being able to interrogate him, we'll always have to watch our backs—which gives him a small victory."

"Either way," said Janney, "you have the right idea. Hope for the best and plan for the worst." He paused. "I understand a duplicate of Jenna Morrison survived."

"This is true."

"How did you handle *that*?"

Cargill blew out a long breath. "As usual, I was forced to make some tough calls. Aaron volunteered to be duplicated, knowing the duplicates were being sent on a suicide mission. But Jenna wasn't a volunteer. It wasn't her fault Knight did this to her."

"So did you make an exception like you did with the final copy of Aaron?"

"I did," replied Cargill. "I've done some horrible things, but nothing on Earth could get me to call for her death. She's agreed to abide by the Aaron Blake rules, to change identity and let the other Jenna live her life. Nathan was heartbroken about the situation. He insisted we duplicate him so he could join her in exile."

"And?"

"I refused. It wasn't a popular choice with either of them, but I couldn't let him do it. Even for Jenna. I couldn't let him purposely create a double who would also be forced to abandon his prior life. I've allowed duplication before, but only to take out the two greatest threats facing the world. I'm not about to allow it for anything less. Where would it end? Jenna and Nathan would surely miss their friends and colleagues on the team. So if I allowed Nathan to be duplicated, why not the entire team?"

"You made the right call," said Janney.

"I did give her and Aaron the option of teaming up. Both are duplicates, in the same boat. They think highly of each other. They worked together when they thought Nathan was dead and made a remarkable team. The same was true when they teamed up to bring Knight down at Lake Las Vegas. And from what Jenna reports, they worked as a team at Knight's guesthouse in Wyoming."

"Did they take you up on it?"

"They jumped at the chance," said Cargill. "They knew that after they left Q5 and assumed new identities, they'd be totally alone, otherwise."

"And you've already given them new identities?" asked Janney.

"Yes. They won't be living together, since they aren't romantically involved, but they've agreed to work together on Q5 missions that I give them. She's brilliant, and has shown herself to be resourceful and brave. And they've proven to make a potent combination."

"Are you funding them?" asked Janney.

"Initially with a million dollars each. But there's more if they should ever need it."

Janney nodded. "The debt we owe them is immense."

"That was my thinking," said Cargill. "Even if this weren't true, I expect them to be worth every penny going forward."

"Of that I have no doubt," said the president.

"They left yesterday," said Cargill. "It was a teary farewell. I can't describe the emotions. We were saying goodbye to good friends, but at the same time, we knew that these friends would still be by our sides. And we felt horrible exiling them. Nathan and the version of Jenna who remained on the team felt the worst."

"A situation unlike any in history," noted Janney.

Cargill smiled. "Or just another day in the life of Q5," he said. "Once time travel is on the scene, almost everything that follows becomes unprecedented. Speaking of which," he added, raising his eyebrows, "there is something else I need to tell you before you go. One last item I didn't bring up when I first came clean. It wasn't vital to our discussion, and I'd already hit you with so many bombshells I thought I'd save it for another time."

"So is this something fairly minor?" said Janney.

Cargill couldn't help but laugh. "Well, sir, if by *minor* you mean the most important discovery in all of human history, then yes, it's minor."

"Come on, Lee," said Janney, shaking his head. "Be serious. Q5 discovered time travel. You're on your way to conquering teleportation and interstellar travel. No way any discovery can trump these."

"That's what I thought," said Cargill. "So I'll let you be the judge. Have you ever heard of something called Tabby's Star?"

"Can't say I have."

"Then let me make a long story short. It's complicated, but Nathan has unimpeachable evidence that this star is at the center of a time travel suppression field. One that covers a three billion cubic light-year volume of space."

Janney stared at him for several seconds, stunned. "Are you saying you don't think this is a natural phenomenon?"

"No, sir. I'm saying we *know* it isn't. Someone built it. And it sure wasn't us. This is absolute evidence of an advanced galactic civilization."

"And you have no doubt of this?" asked Janney.

Cargill blew out a long breath. "None," he replied.

"Maybe not so minor, after all," whispered an awestruck president.

73

Blake gazed at his traveling companion and tried not to show his true feelings for her, something that seemed to get harder every minute. It had only been ten days since Knight had snatched her from the future, a version of Jenna Morrison that, by rights, shouldn't exist here, and had tied her on the floor of a rec room in a mansion.

It had only been six days since Cargill had given them both forged documents. Jenna Morrison and Aaron Blake had become Alissa Henderson and Cliff Webb, and Cargill had deposited a million dollars into Henderson's and Webb's personal accounts.

Cargill promised to provide updates twice a month so they could be kept apprised of developments within Q5, and they were free to talk to him and their duplicates whenever they chose. They would need full knowledge of all activities to be effective on the missions to which they were assigned, and they weren't about to miss out on the progress the group was making to achieve a variety of wonders.

In addition to these communications, Cargill had agreed to send them transcripts of all meetings so they could offer additional perspective on the subject matter. There were so few people who knew about time travel that Cargill welcomed their input, even though, at the start, their opinions were unlikely to diverge from those of their duplicates.

Once their identities were in place, they had decided to travel, as if on an extended vacation, to ease into their new lives and get their heads on straight. They weren't a couple, so there was no reason for them to remain together, but they shared a past, shared monumental secrets, and were fond of each other, so why wouldn't they? Who else did they have? Alissa Henderson and Cliff Webb were newborns, and the only people in the world who knew anything about them were Alissa Henderson and Cliff Webb.

The problem was that now that Blake realized he was in love, being around Jenna only made these feelings grow stronger. So much so that his struggle to hide these same feelings was becoming painful.

Not that she wasn't suffering herself. Mostly she was cheerful and upbeat, but there were times when she would break into tears, mourning the loss of her old life, and the loss of Nathan Wexler. But this was happening less and less as she began to come to terms with her new life.

Wexler hadn't died, after all. He was alive and well and happy. He was doing what he was born to do, with her by his side. She was now the odd woman out, but he had never stopped loving her, and the only reason she couldn't have him was because she *already* had him. He was sleeping with another woman, yes—but he wasn't cheating on her.

It was Knight who had cheated. Cheated nature by creating a second copy of her in the first place.

But what was a curse for Jenna was a godsend for Blake. After Camp David, he had expected to be adrift and alone, not spending time with a woman who had come to mean so much to him.

Blake had chosen an Alaskan cruise to begin their journey, managing to book two cabins only four rooms apart from each other.

"Have you ever seen a more incredible view?" asked Jenna, standing with him on the port side of the cruise ship, gazing out over the balcony. A magnificent blue-green ocean extended for about fifty yards before ending at a twenty-story wall of gleaming blue ice.

Blake smiled. How many times had a similar question been asked in a romantic movie? This exact situation was beyond cliché. The male part of the duo would stare longingly at his female companion, *not* the scenery, and declare how spectacular the view really was. And yet Blake found himself wanting to repeat this tired cliché, despite knowing it would be a huge mistake.

"Nature always helps me get my head on straight," he replied instead. "I'm glad you like it. You get next choice of travel destination."

She sighed. "The problem I'm having is that there are *too many* choices. I've never planned a vacation when I've had unlimited time and unlimited money."

"Well, yeah," said Blake wryly, "who *wouldn't* complain about that?"

Jenna laughed. "Okay," she said, "maybe it isn't *that* much of a hardship." She paused in thought. "I guess I'm in the mood to avoid civilization for a while longer," she continued. "How do you feel about the Serengeti?"

"Not a bad choice," said Blake. "I haven't been on Safari in years. But I'll bet you that I have an idea you'll like even better. One that you'll find more meaningful."

"So you think you know what I'll like more than I do?"

"In this case, yes," he replied with a grin.

"Okay, you're on. You've got yourself a bet."

He leaned closer, as if he was conveying the secret to existence itself. "The Galapagos Islands," he whispered.

Jenna's eyes widened. "How did you do that?" she said in delight. "Maybe you do know me better than I do. Why didn't I think of that?"

"It isn't an obvious destination," he said. "But I knew you'd love having the chance to retrace Charles Darwin's steps as he made the observations that changed the world."

"It's perfect," she said excitedly. "Thank you."

Blake nodded, but quickly turned away, not wanting her to see what he knew was so clearly written in his eyes.

Jenna sighed. "When I told you and the team what happened in the guesthouse," she said. "I left something out. Your duplicate did go on a suicide mission, and he did lie to me so I'd be safe. But what I didn't tell you was that, just before he left . . . " She paused, as if unsure she was making the right decision to continue.

"Go on," urged Blake.

Her look of indecision remained. "Well," she began again finally, "in short . . . he told me he was . . . in love with me."

Blake's face whitened. What?

His double must have had the same epiphany *he* had experienced at Camp David. When he had thought she was dead, killed inside a pickup truck, his own true feelings had ripped free of their shackles.

So why wouldn't the same happen to his double when he saw her being marched off by a would-be rapist?

But while this explained how his double had come to realize his true feelings, it didn't explain why he would ever share them with *Jenna*. What a horrible thing to do to her. Especially knowing she was in love with another man. How could he have burdened her like that?

"I'm so sorry, Jenna. The other me should never have told you. But I promise I won't let this interfere with our friendship, or our time together. I know you're in love with Nathan, and I know you just lost him. So don't worry about my feelings for you. I know that you can't return them."

Jenna looked both happy and miserable at the same time. "No, I'm the one who's sorry," she said timidly. "Because I lied to you."

Blake blinked in confusion. "I don't understand. Lied about what?"

She took a deep breath and then let it out. "In truth, you never did tell me that you loved me. You're too good of a man to do that. But I've been getting this strange vibe that it might be true. And my feelings for you have been getting awfully . . . warm. So I threw it out there to see what you would say."

"You mean to see if I'd confirm it," he said.

"Yes."

"Which I just did."

Jenna gritted her teeth guiltily. "It was horrible of me to do. I know that. It was a spur-of-the-moment thing. I was feeling so close to you just now that I had to know. If I asked you directly, you'd deny it. So I tricked you." She tried to force a smile. "But you can't say I didn't learn this kind of maneuver from the best."

Blake knew he should be angry, but he found himself feeling relieved instead—and suddenly hopeful. "When you say your feelings for me have been getting *awfully warm*," he said, "what do you mean by that?"

"I mean I'm not in love with you," she said, "but I'm beginning to think I'm headed in that direction. I'm still not over Nathan, and I'm sorting out a lot of emotions. So I can't return your feelings now. Maybe not for a while. But you're an amazing man. I have a feeling that once I'm able to let go of my past, I'll catch up with you. If you can be patient, I have a feeling we can be more than friends."

Blake felt like fireworks were going off inside his head, but fought to stay low-key. "Take all the time you need," he said as calmly as he could. "We can let this evolve the way it evolves."

Jenna laughed. "Maybe this will happen on the Galapagos Islands," she said. "A lot of things seem to evolve there."

Blake nodded, but didn't trust himself to respond. They both fell silent, staring at the glistening combination of ocean and ice for several minutes, alone with their thoughts.

"Not to change the subject," said Jenna with a contented smile, "but I wanted to ask you if you'd be willing to train me."

"Train you how?"

"Basic stuff. Some hand-to-hand, some weapons training, and a lot of instruction on tactical and strategic thinking. I'll never be nearly as skilled as you, but if we're going on missions together, I want to be prepared."

"Of course I'll train you," said Blake. "But I like the idea of me being the muscle and you being the brains. You know, I'd be the guy in the field, and you'd be the guy in the truck, talking into my ear."

"No deal," said Jenna. "We've been in danger zones together before. If it makes sense to include me on a mission, I won't shy away. And we both know you have plenty of brains to go along with your brawn. As for me, I'm getting to be more of a badass all the time."

Blake laughed. "Are you kidding? You're a *total* badass."

"Then it's settled," said Jenna happily.

"Great," said Blake. "While we're at it, let me bring up something else. I wasn't going to for a while, but we seem to be going in a lot of unexpected directions suddenly."

"Of course," she said. "What is it?"

"At some point, we have to decide on what we do going forward. We're here for Q5 as necessary, but there may not be that many missions required. We can only travel the world for so long before we get tired of it, or bored to death."

"Okay," said Jenna. "So what did you have in mind?"

"What if we opened up a private detective shop? We could limit the number of cases since we don't need the money. It would keep our minds active in between assignments. I know this is my dream, not yours, but you'd make a great detective. I've seen how your mind works. And this experience will serve you well on any missions we take on."

"As Cliff Webb, you don't have a PI license. And I *never* had one."

"Consider that a minor technicality," said Blake impishly. "You and I have fake passports and fake histories. And we have friends in high places, including President Janney. So we can get any credentials we want. Well, we couldn't get a license to perform open-heart surgery," he amended with a smile, "but I'm pretty sure that wouldn't end well anyway."

"Didn't you say that PIs spend most of their first year in business catching spouses in the act of cheating?"

"What are you saying, Jenna, that you aren't thrilled about the idea of filming other people having wild sex?"

Jenna laughed. "It wouldn't be my first choice."

"Or your hundredth," said Blake with a smile. "But we wouldn't have to do that. Cargill can plant a history for Cliff Webb that paints him as the best of the best. And I spoke with the president recently. He said he'd be happy to pull strings so it leaks out that I'm the guy you go to with challenging cases. We can work on them together, picking and choosing the cases we like."

Jenna considered. "I think it would be fun, but only every once in a while. I'll let you handle most of them solo. Turns out I have another idea for how to spend the bulk of my time."

"How?"

"Jenna back at Q5 is working on the optimal strategy for rolling out a worldwide time travel suppressor, once Nathan perfects it. She's trying to figure out the best way to manage a world with time travel in it. Well, she can use all the help she can get. And I'm just the woman for the job."

"I think it's a great idea," said Blake. "And you know what they say: God helps those who help themselves."

She laughed. "I don't think me helping my duplicate is what they had in mind."

"Was this something you intended to do from the start?" asked Blake.

"I thought about it, but I didn't decide until just now. I was afraid having her share some of her workload with me would be too painful. It would require me to interact with her too much, each time knowing she was living my life. Each time a reminder of what I had given up. But suddenly, I have reason to hope I can have a great life of my own. Not the one I thought I'd have when I was *single*, but a great life."

"And by single," said Blake in amusement, "you don't mean *not in a relationship*."

"I'm glad you caught that," she said playfully. "No, by *single*, I mean when I was the only me in existence."

"Ah, the good old days. We were young. Reckless. But now we've finally multiplied."

Jenna laughed. "I think we have a plan. Let's say another two or three months of travel, and then we'll settle down somewhere and begin our new lives."

"Settle down in separate residences?" asked Blake.

Jenna sighed. "I honestly don't know. I can't say for sure how fast my feelings for you will evolve. But judging by how things are going," she added, "I wouldn't be surprised if one residence would do the trick."

AUTHOR'S NOTES

Table of Contents

1) *Time Frame*: What's real and what isn't

Thanks for reading *Time Frame*. I hope that you enjoyed it.

As you may know, in addition to trying to tell the most compelling stories I possibly can, I strive to introduce concepts and accurate information that I hope will prove fascinating, thought-provoking, and even controversial. *Time Frame* is a work of fiction and contains considerable speculation, so I encourage you to explore these topics further to arrive at your own view of the subject matter.

With this said, I'll get right to it: what's real in *Time Frame* and what isn't. I've listed the categories I'll be covering in order of their appearance, so if you aren't interested in an early category and want to skip ahead to one that might interest you more, I encourage you to do so.

- Kim Jong-un—a scary choice of character
- Kettles, selling my home, and refrigerators
- Tabby's Star
- Smart contact lenses
- The decision to drop the bomb
- Outtakes
- Sperm is cheap
- The fifth dimension
- Sonic weapons and vomit-inducing smells
- Supercoiled DNA and the dead space inside atoms
- Oxytocin

Kim Jong-un—a scary choice of character

Many writers protect their fiction from becoming obsolete by not using actual people as characters, instead drawing characters that are clearly meant to serve as stand-ins for real life figures. Rather than using Kim Kardashian in your novel, you create Cat Chrysanthemum, who looks and acts exactly like Kim, and who has built the same reality show empire. Most readers know the archetype, and if the real Kim goes to jail for cheating on her taxes, or shaves her head bald and becomes a Buddhist monk, this doesn't impact the novel.

Which brings me to another Kim. Kim Jong-un.

As you know, I chose to use the real North Korean dictator as a character, despite the perils of featuring someone who is alive, prominent on the world stage, and prone to making headlines. I felt compelled to do this for two principal reasons. One, the real Kim is already so much stranger than fiction that it would be hard for a fictional stand-in to compare. Two, I had introduced the idea of using time travel to duplicate and kidnap Kim Jong-un in *Split Second*, written in 2015, and had long planned to make this happen in a sequel.

But back in 2015, Kim was *relatively* (key word here) well-behaved, at least compared to the version of him that emerged after I began *this* novel, after I had written key early scenes about Cargill's plans to remove him as a threat.

As I was writing about Kim, his bad behavior intensified by the day. As I was describing a future world in which Kim had become far more dangerous than ever, he was becoming far more dangerous than ever—for real. Everything intensified, escalated: the saber-rattling, the heated rhetoric, his WMD capabilities, global tensions, and so on.

I thought I was introducing readers to information about Kim and the North Korean situation they might not know, like the fact that China might pretend to honor sanctions while being Kim's benefactor behind the scenes, or that America feared he would massacre the large population next door if he was ever attacked—only to see this information become a mainstay of television and print news. Still, while this reduced the novelty of the information, it did increase the veracity of the book.

As I sit to write this note (November 2017), world events have yet to contradict anything I've written about Kim and the future history of the world. But who knows what might be ahead? Who knows how long this might be true? Kim could be removed from power. Assassinated for real. Or other actual events could occur that overtake my novel—events that are too troubling to even speculate about.

I thought long and hard about erasing Kim Jong-un from the novel. I wondered if, given the current escalation and tension, it was appropriate to have him as a character. I also wondered if I could live with the growing likelihood that portions of my novel might become obsolete before I even finished. In the end, I decided not to change the scenes pertaining to North Korea and Kim, believing them to be too integral to the novel to remove.

If events have changed by the time you read this novel, such that the history I paint no longer holds up, I apologize, and hope you were able to see past this. On the other hand, if, by the time you read *Time Frame*, this dangerous tyrant is somehow brought to justice— via time travel or otherwise :)—I will be celebrating my heart out, delighted that my narrative is no longer valid.

Finally, I should mention that there really are credible sources who speculate that Kim is more cunning than he seems, and that he purposely set out to mimic his grandfather. Much of the background on Kim that I used in the book, including this chilling speculation, came from a long article in *Vanity Fair*, written in 2015 by Mark Bowden. If you Google, "Understanding Kim Jong-un, The World's Most Enigmatic and Unpredictable Dictator," you can find it. If you Google, "Inside the luxury world of Kim Jong-un," you will find an article that appeared in *The Telegraph*, also in 2015, that gives a sense of how much money he wastes on palaces and luxuries while his country remains among the poorest in the world.

Kettles, selling my home, and refrigerators

As I was writing, it became clear I would need to name the time machines in *Time Frame* something other than time machines. I needed to refer to them too often, and if I was forced to call them time machines on every occasion, this would quickly become clumsy and tedious. I chose to use the term *kettle,* to honor Isaac Asimov, my childhood idol, and his brilliant time travel novel, *The End of Eternity,* which I had loved as ten-year-old (and in which time machines were called *kettles*).

Time Frame was tricky to write because there was so much going on in my life while I was working on it. After living in the same home for twenty years, my wife and I had become empty nesters, and decided to downsize. We wanted a home that had a master bedroom on the first floor and was smaller and less expensive than the one in which we were living.

Naturally, we ended up with just the opposite. We live in San Diego, where space is at a premium, and we also wanted a view, and not to have neighbors within six inches of us. Smaller and less expensive wasn't working, especially since I work out of the house, and being crammed too close together 24/7 is probably not great for any marriage.

So after months of looking at homes all around San Diego County (since, as a writer, I can work anywhere—on the Moon if it had an Internet connection), we finally decided on a lot in a new development, one that didn't have so much as a slab of concrete upon it.

Wow. New construction. I won't be doing that again. Not only was my writing time interrupted for several months as we toured endless homes for sale, once we decided on new construction, I had to go with my wife to pick out flooring, and window coverings, and lighting, and tiles, and arghhhhh—please make it stop! (To be fair, my wife did almost all of the choosing, and I did almost all of the wanting to kill myself.)

Then there were visits to the construction site every week. "Is that sliding glass door *supposed* to be broken like that?"

Seeing a home being built is like seeing sausage being made, except the sausage isn't the most expensive thing you've ever bought, and you don't have to live the rest of your life inside a Bratwurst.

But let me back up to the real point of this section: refrigerators. The large built-in model we had owned for twenty years finally decided to call it quits in the midst of all of this. No problem. We were working hard to put our home on the market, but we had two weeks until the caravan of realtors was scheduled to descend on our home like locusts.

Two weeks is plenty of time to get a replacement refrigerator. We shopped and found one, nice enough to be in line with those found in homes priced similarly to ours, but not so nice that we had to win the lottery to buy it. It had to be shipped to the San Diego store we bought it from, and it was back-ordered, but we were assured it would arrive in plenty of time.

Finally, the arrival date was set—not only set but guaranteed—a day before the caravan of realtors would be descending on our home. Mind you, this is a demanding group of individuals who haughtily insist that a working refrigerator is a must-have in any modern house (wow, people have become so spoiled). Our realtor even had the audacity to suggest that not only do buyers expect this appliance to be present in a home, they also expect electricity, plumbing, and running water.

So I called the appliance store four times the week before the refrigerator was due to arrive, explaining that I *had* to have it when it was promised because I needed to install it that very day. Explaining that I couldn't show my home to this many realtors with a massive refrigerator-sized gap in my wall of cabinetry, and asking them to confirm it would arrive as scheduled. They assured me each time that it would.

The morning it was due to arrive, I called again. To my delight, it had made it! Outstanding! "Yes," I was told, "your refrigerator has made it to Chino, right on schedule."

"Chino?" I said worriedly. "Where the heck is Chino?"

Turns out this is in Los Angeles, where their national distribution center is located. You learn something new every day. It wouldn't arrive in San Diego for another few days.

Now you tell me.

I had made it *very* clear—multiple times—that I needed it installed in my San Diego home the day it arrived, and was assured this would happen. No one had once told me the date they were quoting was the arrival time to LA, which might have been useful information for me to have. I wasn't asking when it would make it LA—or to Dubai,

South Africa, or even France. I wanted to know when it would arrive in *San Diego*.

So I asked for the manager, and after explaining the situation, he agreed to let me take one of his floor models that was the right size to fill the giant hole in my kitchen. Problem solved.

Except that when I called the installer to confirm, I learned that he had called the store a few hours earlier and had been told the unit wouldn't be in San Diego for two more days. So he had sent his guys to the opposite side of town to do jobs there. There was no way he could install it now.

I could go on, detailing how I called a half-dozen installers in San Diego, offering them extra money if they could squeeze me into their schedule, and so on. Suffice it to say that the next day, an hour before the caravan arrived, the installers I had bribed were racing to complete the job, which they did with just minutes to spare.

It was right around this time that I was thinking about a good way to disguise a time machine for *Time Frame*. I was racking my brain. What could I use? What might possibly work?

And then, like a lightning bolt out of the blue, it came to me. I could disguise a kettle as a large Sub-Zero refrigerator.

Genius! Sometimes I amaze myself. Where do I get this stuff?

I guess creative people never really know where their inspirations come from.

Who knows, had I been shopping for a dresser or a casket at the time, this novel could have been quite a bit different. :)

(After the caravan arrived, the interest in our home was tremendous. Which meant my wife and I were kicked out of it for three to five hours a day for weeks—effectively shutting me down, since I'm not the kind of guy who can write a novel on a laptop at Starbucks. I need a full-sized keyboard and isolation. But this has nothing to do with refrigerator time machines, so I'll stop here.)

Tabby's Star

Everything written in *Time Frame* about Tabby's Star is accurate, except for the part about its peculiarities being explained by a light-years spanning time-travel suppressor—at least I *think* this isn't responsible :). If you google "Tabby's Star" you'll find any number of articles about these inexplicable observations that have captured the imaginations of so many, both inside and outside of the astronomy and cosmology communities. Many of the articles you will find try to come up with possible natural explanations, but each of them have at least one fatal flaw (at least from my reading).

One possibility scientists have taken seriously is that the dimming of Tabby's Star is the result of an alien megastructure, such as a Dyson Sphere, which would consist of an incomprehensibly large array of solar collectors ringing the star. This would allow an alien civilization to harness a significant fraction of the star's energy. (I tried to confirm this by reading literature from a San Diego solar company. Inexplicably, it didn't mention anything about the efficiency of their solar panels increasing if they were placed near the surface of the sun. Still, I'm willing to take these scientists' word for it.)

Here is an excerpt from an article published on May 20th, 2017, in the *Verge* entitled, "Why astronomers are scrambling to observe the weirdest star in the galaxy this weekend."

EXCERPT: *It was early Thursday morning when astronomer Matt Muterspaugh noticed something strange with the star he had been observing for the last year and a half. Telescope data taken from the night before showed that the brightness of the star had dipped significantly. He contacted other astronomers who had also been observing the same star, to let them know what he had seen and to keep an eye on it for any more changes. Then by the following morning, the star had dimmed even more.*

That's when he and the others knew it was time to signal the alarm: the weirdest star in our galaxy was acting weird again. And it was time for everyone to look at this distant celestial body—to figure out what the hell is going on. "As far as I can tell, every telescope that can look at it right now is looking at it right now," Muterspaugh, a professor at Tennessee State University, tells The Verge.

The star Muterspaugh has been looking at is KIC 8462852, though it's also known as Tabby's Star. That's because Tabetha Boyajian, an astronomer at Louisiana State University, first noticed this strange star a couple years ago after looking through archive data from Kepler. The data showed that KIC 8462852 experienced some extreme fluctuations in brightness, way more than what a passing planet would cause. At one point, the star's light dimmed by up to 20 percent. It was a huge dip, like nothing that had ever been seen before, indicating something big and irregular may be orbiting around the star.

Then in late 2015, astronomer Jason Wright from Penn State suggested a tantalizing scenario for the dips. Perhaps large megastructures created by an alien civilization were orbiting around the star, explaining the weird changes. "Aliens should always be the very last hypothesis you consider," Wright told The Atlantic at the time, "but this looked like something you would expect an alien civilization to build." That's when Tabby's Star became popularly known as the "alien megastructure" star.

The problem, though, is that Tabby's star is unpredictable. The fluctuations aren't exactly repetitive and don't seem to follow any known pattern—making it hard to know when the strange star will be strange again. "Things that change the brightness of a star happen in a very regular pattern," says Muterspaugh. "And from what we can tell so far, [this star] is not periodic. We cannot predict when it happens, and that makes it very weird."

That's why astronomers have been observing the star basically around the clock since they first learned of its dimming behavior. To do this, Boyajian started a Kickstarter campaign called "Where's the Flux?" to secure funding for enough telescope time to continuously monitor the star. The campaign successfully raised more than $100,000, which helped Boyajian and others set up a year-long observation program.

. . . So all the theories are still on the table—including the alien megastructures. "That theory is still a valid one," says Muterspaugh. "We would really hate to go to that, because that's a pretty major thing. It'd be awesome of course, but as scientists we're hoping there's a natural explanation."

As of this writing (November 2017) I've searched for the latest news about Tabby's Star to see if scientists have been able to solve this mystery. They haven't. The latest theory I read is that these strange fluctuations are due to an uneven dust cloud moving around the star. But while this theory can account for many observations, it doesn't address a number of dimming events, especially the huge twenty-percent dip in brightness that Kepler has previously observed.

Finally, during this section, I was tempted to repurpose a joke I had once heard on the Simpsons that had made me laugh out loud. I can't remember it exactly, but somehow the death of Lou Gehrig came up. Homer asked what Lou Gehrig had died from. The answer was *Lou Gehrig's Disease*.

Homer's eyes widened in amazement, and without missing a beat, he said, "Wow, what are the odds of *that*?"

The obvious corollary for *Time Frame*, which I decided not to use, would go like this:

"Who discovered Tabby's Star?"

"A woman named Tabby Boyajian."

"Wow, what are the odds of that?"

Smart contact lenses

I found the addition of a smart contact lens in the novel good fun. Sometimes I come up with ideas I think are futuristic and creative, only to later learn that others are already working on them. But in this case, I read about the technology first, and then decided it would be fun to use. I would have never gone so far as to suggest a contact lens could have a night-vision feature—until I read that this capability was actually being worked on at the University of Michigan.

Here are a few excerpts from articles I found interesting. The first is from an article on *Trustedreviews.com* (*news*) in April 2016, entitled, "Samsung's smart contact lenses turn your eye into a computer," by Sean Keach.

EXCERPT: *The human eye is an incredible feat of natural engineering, but it's not smart enough for Samsung. Samsung has been granted a patent for smart contact lenses that would revolutionize the way we see.*

The filing details a smart lens that would imbue a user's eye with computing capability.

The lens would come equipped with an antenna, presumably to connect to a peripheral device like a smartphone, which would likely provide the brunt of the computing heft.

Samsung says users will be able to control the lenses through gestures like blinking, which will be registered by tiny, embedded sensors that detect eye movement.

The second excerpt is from an article by Mark Elgan that appeared in the May 2016 edition of *Computerworld*, entitled, "Why a Smart Contact Lens is the Ultimate Wearable."

EXCERPT: *Smart contact lenses sound like science fiction. But there's already a race to develop technology for the contact lenses of the future—ones that will give you super-human vision and will offer heads-up displays, video cameras, medical sensors and much more. In fact, these products are already being developed.*

Sounds unreal, right? But it turns out that eyeballs are the perfect place to put technology.

Smart contact lenses are like implants but they don't require surgery and can usually be removed or inserted by the user. They're neither on nor under the skin full time. They're exposed to both air and the body's internal chemistry.

Contact lenses sit on the eye, and so can enhance vision. They're exposed to both light and the mechanical movement of blinking, so they can harvest energy.

What you need to know is that smart contact lenses are inevitable for all these reasons.

University of Michigan scientists are building a contact lens that can give soldiers and others the ability to see in the dark using thermal imaging. The technology uses graphene, a single layer of carbon atoms, to pick up the full spectrum of light, including ultraviolet light.

Sony applied for a patent for a smart contact lens that can record video. You control it by blinking your eyes. According to Sony's patent, sensors in the lens can tell the difference between voluntary and involuntary blinks. When it detects a deliberate blink, it records a video. Sony's contact lens would be powered by piezoelectric sensors that convert eye movement into electrical power. It would involve extremely small versions of all the parts of a modern digital camera—*an auto-focusing lens, a CPU, an antenna and even on-lens storage.*

The decision to drop the bomb

I feel it's important that my characters recognize the collateral damage that their decisions bring about, and wrestle with the ethics of this. Often in fiction, it's easy to get caught up in grand explosions without really focusing on the human cost. How many movies have we seen in which the hero fights the villain, but at the cost of thousands of innocent lives?

To be honest, I had never learned anything in school about the deliberations preceding Truman's decision to drop the bomb on Hiroshima and Nagasaki, surely the most difficult ethical decision in human history. When I began researching this topic, I found much more than I thought I would. I was especially surprised to learn that even some on the Japanese side were suggesting it may have been the right call.

If you Google, "The decision to drop the bomb on Japan," you will find any number of articles, some condemning the decision and some in support. As always, I urge you to find your own sources and draw your own conclusions. One article I found useful, which can be found on *historyonthenet.com*, is entitled, "Arguments Supporting The Bomb," by Michael Barnes.

Another article I read, written in 2015 by Tom Nichols in *The National Interest Magazine,* was entitled, "No Other Choice: Why Truman Dropped the Bomb on Japan." This was much shorter, but made an interesting point I chose not to include in the novel, but which I will excerpt below.

EXCERPT: *Still, let's assume, as some historians have done, that Harry Truman was either duped or made an honest mistake, and that the invasion casualty estimates were way off. (One historian has suggested that these estimates were ten times too high.) What should Truman have done? If the figure of 500,000 casualties was wrong, perhaps Truman would have been risking only—only—50,000 lives. But would even **one** more Allied death have been worth not dropping* *the bomb, in the minds of the president and his advisors, after six years of the worst fighting in the history of the human race?*

Imagine if Truman had decided to hold back. The war ends, with yet more massive bloodshed, probably at some point in 1946. Truman at some point reveals the existence of the bomb, and the President of the United States explains to thousands of grieving parents and wounded veterans that he did not use it because he thought it was too horrible to drop on the enemy, even after a sneak attack, a global war, hundreds of thousands of Americans killed and wounded in two theaters, and years of ghastly firebombing. Seventy years later, we would likely be writing retrospectives on "the impeachment of Harry S. Truman."

Germany desperately wanted the bomb for itself, of course, and my research suggests they might have won this race had Hitler not insisted on the extermination of a group of people who could have helped him the most. For a rundown of the many Jewish scientists, including those who fled the Nazis, who contributed to the bomb, I can refer you to two articles, "Scientist Refugees and the Manhattan Project" (from *Atomic Heritage Foundation*) and "Jewish Scientists Helped Build the Atom Bomb," (from *American Thinker*), which you can find by typing these titles into a Google search bar.

I find it highly ironic that had Hitler valued the Jewish people, rather than massacring them, he could well have won the war. Ironic, but not surprising, as further research shows that while Jews make up 0.2 percent of the world population, they make up 27 percent of Nobel physics laureates. ("The Tel Aviv Cluster," by David Brooks, *New York Times*, January 11, 2010).

Outtakes

Writing a novel is an evolutionary process, and scenes are frequently added, deleted, or changed. I wanted to share just a few paragraphs that I cut from the novel, which I thought might be of interest to readers. I made many other changes that were far more extensive, but I won't burden you with these.

The McEnroe Anecdote: (Knight remembering the past)

Cargill was largely a talentless hack, with only a rudimentary knowledge of science. His only skill was in recognizing the talents of others, assembling and fitting together the best people across a wide range of disciplines and inspiring them to work together, herding these cats to achieve his goals with carrots, sticks, and dreams of glory, and then largely getting out of the way.

He had lobbied hard to get Knight to run the technical side of the project, which, all by itself, was enough to ensure a win. The Cargill/Knight pairing was similar to the once-famous team of Peter Fleming and John McEnroe in tennis doubles. When Fleming was asked if he was proud to be part of the best doubles team in the world, he had humbly told the truth—that he had little to do with it. The best doubles team in the world, he had said, was John McEnroe—and *anyone* else.

In this case, the best team to exploit dark energy was Edgar Knight—and anyone else.

Tesla and dark energy: Thirty months earlier, Knight had discovered a way to tap into the mysterious dark energy that physicists had found made up more than fifty percent of all energy in the universe—as nearly all-pervasive and infinite as a human mind could comprehend. Remarkably, Nikola Tesla, genius that he was, had not only sensed the existence of this invisible, unknown energy source that permeated all of space, but that it would one day be harnessed. Tesla had written, "Throughout space there is energy. It is a mere question of time when men will succeed in attaching their machinery to the very wheel work of Nature. Many generations may pass, but in time our machinery will be driven by a power obtainable at any point in the universe.'"

As was often the case, Tesla's intuition had been remarkable, no surprise since he was one of the most brilliant inventors of all time, second only to Michael Faraday and Edgar Knight.

Gravity and the 5th dimension: (Nathan Wexler speaking) "One last thought before I move on to another topic. I mentioned gravity is thought by some to be a higher dimensional phenomenon. I don't want to get into the complexities of the arguments, but gravity is a trillion trillion times weaker than the other forces we know of. It seems strong because there is so much matter in the universe. The entire mass of the Earth is holding you down, but you can still slam dunk a basketball."

"*You* can slam dunk a basketball?" said Jenna with a grin.

Wexler laughed. "Not even with a ladder," he admitted. "I probably should have said, 'but there are *some people* who can slam dunk a basketball.'"

"Probably," agreed Blake. "But who does society value more, those who can defy gravity and slam dunk? Or those with a deep knowledge of the laws of nature who allow the slam dunkers to succeed?"

"Are you kidding?" said Wexler.

"Okay, yeah," said Blake in amusement. "I see how this might be rubbing it in. But we all know who society *should* value more."

"Nice try," said Wexler wryly, "but that doesn't make me feel any better about my one-inch vertical leap. Anyway," he continued, "as I was saying, gravity is ridiculously weak. One theory to account for this weakness is that it's as strong as the other forces, but its strength is focused in higher dimensions, and just a hint of its power touches ours. This is very controversial, as is much of physics, actually, but our tech should give us a way to prove or disprove it."

The complexity of general relativity anecdote: (This was part of the scene in which it was revealed that only Tini and Wexler could reproduce Wexler's work.)

According to an old anecdote, someone approached the great Arthur Eddington at a scientific meeting in 1919, asking him if it was true that he was one of only three scientists in the world who truly understood Einstein's theory.

When Eddington didn't confirm this right away, the questioner praised him for his humility.

"Not at all," responded Eddington, "I'm just trying to think of who the third one might be."

This made for a great anecdote, but was probably not true. In the case of Nathan's theory, however, it was absolutely the truth.

Sperm is cheap

I find certain segments of our society to be more sensitive than ever about discussions that touch upon gender. I tried to present this theory as inoffensively as possible, making it clear that there are differing interpretations of the data—which, as always, I encourage you to read on your own so you can draw your own conclusions.

I chose to include this in the novel because I wanted to show that Jenna had become attracted to Blake, despite herself, and I felt that a biologist like her would be confused by how this might have happened and want to analyze it scientifically. I also find it fascinating to think about how our behaviors can be molded by our genes without our conscious permission, and I never cease to be amazed by the power that sex exerts on our species.

Not that this should be surprising. The power of sex is universal across all species. After all, no quality is more essential for life than the ability to reproduce.

How powerful are these gene-driven reproductive compulsions? Ask male Australian redback spiders, who offer themselves up as post-coital snacks for the lovely females with whom they mate. I suspect that if these male spiders had human intelligence, they would strongly resist this strategy for passing on their genes, embedded in their DNA. I also suspect they would insist that any suppressed desire on the part of their fellow males to be eaten alive after mating wasn't a real thing.

This last paragraph reminds me of a humorous segment from *Futurama*, one of my all-time favorite shows. One of the main characters, a human named Fry, is on the planet of his lobster-like alien friend Zoidberg, and comes to learn that members of Zoidberg's species mate only once, and then die immediately thereafter.

FRY: So you have to choose between life without sex or a hideous, gruesome death?

ZOIDBERG: Yes.

FRY: Hmm—tough call.

With respect to the *sperm is cheap* theory, you can Google this and get many different viewpoints. One article I found of interest was written by John Tierney, and appeared in the August 20th, 2007 edition of the *New York Times*, entitled, "Is There Anything Good About Men? And Other Tricky Questions."

But I will end this note with an excerpt from a 2012 article in *Psychology Today*, written by David J. Ley, entitled, "Why Men Gave Up Polygamy," which presents some interesting conjectures that weren't covered in the novel.

EXCERPT: A question I've pondered over recent years has been why men in so many cultures gave up the right and tradition to have multiple wives? Historically, polygamy has been one of the most common and prevalent forms of marriage, worldwide. But, in modern Western culture, men with multiple wives are seen as sinners and lawbreakers.

This flies in the face of increasing evidence that for many men (though not all), there are genetic, biological and psychological factors that dispose them to not be monogamous. As my colleague Eric Anderson argues in his new well-researched book, The Monogamy Gap , there is increasing evidence that monogamy is not a natural state for males, a dilemma which contributes to high rates of pornography use, infidelity, and marital difficulties.

So, as I've seen this rising evidence, I've wondered why and how it is that societies came to adopt monogamy. If Western culture and American society really have been dominated by patriarchal control, why would these men in charge give up the right to have multiple wives?

And now, here's the answer. In "The puzzle of monogamous marriage" by Henrich, Boyd and Richerson, the authors present evidence that monogamy actually has significant social benefits. In polygamy, powerful men gather the most desirable women for themselves. And less powerful men "go hungry," wifeless. In fact, throughout human history, while 80% of women have reproduced, only 40% of men have. Those men who couldn't compete, didn't get to have even a single wife, and thus didn't have children. So, what did those men do with their time? According to Henrich, Boyd and Richerson, it appears they got into lots of trouble. Polygamous societies have higher rates of violent crime, poverty, and other types of crime such as fraud.

Apparently, if you can't get a wife, what's the point of following the rules?

So, through a (probably unconscious) social process, societies have gravitated towards emphasis and requirement of monogamous marriages, because it smooths out some significant social problems. By allowing all men a democratic chance to get married, men spend more time worrying about looking like good potential mates, and have less time and energy to break the rules and get in trouble.

The fifth dimension

Or the fourth *spatial* dimension—but who's counting. :)

This isn't a subject that the human brain can readily comprehend. I tried to get these concepts across as best I could, but I encourage you to do further research, since I'm sure I didn't do it justice. This is a subject I think is very cool, so I wanted to include it, but I'm far from an expert. Thinking about it too hard hurts my head as much as anyone else's.

I'll end this note by providing an excerpt from an article written by the esteemed physicist and science popularizer, Michio Kaku. The article is entitled, "Hyperspace—A Scientific Odyssey: A Look At The Higher Dimensions," and can be found on *mkaku.org*

EXCERPT: *Do higher dimensions exist? Are there unseen worlds just beyond our reach, beyond the normal laws of physics? Although higher dimensions have historically been the exclusive realm of charlatans, mystics, and science fiction writers, many serious theoretical physicists now believe that higher dimensions not only exist, but may also explain some of the deepest secrets of nature. Although we stress that there is at present no experimental evidence for higher dimensions, in principle they may solve the ultimate problem in physics: the final unification of all physical knowledge at the fundamental level.*

We live our lives blissfully ignorant of other worlds that might co-exist with us, laughing at any suggestion of parallel universes. All this has changed rather dramatically in the past few years. The theory of higher dimensional space may now become the central piece in unlocking the origin of the universe. At the center of this conceptual revolution is the idea that our familiar three dimensional universe is "too small" to describe the myriad forces governing our universe.

Although the theory of higher dimensional space has not been verified (and, we shall see, would be prohibitively expensive to prove experimentally), almost 5,000 papers, at last count, have been published in the physics literature concerning higher dimensional theories, beginning with the pioneering papers of Theodore Kaluza and Oskar Klein in the 1920's and 30s, to the supergravity theory of the 1970s, and finally to the superstring theory of the 1980s and 90s.

In fact, the superstring theory, which postulates that matter consists of tiny strings vibrating in hyperspace, predicts the precise number of dimensions of space and time: 10.

However, try as we may, it is impossible for our brains to visualize the fourth spatial dimension. Computers, of course, have no problem working in N dimensional space, but spatial dimensions beyond three simply cannot be conceptualized by our feeble brains.

(The reason for this unfortunate accident has to do with biology, rather than physics. Human evolution put a premium on being able to visualize objects moving in three dimensions. There was a selection pressure placed on humans who could dodge lunging saber tooth tigers or hurl a spear at a charging mammoth. Since tigers do not attack us in the fourth spatial dimension, there simply was no advantage in developing a brain with the ability to visualize objects moving in four dimensions.)

Sonic weapons and vomit-inducing smells

The military is working on scores of secret weapons, many of them more creative, or more bizarre, than can be readily imagined. The hidden weapons I had Hank Vargas bring to the table are all being worked on today. I will briefly present some information on both vomit-inducing and sonic weapons below.

<u>Vomit-Inducing Weapons</u>

Here is an excerpt from a March 2017 article in *Wired*, by Sharon Weinberger, entitled, "Son of Vomit Beam."

EXCERPT: *Yesterday's post on the "vomit beam" drew some great comments from readers who noted that the idea of a nausea-inducing device is hardly new (although arguably Invocon's method of achieving the desired vomit effect—through the equivalent of sea-sickness—is rather novel).*

In science fiction, there's the "vomit tube" (or puke grenade) used in the movie **Minority Report,** *which induces people to vomit on demand. But what about real life?*

I decided to take a look at weapons the Pentagon has explored that are intended to make you puke, pee, or otherwise lose control of bodily functions. I drew on some old ideas out in the literature, as well as my own past reporting that was just, well, a little too gross to put in any article. Here's what I found

Stink Bombs: *Sometimes grouped together with "gastrointestinal convulsives," malodorants, as they are formally called, are basically things that smell really, really bad. Nausea can be one effect of malodorants, as anyone who has ever been sensitive to certain smells can attest. The wild and crazy folks at the Defense Advanced Research Projects Agency apparently continue to do research in this area, which has been around as an idea for several decades.*

My reading suggests that the stink bombs being explored smell pretty much like decaying flesh combined with rotting garbage combined with concentrated skunk anus combined with vulture vomit.

Sounds delightful.

Sonic Weapons

With respect to sonic weapons, some experts believe these are in the works and making good progress, and others believe (based on their study of hearing and the ear) that these will never work. I'll forgo this discussion for something more topical, at least as of this writing, namely, reports that some kind of sonic weapon was used on diplomats in Cuba. These reports came out after I had already decided to use such a weapon in *Time Frame*, once again turning something that was supposed to be science fiction into something more on the *non-fiction* side of the ledger.

Below is an excerpt from a September 2017 article in *Business Insider* (*Science*), by Kevin Loria, entitled, "The US is slashing its staff in Cuba after diplomats reported brain injuries and hearing loss, perhaps from mysterious sonic weapons."

Excerpt: *No one knows exactly what happened to the growing number of Americans and Canadians who returned from diplomatic missions in Cuba with mysterious and disturbing symptoms.*

Some can no longer remember words, while others have hearing loss, speech problems, balance issues, nervous-system damage, headaches, ringing in the ears, and nausea. Some have shown signs of brain swelling or concussions.

Some of the victims remember strange occurrences before the symptoms appeared, though others didn't hear or feel anything.

Almost a year after the reports began, the AP reported on Friday that the US State Department had determined that the incidents were "specific attacks" on diplomats and had moved to cut its Cuban embassy staff by 60%. The State Department is expected to warn Americans against visiting Cuba, noting that the attacks have occurred in hotels—even though no American tourists seem to have been affected.

The vibrations, piercing sounds, balance issues, and hearing loss have led some to surmise that some kind of never-before-seen acoustic or sonic weapon was used against the diplomats.

Supercoiled DNA and dead space inside atoms

Our scientific achievements to date, as impressive as they are, pale in comparison to nature's capabilities. Nature can create a human being from a single fertilized egg, *including* the human brain, the most complex structure we have ever encountered.

As part of this feat, nature had to find a way to embed the entire blueprint for a human being into every human cell. Since I once chose to devote my life to genetic engineering, I'm particularly fascinated by DNA and the genetic code, and well aware of the degree of DNA supercoiling inherent in the structure of our chromosomes. When I needed an example of how beings of a higher dimension could take dramatic shortcuts between two points in a lower dimension, DNA immediately came to mind.

Here is an excerpt from an article entitled, "How Long is Your DNA," on a website called *ScienceFocus.com*.

EXCERPT: *The DNA in your cells is packaged into 46 chromosomes in the nucleus. As well as being a naturally helical molecule, DNA is supercoiled using enzymes so that it takes up less space.*

Try holding a piece of string at one end, and twisting the other. As you add twists, the string creates coils of coils; and eventually, coils of coils of coils. Your DNA is arranged as a coil of coils of coils of coils of coils! This allows the 3 billion base pairs in each cell to fit into a space just 6 microns across.

With respect to the dead space inside atoms, here is an excerpt from an article by Ali Sundermier that appeared in the science section of *Business Insider* in September of 2016, entitled, "99.9999999% of your body is empty space."

EXCERPT: *Some days, you might feel like a pretty substantial person. Maybe you have a lot of friends, or an important job, or a really big car. But it might humble you to know that all of those things—your friends, your office, your really big car,* **you** *yourself, and everything in this incredible, vast universe—are almost entirely, 99.9999999%, empty space.*

Here's the deal: As I previously wrote in a story for the particle physics publication Symmetry, the size of an atom is governed by the average location of its electrons—how much space there is between the nucleus and the atom's amorphous outer shell. Nuclei are around 100,000 times smaller than the atoms they're housed in.

If the nucleus were the size of a peanut, the atom would be about the size of a baseball stadium. If we lost all the dead space inside our atoms, we would each be able to fit into a particle of dust, and the entire human race would fit into the volume of a sugar cube.

Oxytocin

The effects of oxytocin on the human body are many and varied. I've been following this molecule for years, and there have been a number of intriguing studies done with it, but also several whose conclusions have subsequently been called into question.

In general, this hormone and neurotransmitter has been associated with sex, trust, empathy, and relationship-building. For example, a study published in Psychopharmacology found that intranasal oxytocin increased levels of warmth, trust, altruism, and openness.

A while back I considered writing a novel in which someone had developed a super-oxytocin, similar to T-4 in the novel, that made people trust him or her implicitly. He or she could use this chemical as a sort of mass brainwashing agent to accomplish all sorts of nefarious ends. Although I decided against such a novel, I thought a combination of oxytocin and a standard truth serum, perfected and amped up a hundred fold, would serve my needs for *Time Frame* quite nicely.

That's It—For Now

So that's it. Once again, I've come to the end of a novel, and the end of my notes. I hope that you found at least some of these notes interesting or helpful.

Thanks again for reading *Time Frame*. Until we meet again . . .

Douglas E. Richards

2) Author bio and list of books

Douglas E. Richards is the *New York Times* and *USA Today* bestselling author of *WIRED* and numerous other novels (see list below). A former biotech executive, Richards earned a BS in microbiology from the Ohio State University, a master's degree in genetic engineering from the University of Wisconsin (where he engineered mutant viruses now named after him), and an MBA from the University of Chicago.

In recognition of his work, Richards was selected to be a "special guest" at San Diego Comic-Con International, along with such icons as Stan Lee and Ray Bradbury. His essays have been featured in National Geographic, the BBC, the Australian Broadcasting Corporation, Earth & Sky, Today's Parent, and many others.

The author has two children and currently lives with his wife and two dogs in San Diego, California.

You can friend Richards on Facebook at Douglas E. Richards Author, visit his website at douglaserichards.com, and write to him at doug@san.rr.com

Near Future Science Fiction Thrillers by Douglas E. Richards
WIRED (Wired 1)
AMPED (Wired 2)
MIND'S EYE (Nick Hall 1)
BRAINWEB (Nick Hall 2)
MIND WAR (Nick Hall 3)
QUANTUM LENS
SPLIT SECOND (Split Second 1)
TIME FRAME (Split Second 2)
GAME CHANGER
INFINITY BORN

Kids Science Fiction Thrillers (9 and up, enjoyed by kids and adults alike)
TRAPPED (Prometheus Project 1)
CAPTURED (Prometheus Project 2)
STRANDED (Prometheus Project 3)
OUT OF THIS WORLD
THE DEVIL'S SWORD

48926884R00235

Made in the USA
Columbia, SC
14 January 2019